Attack of the Seawolf

"Thrilling, fast-paced, action-packed . . . not to be missed."—*Associated Press*

"As much fun as *The Hunt for Red October*, both as a chase and a catalogue of the Navy's goodies."—*Arizona Daily Star*

"Superb storytelling . . . suspenseful action . . . Michael DiMercurio, a former submarine officer, delivers a taut yarn at flank speed."
—*Virginia-Pilot and Ledger Star*

"Nail-biting excitement . . . a must for techno-thriller fans."—*Publishers Weekly*

"Gobs of exciting submarine warfare . . . with a supervillain who gives new meaning to the word 'torture.' "—*Kirkus Reviews*

Voyage of the Devilfish

THREAT
VECTOR

Michael DiMercurio

AN ONYX BOOK

ONYX
Published by New American Library, a division of
Penguin Putnam Inc., 375 Hudson Street,
New York, New York 10014, U.S.A.
Penguin Books Ltd, 27 Wrights Lane, London W8 5TZ, England
Penguin Books Australia Ltd, Ringwood, Victoria, Australia
Penguin Books Canada Ltd, 10 Alcorn Avenue,
Toronto, Ontario, Canada M4V 3B2
Penguin Books (N.Z.) Ltd, 182–190 Wairau Road, Auckland 10, New Zealand

Penguin Books Ltd, Registered Offices: Harmondsworth, Middlesex, England

First published by Onyx, an imprint of New American Library,
a division of Penguin Putnam Inc.

First Printing, March 2000
10 9 8 7 6 5 4 3 2 1

PUBLISHER'S NOTE
This is a work of fiction. Names, characters, places, and incidents either are the product of the author's imagination or are used fictitiously, and any resemblance to actual persons, living or dead, business establishments, events, or locales is entirely coincidental.

To the woman I cherish more than my next breath,
Patti DiMercurio,
my wife, my love, my world.
I love you and I will always love you.

Acknowledgments

Deepest thanks to my wife, Patti, the love of my life, who fills me with inspiration and makes my life worth living.

Thanks to my son, Matthew, and my daughter, Marla, who have filled my life with love and hope and joy.

Thanks to my mother, Patricia, who never wanted me to climb down the hatch of a nuclear submarine but kept her peace nonetheless.

Thanks to my father, Dee, who once reminded me that he had been commissioned as a naval officer at twenty— while at that age I was a mere third class midshipman— and kept my feet on the ground.

Thanks to Joe Pittman, the best damn editor in the business.

Thanks to Nancy Perpall, a great friend and a talented writer.

Thanks to Bill Parker, the brilliant computer architect of Parker Information Resources (www.parkerinfo.com), who made the ussdevilfish.com website explosive. Please visit it at www.ussdevilfish.com.

Thanks to my friend and enlightened critic Craig Relyea, who kept me enthusiastic when I was buried.

Thanks to the men and officers of the USS *Hammerhead*, SSN-663, and to the immortal spirit of that venerable ship, for giving me dolphins and making me a submariner.

And thanks to the late Don Fine, who, in the Hereafter, is reading this, frowning, and holding a red pen.

Author's Note

Comments, reviews, and letters are always welcome, whether they come from a critic from the *New York Times*, a reader on a jet touching down in L.A., a housewife on a break from the kids, or a fifth-grader doing a school project.

If you are online, you can reach me by e-mail at:
readermail@ussdevilfish.com.
Or by visiting the website:
ussdevilfish.com.

If you don't have electronic means, jot a note to the publisher. I answer every letter received—not always on the day I receive it, but eventually, so let me hear from you.

For those readers who've followed Michael Pacino from the day he commanded the Piranha-class submarine *Devilfish*, I want to express my thanks. For those who have not, if you like *Threat Vector*, please check out *Voyage of the* Devilfish, *Attack of the* Seawolf, *Phoenix Sub Zero*, *Barracuda Final Bearing*, and *Piranha Firing Point*, all of them available at ussdevilfish.com, Amazon.com, or BarnesandNoble.com.

Welcome aboard and rig for dive. . . .

—Michael DiMercurio
Princeton, New Jersey
www.ussdevilfish.com

"...it is appropriate to comment on the relationship between goodness and stress. He who behaves nobly in easy times—a fair-weather friend, so to speak—may not be so noble when the chips are down. Stress is the test for goodness. The truly good are they who in times of stress do not desert their integrity, their maturity, their sensitivity. Nobility might be defined as the capacity not to regress in response to degradation, not to become blunted in the face of pain, to tolerate the agonizing and remain intact. As I have said elsewhere 'one measure—and perhaps the best measure—of a person's greatness is the capacity for suffering.' "

—SCOTT PECK, M.D.
PEOPLE OF THE LIE, 1983

"Once you accept the idea of demolition as a problem it is only a problem. But there was plenty that was not so good that went with it although God knows you took it easily enough. There was the constant attempt to approximate the conditions of successful assassination that accompanied the demolition. Did big words make it more defensible? Did they make killing any more palatable? You took it a little too readily if you ask me, he told himself. And what you will be like or just exactly what you will be suited for when you leave the service of the Republic is, to me, he thought, extremely doubtful. But my guess is you will get rid of all that by writing about it, he said. Once you write it down it is all gone. It will be a good book if you can write it. Much better than the other."

—ERNEST HEMINGWAY
FOR WHOM THE BELL TOLLS, 1940

"There's a certain knowledge you and I have because we were sub officers, Mikey, and until you've looked at a cruise ship at close range off Club Med, seen it in periscope crosshairs, knowing you could take it down with one shot, with no one knowing it was you, you don't know what being a submariner is. Warner's officials don't know and they don't want to know."

—ADMIRAL RICHARD DONCHEZ
LATE DIRECTOR OF THE NATIONAL SECURITY AGENCY
EAST CHINA SEA CONFLICT

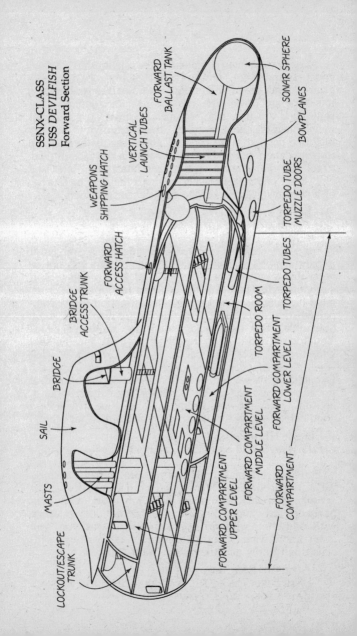

SSNX-CLASS
USS DEVILFISH
Forward Section

FORWARD
BALLAST TANK

VERTICAL
LAUNCH TUBES

SONAR SPHERE

BOWPLANES

WEAPONS
SHIPPING HATCH

TORPEDO TUBE
MUZZLE DOORS

FORWARD
ACCESS HATCH

TORPEDO ROOM

TORPEDO TUBES

BRIDGE
ACCESS TRUNK

BRIDGE

SAIL

MASTS

LOCKOUT/ESCAPE
TRUNK

FORWARD COMPARTMENT
UPPER LEVEL

FORWARD COMPARTMENT
MIDDLE LEVEL

FORWARD COMPARTMENT
LOWER LEVEL

FORWARD
COMPARTMENT

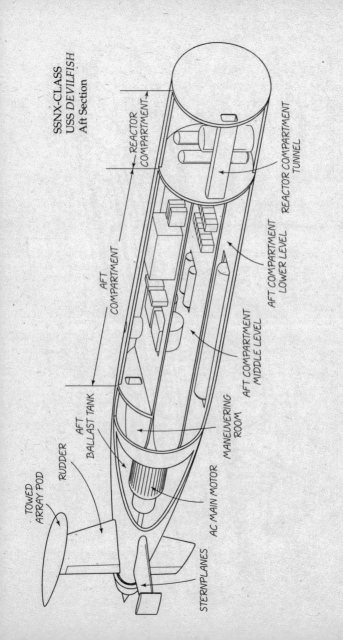

SSNX-CLASS
USS *DEVILFISH*
Aft Section

REACTOR
COMPARTMENT

REACTOR COMPARTMENT TUNNEL

AFT COMPARTMENT
LOWER LEVEL

AFT
COMPARTMENT

AFT COMPARTMENT
MIDDLE LEVEL

AFT
BALLAST TANK

MANEUVERING
ROOM

RUDDER

TOWED
ARRAY POD

AC MAIN MOTOR

STERNPLANES

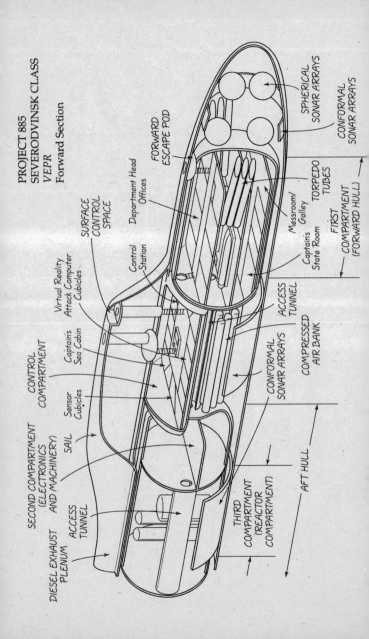

PROJECT 885
SEVERODVINSK CLASS
VEPR
Forward Section

SPHERICAL SONAR ARRAYS

CONFORMAL SONAR ARRAYS

FORWARD ESCAPE POD

TORPEDO TUBES

FIRST COMPARTMENT (FORWARD HULL)

Messroom/Galley

Captain's State Room

Department Head Offices

SURFACE CONTROL SPACE

Control Station

Virtual Reality Attack Computer Cubicles

Captain's Sea Cabin

ACCESS TUNNEL

COMPRESSED AIR BANK

CONFORMAL SONAR ARRAYS

CONTROL COMPARTMENT

Sensor Cubicles

SAIL

AFT HULL

THIRD COMPARTMENT (REACTOR COMPARTMENT)

SECOND COMPARTMENT (ELECTRONICS AND MACHINERY)

ACCESS TUNNEL

DIESEL EXHAUST PLENUM

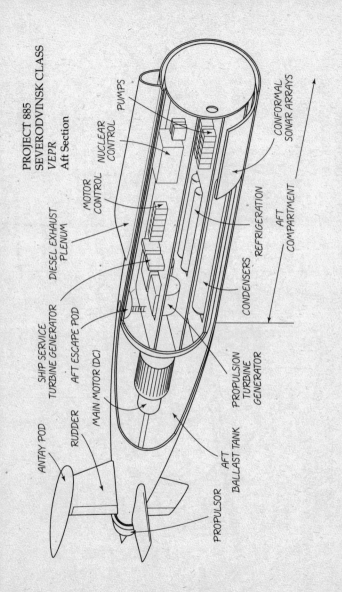

PROJECT 885
SEVERODVINSK CLASS
VEPR
Aft Section

ANTAY POD

RUDDER

SHIP SERVICE
TURBINE GENERATOR

AFT ESCAPE POD

MAIN MOTOR (DC)

DIESEL EXHAUST
PLENUM

MOTOR
CONTROL

PUMPS

NUCLEAR
CONTROL

CONFORMAL
SONAR ARRAYS

REFRIGERATION

AFT
COMPARTMENT

CONDENSERS

PROPULSION
TURBINE
GENERATOR

AFT
BALLAST TANK

PROPULSOR

Threat Vector—U.S. Navy term meaning the direction from which the enemy's most lethal and immediately dangerous element approaches.

The definition assumes that the afloat commander knows who the enemy is. . . .

BOOK I

Targets

1

The battle raged all day and well into the night.

The sun had barely risen over the mountain when it began. She took her first sip of the steaming cup of coffee he handed her, sitting deep in one of the old leather chairs in front of the fire he'd stoked to warm the cabin. The old Wyoming family mountain house that had been presumed lost in the lawsuit surrounding Grandfather Earl's estate, had landed in his lap after he returned from a long sea voyage. The cabin was so remote that the electricity worked only sporadically, water came from a hand-pumped well in the grassy town square, and the nearest phone was an hour's walk away, or a drive taking almost that long over a rutted dirt road replete with craters, mud, and protruding roots. The valley was more of a canyon, where no satellite phone would reach, no pager would beep, and no handheld computer would uplink to the Web. That was the idea—to escape from all that. The resulting peace promised to make this a perfect place to make it right with Diana.

Her cheeks were rose-colored in the glow of the fire. Her fine blond hair fell uncombed over her blue eyes, and her full lips smiled at him over the rim of the cup. He poked up the fire, settled into a chair opposite Diana's, and looked into her eyes.

"You said you had something important to say," he prompted.

"Kelly, I want you to leave her," she said over her coffee, no longer smiling. "This affair has gone on long enough."

He almost choked on the coffee. He held his hands apart and protested innocence, babbling.

"I don't mean a woman," she said, a frown forming on her brow. "It's the other her."

"The ship," he said, his voice dead.

"The ship. I want you home. With the baby coming, you need to do something else with your life. The time for Boy Scouts is over, Kelly."

She'd never understood. The sea wasn't just what he did. It was who he was. It defined him. It was as much a part of him as his voice or the shape of his face.

Though the argument began gently enough, it escalated over the course of the day. He didn't care about her or the baby, she accused. She didn't give a damn about his point of view, he shouted. His point of view should be for the welfare of the child, she shouted back. As if the kid would stop breathing the instant he went to sea, he said, and then more came. This was her insecurity talking. She was being selfish and childish. She returned fire: the ultimate in childishness was clinging to a seafaring career when he could easily make a fortune working for her father. He let loose on her: *that* was what this was really about, that he wasn't making enough money for her, or enough to suit her father, the industrial baron who'd brought three-dimensional projections to the marketplace. Why the hell had she brought this up now, when she was pregnant? She'd known who he was when she married him.

He left to let things cool off, taking a long walk across the river on a century-old trestle bridge, the rails long removed for scrap. He returned as the sun began its descent toward the western range. He found her silent and annoyed. He tried to apologize, but made the mistake of restating his insistence that the sea was part of his identity, that it was his career.

She interrupted that when they were newlyweds he'd planned to leave the sea behind to seek a job elsewhere. How the hell, he shot back, was he to know he would be so good at this? The core of his argument came to him, landing in his mind with a thump. He looked at her swollen belly and said, "It would be like me telling you I don't want you to be a mother, that I want you to be like you were before." An expression of shock flashed across her face as if he'd slapped her. Her face closed like a fist. Her eyes shut, tears leaking from them. She ran to the bedroom and slammed the door behind her. Her disappearance was so sudden and so final that a sense of unreality flooded him. One moment they were having a disagreement; the next their relationship was dead. It was as if, after carefully constructing his argument, his logic building on the idea before, one step after another, the last step had led him over a cliff, and he was plummeting headlong, stunned. And when it happened, he began to wonder whether it was the last step he regretted or the entire torturous journey.

He started after her, pounding on the door, calling her name, begging her to come out, to forget that last thing he'd said—he'd only meant that the sea was as important to him as the baby to her, not that he didn't want her to be a mother. The only thing she said, in a choked voice, was, "If the fucking sea is so important, go back to it and leave me alone." After that no amount of pleading would bring her out. He knew it was useless. With darkness overtaking the valley, he retired to the back bedroom, the cabin's addition behind the kitchen.

In the light of the moon, he stared up at the knotty pine paneling. His marriage was a tomb. Like pulling over a refrigerator, it would rock back and forth hard before it would come down, and their marriage had been rocking hard. This might just be more than an argument. It could be Diana's last straw.

To remain with her meant leaving the sea, and he was not sure he could give that up. He stared at the ceiling, wondering if he could live life without the boat, and it was as hard as thinking about living without Diana. He knew he had to choose. But how could he? He drifted in and out of sleep, his dreams torture, awakening in a sweat. He pushed off the blankets, close to a decision. He was a husband and father first, he told himself. He sat up in bed, scratching the back of his neck, and wondered whether he should tell Diana now or wait for the morning. He found his diving watch by the bed, its luminescent dial reading shortly after 2 A.M., mountain time. He yawned, then froze.

A sound, a sound that had no business here—a chopping noise, coming from the wider part of the valley, distant helicopter rotors. As soon as he thought he'd heard it, it faded away, and he knew he'd been dreaming. He checked the watch again, and it read 2:30. He must have dozed sitting up in the bed. He tried to blink back the sleep, then stood. He had to tell Diana.

The floor creaked under his feet. A shadow passed across the moon, just for a moment. He paused, scanning the hallway in the moonlight, then shrugged. He stepped toward the front room on the way to the master bedroom. He was almost at her door when something hit his face, a spider or a bug. He reached up to bat it away, but it was wet. A rushing noise sounded, and the air near his face was filled with mist.

An aerosol spray, part of his mind reported. Inexplicably, he felt himself go limp and begin to sink to the floor, yet his mind was fully alert. Was he having a stroke? Did he need to go to a hospital? Almost in slow motion he reached the floor, his head striking the wood, the ceiling panels in view, and he could not move his arms. He couldn't move his legs. He could barely blink his eyes. He could feel his limbs, but they would not respond to commands. He could still breathe, and his heart was racing, the fear pumping through him. Paralyzed, perhaps dying, he tried to see through the moonlight, tried to move so that he could make a noise, to wake Diana, to try to get her to take him to the nearest doctor in Saratoga.

As he looked up at the ceiling, a black shape came into view and then came closer to him. The man wore a black ski mask, and black gloved hands reached out for him, a rectangle of something in the hands. Duct tape was slapped over his mouth. The big man rolled him over and taped his hands together and his paralyzed legs. Strong arms lifted him up and he felt himself carried by the first man and three more out the door.

Slowly the men carried him across the grassy center of the town, past the old log town hall, past the well-water hand pump to the other side where the trail dead-ended. Ahead in the moonlight was a buggy with a roll bar and a rear deck, like that of a pickup truck. The man he'd seen first gave a hand command, and the buggy rolled quietly, perhaps powered electricially, bouncing up over the trail and on into the thick woods. Some time passed, perhaps five minutes, before the vehicle came to a halt. The men came out and pulled him from the back, carrying him again.

A fugitive thought flashed through his mind: what about Diana? What would she think when the sun rose and he was gone? Would it ever occur to her that he'd been kidnapped? Of course not— she'd assume he had left her. But there was no time to consider that, because looming ahead in the moonlight high over his head was the biggest helicopter he'd ever seen. It was a flat gray color, with a large star inside a circle with stripes on either side, and beside the logo were block letters spelling U.S. NAVY. As he was carried toward the gaping door in the flank of the aircraft, the engine turbine began to spool up, whispering, whistling, screaming a high-pitched shriek. The second engine came up to full revolutions. He was lowered into a canvas seat and strapped into a five-point harness, the duct tape still on his mouth, wrists, and ankles.

The men who'd carried him to the helicopter took off their balaclava hoods, wiped the black makeup off their faces, and donned flight helmets, taking their positions. The first one he'd seen climbed into the pilot-in-command seat. Overhead the rotors slowly began to turn. The huge blades moaned as the pilot engaged the clutch, and the aircraft shuddered as the rotor came up to idle. The jet helicopter took off, the mountainside shrinking below, and the pilot glanced at the copilot and climbed back to the cabin.

The man pulled the duct tape off as gently as he could, saying in a deep voice over the roar of the rotors: "Commander McKee, sir, I'm Lieutenant Commander Sonny Sorenson, Second Platoon Commander, Seal Team Seven. Sorry about the black-bag job to get you here. Very specific orders from Admiral Phillips. The aerosol should be wearing off in a few minutes. We're taking you to the Saratoga airport. The admiral has a supersonic transport for you with some weird spooks onboard. I don't know anything else, sir, but it must be damn important."

Commander Kyle Liam Ellison "Kelly" McKee, U.S. Navy, stared at the Seal commando, his mind racing. He had been on leave, and no one, not

even his relatives, knew where he had been going.
Feeling returned to his neck, and he could move
his head, the muscles spasming and aching. Then
his arms and legs, pins and needles running through
him. When he could move his arm, he checked his
watch. It was three in the morning. Out the window
the mountains rushed by, too close and too fast.
The noise was too loud to shout over and be heard.
McKee kept his peace, waiting for the chopper to
land. It took less than ten minutes to reach the
Saratoga airport. When the chopper settled, the
Seal officer handed McKee a naval air service jumpsuit, socks, and combat boots. McKee looked
down, realizing he was wearing only boxers and
a T-shirt. The Seal platoon commander grabbed
McKee's arm and led him to the Gulfstream supersonic private jet in the shadow of a hangar.

In the dim light of the parking lot lamps, McKee
climbed into the jet. The twelve seats were empty,
and two men in dark suits stood in the aisle with
grim expressions on their faces. The Seal officer
saluted and withdrew.

"What's going on?" There was no sign of a flight
crew, just the yellow glow of the cabin lights and
the two stiff men.

"Commander McKee, sit down, please." The
older one pointed to the mid-cabin seat. "I'm Special Agent Calvert, NIS."

Naval Investigative Service, McKee thought, trying to piece the puzzle together but coming up
blank. He sat in the seat and looked up at the
spook.

"Read and sign," Calvert said, handing him a

folder with a document full of tiny print. McKee squinted at it.

"Million-dollar fine? Death sentence or a hundred years in prison? What is this?"

"Release Twelve security clearance paperwork. The term 'Release Twelve' is top secret code word, by the way. I'm sure you're aware of the punishment for release of TS code word material?"

"You guys drag me out of my vacation house at three in the morning to threaten me? Excuse me, I'm making a phone call." As he stood to go to the front of the plane, he felt four hands forcing him back into his seat. Calvert's coat came open, revealing a shoulder holster and MAC-12 machine pistol.

For the next half hour the spooks read him the harsh government regulations surrounding the Release Twelve security clearance, then made him stand and raise his right hand and swear he would never divulge Release Twelve information on pain of execution. He signed the paperwork, they signed as witnesses, a notary seal was applied, and the NIS agents left. As they filed off the plane, a Navy pilot in a jumpsuit similar to McKee's climbed on, a younger one behind her. She threw a salute at McKee, said her name was Lieutenant Davis, and vanished into the flight deck.

"Give me the phone," McKee said, leaning in the flight deck door. His wife would be furious when she woke up to an empty cabin. She had to know he hadn't left her. If he were unable to get through to her, she'd assume he was finished with her, with their marriage.

"No phone, Commander," the pilot said. She reached into the overhead console and snapped a breaker, bringing the cockpit avionics to life. "Express orders of Admiral Phillips." A second breaker caused a hum to the left of the cockpit—the hatch coming shut with a thud. The outside wind noise was replaced with a sudden quiet. "I recommend you take a seat and strap yourself in, Commander," she said, her ponytail flipping as she looked over her shoulder at him. "We'll be airborne in two minutes, transonic in three." She turned back to her console and hit the starter button on the port engine. The jet growled as it turned, then caught and whispered to life. Within a minute the plane tilted dramatically toward the black sky. The cabin became whisper-quiet as the Mach indicator changed from 0.99 to 1.00, the numerals scrolling up to Mach 1.80. When the supersonic jet leveled off, McKee was loosening his belt to get up to ask the lieutenant where they were going, but she walked back down the aisle instead, a black portfolio in one hand.

"Here," she said, tossing the folder down on the table in front of McKee. "You should be cleared to get into that. Admiral Phillips' instructions were for you to enter your midshipman number from the Academy when the computer asks for a password." She headed aft to the bathroom, leaving McKee staring at the portfolio.

He opened it up, finding a small WritePad hand-held computer inside, but with an elaborate passkey system, one part reading his fingerprint, a second scanning his retina, then lighting up and asking his password. He typed in his midshipman number from sixteen years before, a number so ingrained in memory he used it for all his personal passwords.

The computer didn't come to life with the usual Windows/Linux 2017 display, but showed just a flat white sheet with black print, almost as if he were looking at a sheet of paper. Past the first paragraph, a definition of Release Twelve, the next line identified the code word Alpha. This was defined as information about developments in the Ukraine.

Alpha information went beyond recent Ukrainian history to a war between Argentina and Uruguay in South America, a subject McKee hadn't heard about. The next page of computer text revealed that both had acquired nuclear weapons in large quantities and had been threatening each other for the last five years. In 2013, both nations had manned up their conventional militaries, mostly land armies.

The next page reported the intentions of Argentina, gathered from electronic eavesdropping of phone conversations and computer e-mail. The country had struck a deal with the ever insolvent Ukraine involving its Black Sea Fleet. Ukraine had agreed to sail south to the coast off Montevideo, Uruguay, and attack from the sea while Argentinean forces crossed the border on land.

McKee whistled aloud—none of this had ever made its way to the *New York Times*. He'd assumed the massive Ukrainian Black Sea Fleet was rusting away in mothballs at the Sevastopol piers.

Yet he certainly believed that they'd want to get some use out of all that firepower.

McKee looked up and found the naval air lieutenant sitting opposite him, watching him intently.

"Yes?" he asked.

"Can I get you anything?" she asked.

"Coffee would be great," he said. "And I'd like to smoke, but I don't imagine you have a stock of cigars."

"Admiral Phillips said to give you whatever you need," she said, standing. From an overhead compartment she withdrew a small humidor and opened it to reveal a half-dozen Cuban Montecristo cigars, a cutter, and a lighter, then moved aft to the bar.

"What I really need is a phone," McKee growled.

"Except for a phone," she called back from the bar, smiling.

"Goddammit," McKee muttered. Clipping the tip from the torpedo-shaped cigar, he fired it up with a lighter with the skull-and-crossbones emblem of the U.S. Unified Submarine Command on it. When the coffee landed in front of him, he waved at the lieutenant and paged the computer display through another page of dry text.

The next section was a file of e-mails and encrypted radio messages, going as far back as 2013, five years ago. They detailed the hostility breaking out between the two South American countries— over trade, border disputes, and what seemed to boil down to a personality conflict between the respective heads of state. Then in 2014, Uruguay detonated an underground nuclear test. Early in 2015, Argentina blew up four test warheads. A cargo ship sailed from Red China and made port in Comodoro Rivadavia, Argentina, off-loading twenty missile bodies, ready for warheads. In 2016, Uruguay's army was a paltry thirty thousand men. By 2017, Uruguay had put a whopping 700,000 in uniform, out of a population of twelve million. And by that time Argentina's army had grown to two million, but Uruguay had imported over three hundred of the newest Indian Madras battle tanks. Argentina's sparse navy had been ordered to maximum readiness, while the Argentinean talks with Ukrainian President Dolovietz progressed from the theoretical to compensation details. As Argentinian money was wire-transferred to Swiss accounts, the Black Sea Fleet's maintenance went from poor to substandard to fair. Over the course of two years the destroyers, frigates, cruisers, and aircraft carrier of the Black Sea Fleet were tended to with loving care, being prepared for action.

There was one lengthy e-mail to the President from the Secretary of State, acerbic Lido Gaz, going over the five-year history of the failed American diplomatic initiatives to bring the Urguay-Argentina feud to an end. This included the recent intervention in the Ukraine, when Gaz had gone to speak to—or threaten—President Vladimir Dolovietz, but the entreaty had been ignored.

The messages in the file grew recent. On April 14 of this year, three Ukrainian destroyers had transited the Bosporus Strait and Dardanelles and made their way into the Mediterranean Sea, on an

exercise. They made port in Toulon, France, for
what they called a foreign exchange port call. On
April 20, another squadron of three destroyers left
the Black Sea, also stopping in France. On April
25, all six destroyers departed Toulon and transited
Gibraltar to the deep Atlantic. U.S. satellite reports
showed them conducting exercises in a square
block of ocean two hundred miles off Spain.

On April 28, the engine room of the huge nuclear-powered aircraft carrier *Admiral Kuznetsov*
lit off, the heat blooms captured in American spy
satellite passes. Later that day the nuclear reactor
of the Severodvinsk fast attack nuclear submarine
Tigr was started. On April 29, four cruisers departed Sevastopol, Ukraine, and headed west, followed by four fast amphibious attack ships, all of
them stuffed to the gills with Ukrainian marines
and tanks. Following them were two oilers loaded
with fuel for the fleet, enough for a long voyage.
On April 30, three squadrons of frigates made their
way to the Mediterranean. That same day the Severodvinsk submarine departed the Sevastopol pier
and within twenty kilometers dived and disappeared. On the first of May the aircraft carrier
tossed over her lines and made for the seaway behind the frigates and cruisers. On May 10, satellite
scans showed the late-departing flotilla going westward through Gibraltar into the Atlantic, one ship
at a time, casually, so as not to attract untoward
attention. By May 11 the entire fleet was in the
Atlantic, conducting independent maneuvers in the
square of ocean off Europe.

On May 12, a flurry of e-mails, phone calls, and

radio messages passed between Buenos Aires, Argentina, and Kiev, Ukraine. On May 13, the Ukrainian Black Sea Fleet formed up and headed south-southwest at maximum speed, thirty knots. On May 14, three squadrons of Flanker supersonic attack fighter-bombers took off from Sevastopol and landed on the deck of the *Kuznetsov,* followed by a dozen attack helicopters. By May 16, the Ukrainian battle group had crossed the Tropic of Cancer en route to the equator, the headlong rush to the South Atlantic still in progress.

McKee looked down at his fist, where the cigar had gone out. His coffee had long gone cold, but he slurped the remainder down anyway and relit the cigar. He returned to the message file, where he found the name of one particular American ship mentioned more and more, the USS *Devilfish.* This was the prototype ship of the NSSN new attack submarine class, designated SSNX, SSN standing for submersible ship nuclear, the X for experimental. The NSSN program was designed to replace the Seawolf class and take the fleet into the twenties and thirties. And as a prototype, SSNX was a one-of-a-kind ship, not quite the same as the follow-on USS *Virginia,* the true first NSSN on the building ways in Groton, Connecticut, at the Dyna-Corp New Construction Facility. Three other NSSN hulls were in various stages of construction, but until *Virginia* joined the fleet a year from now, *Devilfish* was considered the most formidable submarine in the world. The messages began to suggest that *Devilfish* might be tasked to intercept the Ukrainian task force. The suggestion had originated at a low level, then made its way higher, becoming recommended by Admiral Bruce Phillips himself. As commander of the Unified Submarine Force, Phillips carried tons of weight in the Pentagon. The next few messages were e-mails exchanged between Phillips and Admiral Kane, the Vice Chief of Naval Operations for Submarine Warfare, then a few exchanges between Phillips and the Chief of Naval Operations, the commanding admiral of the entire U.S. Navy, Admiral Michael Pacino.

Pacino's messages were full of questions about tactics, survivability, purpose of the operation, and exactly how *Devilfish* would be employed. What kind of weapons she would fire, whom she would target. The e-mails then went to even higher levels, Admiral Pacino's recommendations to Fleet Admiral Richard O'Shaughnessy, Chairman of the Joint Chiefs of Staff, and to Freddy Masters, the Secretary of War, that *Devilfish* be loaded out with surface-ship- and sub-killing weapons and sent at maximum speed to intercept and sink the Ukrainian battle fleet. The next e-mails in the file were from Freddy Masters to President Warner herself, the reply the convening of the National Security Council at Camp David that weekend. The meeting transcript from the Saturday meeting was thirty-two pages long; the meat of it was that the Black Sea Fleet should be put on the bottom of the Atlantic to attempt to defuse a possible nuclear war.

The message traffic had grown heavy on May 15, a few days ago, when the upper levels of the Pentagon suddenly realized that the commanding officer of *Devilfish* had gone on leave, to parts unknown, and could not easily be called back. Glitches like this became commonplace when information was as tightly controlled as Release Twelve, since even Admiral Phillips was unaware of the coming conflict when he had approved the *Devilfish* captain's vacation plans. On May 17 the executive officer, the second-in-command, of the *Devilfish* was ordered to set sail for the Atlantic, making a maximum speed run for the equator. When the captain was located, he would be taken to a rendezvous point and reunited with his submarine. On May 19 the captain was traced to a remote Wyoming location. Today, May 20, he would be airlifted to the rendezvous point, the operation already three days old.

May 23, three days from now, was the date set for the interception of the Ukrainian battle group, at latitude thirty degrees south, off Porto Alegre, Brazil, just out of Ukrainian aircraft range. It would be cutting it close, but the submarine was in a tail chase at flank speed, and would need all the time the White House could grant her to speed ahead of the enemy fleet and ambush it.

The last message was from the Seal Team Seven platoon commander, reporting that the *Devilfish* commander had been located and was being airlifted to his ship. McKee shut off the computer and closed the portfolio. Out the window the morning sun was glimmering over the deep blue water of the Caribbean Sea, or at least what he imagined was the Caribbean Sea.

So that was why he'd been pulled out of the

cabin. But couldn't they just knock on the door
like anyone else? he wondered. But then, after
seeing what Release Twelve meant, he began to
see that they couldn't afford to have him say no.
Someone would have had to say, 'You have to, it's
war,' and at that point Release Twelve code word
Alpha information would be compromised. What a
tangled web, McKee thought.

He stared out the window some more, amazed
that a week ago he had been doing little more than
political infighting in a peacetime Navy. Now he
was going to war. It was too much to process. Despite the queasiness he felt from the aftereffects of
the drug the Seals had used on him and the jitters
from the coffee and cigar tobacco, he decided to
try to sleep. He reclined the seat, pulled down the
window shade, and shut his eyes.

What sleep he got was troubled. He kept seeing
Diana's face, her cheeks wet with tears. He woke
after less than an hour, feeling deeply disturbed,
and promised himself he'd quit the Navy as soon
as this operation ended.

2

Commander Kelly McKee sat strapped into a body harness tied by a steel cable to a pulley system hanging from the overhead of the Sea King helicopter, which banked hard over the shimmering blue water of the West Indies. The chopper circled a particular spot over the ocean. As McKee watched, a spot of white foam appeared, then blew upward in an explosion of white. A fat black elliptical shape roared out of the sea, the bulbous conning tower a streamlined teardrop on the top of the hull, a fat cylinder of metal.

The hull continued out of the sea, still angled upward, until the rudder at the tail end came out. After hanging motionless for a half second, the ship came back down. The splash caused a second explosion of white foam and spray that reached up to the helicopter's open door a hundred feet above the water. In the turbulent foam the ship vanished, having sunk back into the sea, until like a cork it returned to the surface. This time it was horizontal, showing just the top of the deck and the streamlined conning tower. At the aft end, the rudder rose over the water, a teardrop-shaped pod on top. From the leaned-back sail a tall mast like a telephone pole rose upward, followed by an even taller,

fatter pole. The first was a type 20 periscope, the
second a Bigmouth multifrequency antenna.

At the top of the sail, clamshell trap doors were
lowered into a cavity, forming a crow's nest, the
bridge. Two men appeared, both wearing at-sea
parkas and ball caps. One of them hoisted a stainless-steel flagpole aft of the bridge, raising a huge
American flag from one halyard. Following was the
black emblem of the Unified Submarine Command,
a skull-and-crossbones pirate flag with script printing above the skull reading DEEP—SILENT—FAST—
DEADLY, and below, UNIFIED SUBMARINE COMMAND.
The flag had been designed by Admiral Phillips'
predecessor, Admiral Michael Pacino.

On the top of the deck two massive steel hatches
opened upward. From them a dozen men wearing
safety harnesses and cables appeared, manning
the deck.

The submarine below was the USS *Devilfish.*, It
was 377 feet long and 34 feet in diameter and dis-
placed 7,700 tons, carrying a torpedo room of
twenty-six weapons, with twelve vertical launch
tubes. The ship was powered by an S9G DynaCorp
pressurized water nuclear high-density power-reac-
tor driving two grip-service electrical turbines and
two steam turbines, called main engines, turning
the alternating-current propulsion generators supplying the single oil-enclosed AC main motor for
the propulsor. The reactor made 230 megawatts
thermal with an incredible sixty thousand shaft
horsepower at the propulsor.

"We're ready for you, Commander," a crewman
shouted from behind McKee's perch. McKee nod-

ded, and before he had time to think, he was suspended in empty space over miles of ocean. He dropped until he was caught by several men and guided to the foam-tiled deck of the ship. The anti-sonar coating felt strange when feet expected solid steel underneath. The harness was released and withdrawn up to the chopper, which was already banking hard and flying away. McKee walked quickly to the open hatch on the deck aft of the sail, lowered himself into the gaping maw, and went down the ladder. The interior seemed pitch-black in contrast to the midmorning Caribbean sunshine. The escape hatch chamber was a large cylinder of steel fully one deck tall, leading to the middle level of the three-deck-tall forward compartment.

There an officer stood waiting by the ladder, dressed in an at-sea blue jumpsuit. A wailing bosun's whistle sounded throughout the ship. "*Devilfish*, arriving!" The PA system boomed on all levels the announcement that the ship's commanding officer had just arrived aboard. It sounded strange here, over two thousand miles from the pier the ship had departed three days ago. The bosun's whistle sounded again at the same time Commander McKee's boots hit the floor plates of the deck at the base of the ladder. When McKee let go of the ladder, the officer came to attention.

"Welcome back, Captain," she said, her voice deep for a woman.

The slim, tall lieutenant commander with the brunette ponytail tied tightly behind her skull looked at McKee. Her embroidered name patch read

PETRI. Her collars carried gold oak leaf insignia. Above her pocket was an embroidered dolphin pin. On one sleeve her coveralls bore an American flag patch. On the other sleeve she wore the Unified Submarine Command patch and a second one with the emblem of the *Devilfish,* a snarling ram's head above, a nuclear submarine below, the hull numbers of all submarines having carried the name at the bottom.

"XO," McKee said tersely, using the universal Navy nickname for the executive officer, looking at her with what appeared to be at once relief and annoyance. Petri presumed that the relief was that he was back in his world, and the annoyance came from his being away long enough for Karen Petri to assume temporary command, infringing upon McKee's turf. Her stint as acting captain was now over, and she realized that she had mixed emotions about it. The emergency orders to get underway from Norfolk without the captain had at first made her anxious, but then as she had risen to meet the task, the feeling of command had started to grow on her, and she had learned what ancient seafarers had known since the beginning, that command at sea is a drug like no other. And with the appearance of Commander Kelly McKee, her mentor and captain, she was disappointed and half angry that she'd have to return command of the ship to him. But the feeling of happiness to see him prevailed. It had been a difficult voyage so far, and McKee brought an air of confidence to every task. With him around, nothing was difficult.

McKee was of average height, but his style made

him seem taller. His hair was a dark brown, his eyes likewise dark. His facial features were rugged, his lips too full for his otherwise bony skull, his hairline a strong arch over his bushy eyebrows, the overgrowth of them striking for a forty-year-old man.

Petri had worked with McKee for the last two years, and she felt she had grown to know him better than anyone on earth, even his wife. She studied him, was next to him all day, in the pressure cooker of a sub, while Diana sat in her gilded cage and expected McKee to pamper her. Diana was not Petri's favorite person, but Petri was a diplomat, something that had served her well in her career to date. She was one of the first female officers granted admission to the previously all-male submarine force.

When the word came down from Congress to allow women into the force, Admiral Phillips had made a decision that the way to do it wrong would be to bring them in from the bottom, where the men might be tempted to harass and bully the women. He had decided to inject them into the force at the top of the command ladder, where their authority would not be questioned. He'd hand picked two dozen female officers, all of them surface-ship executive officers, all with the best fitness reports, all deep-selected for command at sea. Petri had been in line to command a nuclear cruiser, having completed her executive officer tour on the *Port Royal,* when the call had come in from Phillips' office. His staff had offered her the chance to serve in submarines, taking an implicit demotion back to executive officer, with the promise that superb performance would merit a sub command of her own.

The training had been grueling. She'd had only two years to master what most men had taken sixteen years to accomplish. There had been months of little sleep, with attack simulator run after run, finally giving her the better part of the knowledge she needed. She already knew the Navy and knew how to command men. It was the knowledge of the machine that had been missing, or so she'd thought. But it wasn't just learning a machine, it was learning a new language, a new culture, a new world, and without Kelly McKee she would never have gained entrance to that world. He had spent hours training her, putting her on the conn during battle drills, infusing her with every scrap of experience and knowledge he'd gained in the decade and a half since Annapolis graduation.

There were times she thought of him as more than just a mentor, more than her commanding officer, but she was a woman of extreme discipline, and thoughts such as these she did not admit even to herself.

As Kelly McKee looked at Karen Petri, a comfortable feeling came to him that things were under control, a feeling he always had when she walked into a room. She was the most competent executive officer he had ever known. She was two inches taller than he was, her figure slim in the sexless submarine coveralls, but the fabric unable to conceal the swelling of her chest. She had the cheekbones of a Cherokee, with the jet-black hair to go with it. Her eyes were large, almond-shaped, their darkness impenetrable. While each of her features would be considered pretty, the overall effect of her face was one of hardness. In a word, she looked tough. It was not a look that appealed to McKee as a man—he preferred soft femininity in a woman—but it was one he appreciated in his second-in-command.

Behind him the men who had brought him down to the deck were climbing down the ladder into the ship. The last of them looked at McKee and said, "Last man down, sir." The smell of the submarine filled McKee's nostrils, a complex brew of cooking grease, cigar smoke, various lubrication oils from the machinery aft, ozone generated by the electrical equipment, chemicals from the atmosphere control machinery. In all the smell was pleasant, a reminder of a place where he was comfortable, akin to the smell of the log fire at the cabin. With that thought, a momentary memory of Diana invaded his mind, but he quickly choked the thought and returned to the present.

Petri turned to the hatch operation panel and moved a hydraulic control lever, dropping the upper hatch into position with a solid thump. The sunlight from above vanished. A hydraulic control ring in the hatch rotated, locking the massive steel of it against sea pressure; then the lower hatch directly above them shut. Petri muttered into the phone that both hatches were shut, then nodded to McKee.

"Let's go to control, XO," McKee said, leading

the way down the dark wood-paneled passageway.
The passageway led past the door to the VIP stateroom, Petri's cabin, and the captain's stateroom,
opening into the control room. It took up the entire
width of the vessel, the elevated periscope stand in
the center, the battlecontrol virtual-reality stations
on the starboard side, the electronic sensor stations
on the port side, the ship-control station forward.
The door to sonar, radio, and computer rooms was
at the forward exit of the room. While the room
was large, every single cubic inch was used.
Crammed in were cables, valves, widescreen flat-
panel displays, consoles, handrails, phones, gas
mask hose stations, navigation tables. At battlestations, when some two dozen watchstanders further
crowded the room, it could become claustrophobic.
No matter how big a submarine was, the control
room would always seem this way, McKee mused,
and perhaps that wasn't a bad thing.

No other place in the world did to him what
the control room of his nuclear submarine did. He
imagined that this was the feeling a pilot had for his
cockpit, a cruise ship captain for his wheelhouse, a
parson for his pulpit, a president for his podium.
This was where McKee realized the most of his
human potential, he thought, and with a pang of
regret he wondered how he could ever give up
his command.

McKee frowned up at the officer of the deck, the
man in tactical control of the ship for this six-hour
watch. The ship's chief engineer was a young lieutenant commander named Todd Hendrickson. The
lanky, blond-haired engineer was an odd case, an

individual so introspective that from the outside he had no discernible emotions. When he turned to face McKee, his eyes were clear and alert. He came to attention, snapping in a crisp voice, "Good morning, Captain, welcome home."

"Report," McKee said, his hand out. The chief of the watch at the port sensor panels handed him a Cohiba cigar like a nurse slapping a scalpel into a surgeon's hand. A second pass transferred McKee's lighter with the *Devilfish* logo. The cigar erupted into a cloud of mellow smoke as he listened to the engineer.

"Ship's rigged for dive, Captain, checked by Mr. Evans. We have message traffic onboard, with a flash transmission marked 'Personal for CO.' Plant's in a normal full-power lineup, propulsion is on the main engines. Artificial intelligence network is nominal. Battle-control system has a class II discrepancy, being worked by Mr. Van Dyne. We're ready to dive and return to PIM, depth six hundred, course one one zero, speed forty knots. We've been flanking it, sir—I've never seen PIM go so fast."

PIM was a submarine term for "plan of intended motion," the direction, depth, and speed the ship's operation order dictated she follow to arrive where she was scheduled to be, which in this case was the South Atlantic off Brazil.

McKee leaned over the starboard chart table aft of the elevated periscope stand. "Where are we?"

"Here, Captain, about eighty-three miles from Barbados. Course one one zero will lead us over the equator past Cape San Rogue, Brazil, where we make the turn to course two zero zero and follow the contour of the continental shelf. Destination is Point Zulu, our hold position. That's part of a top secret operation order, by the way, Skipper. And that's all its says, follow this PIM and get there damned quick. I have no idea why *that* would be TS. Maybe the flash message has the answer. But one thing is for sure, Captain—we're ten miles behind PIM and we need to catch up. We'll need to be deep at flank for the next twenty-four hours if we are going to keep up with this. There won't be time to ascend to periscope depth until Tuesday at the earliest. That's another strange thing—that's perfectly okay with the op order. I've never seen that before. Something is very odd about this op."

McKee narrowed his eyes at the youth. The thought dawned on him that he would have to come up with a briefing for the crew on this mission, and he had no idea what of the Release Twelve code word Alpha information he could divulge.

"Very well," McKee said, his voice low and clipped, the feeling of authority coming to him automatically. "Submerge the ship to six hundred feet and return to base course, and all-ahead flank."

"Submerge to six hundred, base course, and flank it, aye sir," Hendrickson said so rapidly it was a single word. "Pilot, submerge the ship, depth six hundred, all ahead two thirds!"

The pilot, the watchstander who had replaced the older submarines' diving officer, helmsman, and planesman, either a senior chief or a commissioned officer, sat in the enclosed wraparound panel forward. The console resembled a fighter jet cockpit simulator, engulfing the officer in a hemispherical array of computer screens and panels. The control stick between his knees and rudder pedals at his feet worked on the control surfaces of the ship exactly as they would for a fighter jet. He responded, repeating back his orders, then pushed a button on his stick, and an alarm sounded throughout the ship. The klaxon OOH-GAH of the diving alarm was followed by a computer-generated voice pronouncing the words "Dive, dive!" followed by a second OOH-GAH, the traditions of the 1930s remaining almost a century later, though now spoken by electronics rather than gongs, bells, and human voices. The officer pushed the throttle lever forward. The main engine turbines several hundred feet aft came up to revolutions for fifteen knots, all ahead standard. He pushed his control stick forward, causing the bowplanes to rotate to the dive position.

As the ship accelerated slowly, the officer of the deck raised the type 20 periscope with a hydraulic control ring set in the crowded overhead. The optic module came smoothly out of the periscope well, and the officer of the deck pressed his face to the optics and rotated the instrument around in slow circles. The pilot hit a second button on the stick, opening the forward ballast tank vents. That released the air stored there and let seawater in through the vents at the bottom.

"Venting forward," the pilot announced.

Up in the overhead was a television wide-screen display showing the view out the periscope. The waves came faster toward the view as the ship sped up. Then a geyser of water and air blasted out of the forward deck. As the ship inclined forward, the deck plates began to feel more like a ramp than a floor.

"Depth eight five," the pilot called. "Venting aft."

The deck continued to incline, trembling slightly as the ship accelerated. The view out the periscope grew closer to the optics. The waves rushed toward the reticle until they washed up against the lens in a blast of white foam.

"Scope's under," Hendrickson announced.

The lens cleared, showing the underside of the waves, reflecting silvery light from above.

"Lowering number two scope," Henrickson announced. He clicked the scope grips upward, pulled on a large circular handle in the overhead, and stepped back as the large optic module sank into the deck. The stainless-steel pole followed it down into the periscope well. "Pilot, all ahead standard."

"Ahead standard, aye, sir. Depth one hundred, ship's angle down ten."

The deck had become a steep downward ramp. A ship-control repeater panel in the overhead of the periscope stand featured a large digital depth meter. It rotated large numbers as depth increased, from 120 rapidly to 150, 170, 200, then 250.

"All ahead full," Hendrickson called.

"Full, aye, sir, speeding up to thirty-five knots."

The periscope stand, called the conn because it was where the officer of the deck controlled the ship's motion, was a platform rising eighteen inches. McKee took the three steps up to the conn and slowly turned to examine the room. His gaze stopped on the ship-control repeater panel in the overhead, showing the vessel gliding through the water at thirty knots and still accelerating.

"Ahead flank," Hendrickson ordered.

"Flank aye, throttle advancing to forty-five knots," the pilot called.

"Very well."

The deck trembled slightly as the ship accelerated to her maximum speed, then quieted. There was no discernible vibration, but there was something different to the feel of the ship at flank. Somehow McKee could sense the ship was running full out.

"Depth five-five-zero, fifty feet from ordered depth, pulling out now, ship's angle down five, down two, depth five-nine-zero, depth six hundred feet, all-ahead flank, sir."

"Officer of the Deck," McKee said, "I'll be in my stateroom. XO, meet me there in twenty minutes."

McKee's cabin aft of control was spacious for a submarine. It featured a foldaway bed, a desk, a conference table, and a high-backed leather chair. Set into the soffit above the door was a row of wide-screen video displays that could be configured a thousand ways, showing video camera views of critical stations, the chart, the readout of his WritePad computer, or video conferences. He stripped off the sweaty Nomex flight suit and stepped into the bathroom, the head, he shared with Petri. The walls and overhead were done in stainless-steel, the deck a troweled stone. After he showered and put on his customary at-sea submarine coveralls and running sneakers, he felt more himself than he had in the last week. He thought momentarily about Diana, and wondered if there were some message he could get out to UsubCom Headquarters that would get them to check on her. Would they tell her he was at sea? Probably not, he realized. And if not, what would be the point? It was a bad idea, yet he still wanted to do it.

He rubbed his hand on his neck, sank into his command chair, and pulled his personal WritePad computer from the slot in the wood surface. The officer of the deck had said there was a flash transmission message for him. Under normal circumstances he would have hopped to look at it—a flash message would need to be read within thirty seconds of receipt—but here, with no reply possible because of the depth, there could be very little that would be urgent. McKee clicked into the software and called for the message.

It was Release Twelve code word Alpha. Before the computer would let him see it, it demanded his password. He entered his midshipman number, and the message flashed on the display, another white field with black letters. McKee grimaced as he read the short and simple message. He could tell his crew exactly nothing. The charts and navigation equipment and control room were to be barricaded, with access only to officers with special compartmented clearances, and only then to the ones with the need to know. When they were at the Point Zulu hold position, he would be sent an emergency action message with orders to fire on the Black Sea Fleet.

An EAM would come in a coded format, requiring his officers to pull an authenticator package out of a dual safe. No one who knew the inner combination knew the outer combination, and inside the inner safe were silver-dollar-sized packets wrapped in foil with six alphanumeric symbols inside. The authenticator was required to be under two-person control from manufacture to destruction, and the little packets were able to make a meaningless group of symbols a nuclear release order. The EAM's title block would contain the name of the particular authenticator to use, and when it was checked as valid, the orders to fire on the fleet would be official.

Until then McKee could say absolutely nothing, not why the ship was flanking it south, not why the charts were barricaded from the crew, not the characteristics of the targets—the fleet order of battle, how many frigates and what type, how many cruisers and what they would look like and sound like, what type of helicopters the fleet carried, and above all, whether the Severodvinsk submarine had joined up with the flotilla, screening ahead for them.

McKee closed the message and pushed the computer aside, staring at nothing, running his hands through his hair. A knock came at the door. He looked up to see Karen Petri.

"Yes, XO?" he asked.

"You wanted to see me, sir?"

McKee remembered, realizing he was distracted.

"Call the department heads to my stateroom." He might as well brief them on nothing, he thought.

While he waited, he wrote a message into his WritePad computer, an instruction to UsubCom HQ to contact Naval Personnel and ask them to check up on Diana, both in Wyoming and in Virginia Beach. By now she'd be long gone from the cabin, but he might catch her at home. He called for a radioman to bring him a baseball-bat-sized slot buoy, a radio transmitter that could be ejected from a tiny torpedo tube, where it would float to the surface and transmit its message to the orbiting communications satellite overhead. Once the message was coded into the buoy, he called the engineer on the conn, told him to shoot it, and told him to get one of the junior officers to relieve him to come to the captain's briefing.

The briefing was an anticlimax. He told them their orders only said to hightail it south to a point off Brazil, where they would receive further word. The officers took the news stoically. McKee collected status reports on the ship, in the process beginning to feel more plugged into the vessel and the crew. After five minutes he dismissed the men and Petri. For the next hour he sat at his table, looking through the computer at the characteristics of the Ukrainian Black Sea Fleet, particularly what each ship looked like from the viewpoint of the periscope. That done, he sank into his bed and tried to shut his eyes. Where the day had started, in Wyoming, seemed a lifetime away.

3

The day began, complete with the usual rituals, as all his days at sea did.

The wake-up call came promptly at 6 a.m. on the third day of the mission. McKee opened his eyes to a carafe of steaming hot coffee and his *Devilfish* mug. He sat in his command chair at his table, reading the WritePad computer's download of message traffic from the last periscope depth. The boat had come up only once during their long journey from the Caribbean, and that was late last night. There was a lone message to him from Admiral Phillips, Commander Unified Submarine Command, confirming phase two of the operation order previously downloaded to McKee's computer. Phase three would begin in a few short hours.

McKee was ahead of schedule this morning, since the message traffic was so slim. He downed the last of the coffee and headed into the shared bathroom between his stateroom and the executive officer's. He had shut the stainless-steel door behind him when he realized the room was oddly steamy. He looked up to see Karen Petri's naked body. This certainly was not part of the morning at-sea routine. He had been so lost in his thoughts that he completely forgot to knock. But seeing his second-in-command naked had happened before, perhaps three times, and she had come in on him at least twice. It was unavoidable, given the tight quarters of the ship and the round-the-clock schedule. He and Petri even had an unofficial routine when this happened—he wouldn't call her "XO" and she wouldn't call him "Captain." When one of them was naked, it was strictly a first-name event.

Sheepishly he looked away, saying, "Sorry, Karen." He caught her smile in the mirror as she replied, "It's okay, Kelly. Good morning, by the way. I'll be out in five." He had waved over his shoulder, leaving the room to her. In the privacy of his stateroom, the image of her body returned to him, all long tanned legs and upturned full breasts, downy fur between her legs, her eyes large and dark and unreadable.

When he had showered and donned a fresh pair of at-sea coveralls, he walked to the control room. Artificial Intelligence Officer Bryan Dietz had the officer of the deck watch. At thirty-four, the lieutenant commander was bald and wore thick glasses. Dietz was completely in his element as the computer officer, dealing more easily with machines and other computer operators than with laymen. He was a professional and he was good, but he needed some help with his people skills if he wanted command at sea, McKee thought.

McKee nodded as Dietz made his terse report, just the way McKee had trained him. Ship's depth, course, and speed first, then position in the sea, position with respect to PIM—the moving dot in the sea that marked where the brass expected them to be—status of the mission, status of the Cyclops computer, status of the reactor plant, status of the forward spaces, and status of the crew. He took it in while leaning over the manual navigation chart, watching their previous track laid out in pencil with times marked at each waypoint.

Point Zulu was just ahead, twenty minutes at flank. During the night they had passed the Black Sea Fleet's southern track, though the Ukrainians were far to the east still, outside sonar range. Once at Point Zulu, *Devilfish* would slow to five knots and pop up to periscope depth and wait to ambush them. McKee snapped his fingers for more coffee, and while drinking it a thought of his wife came to him.

Reluctantly he admitted to himself that thinking about her seemed an obligation. Here, in his control room, surrounded by a well-trained crew and a tightly run ship, in the middle of a vital mission for national security, he loved this life. The thought of giving it up seemed ludicrous. But if Diana made him choose, could he leave her for this? With a measure of guilt he realized the thought of her divorcing him, the very word "divorce," sounded amazingly like freedom.

"Point Zulu, Captain," Dietz said quietly, snapping McKee back to the present. He took a last pull of the steaming coffee and looked at the officer of the deck.

"Upstairs, OOD, and let's grab the zero-seven-fifteen broadcast." The radio messages would be burst-transmitted from the satellite every fifteen minutes. Any change in their orders and the latest intelligence on the Ukrainian fleet would be on this broadcast.

Dietz turned to the helmsman officer at the ship-control station. "Pilot, all stop. One-five-zero feet, ten-degree up bubble."

The lieutenant at the panel pulled back on the throttle and his stick, the animation on his display revealing the ship's control surfaces responding. Dietz reached for a microphone hanging from a coiled cord in the overhead. "Maneuvering, control, downshift pumps and shift the reactor to natural circulation. Sonar, conn, slowing, coming shallow."

"Conn, Maneuvering aye," an overhead speaker rattled, the acknowledgment from the engineering control center. "Reactor's in nat-circ."

"Conn, Sonar aye."

The deck came up to a steep incline. McKee listened for the sound of dishes breaking from the galley on the upper level, the ship's stowage for sea his pet peeve, but silence prevailed. The numerals on the conn depth display rolled from 600 feet up to 150.

"Above layer, Captain," Dietz called. The ship had ascended out of the deep cold, above a dividing line where the sea was warmed by the sunshine. Above the thermal layer their sonar gear could hear the noises from the surface. "Sonar, conn, one-five-zero feet, baffle clear. Pilot, right fifteen degrees rudder, steady course south, ahead one third."

The pilot at the ship-control console acknowledged, and the ship came around, making sure there was no one close.

"Conn, Sonar, leg complete, no contacts."

"Pilot, right fifteen degrees rudder, steady course north."

The ship completed its slow circle. Again the report came from sonar—no contacts around them. The sea was empty.

"Officer of the Deck, PD," McKee said, ordering Dietz to periscope depth. The deck came up again, more shallowly this time. Dietz stepped behind the starboard periscope well and called, "Lookaround number two scope."

The pilot answered him: "Depth one four zero, speed four knots."

"Up scope," Dietz called, reaching into the overhead for a circular control ring. With a thump of hydraulics a stainless-steel pole rose up through the hull. The large optic control module emerged. Dietz slapped down the periscope grips, the triggers on them activating the motors that would rotate the heavy instrument. Dietz put his eye up to the rubber eyepiece and began spinning in rapid circles. A television widescreen came on high in the crowded overhead. The view was out of the periscope, complete with the same cross-hairs Dietz saw in his view. The view depicted the undersides of the waves high over the ship. The waves were large, a seastate of at least four, McKee thought. All the better for a periscope approach, since the waves hid the scope.

Dietz called, "No shapes or shadows." The control room was quiet, waiting for the periscope to

pierce the surface above. The room tensed to accept Dietz's command "Emergency deep," should
a surface ship appear.

"Nine zero feet," the pilot called. "Eight five
feet, eight four, eight three . . ."

"Scope's breaking," Dietz said as the view panel
showed white foam splashing against the eye piece.

"Eight zero feet, sir."

"Scope's clear," Dietz announced, speeding in
circles around the periscope. The view out the
widescreen blurred as the OOD spun the scope in
four rapid circles, looking frantically for close hulls,
but the widescreen was empty.

"No close contacts," Dietz said. "Low-power surface search." He slowed his rotation, now studying
the sea with a sixty-second-long circle. Still no surface ships. "High-power search." Dietz's circles
slowed, taking four minutes to scan the sea. Still
the view showed only a featureless overcast sky and
the dark blue sea.

"Conn, Radio." A new voice came from the
overhead speaker. "Request the Bigmouth."

"Pilot, raise the Bigmouth," Dietz commanded
from the periscope, his voice muffled by the optic
module. With another hydraulic thump the large
multifrequency antenna came out of the sail and
extended skyward to receive the burst transmission
from the orbiting Navy satellite. McKee checked
his watch—0714 and a few seconds. The antenna
would dry off, and at 0715 the communication
would begin.

"Radio, Conn, broadcast received, Bigmouth
coming down." A hydraulic thump again sounded

as the radiomen lowered the antenna themselves. "Captain, Radio, flash traffic in the computer, sir."

McKee turned to take the radioman's WritePad as the youth hustled it into the control room. This would be it, McKee thought. Either the White House had decided to scrub this mission, or they would have orders to attack.

McKee scanned the message list. There were three, the first an emergency action message, the second a brief operation order, classified merely top secret so McKee could share it with his officers, the last a secret-classified intelligence message. Unfortunately, the most important message to McKee was the one he would get to last. The emergency action message, at flash precedence, would wake up the ship's officers who'd just gotten to sleep after their all-night midwatches and would empty the officers' wardroom, where the remainder were starting their mornings over eggs, fruit, and coffee.

McKee looked up at Dietz. "Emergency action message, OOD."

"Aye, sir." Dietz reached for another microphone cord, this time for the shipwide PA system. "Communications emergency!" he called, his voice booming throughout the ship. "Communicator, navigator, radio senior chief lay to radio! Communications emergency!"

McKee looked at his watch, timing the arrival of the three tactical crewmen. It took all of thirty seconds. The navigator, heavyset Kiethan Judison, led the brigade. Judison was a Texan with a mop of hair obscuring his eyes. His drawl and loud voice usually announced his coming long before he was

even on the deck level of his destination, but he
had a piercing intelligence and an explosive wit, the
two catching by surprise anyone foolish enough to
judge him on appearance alone. Behind him was
David Dayne, the communications officer, a sloppy
and lackluster kid McKee was having trouble shap-
ing up, and then the radio chief petty officer, Senior
Chief Morgan Henry, a Maine fisherman's son with
a barrel chest, shaved skull, and pallid skin. Lieutenant Commander Judison stepped up to the railing of the periscope stand on the starboard side
where McKee stood, his face expectantly raised.

"Communication party present," Judison announced unnecessarily, the loudness of his voice
piercing the previous churchlike quiet. "What've
we got, Skipper? Emergency action message?"

"EAM's aboard, Nav," McKee said, thrusting
the WritePad at Judison. Judison's manner changed
from brash to meek in a heartbeat. The EAM had
just put the ship on a wartime status, and the message required the communications team to authen-
ticate it with one of the sealed packets in the double
safe. Judison passed the message on to Dayne and
Henry, then the three filed out of the room through
the aft door to get to the sealed authenticator safe
in the executive officer's stateroom. Within sixty
seconds they were back, Judison holding a foil
package over his head.

"Authenticator juliet papa delta hotel eight
mike," Judison said, putting the Alka-Seltzer-sized
packet in front of McKee. McKee read it and compared it to the EAM's authentication line, which

demanded authenticator number JPDH8M. It matched.

"Open it," McKee said.

"Open it, aye sir," Judison said formally. He was shaken, McKee thought. A sight he'd never thought he'd see. The navigator's fingers shook slightly as he ripped open the package. Inside was a small sheet of heavy paper with alphanumerics written on it. "Authenticator reads, 'November whiskey five four zero tango,'" Judison said. Senior Chief Henry looked over Judison's shoulder.

"NW540T," Henry said. "Confirmation."

"Mr. Dayne, read the message authentication requirement," McKee ordered. It seemed ridiculous, but the level of formality was required. *Devilfish* was being ordered into combat—those orders would be as official as the Navy would get.

"NW540T, sir."

"Very well. Navigator, scan the operation order," McKee said, handing the computer to Judison.

Judison read, his eyes becoming wide. He looked up. "We're shooting," he said. Dumbly, he said it once more.

McKee looked up to see Petri looking at him. For a second he thought she looked good, attractive in a different way for a woman. That he'd ever think a woman would be sexy in submarine coveralls would have been inconceivable before the fight with Diana. Now maybe he was changing, a psychological glacier moving a tenth of an inch at a time, but moving all the same.

"XO, convene the officers in the wardroom with

Mr. Dayne on the conn, Mr. Horner aft," McKee said. He looked around the now deserted control room. An odd feeling overtook him. Soon a combat watch would be manned here, and he would be shooting torpedoes in anger.

It wasn't much of a briefing, McKee thought. There was just not much to tell the crew. But they couldn't go into battle without an officers' briefing.

"Good morning, gentlemen, Captain, XO," Judison drawled. The navigator stood in front of the projection flat-panel display, which was blank. The room was full of the ship's sixteen officers, the department heads gathered at McKee's end of the table, Petri on his right, the engineer on his left. Judison had put on some half-frame reading glasses. "You've all probably been wondering why we left Norfolk in such hurry, flames coming out of our assholes, not even any time to, say, pick up the captain. Then we pick him out of the sky and flank it south off of Brazil to some godforsaken hole in the ocean labeled Point Zulu." He paused, his sense of drama inflating him. Get on with it, McKee thought, but let the navigator continue.

A map of the South Atlantic flashed up behind Judison with their track shown from the equator south, Point Zulu the track's termination. "Turns out we've got an EAM aboard. Mr. O'Neal, what's an EAM?"

The young electrical officer looked up. He'd been aboard for less than a year and still was working on qualifying in submarines. His first name was

Ryan, but his nickname was Toasty, and the officers all called him that.

"Emergency action message?"

"Correct. And what's that mean?"

"Orders to go into combat."

"From whom?"

"Uh, Unified Sub Command?"

"No. The term 'NMCC' mean anything to you?"

"NMCC," Toasty stammered. "Naval . . . Military . . . Communications . . . Central?"

The experienced officers roared in laughter. Judison scowled over his glasses, amused.

"Try National Military Command Center," he said gently. "Read 'Pentagon.' Read 'President.' Men, these orders come from the top, from the President herself." Judison turned to the display. "Over the horizon, sailing directly toward us, is a carrier battle group, owned by the Ukrainians, hailing from the Black Sea." He turned to Toasty O'Neal. "That's why, Mr. O'Neal, we call it the Black Sea Fleet." O'Neal waved off the sarcasm, smiling. "Our orders are simple. Sink it. Sink every ship while remaining undetected." Judison took the glasses off, his face serious and cold.

McKee scanned the crowd, gauging their reactions. The officers were frowning, not in anger but in concentration. Karen Petri's mouth had dropped open for just a second, then shut, her jaw clenching, her dark eyes smoldering. She glanced over at McKee. She was worried, he realized, and the look at him was her attempt to find solid ground. Still, despite whatever fears she felt, no one else would see them, and for that she received high marks.

McKee took a moment to look at the officers, suddenly feeling extraordinarily lucky that these men were under his command. The ship was top-of-the-line, the crew the Navy's best, the mission clear-cut and unambiguous.

"Okay, order of battle." Judison stood to the side of the flat panel, while video clips began to roll. "Lead ship of the flotilla is the *Admiral Kuznetsov,* a huge aircraft carrier, the Ukrainian answer to the Nimitz class." The video showed the carrier from the air as it plowed the sea. "This is target number one, the high-value unit. Next, the cruisers, four of them."

The navigator continued, profiling each ship of the fleet. McKee bit the inside of his lip as he realized that with one carrier, four cruisers, eight frigates, six destroyers, two oilers, and four amphibious transports, there were not many torpedoes to spare, particularly if he targeted several torpedoes per high-value unit.

"Finally, gentlemen, the wild card. The Black Sea Fleet has a small squadron of Severodvinsk Generation Four nuclear submarines attached. We think one of them got underway with the fleet when it sortied through the Med. If the Severodvinsk is screening the fleet, we may have some company."

Without an antisubmarine screen, the fleet would be easy pickings. An antisubmarine attack submarine, though, could blow the whole assault. But there was nothing they could do but stay alert.

"And gents, that's all we have for you. Contact time is eleven hundred, so you have about an hour to take a dump and study the war plan op-brief. We'll be manning up at ten forty-five. Any questions?"

There was only one, from the rider. A "rider" was an officer not of ship's company, usually from the squadron staff, who rode with the boat on an operation to gain experience or to evaluate the ship. This run, Lieutenant Commander Mike Kurkovic was onboard, the surgeon general from Unified Submarine Command HQ, a surgeon who was riding to see if there was any merit to the idea of assigning medical doctors to the crews of subs. Up to now, noncommissioned medics had taken the load. Kurkovic was a tall youngster, blond and stern and Slavic, wearing round metal-rimmed glasses. He had the top secret clearance for everything they were discussing, but for him to come to a war briefing and then ask a question seemed out of line. McKee raised an eyebrow and looked over at the doctor.

"There's a lot you've discussed about the 'how' but not much about the 'why,'" Kurkovic said. "If that carrier is anything like the old Nimitz-classes, it has about three thousand people onboard. Maybe five. Add the other ships, and we're talking about seven or eight thousand sailors steaming in that fleet. God knows how many men are in the troop transport amphibious ships, but say that's ten or twenty thousand more souls. Captain, we're about to kill the population of a small town. Why? Who are these guys? What do they mean to us?"

McKee frowned, aware of the staring eyes of the men. This was his test, he thought. Had it not been for the USubCom doc, they would have dismissed, manned battlestations, and started firing. With this question, every officer in the room would have his doubts. Why would they ambush a fleet on the basis of what boiled down to an e-mail with a few letters and numbers?

McKee stood up. "Gentlemen, XO, a few words if I may." The officers were watching him, not missing a word. "We're all officers in the U.S. Navy. The American Navy. Now, would America ever go out and ambush a foreign fleet—with twenty thousand souls aboard—without a damned good reason? Does anyone here, *anyone,* think that this operation was ordered without first having our diplomatic people do a full court press on the Ukrainians?" He paused. There were no hands raised. "And are we diplomats? No, we're not. So, are we privy to the results of diplomacy? Again, no. But we are America's enforcers. And as enforcers we've been called on to do what we're trained to do. What we've been ordered to do."

He continued, holding up a printout of the emergency action message. "This EAM, this sheet of paper . . . let me ask all of you a question. The married men in the room, raise your hands." Ten hands came up. "Do any of you think that your marriage license is a mere piece of paper?" No one spoke. "Now, the marriage vows you took . . . anyone here feel like they were just words?" Still silence. "Each man in this room, including you, Doc, took an oath of office. Does anyone here remember what it said? Let me quote for you." McKee raised his right hand, his glare darkening. 'I do solemnly swear that I will support and defend the Constitution of the United States against all enemies, foreign and domestic, that I will bear true faith and allegiance to the same, that I will obey the orders of the officers appointed over me, that I take this obligation freely, without any mental reservation or purpose of evasion, and that I will well and faithfully discharge the duties of the office on which I am about to enter, so help me God.'" McKee stared hard at the men. "Does anyone here feel those were just words? No? Well then, men, this EAM, this emergency action order, came to us from the President of the United States, and it orders us into action. Doc, it orders us to kill, to ambush, to assassinate twenty thousand men. I can only speak for myself, but that oath of office and that officer's commission in the Navy, they aren't just words, and that commission isn't just a piece of paper. It's a commitment. It's a message. A message to the President, that when she says 'go do this,' I do it. I don't ask why. I don't wonder what the results will mean to the greater world order. I just do it. That's what we're here for, Doc. This is what we do. It's more than our job. It's our duty. Yesterday our duty was to steam at damn near fifty knots at six hundred feet under the Atlantic to reach this square mile of ocean. Today our duty is to take the contents of our torpedo room and the fleet coming over the horizon and connect the two, to deliver the cargo we've carried from Norfolk at top speed. Our orders are to put a fleet—weapons of war, in case anyone here has forgotten—on the bottom of the sea. In less than an hour, I'll be on the conn lining up the battlecontrol system to shoot those targets. I suggest that all of you join me. Officers, dismissed."

4

The Circuit One shipwide announcing system boomed throughout the ship. "Man . . . battlestations!" The general alarm sounded then, a loud bonging noise tolling three times, then the magnified human voice again: "Man battlestations!"

McKee stood on the conn periscope platform, timing the arrival of the men in the room. Within thirty seconds the battlestations officer of the deck, Lieutenant Commander Dietz, looked over at him. "Battlestations manned, Captain."

McKee strapped on his headset, a device with one earphone, a boom mike, and a wireless transmitter, leaving one ear for the room.

"Attention in the firecontrol team, attention in sonar," McKee announced. This was it, he thought, the moment he'd trained for his entire adult life. The watchstanders' eyes were all on him, the room quiet. "Here's the plan. We're going with the OTH intel." OTH, for over the horizon. "The Keyhole spy satellites will feed Cyclops at the far-distant range. We'll supplement with two tube-launched Mark 5 Sharkeyes." Sharkeyes were sonar sensors loaded into the warhead compartments of Alert/ Acute Mark 58 torpedoes. At their destination the sensors would detach from the torpedo bodies, sink to best-listening depth, float a small radio transmitter to the surface connected to a thin wire to the sensor, and relay the data of what it heard to the Navy CombatStar satellite, which would then relay it to the Cyclops computer. "One of the Sharkeyes goes to the right of the fleet, the other to the left, the right unit twenty miles away, the left forty. When the fleet steams into the middle range, thirty miles, we'll open fire with the Alert/Acutes."

Alert/Acute was the inevitable nickname for the extreme long range torpedo/ultraquiet torpedo, or ELRT/UQT, the Mark 58. The advanced torpedo was the latest generation of active-quieted units, which put out sound into the water intentionally, but sound in reverse phase to the sound emitted by the propulsor pump jet. Because the broadcast sound canceled out the machine-generated sound, the heavy torpedo could sneak up on targets invisibly. The Mark 58 could carry either a two-ton conventional PlasticPac explosive or a small plasma warhead. For this run, *Devilfish*'s torpedo room had been loaded out with Mark 58 Mod Alphas, the PlasticPac-warhead variety.

"We'll put out a filtered salvo of twenty-three torpedoes." Filtered salvo, each torpedo fired at almost the same time, but each one tuned to listen to a particular ship so that twenty-three fish would not gang up on a single target. "The firing sequence is as follows—Navigator, Weapons Officer, listen up—the first fired unit to target one, aircraft carrier. Unit two to target two, one of the cruisers. Then the other three cruisers get one fish each. That's five launches for the five high-value targets.

Then one torpedo for each of the eight frigates, that's thirteen total. One torpedo for each of the six destroyers and four amphib transports, that's twenty three, leaving three torpedoes. I'm going to fire ten Vortex Mod Deltas from the forward vertical launch system to target the two oilers and any surviving surface hulls."

Vortex Mod Ds were solid-rocket-fueled torpedoes that traveled at three hundred knots. The Deltas were new, fired from the forward vertical launch tubes in the forward ballast tank near the bow. Each of the missiles could be launched only from deep depth, swimming upward and turning to the horizontal, then lighting off the solid rocket charge to make their way to a surface target. Once close to a surface ship, the Delta would dive deep—over a half mile—then turn and "fly" straight up at three hundred knots with the blue laser seeker looking for a surface-ship hull. The combination of high-density PlasticPac explosive and the upward velocity would blow most ships into a half-dozen pieces, all of them bursting into flames. It took only one to put down an aircraft carrier.

"That will give us a reserve of three torpedoes in the room and two Vortex Mod Deltas in case the Severodvinsk is with the task force, and in case any of the units of the filtered salvo double-team the targets instead of discriminating. By the time the fleet is within ten miles of us, within our visual horizon, the weapons should begin hitting. We need to be alert for antisubmarine jets off the carrier, ASW helicopters from the carrier or the destroyers and frigates, and the Severodvinsk. We'll begin the assault from periscope depth. Later on we may go deep and disconnect from the topside datalink. Everyone clear? Carry on." He looked over at Dietz. "Take her up to PD, sharp angle, no baffle clear."

As Dietz shot the ship up, the reports and commands only dimly registered in McKee's mind. Yet he was plugged into the sounds and rhythm of the ship.

Dietz hugged the periscope optic module as the ship rocked in the swells at periscope depth. "Raining outside, Captain. Coming down pretty hard now. Sky's dark, too."

"Dammit," McKee cursed, glancing at Petri. "That's going to hose the overhead satellite view."

"We'll still have infrared, sir."

"Better than nothing."

"Plus it'll shield the periscope."

McKee was deep in thought, wondering where the surface force was.

"Sonar, Captain," he called into his boom mike. "Report all contacts."

"No contacts, sir," the sonar chief, Chief Cook, replied. Cook seemed to have stepped aboard from the 1950s, sporting a whitewall haircut, black frame glasses, a pocket protector, and white socks. He was the ultimate sonar geek, and proud of it.

McKee pulled out a Cohiba torpedo cigar and lopped the end off with the cutter Diana had given him, the inscription *For my dearest Kelly* seeming odd in this setting. But McKee was so deeply involved in the moment that the memory of her face was lost to him. The lighter flared up, the smoke making a cloud around him, the first cigar of the

day smooth and calming. He wanted his crew to
see him like this, a cigar clenched between his teeth
as they went into battle.

"Nothing to do now but wait, XO," McKee said
to Petri, glancing over at her to see how she was
bearing up. She seemed calm enough, nodding back
at him.

McKee looked at his watch. Eleven o'clock on
the nose. The Keyhole intelligence satellite would
have broadcast its data to the CombatStar satellite,
which would be ready to link them in. The antenna
in the periscope would receive the data and make
the Cyclops computer a node in the theater battlespace system, all obtainable information on the
approaching enemy fleet available in seconds. The
navigator, who was responsible for the information
from the datalink, had ducked into the forward virtual-reality station, an egg-shaped hood some five
feet in diameter rolled down from the overhead all
the way to his feet. The interior was the display
field for the Cyclops computer.

"Captain, Navigator, datalink is up. We have the
surface force."

McKee stepped into the aftmost eggshell, VR4,
and leaned against a rail while pulling on a hood
with wide-aperture glasses, allowing the three-dimensional view the computer would use to display
the approaching fleet. "Battlescreen up," he commanded the computer.

Instantly McKee was in a different world. Instead
of standing on the deck plates of a nuclear submarine, he was standing in a virtual computer world,
which looked like a huge valley, the floor of it flat.

At what looked like a football field away, the floor of the valley sloped upward, gradually at first, then steeper as the distance grew. It was like being inside a stadium, but without seats, just a smooth surface colored an olive drab. Superimposed on the olive bowl of the valley were lines, circles around him climbing up the sloping walls, and lines drawn out radially from his position at the center of the bowl. The lines were range and bearing marks, and the slope of the bowl was the computer's depiction of the earth. The flat part of the bowl, the floor, represented the space near them, the flats inside the horizon. If he could see a ship through the periscope, the computer would show that contact somewhere on the flat part of the bowl floor.

Contacts outside the area of the horizon would show up on the sloping portion. The more distant the target, the higher it was up the wall. When the surface battle group appeared in the computer's battlespace, they would be high up the bowl on the line representing their bearing from the submarine. The battle group would descend closer and closer, until they reached the floor of the bowl. The color of the bowl changed from olive to pink at about halfway up the rise. The change in color showed the far range of their weapons. The virtual setup took some time to get used to, but after a few weeks it was hard to remember how they had ever put weapons on a target before.

"Captain, Navigator, datalink contact information coming into the battlespace now, bearing zero one zero, range eighty-seven miles."

"Very well," McKee replied. He turned so that

he was facing true north, and ten degrees to his right, far up on the sloping bowl, the dots of the battle group appeared.

"Datalink cascading into Cyclops, Captain," Judison said. The dots changed from simple spheres to shapes. One grew into a beachball-size three-dimensional diamond, its color changing to bright red—the aircraft carrier. A second turned into a blue box the size of a hat box, a frigate. The other dots dissolved into shapes until the cluster was as bright as a Christmas tree, all of them descending slowly down the sheer smooth wall of the otherwise empty virtual arena. Kelly blinked, and a cursor floated in front of him. He moved his eyes, and the cursor moved with it. He rolled the cursor to the diamond shape, then blinked. A mass of data appeared in space floating in front of him, to the right of the diamond, but at a distance that allowed him to see the text and the diamond without refocusing his eyes. The text was the computer-stored information on the carrier.

"Time," Kelly said to the computer, and a time display came up in front of him, also floating in space. "Cyclops recommendation on Sharkeye launch, unit two on left flank, range eighty-thousand yards from own ship, unit one on right flank at forty thousand yards, transit speed low. Calculate."

In front of McKee two orange beams of light shot out from the center point of the bowl, from his feet. One of them extended up to the right of the surface force, the other to the left. Launch times came up in front of him in countdown style. Two minutes to launch the left-running Mark 5

Sharkeye pod, seven minutes until they had to launch the one to go right.

Ten minutes later, the Mark 5s had been launched from the *Devilish*'s tubes, and McKee watched the units climbing up the walls of the virtual bowl. He puffed his cigar, the ventilation system high in the egg pulling out the smoke, fresh air blowing in the bottom. He waited another ten minutes while the Mark 5s ran to their positions and detached from the torpedo bodies, streaming their cables to small buoys on the surface, which would communicate with the CombatStar satellite, which would communicate with the *Devilish*.

"Captain, Navigator, Mark 5s deployed. We have the battle group on own-ship datalink." The incoming fleet was now detected on sensors launched by the ship rather than something boosted to earth orbit, the navigator's report indicated. The fleet was still too far distant to be heard on the Cyclops sonar system. By the time it was, half the weapons would be fired. The color of the fleet's shapes, still coming slowly down the incline of the bowl, brightened, showing the data to be another notch more reliable. The shapes approached, crossing the sixty-mile-range circle high over McKee's head. A few more miles and the fleet would cross from the pink section down into the olive-drab area, within weapons range.

"Navigator, tube status," McKee called to his boom mike.

"Sir, all four loaded with Mark 58s, programmed for medium-speed transit," Judison's voice said in his headset.

"Very well. Officer of the Deck, shift to computer control of the tubes," he ordered, placing the torpedoes and the tubes at the hands of the Cyclops battle-system computer. The system would ram new torpedoes in the tubes, pressurize them, flood them, open the outer doors, launch the weapons, shut the outer doors, drain down the tubes, open the inner doors, and ram in new weapons. *Devilfish* would pump out torpedoes at the rate of one every fifteen seconds, the twenty-three torpedoes ejected in less than seven minutes.

"Cyclops has the torpedo room, Captain," Dietz said.

McKee watched the two dozen shapes of the surface battle group crawl into the olive-drab zone, then down the range circle at forty miles where the left-flank Mark 5 sensor hovered.

"Conn, Sonar," Chief Cook's deep voice sounded. "We have acquisition of the surface force on acoustic daylight imaging. We show targets one through twenty-five. Bearings and bearing rates correlate with Mark 5 data."

"Sonar, Conn aye," Dietz said. "Captain, Cyclops shows ten seconds from torpedo autosequence."

"Captain aye."

A loud crash suddenly sounded from below McKee's feet—the first torpedo tube firing.

A bolt of blue light shot out from McKee's feet and zipped outward to the surface force. The first was followed by another fifteen seconds later, then another, the weapons represented by blue streaks of light moving quickly outward at first, then slowing as the range circles compressed. After six min-

utes, the last of the torpedoes had been fired. As
the shapes of the surface force neared the twenty-
mile-range circle, at the corner of the bowl flats,
the first blue bolt hit. The diamond shape pulsed
slowly, fading in and out. A second flash of blue
hit the diamond, the pulsing speeding up.

"Conn, Sonar, we have detonations at the bearing to Target One."

Over the next few minutes, the other symbols
began pulsing as blue flashes connected. Twenty
miles away to the northeast, the ships of the surface
force were taking hits, if the sensors were correct.

"Conn, Sonar, acoustic daylight deflection/eleva-
tion angle shows surface force vessels sinking."

"Sonar, Captain, how many?"

"We've got ten hulls going down."

"Target One?"

"Still on the surface."

McKee blinked for more data. The headset monitoring his eyes fed the blinking to the Cyclops. Several shapes displayed data, a dozen of them coming
up with the label HULL SINKING. It was time to
launch the Vortex Mod Deltas.

"Officer of the Deck, take her deep, eight hundred feet, fifteen knots."

The deck angled down as the ship dived. The
virtual bowl beneath McKee's feet changed, as if
he had sunk through the floor of the arena, the
gridlines above him, radiating out from him, and
beneath him. The display was the antisubmarine
setup, useful to determine the location of an enemy
in the space around them.

"Navigator, ten Deltas targeted toward the remaining heavies."

"Targeting by remainder priority, Captain."

"Eight hundred feet, Captain," Dietz reported.

"Shift vertical launch system to Cyclops control," McKee ordered.

The vertical tubes then launched one after the other, with a one-minute firing interval. The Cyclops display showed the missile tracks in red. The speed of flight was much faster, the weapons covering the eighteen-mile range to the target in four minutes. The first of them impacted while the computer was still launching the last six weapons.

"Conn, Sonar, detonations from remaining targets."

McKee blinked to call for more data. There were some ships indicating they were sinking, but there were tenacious vessels still on the surface. Finally the computer was finished firing the Vortex missiles. He decided to drive in close and see the result of the attack. He pulled off the computer headset and rolled up the eggshell enclosure, feeling as if he were walking out of a matinee into sunlight. He tossed the cigar butt, long cold and soggy from being chewed on, into a trash can.

"I have the conn," he said to his headset and to the room.

Dietz called out: "Captain has the conn."

"Pilot, right five degrees rudder, steady course one zero zero, all ahead full. Sonar, Captain, speeding up and heading to the southeast." McKee stepped up to the periscope stand. "Attention in the firecontrol team. I intend to approach the surface fleet at close range and observe the results of the assault. First we'll move off the track of the weapons. We're turning southeast to clear torpedo tracks, and when we're ten miles from the firing point, we'll turn north. When we're abreast of the fleet, we'll approach slowly out of the east. Carry on."

The minutes ticked on as the ship made its maneuvers. Before they turned to the north the computer reported the impact of all ten Deltas. Sonar could not confirm the remaining hulls sinking—the Vortexes could have blown their targets to such small pieces that they showed up as dust to the acoustic daylight imaging system.

McKee tried for a minute to focus inward, to see what his conscious thoughts were about attacking the surface force, and he realized he had none. There was no pity, no exhilaration, no feelings of loss, none of victory. He was as empty as if he'd played a computer game, and in point of fact, that was all he had done. The enemy had never been more than computer-generated shapes in the distance of a virtual arena.

"Pilot, depth seven five feet, twenty-degree up bubble, all ahead full." With a burst of speed McKee was bringing the vessel shallow, from eight hundred feet to seventy-five. "Mark speed twelve knots."

"Pilot, aye, ahead full, seventy-five feet, twenty up. Ship's angle is up ten, up fifteen—"

As the deck became a steep ramp, McKee's fist on the conn handrail turned white-knuckled.

"Five hundred feet, sir."

McKee waited, checking the weapon tube display

panel—three torpedoes left in the room, all tube-loaded, outer doors open. Two vertical launch tubes were ready with Vortex Deltas. Their outer doors were shut but ready to be opened at a moment's notice.

"Two hundred feet, sir, speed twelve."

"All back one third," McKee ordered. "Flat angle, up bubble five degrees, mark speed five!"

"Back one third, aye, sir, bubble down to up five, up three, one five zero feet! Speed five knots, sir."

"All ahead one third. Bring her up, Pilot!"

"One four zero feet, Captain."

"Lookaround , number two scope!"

"Speed five, depth one hundred feet."

"Up scope." McKee rotated the hydraulic control ring, and the periscope mast rolled upward out of the well. McKee put his eyes to the cold rubber eyepieces when they were at waist level. With his left grip he trained the view field high upward, looking above them to the nearby waves.

"Nine zero feet, sir."

The periscope was ten feet underwater. The waves rolled closer to them. McKee took a quick spin to look overhead, then kept the view trained ahead, in their direction of motion. They were steaming toward the task force, which was less than five miles ahead, less than ten thousand yards. When the scope cleared, the remaining ships should be visible.

"Eight five feet, eight four, eight three . . . eight three."

"Get us up, Pilot!"

"Eight two—"

"Scope's breaking, scope's breaking." Foam washed over McKee's view. He cursed under his breath, knowing that 7,700 tons of submarine at dead slow could take a minute to rise five feet.

"Eight zero feet, sir."

"Come on, get us up. Scope's clear. No surface search."

The control room was dead quiet. McKee's view was barely above the waves, the troughs of them low but the crests keeping him from seeing farther ahead.

"Seven nine, seven seven, seven six feet . . . seven five feet, sir."

The periscope rose over the last wave crest, and then McKee could see. Nothing in his sixteen years of operating submarines had prepared him for what was ahead in his periscope view. Because the view was piped down to the control room, Petri and Judison and the others also were able to see what McKee saw. At once a gasp rose up in the control room.

Ahead of them on the rain-swept sea was a mammoth aircraft carrier, gray in the haze. The ship was listing pitifully to port, the island leaning over, the deck dipping toward the sea, fires ripping across the deck. There was no sign of life, but then the entire deck was engulfed in flames. To the left of the carrier was a cruiser, once a mighty blue-water ship, now bow down, the superstructure underwater, the aft helicopter deck and the fantail and the screws reaching for the clouds. There were no lifeboats, no helicopters, no men floating in life jackets. To the right was an amphibious ship, a cruise

ship painted gray and converted to a troop transport. While McKee watched, the amphib transport
began to roll, the side closest to the periscope dipping into the sea, taking the rows of lifeboats—
oddly still attached to the upper decks, the covers
lashed on—into the water. The ship slowly capsized, rolling into the sea with a massive splash of
white foam. The two large stacks for the diesel engines went under, then the deck, until only the
rusty, featureless hull remained, the brass screws
pointing forlornly toward the rainy sky.

McKee increased the visual power to search for
survivors. With his right periscope grip he hit the
doubler trigger so that the scope went to forty-eight
power, the magnification making the image jump.
He saw no one. No floating corpses, no swimmers,
just a few empty life jackets and some floating debris. There should have been twenty thousand men
on the transport, maybe more, but the lifeboats had
all gone under when the vessel rolled. There was
an ocean of flotsam scattered over the sea, but not
a single human face.

He turned the periscope back to the carrier. The
entire deck was engulfed in flames, the angle growing steeper as the bow sank. The image focused on
the huge island. The upper decks of it emitted rolling clouds of orange flames and black billowing
smoke. The lower decks' windows were broken
open but empty. The sea around the carrier was
dirty with debris and patches of oil fires, and still
no sign of life.

To the left the cruiser departed the surface, the
stern vanishing below a wave, a field of foam and

bubbles on the waves the sign of its passing. A mournful groaning creak sounded loudly through the hull, filling the control room.

"Conn, sonar, the cruiser's bulkheads are collapsing."

Something made McKee look back at the carrier. From behind the island emerged an antisubmarine attack helicopter.

"Aircraft! Chopper, bearing mark!" he shouted.

"Mark 80 panel armed in auto, Captain, outer doors coming open, Mark 80s ready in all respects." Dietz had immediately armed the Mark 80 sub-launched antiair missiles in the sail, the automatic response to the appearance of a hostile air contact.

"SLAAM 80," McKee said, a little too loud for his own liking, while he punched a red button on the left grip. High over his head a small missile— eight feet tall and eight inches in diameter—was launched from a vertical tube in the sail. McKee kept his crosshairs on the chopper as it banked around the carrier. The flame trail of the missile was ruler-straight as it flashed past the chopper, seeming to keep going a few hundred feet beyond while the helicopter exploded in a huge ball of flames.

"Air search," McKee called, scouring the skies for another helicopter or antisub aircraft, but the sky was empty. He felt his heart rate decline to normal, his breathing slowing as if he'd run a mile. He pulled a hand from the right grip and wiped the sweat from his forehead.

In the periscope view, there was nothing left of the fleet except for the carrier, which stubbornly remained on the surface, bow slightly down, the fires on her deck calming now, the flames from the island just black heavy smoke.

"Attention in the fire-control team," McKee announced with his face still pressed up to the periscope. "I'm going to drive us in closer to observe the carrier. All other contacts have sunk. Pilot, left fifteen degrees rudder, steady course two six zero, turns for eight knots."

After twenty minutes, the ship had closed range to two thousand yards, a mere mile from the carrier, which now lay trimmed bow down with the flight deck forward edge just under the waves. The fires had gone out, the huge vessel's paint, once gray, now streaked in black. The ship sat there silently, floating. This was not allowed by Admiral Phillip's op order, McKee thought. Leaving the carrier floating would broadcast to the world that no natural disaster had befallen the Ukrainians but foul play. Their position would be marked, and salvage ships would easily find the torpedoed hulls on the ocean floor. Once the carrier went down, only a few people would know that the convoy had happened to be in this particular location.

"Attention in the fire-control team. I intend to shoot a Mark 58 at the carrier, target one, in direct contact mode, shallow transit, immediate enable."

Four minutes later, explosions rose from the carrier hull. Renewed orange flames and black smoke rose from the hulk for all of ten minutes as she finished dying. The ship finally plunged into the waves, bow first, the island splashing into the sea, then the stern. Bubbles and foam and oil fires marked her passage. At eight hundred feet depth the hull shrieked as the main deck and central compartments imploded. The acoustic daylight imaging of the sonar system tracked the hull until it smashed into the rocky bottom three miles down, then broke in two and become lost in the bottom clutter.

The fleet was gone, and with it McKee's enthusiasm for the mission. What had the good doctor said—twenty thousand men, maybe more, killed from the day's shooting. McKee's stomach hurt. He blinked in disgust, as if trying to banish the sickening images of the fleet's sinking.

"Officer of the Deck, secure battlestations. You have the conn." He snapped up the periscope grips and lowered it into the well. "Take her down and orbit Point Zulu at five knots. I'll be writing the situation report. Keep a max scan enabled for the Severodvinsk submarine. If she shows up, prepare for an immediate quick-reaction Mark 58 shot."

Without another word, McKee stepped down from the conn and walked to his stateroom, preoccupied. He shut the door of his cabin behind him and sank into his command chair. The thought nagged at him that he hadn't seen a single body or survivor. How could that be? It had to be the killing force of the Mark 58s slamming into each hull, causing massive shock to the crewmen, dropping the sailors where they stood, so that the hulls of their ships took them down. But the troop transport—what about it? Surely a vessel loaded with thousands of marines would have dozens standing topside getting fresh air or smoking, despite the rain?

McKee's thoughts were interrupted by the clicking of the Circuit One PA system, The voice of Bryan Dietz was inexplicably an octave too high as he shouted, "Snapshot tube one!" Dietz had just ordered the ship to prepare to fire an emergency quick-reaction torpedo at an enemy submarine.

One moment McKee had been sitting with his head in his hands. In the next he was hurtling into the brightly lit control room. He snatched up a headset and whipped it on. He ducked into virtual-reality station 4, the eggshell rolling down in annoyingly slow motion, the computer display lighting up.

He shouted at the computer to display Dietz's face on his eggshell canopy surface. Dietz looked pale, with eyes larger than hard-boiled eggs. Dietz began stammering his report even before McKee demanded it.

"The Severodvinsk, Captain, bearing two seven five. He got close in, within his weapons range, came in from the north, from the other side of the sinking site. Acoustic daylight sonar didn't pick him up because the bubbles from the sunken hulls were interfering with the noise on that bearing and—"

"How do we hold him now?"

"Acoustic daylight imaging. Nothing on frequency analysis or broadband noise—"

"Status of battlestations?" McKee barked, trying to keep Dietz's panic in check. The previous command "Snapshot tube one" automatically notified the crew to man battlestations.

"Wait one, sir. Chief of the Watch?"

Another voice: "Battlestations manned, sir."

McKee called out to Petri, "XO?" He muttered to the computer to display her face on the canopy next to Dietz's.

"Here, Captain," she said. Her face was dark, her brows curving into a frown.

"Target designation?" he asked.

"Target twenty-six," she snapped.

McKee looked out at the display field in front of him. Once again he was surrounded by a grid of range marks, bearing lines, and depth planes. On the far side of the virtual pool slightly above him was a pulsing object, appearing as if it were forty feet away, a Zeppelin shape about three feet long. It oddly seemed to vibrate slowly, closer, then farther. The sliding back and forth was the computer's way of showing that the exact distance to the target was uncertain. At its closest it was twenty miles out, at its farthest some thirty-five. But at either of the possible distances, the Severodvinsk attack submarine was much too close for McKee's liking. The question was how to shoot him without him knowing about it, since the loudness of weapons could potentially give them away.

If McKee lived by the book, he would launch a Mark 58 Alert/Acute torpedo in ultraquiet swimout mode, the propulsion drive of the torpedo at its quietest, but also at its slowest. The weapon would take up to an hour to traverse the distance to the Severodvinsk. In that time the enemy submarine could pump out two dozen weapons, McKee thought. The Mark 58 tactic would not fit. McKee realized he might be accused of impatience or even fear, but he didn't care. This situation demanded that he strike quickly.

"Navigator, program Vortex Mod Delta units eleven and twelve in submerged target mode."

The navigator's voice was surprised but obedient. "Units eleven and twelve set up in antisub mode, Captain," he said after twenty long seconds of dancing with the Cyclops computer's weapons control module.

"Attention in the fire-control team," McKee said. His voice was level and deep, he noticed. A part of him was glad, but another realized the tone of voice was a lie. He was far from confident. The tight feeling in his throat and the coppery taste of his tongue attested to that, but if the crew knew that, this attack would derail in its first minute. "I'm putting two Deltas down the Severodvinsk bearing line. At submerged weapon transit speed of three hundred knots, we'll have ordnance on target in five to eight minutes. However, with the noise of the solid rocket propulsion, the Severodvinsk will very likely fire back at us. I don't think he's heard us yet, but when he hears the missiles, he'll shoot down the bearing line. Our plan is to shoot and then drive off track. We'll remain in-theater long enough to observe the Severodvinsk sinking." McKee took a breath. "Firing point procedures, vertical launch tubes eleven and twelve, Delta missiles in antisub mode, target twenty-six."

"Eleven and twelve on Cyclops control, Cyclops in autosequence, sir," Judison said.

"Very well." McKee waited, his heart pounding.

A few seconds later the forward vertical launch tubes barked. Blue streaks extended from McKee's position, slowly swimming toward the Severodvinsk. McKee waited for the rocket motors to ignite, and within a minute both rocket motors had lit off, the sound of their ignitions loud in the room, then fading away. The Cyclops virtual display showed the blue streaks speeding up dramatically and dashing toward the target. McKee watched the target for signs of it detecting the incoming missiles. The Deltas were within a half mile of the target, and still no sign of the Severodvinsk fighting back. McKee smiled to himself. Perhaps this battle would be over soon. He watched the first missile connecting with the target, then the second, and the target disappeared in a pulsing bright cloud.

"Conn, Sonar, target twenty-six going down."

"Conn, aye," Dietz replied, the men in the control room erupted in a cheer.

"Keep it down, people." Petri's voice said in McKee's earphone circuit, but he was too preoccupied to notice. He squinted at the position to the target, waiting. If it had put a weapon in the water, it would be coming now.

"Conn, Sonar, torpedo in the water, bearing to the position of the Severodvinsk."

Goddammit, McKee cursed to himself. The Severodvinsk had gotten off a counterfire, and now the *Devilfish* was under attack.

"Sonar, Captain, classify the torpedo," he said, intentionally injecting venom into his voice to keep the crew moving. "I have the conn," he said. He considered leaving the eggshell so he could pace the control room floor as he had during the surface attack, but he needed the three-dimensional data from Cyclops inside the canopy. He compensated by displaying the key officers in front of him. They also had an image of him in their views, from the tiny camera embedded in his canopy. "Pilot, all ahead flank, cavitate the propulsor, right ten degrees rudder, steady course east!"

"Cavitate flank, my rudder's right ten, course east, aye."

Dietz's Circuit One PA announcement rang out in the room and throughout the ship: "Torpedo in the water! Torpedo in the water!"

"Turns for flank, sir," said the pilot at the ship-control panel.

"Take her down to test depth, fifteen hundred feet," McKee ordered. The ship might be just a hair faster deep. With the water a degree cooler, it would be less likely to boil into vapor from the low-pressure side of each propulsor blade, making the thrust greater. Also, the torpedo might not be designed to go so deep.

"Pilot, emergency flank, two hundred percent power," McKee called. At that speed the ship might gain another five knots, but McKee had just committed the ship to three months in the drydock, replacing fuel modules after overpowering the core. Plus, the entire aft two thirds of the submarine would become a high-radiation area. Small potatoes when an incoming torpedo was chasing them.

"Sonar, Captain, classify the goddamn torpedo!" They still hadn't said a word about it. Was it a Severomorsk 52-centimeter? Chinese-designed Cultural Revolution 52-centimeter? Or, God help them, a Russian-designed 100-centimeter Magnum with a plasma warhead?

"Captain, Sonar, the torpedo is putting out the frequency spectrum of a Russian Magnum," Senior Chief Henry's voice said on McKee's headset.

We're dead, McKee couldn't help thinking.

"But it has the propulsor low frequencies of an American Mark 48 Adcap torpedo, sir."

McKee swallowed. His sonarmen had either lost their minds or this was some sort of variant on the Russian Magnum. But the Ukrainians could have grabbed an old Mark 48 Adcap "advanced capability" from twenty years ago and inserted some kind of new motor in the weapon casing. It was bad news if this were a retreaded Adcap. The Adcap could go fifty-five knots, faster than their emergency flank speed of—McKee craned his neck to see the speed indicator—fifty-two knots, not good enough. The torpedo would catch up to them. Even if it took an hour, it would catch up and it would detonate.

But if it were an Adcap, there was also some good news. The Adcap had a "floor" of 1,850 feet. Below that it would implode from the pressure of all the tons of water above it. That depth had been verified dozens of times in tests. There was only one problem. *Devilfish*'s own crush depth was 1,800 feet.

"Torpedo closing, Captain," the sonar chief reported.

McKee looked out at the virtual landscape. Under him was a submarine shape indicating ownship. In the far distance was a blurry cloud where the Severodvinsk had exploded when the two Deltas had blown it apart. In between the Severodvinsk wreckage and *Devilfish* was an incoming blood-red shape about the size of a banana, now about ten feet away in the make-believe pool.

"Conn, Sonar, torpedo range three thousand yards, torpedo becoming active."

"Sonar, Captain, the torpedo noise—any change in classification?"

"Cap'n, Sonar . . . we, uh . . ."

Silence.

"Sonar, Captain, report!" McKee's fury suddenly overcame his fear.

"Sir, definite Mark 48 Adcap."

"Pilot, take us down slowly to depth nineteen hundred feet, very shallow angle, no more than ten feet per second, flat angle."

"Say again, sir?" the pilot stammered. Most orders were followed instinctively, but this order could crush the ship.

"Goddammit! Take her the hell down! Flat angle, ten feet per second, nineteen hundred feet."

Petri chimed in. "Mr. Phelps, you heard the captain. Take her the fuck down!"

Perhaps it was McKee's voice, or the unexpected sound of the female officer cursing, but in any case he put his control stick down.

The hull angled downward sharply, the pressure causing a groaning sound. Usually McKee paid the creaks no mind—the ship was fabricated of the finest high-yield HY-120 steel, the entire ship a giant pressure vessel with steel almost two inches thick. But now he would be taking the whole ship, with 133 souls onboard, down into a depth where the warranty was off. DynaCorp's Electric Boat Division, headquartered in Groton, Connecticut, stated that test depth was fifteen hundred feet. Design failure depth with a safety factor of 1.0—with no margin—was calculated, assumed to be, eighteen hundred feet. But no one could really say. Crush depth might be nineteen hundred or even two thousand feet. Or a main seawater cooling pipe, two feet in diameter, could fail at seventeen hundred and fifty feet and fill the hull with water within a minute, a flooding accident from which they couldn't recover. And they were going faster now than any DynaCorp engineer had envisioned when the crush depth calculations were made. A gram of incorrect pressure on the control stick could take them instantly down hundreds of feet as the bowplanes and sternplanes screamed through the water flow.

Hell with it, McKee thought. Taking her below calculated crush depth would either lose the torpedo or kill every man onboard.

Just then a piercing shriek sounded through the hull, the sound of the torpedo sonar. A shiver crawled up McKee's spine.

"Depth seventeen hundred feet, sir, proceeding deeper," the pilot said uncertainly, as if hoping the order would be rescinded.

"Take her down," McKee said, his voice hard as steel, but his heart beating like a jackhammer.

The torpedo sonar shrieked again, a high-pitched whistle sounding for five long, ear-splitting seconds.

"Depth seventeen fifty."

McKee waited, then decided to leave the virtual reality eggshell canopy. If the ship went below crush depth, he didn't want to be stuck inside a computer game. He'd stand on the conn and command his crew and his ship. When he emerged, he found that Petri and Dietz had already left their canopies and were standing at the starboard plot table, the one displaying the computer-generated plot of the battlespace. Neither one looked at him.

"Depth eighteen hundred, sir."

"Very well, proceed to nineteen hundred feet." It could be the last order he'd ever give.

"Eighteen twenty-five, sir."

McKee nodded. There were twelve people in the room outside the virtual eggshells. All twelve pairs of eyes were fastened to McKee, hoping for some kind of reassurance. He had none to give them. But image was everything, he thought. To prove the point, he pulled the last Cohiba from his pocket, clipped it with Diana's cutter, and lit it with his *Greenville* lighter. He felt as if he were standing on the gallows. He stared down at the cutter Diana had given him, thinking he should have listened to her months ago. But it was too late now.

"Eighteen-fifty feet, sir."

"Very well."

The floor setting of the torpedo, if it were an Adcap. Why the hell a Ukrainian submarine would carry an ancient American torpedo remained a mystery. He hadn't had time to think about it before, but there was nothing to do now but think.

"Conn, Sonar, torpedo range gating. It's within one thousand yards."

Half a mile, McKee thought. With a closing rate of just four knots, it would take six minutes for the torpedo to catch them.

"Eighteen seventy-five feet, sir."

The hull continued to groan from the depth. The popping of the hull frames sounded like the creaking of an old house in a storm.

"Sir, ship's depth—nineteen hundred feet."

McKee held his breath. A hundred feet below calculated crush depth, with *Devilfish* sailing at 200 percent reactor power. The designers and their margins of safety, he thought, were responsible for their survival so far. *So help me God,* he thought, *if I live through this I will kiss the DynaCorp chief designer. On the lips.*

"Conn, Sonar, we're getting odd noises from the torpedo."

"Sonar, Conn, report." *Come on, what are you talking about?*

"Captain, incoming torpedo is making popping sounds."

McKee paused. "Popping sounds," he prompted.

"Popping sounds, sir."

After all that, his tactics were failing. The torpedo had followed him deep. If *Devilfish* could go deeper than its calculated crush depth, so then could the torpedo.

"Pilot, depth nineteen-fifty."

"Nineteen-fifty, aye, sir. Taking her down."

A ripping, screeching noise sounded through the hull. The pressure was enough to smash them flat, an egg under a car tire.

"Conn, Sonar—"

An explosion threw McKee into the periscope pole. The lights went out. An alarm sounded loudly in the space, but the noise seemed muted to McKee as the room slowly rotated in a hazy red light. He could only croak out two words:

"Emergency blow."

"Pilot, emergency main ballast tank blow!" Petri shouted. Her voice sounded muted and dull to McKee, who now was looking at the deck plates of the conn's elevated periscope platform.

"Blowing forward, blowing aft, sir! Depth nineteen hundred."

McKee couldn't answer, his head pounding, blood in his mouth.

"Conn, maneuvering, reactor scram," the overhead speaker announced.

"Conn, Sonar, incoming torpedo detonated. Range was eight hundred yards."

"Depth fifteen hundred and rising."

"Officer of the Deck, damage reports." Petri's voice.

McKee tried to reach up to one of the handrails around the conn. His head was spinning. He hauled himself up, his mouth bleeding.

"Are you hurt, sir?" Petri's hand on his shoulder.

He waved her off. "I'm fine," he said.

The deck was angled steeply upward, twenty degrees, making it nearly impossible to stand.

"Captain, all spaces report no visible damage."

"Depth one thousand, sir."

He had to abort the emergency surface, he thought. The ship was out of danger, and they couldn't be seen in the area.

"Pilot, vent forward and aft, take off the angle, maintain depth below one five zero."

The pilot fought the depth, the speed of the ascent giving the control surfaces power to keep the vessel down, but the ship was slowing from the loss of the reactor.

"Depth eight hundred, angle up ten, sir."

"Keep us down."

"Depth six hundred, angle down two."

McKee pulled a microphone down from the overhead. "Maneuvering, Captain, status of fast recovery startup?"

"Conn, Maneuvering, fast scram recovery in progress, estimate full propulsion in two minutes."

"Depth four-fifty, sir, we're controlling it."

"Maintain four-fifty feet," he said.

The reactor was back within a few minutes. McKee gave the orders, taking the ship out of the area. Op order or not, he didn't want to be anywhere near the site of the Black Sea Fleet's sinking. He went to his stateroom and drafted a dry situation report on the sinking of the fleet. He took it to radio, went to the conn, ordered an excursion to periscope depth to transmit the report and obtain further orders. Strangely, orders came back immediately, telling them to get back to Norfolk at flank speed. He ordered Dietz deep, ordered flank, and returned to his cabin.

Under the spray of a shower he washed away the sweat of fear. Yet when he was clad in fresh coveralls, he felt no better. He was in his stateroom's command chair when Petri knocked and came in.

He looked up at her, his eyes glassy. He reached for a cigar from his desktop humidor, which was bolted to the desk to keep it in place during large angles. His hands trembled violently as he raised the cigar to his lips.

"Yes, XO?"

"Sir, I thought you did a great job."

McKee nodded, not sure how to take the comment. He tried to raise the lighter to his cigar, but his hands were shaking so badly he couldn't get a flame. Petri gently took the lighter and put the flame to his cigar while he puffed. When she was done, she put the lighter on the table. He felt his eyes water, and he looked up at her, wondering if his gratefulness was in his expression.

"Thanks, XO."

"No, sir, thank you. If it weren't for you, we'd be fish food."

McKee's eyes were suddenly heavy.

"If it's okay with you, XO, I think I'm going to get some sleep." He felt dead. He put his hands under the table so Petri wouldn't see them trembling.

"Good night, Skipper."

The door shut behind her. He sank into his rack and into darkness.

5

The phone rang, the ringing sound changed. Diana must have bought a new phone. And though it was strange, he knew it was Diana calling.

"Hello," he mumbled sleepily, the phone cord dangling over the bed. He remembered that he was still angry at Diana, but he couldn't remember why. "What do you want?" He dropped the phone and had to reach down to the carpet to find it. "Diana?"

"Um, no, Officer of the Deck, sir." It was Judison.

McKee tried to wake up but he was dead tired. "Okay," he said, his voice still heavy with sleep. "What do *you* want?"

"Sir, it's twenty-two hundred, and we're being called to periscope depth by our extreme-low-freq call sign."

ELF radio waves could penetrate deep into the ocean, but were limited in value—it took ten to twenty minutes to transmit one character. *Devilfish* had a two-letter call sign, which had taken some time to receive onboard.

"Request permission to come shallow in preparation to coming to periscope depth."

"Take her to PD," McKee said, violating his own standing orders that the OOD had to come to 150

feet first and fill him in on the ships detected on
the surface before coming above that depth. "And
don't call me again." McKee dropped the phone to
the carpeting and felt the blackness again, sinking
deep into his bed. The bed tilted upward with the
ship, then began gently rocking from the waves at
periscope depth. McKee waited for the bed to tilt
again as the ship went deep, but it kept rocking.

The phone buzzed again. He had to find the
handset on the deck of the dark cabin.

"Captain. Now what?"

"Sir, there's flash traffic in the computer, marked
personal for commanding officer."

A knock came at the door. The radioman was
bringing in a WritePad computer with the radio
message they'd received. McKee put the phone
down and sat up in bed. The door creaked open,
letting harsh white light into the room, silhouetting
the radioman.

McKee took the computer and waved off the
petty officer, then began to read. McKee had half
expected this. The dry written situation report on
the sinking of the fleet was certainly not enough
for the flag officers. They'd want details. But
strangely, the message required him to be in a dress
uniform. That was ominous. They did that when
they relieved a captain of command. McKee had
done nothing that would warrant his sword being
broken. He shrugged into coveralls and took the
computer through the head to the far door that led
to Petri's stateroom. He knocked. Her voice called
him in.

When he opened the door, she was sitting at her

fold-down desk, working on some files, wearing her coveralls and socks, her hair down and spread over her shoulders. "Yes, Captain?"

"XO, we're being called to a videolink. Hope you brought service dress khakis with you."

Petri scanned the message, then smiled. "Brass want the gossip," she said. "They want to know what it felt like sinking that fleet."

Ten minutes later, they sat at McKee's conference table, made up with a green felt tablecloth. McKee wore a starched khaki jacket with its black shoulderboards, each bearing the three stripes of commander, his gold dolphin pin and his ribbons above his left pocket, the submarine capital ship command pin below the pocket. Under the jacket he wore a khaki shirt and a black tie. Petri had chosen the version of service dress that had pants rather than a skirt.

They sat at the side of the table facing the camera and videolink widescreen. When it came up, the camera rotated to face them, and the screen filled with several images. The main image showed Admiral Bruce Phillips in his Norfolk office. The other men were officers in service dress, but McKee didn't recognize them.

"Good evening, gentlemen," Phillips began, blinking momentarily at Petri, whose gender would mess up the official-sounding opening of the videolink. "This is a debrief of the sinking of the fleet." Phillips introduced everyone. One of the men was from Seal Team Seven, another from the Artificial Intelligence Command, another from Naval Intelligence.

McKee looked up at Phillips, who was sitting in a high-backed leather chair behind an oak table, his white officer's cap with the scrambled eggs on the surface, the traditions of the Navy forbidding a hat on a table unless the owner had been to the North Pole—an old rule designed to keep hats off tables, until nuclear sub officers who'd been under ice began to toss hats on tabletops. Phillips had a crewcut that masked his receding hairline over an ordinary round face. If met on the street, Phillips wouldn't gather a second look, one of the reasons he had gone into weight training, his arm muscles bulging out of his shirt. McKee had served for Bruce Phillips several years before, when Phillips was in command of the Seawolf-class ship *Piranha* and McKee had been his navigator. The two men had been friends, as much as they could be separated by their rank and station.

"Gentlemen, please stand by while I patch in the Chief of Naval Operations."

McKee held his breath. Admiral Pacino's listening to his briefing was unprecedented. Pacino was the number one admiral in the Navy and reported to the Secretary of War and the President. He could kill a career with one shake of his head. McKee felt his armpits melting. A portion of the screen blinked, jumped, then focused on Admiral Michael Pacino, a gaunt, hard-looking man with white hair and dark eyebrows, a deep tan, emerald green eyes surrounded by crow's feet and a thin face. The admiral looked barely older than McKee, yet had something in his eyes that made him seem like a very old man. His look was an intense mask of concentration, his brows low over his eyes. He wore a tropical white uniform shirt with his four stars and gold anchors on gold shoulderboards, his eight rows of ribbons over his pocket, a dolphin pin and fleet command pin barely in screen view.

"Evening, people," Pacino said in a deep, scratchy voice. "I asked Admiral Phillips to let me eavesdrop on the debrief before our audience with the President in the morning. Please go on with the briefing as if I weren't here."

Yeah, right, McKee thought in a mental grimace, but keeping his face neutral.

Phillips continued, "Commander McKee, could you take ten or fifteen minutes to describe in detail the operation? Start to finish."

McKee briefed the op, his sentences crisp and complete, from the flank run south to the outrunning of the Severodvinsk's torpedo shot.

When he was done, Phillips looked at him closely. "So, Commander McKee. You had highly classified orders to speed to the South Atlantic, then an emergency action message to sink the Black Sea Fleet, is that correct?"

"Yes, Admiral." An alarm bell was ringing, but McKee couldn't put his finger on the trouble.

"You sank the fleet, shot down an ASW chopper and the fleet-screen submarine, right?"

"Yes, sir."

"And you were fired on by the submarine? A Mark 48 Adcap torpedo?"

"Yessir."

"Did you see any survivors in the water?"

"None." McKee had already gone over all this.

"Did you find that or the Mark 48 a, well, an anomaly?"

"Yes, sir. But we were too busy trying to evade it. There was no time to analyze the situation." Something was wrong. A corner of Phillips' mouth was raised, just slightly. Pacino was smiling.

"Well, Admiral," Phillips said, apparently addressing Pacino. "Looks like the scenario was written better than we thought."

Scenario? McKee thought, glancing at Petri, whose eyes were wide, looking back at McKee.

"Commander McKee," Phillips said, "the operation was an exercise. The Alpha code word information is a category of Release Twelve devoted to system testing. The operation was a test of how fast we could scramble a submarine to intercept a fast-transiting offensive fleet, of how well we could attack a surface action group with a lone sub, of how our command-and-control system functions, and how the crew would function under this kind of pressure. It was even a test of fleet administration—we had let you go on leave to who knows where and suddenly *Devilfish* was sent to sea. It was a test of what we'd do, let the XO take the ship out and insert the captain later by chopper. And it was a great success, although we were worried that having you briefed solely by a computer would take away a lot of the realism, especially since there was no 'context' to the scenario."

A smoldering anger was building inside McKee, but he kept his face absolutely flat.

"Then the scenario began to come apart—we didn't think you'd approach close into the sinking hulls, and we had no corpses, a major discrepancy, and the Severodvinsk submarine was a decommissioned Los Angeles–class with a Severodvinsk noise-spectrum generator. The torpedo was a Mark 48 Adcap with a Magnum noisemaker, but we figured that would be revealed late in the scenario."

McKee felt like a fool. "Admiral, at the risk of looking like an idiot, I can tell you right now, we had no idea. And I fought the ship to the limits, sir. We overpowered the core and took the ship down to nineteen hundred fifty feet, below theoretical crush depth."

"We know you tried, Kelly. We got a transmission of telemetry at your first periscope depth."

"A transmission? I didn't authorize a transmission," McKee said, then bit his lip.

Phillips gave McKee a gentle, almost sorrowful look. "We had the ship wired, Commander. The cameras used by the Cyclops and all the Cyclops battle-recording data were tied into a hard-drive memory module rigged to a burst transmission when you came up."

"But what about my violating the ship's operating limits?" McKee knew he sounded even more foolish, but he needed to know. Something was snapping inside him, and he was finding he no longer cared how he looked.

"We had a safety module inserted into Cyclops. If you tried to overpower the core or take the ship below test depth, the computer would simulate the readings as if it were responding to you, but meanwhile would keep the ship inside limits. You never went over a hundred percent power or deeper than fifteen hundred feet, Kelly. It just seemed like you did. Cyclops had a noisemaker brought onboard before the ship sailed—to simulate the creaking noises of the hull. And we had a safety monitor onboard. The surgeon general, Lieutenant Kurkovic? He's a surgeon assigned to USubCom. He's also submarine-qualified. He was our observer, and had orders that if Cyclops' safety module failed, he'd tell you about the exercise.''

"But the fleet, the chopper, how—"

"A question for the Artificial Intelligence Command,'' Phillips said, and a Navy captain, one of the other faces, began talking about the programming of the robot fleet, each ship a mothballed U.S. Navy ship, painted, modified, and equipped with the robotics to allow them to sail in fleet formation to the South Atlantic. The only problem that cropped up was the submarine. The mockup Severodvinsk had had mechanical trouble and was trying to catch up to the fleet when McKee attacked it, making it arrive on scene much later than the scenario demanded.

McKee listened, his face a mask, until Phillips brought the meeting to a close. The room crashed into silence. McKee kept staring at the wall. The phone buzzed. McKee let it ring.

"Sir?" Petri, looking at him.

"You get it.'' Disgust in his voice.

"XO,'' she said. She listened, then cupped the phone to her shoulder. "OOD wants to go deep and get back on PIM at flank.''

McKee looked at her in disgust. "Fine. Deep. Flank. Chase PIM.''

Petri stared at him for a moment, then spoke into the phone. "Captain orders deep and flank, return to PIM." She put the phone down.

"Sir?"

"Leave me alone."

When the door shut behind her, McKee continued staring at the stateroom bulkhead.

6

"All stop," Dietz ordered into a microphone. He put the bullhorn to his mouth and shouted to the crew on deck, "Pass over line one." A mechanic petty officer tossed the monkey's paw with the lead line to the pier, the thin rope carrying over the heavy Manila line made fast to the forward starboard cleat. McKee watched him from the flying bridge.

The other lines were passed to the pier and doubled up. The gangway came down, the bridge carrying the heavy shore-power cables next. McKee climbed down the sail hatchway below to the upper level of the forward compartment and down a steep ladder to his stateroom. He grabbed his bag and paused in the control room, finding the officer of the deck.

"Shut down the reactor and bring on shore power. Dismiss the crew and station in-port duty section three. You need anything, call Petri."

He climbed the ladder up the forward escape trunk to the deck and over the gangway to the pier, the announcement ringing behind him throughout the ship and the topside deck, "*Devilfish*, departing!" Pier Seven at Norfolk Naval Station was a half-mile-long jetty of concrete, as wide as a runway, with black hulls of submarines tied up on either side. McKee walked solemnly down the pier to the senior officer parking lot. He tossed his bag into an aging Porsche and cranked the motor. He was barely aware of arriving home to a two-story house set in one of the dozens of residential subdivisions behind the beachside resort complex of Virginia Beach.

He walked up to the door and said to the computer microphone, "I'm home." The door unlocked itself and opened, the lights coming on. As McKee stepped in, the house was quiet. There was a smell here, he thought, standing in the foyer. It was Diana's smell, a pleasant mixture of her perfume, her shampoo, her hair, her skin. Here, in her universe, the submarine and the Navy were gone, and there was just her. He walked into the front room he'd taken for his office, glancing at the e-mails sent to the house, much of it junk, the bills all taken care of by the electronic banking system. He looked over at the wall, where a picture of them hung, the wedding picture they'd both loved, McKee in a starched choke-collar white dress uniform, lieutenant's shoulderboards on his shoulders, Diana ravishing in a low-cut gown. Her generous breasts and small hips and straight long blond hair and shimmering deep blue eyes were all part of what had drawn him to her, but there had been so much more beyond the physical—her intelligence, her humor, her serious approach to her family, her joyful acceptance of his, her planning for the baby, even her explosive temper. Suddenly he missed her. And God knew the Navy had nothing for him anymore. Not after the business with the exercise. He glanced at the photo next to it, the one famous in the family. His father, grandfather, and great-grandfather were all standing behind an eight-year-old version of himself on the deck of a fishing boat with a shark on the deck. All Navy officers, the reason he himself was. Annoyed, he looked away. Diana had always hated that he'd chosen the career his family had urged, and only now did he think she might have been right. He turned away from the shark picture and walked up the stairs.

He tossed his bag on the unmade bed, sensing her again even more strongly here. He peeled off the uniform stinking of submarine, ready to step into the shower. It occurred to him that the computer had no messages from Diana, but that wouldn't matter—he would tell Diana that he was finished with the Navy. Then they would get on with their lives, have the baby, and go on. They'd have to sell the house, though, and move someplace where he could get a job. He would do it on his own, the hard way, knowing that he could never work for Diana's father.

The water ran over him in the shower, the water as hot as he could stand it. He stayed in until the hot water ran out, then toweled off and pulled on a T-shirt and jeans and sat on the bed. Looking at the bed, he wondered if she had stayed in Wyoming.

He wandered through the house, glancing at his watch. It was Saturday and the light was fading into evening. He was sitting down to his desk, about to pick up the phone and find Diana, when the doorbell rang. He thought of excuses he could give the neighbors but caught a glimpse of a black Lincoln staff utility truck in the driveway.

When he opened the door, he was eye to eye with Admiral Bruce Phillips. Phillips was wearing working khakis and a cloth garrison cap, which he removed.

"Can I come in?" he asked, the crow's feet at his eyes crinkling, his expression serious.

McKee waved him in, ruffling his hand at the hair on his neck, his habit when nervous or uncertain.

"I think I have some beer in the fridge," McKee said, walking toward the kitchen.

"I brought some," Phillips grinned, motioning to the driver, who brought in a cooler. "You've been at sea for a while, and I figured the cupboard might be bare. It sure used to be when I'd get home."

"Yeah," McKee said, sinking into one of the chairs, "I'm not sure if Diana has even been here, much less gone shopping. I haven't talked to her yet. We were in the middle of a big fight when your Seal commandos stopped by." McKee looked at Phillips. "They didn't bring beer."

"Sorry about that, Kelly," Phillips said. "That's really what I came by about. I wanted to apologize for the exercise. You know we're not in the business of lying to our skippers—"

"But you did anyway," McKee said, his voice cold.

"It was part of the . . . scenario," Phillips said lamely. "It was . . . a prewritten . . . deal."

It was Phillips' way of saying someone else had

written the scenario and it had been rammed down his throat, McKee realized, but as admiral in command of the force, it was all the more imperative that Phillips "own the orders," the Navy's traditions demanding that a commander always act as if the orders he gave came from him.

"Doesn't matter, Admiral. I'm glad you're here. It'll soften the shock when I hand you my letter."

Phillips gulped and put down the bottle. "Say again?"

"I'm giving you a letter. I'm punching out."

"You're resigning on me? Because of the goddamn exercise?"

"Admiral. Bruce. Listen to me." McKee leaned far forward, his eyes drilling into Phillips'. "I took this thing to the mattresses for you. I gave a goddamn speech to my guys—duty, honor, country, the President needs us—which you turned into a bunch of bullshit. Now I look like an idiot to my entire crew. My XO, your Karen Petri, comes into my sea cabin after the attack and sees my hands are shaking so hard I can't light my goddamn cigar. I'm covered in sweat, and all I can think about is the men who supposedly died in that fleet. Sir, it's not just that I lost something in the eyes of my men and officers, it's that I lost something of myself in my own eyes. Admiral, when that torpedo was bearing down on us, I was so scared I think I might have wet my pants, but I'm thinking, it's okay because I saved the ship and I performed the mission, and then you say 'good dog,' and in front of the fucking Chief of Naval Operations I'm sitting there hearing it's a goddamn *exercise*." McKee was now shouting. His hand swept his beer off the table, and the glass bottle shattered on the tile floor. For a moment he stared at it dumbly, then continued in a subdued tone, "Diana was right. It's time to quit the Boy Scouts and do something serious with my life."

"You don't think this is serious?" Phillips' face had turned red.

"No, Admiral. I used to, but I don't anymore, and it's thanks to you. I was about to tell Diana that the submarine was more important than my marriage when she told me to choose." McKee snorted. "Thank God I only wasted another week playing with the goddamn boat."

Phillips frowned and spoke, his words clipped and hard. "Godammit, it wasn't just an exercise. There really is an Argentina-Uruguay crisis, and it gets worse every day. The latest Argentina communications to the Ukraine are about the price of making the Black Sea Fleet a mercenary force. The higher-ups no longer talk about whether Argentina will use the Black Sea Fleet to attack Uruguay, but when. The Ukrainians haven't put to sea yet, but the CIA believes it's just a matter of time before Ukraine agrees to sail for the South Atlantic.

"And, anyway, Kelly, we got more data from that operation than ever imagined possible. The cameras in control—they recorded into the history module. I've looked at the disks. We're making a movie of the run, and it'll be a required course at prospective commanding officer school. Kelly, I'm not good at this—you just have to believe me. You were great out there. You showed them all how it's done. You're our number one skipper. For God's sake, you're commanding our number one boat." Phillips held out his hands. "What more can I say? We can't lose you."

"Listen, Bruce. I believe a man has one battle in him, one chance to stretch beyond his best." He looked at Phillips. "You've already got my battle, and lucky you—it's on videodisk." He stood. "That's all I've got to say. I need to ask you to leave, Bruce. I've got to find Diana and tell her I'm out. You'll have my resignation e-mail by tonight."

Phillips frowned. "I'm not taking your resignation. I'm placing you on leave so you can think about this." He stood, walked to the door, opened it, and headed out into the night. He had turned to say something to McKee, who stood in the doorway, when the black staff truck rolled into the driveway. The vehicle was identical to Phillips', except it had the squadron's markings on it. The rear door opened and a uniformed naval officer stepped out, walking slowly up to the two men on the porch. The newcomer was a lieutenant commander, but looked older than usual for the midlevel rank, his cropped hair gray, his face wrinkled. Ribbons climbed his chest to his gold airborne wings. Above the sleeve stripes of his service dress blues were crosses instead of the usual stars.

"What's a Navy chaplain doing here?" Phillips mumbled to himself. The chaplain approached, and saluted.

"Commander Kyle L.E. McKee?"

"I'm McKee. What's going on?"

"Commander, I'm Chaplain Glenn Morris. I was

sent by the squadron to find your wife after you sent your messages. She wasn't seen by friends or family members out east. I flew out to your mountain cabin. I'm sorry to have to tell you this, Commander. We found your wife's body inside. She had had a miscarriage and lost a lot of blood from a hemorrhage, and was trying to make it to the door to get help. There was nothing I could do. By the time I got there, she had been gone for several hours. I'm so terribly sorry, sir. We've made arrangements to fly Mrs. McKee's body home."

The chaplain had his hand on McKee's shoulder. McKee had gone white, his eyes unfocused. Phillips took over.

"I've got him, Chaplain. Get back to squadron."

"Yessir." The chaplain withdrew, his engine silent as the truck backed out of the driveway and moved down the street.

McKee stared after it, then looked at Phillips.

"I can't believe it. She's gone. Oh my God, I should have been there. I would have been there. Oh, Jesus." His voice cracked on the last syllable, and the strength seemed to leave his legs.

Phillips quickly pulled him inside and sat him at the kitchen table. McKee didn't resist as the admiral filled a highball glass with whiskey. It burned on the way down. After a second, he barely resisted as his friend pulled him up the stairs and gently laid him on the bed. After what seemed like hours, he sank into a feverish sleep.

The phone rang at Michael Pacino's Annapolis waterfront home. "Hello," Pacino answered, clicking into the video widescreen mounted on the wall by the oven. If it was the President, she'd see that he was clad in chinos and an old Naval Academy sweatshirt stained with grease and oil from working on the sailboat all day.

Pacino had been Chief of Naval Operations, the admiral-in-command of the Navy, for a year. He was over six feet tall, weighing the same as he had when he graduated from Annapolis. At forty-nine he was the youngest admiral ever to command the service, but despite his slim frame and unwrinkled face, he hardly appeared young. His face seemed perpetually tanned from an Arctic mission that had given him severe frostbite, along with deep crow's-feet at his eyes, bony cheekbones, and hollow cheeks on either side of a straight nose presiding over full lips. But his most noticeable feature in the roster of odd features was the color of his eyes, a deep emerald green, as if he wore the old fashioned colored contact lenses.

But the caller wasn't the President. The face of the commander of the Unified Submarine Command, Bruce Phillips, materialized onscreen. Phillips started talking immediately.

"We've lost McKee," he said, his voice and his face dead. "He turned in his sword over being treated like a piece of equipment."

"Dammit, I knew it," Pacino said. "I told Warner this would happen."

"It's worse, sir." Phillips told Pacino about Diana's death and the poor timing of the Seal commando raid.

"Where are you?"

"At McKee's. I put him down. I'll stay, make sure he's okay, maybe cook him breakfast in the morning, help him through the funeral arrangements. This time tomorrow we should be pretty drunk, so don't call me."

"Anything I can do, Bruce?"

"Yessir, but it's more in the category of inaction."

"Okay. What can I *not* do?"

"Useless fucking exercises for a President who doesn't understand the Navy, its machines, or its men."

"Bruce, the next sword that gets turned in will be mine. Call me tomorrow and let me know how he is, and I don't care how drunk you guys are."

Pacino clicked off and sat for a long time at the kitchen counter, staring at nothing.

BOOK II

BOOK II

Rafael

7

I am sixty-two years old. I have been a prisoner for the last thirteen years. I do not know the name of the prison. I have been in solitary confinement since I was flown here, somewhere in Siberia, or so I have always imagined.

My contact with the guards is minimal. I say good morning, good afternoon, good evening when they bring me meals or walk me in the yard. I ask them for news sometimes. For the first ten years of my confinement, the guards would try to be pleasant, and then something changed. Their faces and their uniforms were different one morning. I was moved from my cell to a larger cell. The new guards would not say where the old guards went, but there was some news. There had been a change of government. Many prisoners were being released, they said.

One morning a guard, a small boy with a pimply face, arrived with breakfast and an envelope with papers in it. They looked very official. They went on for forty or fifty pages. But they boiled down to an offer of conditional release. Release conditional on a written confession.

Five years ago I would have wiped such papers on my hindside. But now is different. This year I have had trouble breathing as they walk me in the yard. I had chest pains during two days in the winter. They took me out of the cell and to a hospital ward. The doctor said it was not a heart attack, but angina. I take pills for it now.

What is different about this year is that I finally understand that I am old and tired and will die soon. Yes. Up till this year I had always thought that one of the things that made me different from other people was that I was not afraid of death. Did I not go under the flooded water of the control room of the Kaliningrad when she was sinking under the ice? And even then my heart barely beat faster than normal. But now I am sixty-two years old, and I see that all my life I have been more afraid of death than anything else. I was not afraid on the Kaliningrad because I would not let myself acknowledge the fact of my own death. For sixty-two years I have been in denial, and now finally, after sitting on a cold metal table with no clothes and a strange machine strapped to my chest, I realize that death has been my constant fear, my overwhelming fear, and it fills my nightmares and sits behind my eyes and it paralyzes me.

At lunch, when I saw a guard, I asked for a pen and a pad of paper. They will release me if I confess in writing. Always until this moment I saw this as a trick. The minute they had my confession, they would execute me.

Now they tell me to confess and they will let me go. I still believe it is a trick. This paper will go into a file cabinet, and as the drawer shuts, the sounds of bullets will ring out over the courtyard. But I do not care now. I am not only old. I am tired. I no *longer want to live my final days here. So, believing that this confession will seal my fate, I now begin it.*

The gray-haired, craggy-faced man, once barrel-chested but thin in his later years, looked over what he had written. It did not say exactly what he wanted, but what did it matter? He rubbed his neck, suddenly thinking how wonderful a shot of vodka would be, and tried to dismiss the thought. Perhaps they would grant a last request before they "released" him to the courtyard to be shot, he mused. He picked up the pen and began to write.

This is my confession.

My name is Alexi Novskoyy. When I was forty-eight years old I was named the Admiral in Command of the Red Banner Northern Fleet of the Russian Republic. During that time the fleet was being disarmed. The Rodina, the Motherland, was being disarmed. Our nuclear weapons, which up to then had protected us from the imperialism of the Americans, were being destroyed in front of a commission of the United Nations, a group of foreigners.

During that time I became convinced the disarmament of Russia was a crime. I acted to counter that crime. The details of what I did, which was labeled a war crime, have been documented by many people, many firsthand reports. But this is a confession, and in a confession—need I explain the obvious—the confessor must report his own crime. I will keep this short.

First, I substituted dummy cruise missiles for the weapons to be destroyed by the UN commission and loaded what were purported to be exercise weapons onto 120 attack submarines of the Northern Fleet. But the exercise missiles were actually fully armed nuclear SSN-X-27 cruise missiles. I scrambled the fleet out of our northern submarine bases with instructions for them to sail to points offshore of America's eastern coast, where they were ordered to remain at mast-broach depth and await instructions. They formed a loaded pistol pointed at the temple of America. Meanwhile I took under the ice the newest, most revolutionary submarine ever built in world history, the Fleet Submarine Kaliningrad—the submarine called by the West the Omega, the last letter of the Greek alphabet, a vessel I designed with my own two hands. We sailed under the ice of the polar icecap and surfaced at thin ice, in radio communication with the submarines of the Northern Fleet. It had been my original intention to threaten the politicians and military warmongers of the imperialist Americans with my nuclear-tipped cruise missiles and thereby force them to give theirs up, to be destroyed before a UN commission on their soil by foreigners. But under the icecap something happened.

To this day I am not sure how or where my attitude changed. Perhaps my intention was always there and I had hidden it from myself. Or perhaps there is just something about a loaded pistol—the weight of it, the balance of heavy metal, the feel of the trigger, the knowledge that power is but a trigger pull away—that infected me. Instead of using my radio gear to address the evil men in Washington, D.C., I used it to send a molniya—a "go code"—

to the Northern Fleet submarines, ordering them to launch their cruise missiles at the strategic centers of the American east coast. Even though I "went nuclear," the plan would still have worked. With the military-industrial complex of the U.S.A. surgically destroyed, Russia would have stretched out her hand to the Americans and helped them rebuild, and together our nations would have marched into the future, side by side, in peace.

But my vision was not shared by the men in charge of the U.S. Navy. An American hunter-killer submarine was sent to assassinate my Kaliningrad. And perhaps that is what changed my plan from a threat to an action. Kaliningrad was torpedoed, her systems crippled. I fired back with a nuclear-tipped torpedo, meaning to sink the intruder under the icecap so that I could get back to my molniya, but the torpedo missed, and the nuclear detonation further injured the Kaliningrad. She flooded and sank. We got out in an escape pod, and found ourselves on the ice in a miserable Arctic storm, shipwrecked with the same Americans who had fired on us—since it turned out that their vessel had also been mortally injured by our torpedo. We were in a bubble shelter, but the generator died, and when the warmth ended, so did we. There was one other Russian survivor of all the men who had dived with me on the mission. I heard that later the other survivor died of his injuries. Two Americans survived, one of them the captain of the U.S. attack sub sent to kill us.

The storm raged on, but somehow we were rescued. The Americans turned us over to the Russian authorities. I was flown back to Russia in a transport plane. It landed at a strip about five minutes from here. There was no trial, just confinement. I have not seen any more of the world since then, other than the pines outside my cell window. I have not heard any more of the world since then.

Novskoyy paused, his hand cramping from writing. He read over a paragraph, sickened at his own tone of melancholy, then looked away and began writing again.

No confession is complete without contrition. Am I sorry for what I have done? Am I sorry for the men who died, on both sides of the conflict I started?

It has been many years since then, and I have grown older and have had time to reflect on what has been labeled a war crime. At first I was defensive about it. No one could understand what the disarmament of Russia meant to world history. Our way of life would be extinguished.

But there on the icecap I looked into the eyes of the Americans—I was conscious for all of twenty minutes—and I am ashamed to say that these men seemed much like us. Seafarers. Submariners. Navy men. I am ashamed to say that I would have been proud to drink vodka with these men. And in thinking this, I now realize that what I did was wrong, that the target I was launching at was a map drawn in blue with strange names written on it, names like "Norfolk" and "Boston" and "New York" and "Jacksonville." I was not shooting at people, and if I had met these men before I wrote my plan, perhaps things would have been different.

I do not know if that is contrition enough. But it is what I think.

My "confession" is over now. If it is used as my death warrant, so be it. I fully expect that as soon as I sign it and give it to a guard, I will not spend another night here, but will be lashed to the pole outside and feel the bullets ripping into me. Again, so be it. I am ready to die. Perhaps it is not only just, but it is time.

Signed,
Alexi Andrieovich Novskoyy
Prisoner

Novskoyy tossed the pad of paper on top of the other papers on the desk and walked over to look out the window. Time passed slowly until the sun set, the pines going black in the dimness of dusk. The guard came to bring him his dinner tray. Novskoyy gave him the confession, ignored the food, and sat on the bed, awaiting the inevitable.

He thought he would suffer through a sleepless night, but after signing the confession, he felt better. All the folklore about confession being good for the soul was grounded in fact after all, Novskoyy thought, and at eleven o'clock he put his head on the pillow and slept like a baby until sunrise.

Usually when he woke he would go through a morning routine. It consisted of going to the bathroom, shaving, stripping naked, and doing exercises. Then he walked from one wall to the next as fast as he could, bouncing off with his hands and

returning to the other wall, the walls marked with
handprints. He kept this up for forty minutes, then
finished with a round of crunches and push-ups.
He'd stand and stretch until he stopped sweating,
then he'd wash at the sink before putting his jumpsuit on. Then he would sit and read. He had gone
through four to eight books a week since he'd been
here, finishing them whether or not he liked them.
It had been its own form of education.

But today was different. Somehow today he did
not want to exercise. The idea of being found walking from one wall to the other stark naked when
an execution crew arrived seemed too absurd. Even
though morning meal came and went with nothing
happening, it did not alter his state of expectation.
Noon meal arrived, but he was not hungry. He tried
to read, but the words did not hold his interest. He
sat in his chair facing the door and waited. It was
midafternoon before the footsteps came, three men
from the sound of it. He sat back in his chair as
the door gave its buzzing noise before the system
opened it. It rolled open and revealed three men.
Two guards and someone he'd never seen before.

The newcomer did not have the air of a warden
or prison official, but seemed bouncy and restless,
as if his body were unable to contain him and his
energy. He wore a charcoal suit of expensive material, the design of the suit strange to the eye, the
fabric draped over a large, barrel-chested, well-fed
frame. The man kept his hands not at his sides but
angling outward, as if he wanted to reach out and
grab the entire room. He had a beard, much of it
gray, with a thinning head of reddish-blond hair

framing large features, including eyes that stared out intensely. He seemed to be in his forties, though the years did not seem to have been particularly kind to him.

The newcomer held out his massive paw. "Alexi Novskoyy, good to meet you. My name is Rafael. I have a last name, but I never use it. Rafael alone is good enough. Mind if I call you Al? Goddamn small cell if you ask me. And by the way, what took you so long to write that damn confession? I've been trying to spring you out of here for three years. Cost me well over two million U.S. dollars. The Russian Federalists pocketed the wire transfer back in '15, and then I'm told you won't confess. They won't let you read my letters, it's all bullshit, because once they have the confession you're out. God, at last you picked up a pen."

American, Novskoyy thought, with a lilting speech carrying overtones of a European accent, the man's origins indistinct. Novskoyy stood slowly, looking at Rafael suspiciously. The man's speech came out like water from a firehose, Novskoyy thought, and loquaciousness had never been a quality he prized in his officers.

"Alexi Novskoyy," he growled, squeezing the American's hand. "What are you talking about?"

But Rafael could not be slowed, his speech continuing.

"Finally they tell me you've signed the confession. I read it just before they brought me up to the cellblock. 'I realize that death has been my constant fear, my overwhelming fear, and it fills my nightmares and sits behind my eyes and it paralyzes me.' Jesus, where did you learn to write? And God, where did they teach that sense of drama? Remind me to keep you away from the word processor, Al. Come on." Rafael turned to the door. "Anytime now, gents," he said in a raised voice.

Novskoyy gawked at him as the door opened. Rafael was three steps down the corridor before he realized that Novskoyy remained in the cell, staring incredulously.

"Well, come on," Rafael said impatiently. "You don't want to stay here, do you? For God's sake, I doubt the Russian Feds will give me my two mil back. Follow me. I've got a chopper outside the courtyard and a jet at the airport—or what passes around here for an airport."

"Wait," Novskoyy said, his tone of command returning momentarily to his speech. "First you tell me what the hell is going on here. Where are we going?"

"What's going on here, Al, is you and I are getting out of here. We'll be in Africa in ten hours. I'll tell you about it on the way. Come on, we've got clients waiting."

"Clients?" Novskoyy walked hesitantly behind the big American down the corridor, past the massive stainless-steel-sheathed doors of the cellblock. Rafael walked in the exact center of the passageway, forcing Novskoyy to the side. Although it had been over a decade since Novskoyy had been a general officer in the Russian Navy, it irritated him that Rafael gave him no room to walk beside him, and the American's body was too big to walk beside in the narrow hallway. Feeling like a ridiculous subordinate, Novskoyy walked two steps behind Rafael. He was opening his mouth to say something about it when Rafael handed him something over his big shoulder.

"Here. This is your new gig."

It was a card, looking like a plain white blank name card. But when Novskoyy took it, it lit up with a flash, colors and graphics bursting out all over it. In surprise, Novskoyy dropped it as if it had shocked him.

Rafael stopped and looked at him strangely. "What's the matter with you? Never seen a business card before? Jesus. Pick it up, it won't bite."

Novskoyy looked down at the card on the tile floor. It had changed back to a plain white cardboard inanimate object, but when he retrieved it, the colors and graphics lit up again. This time he held on to it, and watched as the colors swirled across the surface of the card, an elaborate sequence of rapidly appearing and fading three-dimensional images flashing over the card—one of them an ancient concept sketch of a helicopter, another a sketch of a man with outstretched arms with the man being suspended inside a wheel, then a sketch of a crustaceans's shell, then finally a bathyscaph. The images then calmed down, and out of blue sky and clouds a series of letters appeared, growing closer, finally spelling out the words *Da Vinci Consulting Group*, and below that the words *Alexi Novskoyy, Executive Vice President, Undersea Systems Division*. At the bottom of the card were the words *A Subsidiary of da Vinci Systems Limited, Rome, Milan, Florence, Paris, New York,*

Berlin, Kiev, Seoul, Jakarta, Bangkok, Koala Lumpur, Beijing and then what looked like a phone number and a website address. Novskoyy stopped and looked up dumbly at Rafael. By then the two men were at the interior main door to the prison.

Seeing the shock on the former admiral's face, Rafael's features softened and he turned and handed Novskoyy another card. This one did the same three-dimensional graphics tricks that the first had, with the same lettering, except the name and title read *Rafael, President da Vinci Consulting Group, Managing Partner da Vinci Systems Limited, Florence, Italia.* A photograph of Rafael's face appeared by the name, the face smiling and animated. Novskoyy looked up. His expression must have appeared as confused as he felt, because Rafael put his hand on Novskoyy's shoulder.

"Listen, Al," he said quietly, a fatherly tone in his voice. "You're a free man now that you signed that confession, but only to a certain extent. You can walk out of here, but here you're two thousand miles from civilization. A hell of a place to start your new life as a free citizen of the Russian Federated Republic. Besides which, you owe me almost three million dollars—I'm calculating interest on my investment—and I will be taking that out of your first year's bonus, by the way, but that should still leave a couple million for you. And don't worry, next year will be even better. We should clear ten, fifteen million each after expenses and taxes."

"Rafael, perhaps my mind is not as sharp as it

once was, but I woke up this morning a prisoner. What, exactly, am I now?"

Rafael smiled. "Until you walk through that door, a prisoner. But once we're out of the country and on our way, you're a businessman and my partner."

"How did you know about me?"

Rafael smiled. "The Russian Feds released the records of the undersea battle you fought thirteen years ago. I saw it, read it, and made a decision to hire you. And the more I read about you, the more I realized you're perfect for what we're trying to do now."

"You keep saying 'the Feds.' What are you talking about?"

"Russia split in two three years ago, Al. From the Urals west—European Russia—is the Russian Republic. From the Urals east to the Kamchatka Peninsula, that's the Russian Federated Republic, where you are now. Siberia. As in damned cold. Can we keep walking now?"

"So . . . what will you have me doing exactly?"

"This is not a good place to talk. Let's just say it involves doing what you were doing before."

"Before, I commanded a fleet of ships and thousands of men."

"That's not all you did. Think of your historical contribution."

"I almost started a world war."

"No, you didn't. The Americans made sure nothing happened. I'm talking about the ship you designed. The Omega."

"Omega. That's right, that's what the West called my *Kaliningrad*."

"Biggest and baddest nuclear submarine in town, right, Al? Well, at da Vinci we're consultants, naval architects, naval designers, and our clients need our skills, our brains, our designs, our—let's just say— strategic plans."

Rafael nodded to the guards behind a glass booth. The door buzzed open, and blindingly bright sunlight streamed into the vestibule. Novskoyy followed Rafael through to the outside, narrowing his eyes to slits in the sunshine. The air felt brisk and cold, but good. He'd had daily walks in the yard, a court not far from this part of the complex, but this air felt different, it felt free. They walked to a wall on the other side of the courtyard, where a tall gate opened slowly, driven by an electrical motor, and outside the gate a black shining Mercedes purred. Novskoyy stared at it for a long moment. It was unlike any car he'd ever seen, streamlined, with small headlights and a curving shape carved from the wind. There were no seams where the doors were supposed to be. And then, oddly enough, Rafael spoke to the car: "Open the left rear," and the door seams appeared just before the door popped open. Novskoyy got in while Rafael walked to the far side and addressed the car, which let him in.

Novskoyy found himself in a deep leather seat sitting in front of a display screen.

"Sorry about the old car," Rafael said. "It was all I could get up here." He touched a console in front of him, bringing lights and quiet humming from the panel. "Airport, please, and crank up the jets on the Falcon."

The car started rolling in mystifying quiet, not a sound from the road coming into the cabin. It was sixty seconds into the drive before Novskoyy realized there was no driver. He looked over at Rafael with his mouth open, pointing to where a driver should be.

"What?" Rafael said, then seemed to notice Novskoyy's prison uniform. "Here, there are clothes in that bag on the floor. You need to wear a suit. We're stopping on the way to Rome, a little client meeting I have scheduled. We can't talk about it here—we have to assume anything we say is monitored in-country—but once we're across the border I'll bring you up to speed. By the way, I hope long hours aren't a problem for you. We've got a lot of work in front of us before the week is up. I've got two more clients lined up and a lot for you to help us out with. Here, have a shot. No more vodka for you. Better get used to red wine and single-barrel scotch. Oh, do you have any family in Russia or the Russian Federated Republic?"

"No. No one. My mother died some time ago."

"Okay. Then it's off to the meeting."

Rafael didn't say another word. The limo arrived at a clearing, where a huge four-bladed helicopter waited, the rotors spinning at idle. By this time Novskoyy was beginning to see that this world would surprise him at every turn, and he must start to get used to that and stop acting like a wide-eyed five-year-old. Still, when the helicopter landed at the newly asphalted airstrip next to the towering

transport plane with its nose open revealing the
mammoth cargo space, he had to stare. The helicopter's rotors were folded back, and it was loaded
into the nose door of the immense jet transport
while Rafael led him to a sleek delta-winged private jet. He climbed in, the engines came up with
absolutely no noise, and soon he was airborne over
the countryside of eastern Russia, the Federated
Republic, wondering what was in store for him.

8

Although Admiral Michael Pacino hated the idea of taking time to remodel an office, the suite left him by Dick O'Shaughnessy was uninhabitable. Back when Pacino's old friend Dick Donchez had owned the suite as Chief of Naval Operations, the walls had been paneled in mahogany, the corners of the room occupied by cherry cases with submarine models inside, an entire wall devoted to the bookcases Donchez had loved. Later, when Dick O'Shaughnessy had moved into the Pentagon E-ring's Chief of Naval Operations suite, he had ordered the paneling ripped out and commissioned a mural to cover every wall in the suite, the mural depicting the bloody invasion of Iran during the Islamic war, which the media had lately taken to referring to as World War III, back when O'Shaughnessy was a Seal captain leading a special warfare brigade of Navy Seals and Army Green Berets and Rangers onto the turf at Cha Bahar. O'Shaughnessy had been badly wounded during the stealth-bombing of the city, an abdominal wound that nearly killed him. Some people, when looking at the mural, swore that in one area to the left of the central window there was a scene of a commando writhing on the ground, an explosion from one of the fuel-air explosives bursting in the scenery behind him. That such a compassionate man as Richard O'Shaughnessy would plaster scenes of grisly warfare on his walls often seemed a contradiction, but Dick would wave it off and insist that they were in the business of war, so they might as well remember that.

But the mural was too extreme for Pacino's taste, and while O'Shaughnessy was parachuting into Iran, Pacino had commanded the submarine *Seawolf* sitting high and dry in a graving drydock. At the time it had seemed the ground war would have little to do with the Navy, particularly the submarine force, but fate had had a different opinion, and the final battle that ended the war had taken place at sea on the business end of one of *Seawolf*'s torpedo tubes. But that would not have made much of a mural, Pacino thought, and murals glorifying himself were not his style. He'd ordered the mural painted over with four coats of white latex paint.

For several months Pacino was content to use the office suite with just its white walls, finally allowing his chief of staff, Rear Admiral Paully White, to bring in a contractor to make the one renovation that Pacino approved of—knocking out the outside wall and replacing it with a floor-to-ceiling window, Pacino having always maintained that a true submariner missed weather more than anything else, including rain and overcast clouds, so that any office should bring as much of that weather inside as possible. On the inside wall the contractor's architect had fantasized about putting in a fireplace, and at first the idea seemed absurd, but after the initial studies were done, Pacino proceeded, and the river-stone fireplace went in on the wall opposite the window. A delivery was made a month later—leather couches and chairs, courtesy of Dick O'Shaughnessy—and the suite began to shape up. Pacino's wife, Colleen, Fleet Admiral O'Shaughnessy's daughter, had commissioned a painter to put on canvas renditions of every ship Pacino had sailed, the result a beautiful series of paintings, from the ancient Piranha-class nuclear submarines *Hawkbill* and *Devilfish* to the recently constructed SSNX, the new *Devilfish,* designed by Pacino personally. Pacino shipped in his old desk from his former United Submarine Command Pacific Headquarters office, the desk made from timbers of John Paul Jones' *Bon Homme Richard,* and with it his massive oak library table. Today Pacino stood between the wide window overlooking the Potomac and the couches, realizing that a visitor to the suite would never know that Donchez or O'Shaughnessy had ever been here, and that was truly sad, both men having been vitally important to Pacino's career and his life.

Richard Donchez had died over a year ago, after being Pacino's mentor ever since he could remember, and Pacino found that he missed the old man more every day. Pacino's father had been gone since Pacino's plebe year at Annapolis, the victim of a submarine incident with the Russians under the polar icecap, and missing his father had seemed like the constant ache of an old war injury. On one wall there were two more paintings, both gifts from Colleen. One was an oil rendition of an old photo-

graph, with the conning tower of a Piranha-class
sub in the background, with two officers in dress
white uniforms wearing ceremonial swords in the
foreground, one bald and older, one startlingly
young with a full head of jet-black hair. The letters
on the conning tower spelled out DEVILFISH SSN-
666. The old man was Donchez, the younger officer
Pacino, back in the days before his hair turned
stark white and he lost twenty pounds. The original
Devilfish had gone down thirteen years ago under
the polar icecap—not three hundred nautical miles
from where his father's sub had been torpedoed—
in an icy confrontation with the Omega-class attack
submarine launched in the last days of the Russian
Republic, and though Pacino had survived, he still
wore the scars of the Arctic frostbite, his face and
arms appearing dark, as if deeply tanned.

The second painting was another rendition of a
photograph, this one of a young boy, perhaps eight
years old, standing next to a tall man with black
hair, another submarine in the background. The
man in that picture looked like Pacino now, except
not as gaunt: his father, Commander Anthony Pacino. Pacino put his hand on the painting, thinking,
Rest in peace, Dad. Finally, the picture that occupied center stage on the wall was a blown-up photo
of Pacino in the dress blue uniform of a full admiral, with the sail of the SSNX, the new *Devilfish,*
in the background, and a tall youngster in a midshipman's uniform next to Pacino. The young midshipman had brown hair and soft features, a face
that on a girl would be considered very pretty,
wearing a frown as if trying to harden it, but there

were shadows of Pacino in the lad. The boy in the picture was his son, Midshipman Anthony Michael Pacino, a plebe at Annapolis when the picture was taken. Pacino was standing and staring at the photo when a knock came at the door.

Putting aside the strong emotions the pictures caused, Pacino called to the door, "Come." His secretary, Joanna Stoddard, appeared, her hair in a bun, her steel glasses obscuring her eyes. "Admiral Phillips, Commander Unified Submarine Command, is aboard, sir."

"Send him in," he said, smiling to himself at Stoddard's attempt to sound nautical and military at the same time. She was an old hand, with him since the days when he'd been named to be the first commanding admiral of the unified sub force, a time that seemed generations ago.

Bruce Phillips was speaking before he was even through the door, his hat under one arm, his briefcase in the other.

"Glad you could see me, sir. Wow, you've redone the office. I like it." Phillips stopped to look at the paintings, ending up at the one portraying young Anthony. "He's really growing up, isn't he?"

"He is," Pacino said, trying to keep the pride from his voice. "He may grow up even faster if they kick him out of the Academy."

Phillips turned to look at Pacino. "I doubt they'd dismiss him, not with *his* connections. Dad's the Big Boss."

"The Academy superintendent is Sean Murphy, my old roommate. He took the 688-class sub *Tampa* into Chinese waters a few years back and

got caught, and I and *Seawolf* had to pull him out.
He owes me a few, and not just from the Chinese
bay incident. I told Sean I'd fire him if he showed
or allowed favoritism to young Anthony."

"Bad connection, I see."

Pacino laughed. "Exactly. Sit down. Can I buy
you a drink? Sun's over the yardarm." Pacino's
scratched Rolex diver's watch read five-thirty.

"Thanks. That'd be perfect, given what I'm pro-
posing today."

Pacino opened the bar to the left of the fireplace,
took two glasses and ice, and poured two generous
portions of the single-malt scotch that O'Shaughnessy had given him as a wedding present.

"I'm more of a Jack Daniel's man myself, Admiral," Phillips said, sniffing the glass.

"Drink it, you'll like it. That's an order."

Phillips sat on the deep leather of one of the
chairs, Pacino sinking into the chair beside it. He
offered Phillips a cigar and watched as Phillips lit
up, Pacino not taking part.

"I feel like I'm in a gentlemen's club in old
London."

"Bruce, you'd be amazed how much better my
results are in an environment like this. People can
relax instead of bracing up like plebes. You should
have seen this place when O'Shaughnessy had it."

"Boss, I'm here to promote exactly that," Phillips
said, sitting up in his seat. "You know you had an
idea for a senior officer retreat? And we were going
to invite our key junior officers, their reward for
good performance? Make it a week in Hawaii, you
said, or the Bahamas."

"I remember. We were thinking about July." Pacino grimaced. He'd become caught up in the administrative burden of running the Navy, with its truckloads of problems and the politics that went with it.

"Someone said it sounded like what the aviators do with their Las Vegas convention every year, what do they call it, Tailhook, and they have a good time but do some business in between."

"I know you have an idea percolating in there, Bruce. You don't have to sell me, just come out with it."

"Why don't we have a fleetwide version of Tailhook, sir? We'll have the sub officers—bubbleheads like us—the skimmers—surface pukes—the Marines and the flyboys, all under one roof. We'll have seminars where we'll learn each other's frustrations, we'll hang out with our hot-running junior officers, see what they're made of, and all away from the drudgery of the fleet and the usual headaches from the headquarters weasels like us. We'll get away from it all and get some real thinking done. You can take one day to discuss equipment, get feedback from the officers about ship problems, gripes about the platforms, what we need for the Navy of tomorrow. Then a day to discuss personnel issues, see how our fleet is or isn't taking care of its people. Then a day to go over our strategic vision for combat in this century, who the enemies are likely to be. Then a day or two just to relax. We'd all come back the better for it."

"Nothing new there, Bruce. That's all in my memo to the type commanders." The "type com-

manders" were the heads of the submarine force—
Phillips—the naval aviation force, and the surface
navy force and the commanding general of the
Marines.

"Roger that, sir. But it occurs to me that going
to a hotel in Hawaii or the Bahamas is not our
style. That's too Air Force for us. That's what our
friends in blue would do. We need to do something
more, well, more Navy-like."

"Go on."

"Picture this, Admiral. We charter an entire
cruise ship and take it out, have our seminars and
parties onboard. In between we can hang out on
the bridge, even take the watch. Some of our old
salts will probably be in the engine room inspecting
the bilges. They'll absolutely love it, criticizing the
captain for his shiphandling as he maneuvers off
the pier on day one, bitching about how he navi-
gates in mid-Atlantic. The boys will love it."

Pacino looked at Phillips, amusement crinkling
the crow's-feet at his eyes. "You've been thinking
about this for a while."

"No, not really. Just since last week." Phillips
blushed slightly. "My company bought a cruise line.
The *Princess Dragon* comes out of her shakedown
in three weeks. I propose we book her maiden
voyage."

Phillips was from old money, Pacino knew, from
Philadelphia's Main Line, where the idea that
someone would work at anything other than charity
was scandalous. His family had cut him off completely until Phillips became a household name
during the East China Sea incident, when his USS

Piranha had turned the tide of an unwinnable naval battle. After that he had become the family hero, entrusted with the entire estate and the corporation shielding the Phillips family's assets from any inheritance taxes. It was just like Phillips to buy something that some in the Navy would consider frivolous, such as a cruise ship, but it was a quality Pacino enjoyed in the younger man, a counter to his own usually melancholy personality. Pacino grinned, giving himself away.

"What's the best time to sail?"

Phillips smirked. "You like it, don't you, sir." A statement, not a question.

"I just want to know when to pack my bags."

"Monday, July 23, we'll depart Norfolk. The Pacific guys will need to fly in the Sunday evening before."

A knock at the door. "Sir, your wife is here. I told her you were in conference."

"No," Pacino said. "Send her in."

Colleen Pacino swept into the room wearing a suit skirt and jacket. She smiled at Phillips, who had come to his feet as she entered. She walked up to him, kissing him on the cheek. "Hi, Bruce." She came up to Pacino and gave him a quick kiss on his lips.

Colleen Pacino, formerly O'Shaughnessy, was the head of a defense contracting company that had pioneered the battle-control system on the SSNX-class submarines. Pacino had met her in the shipyard, losing his heart to her even before her father ascended to the CNO position. She had a head of fine raven-black hair that fell smoothly to her shoulders, framing a soft-featured face with large almond-shaped black eyes and full lips.

"Can I get you something, Colleen? We've got the best cabernet in the Pentagon."

"That'd be great." She smiled, sinking into the couch. "Bruce, I want to know why you're still single," she said, taking the wine from Pacino. "I have a vice president at Cyclops Systems who's dying to meet you."

Phillips blushed, tamping out his cigar and looking at Pacino in appeal. Pacino refilled their glasses and sat back down.

"Bruce and I are putting our heads together for the all-Navy stand-down retreat, the skull session we were talking about before," he said. "Bruce just bought a new cruise ship. He wants us to take the retreat to sea, get some sun, bother the civilian deckhands."

"You'd better tell me next that the wives are invited. Some of your female officers are looking a little too pretty these days."

"What do you think, Bruce? Do we bring wives and girlfriends along?"

Phillips stood. "It's a plan, sir."

Pacino stood, telling Colleen to wait while he walked Phillips to the door. Out of her earshot, he looked into the younger admiral's eyes.

"What's the status of Kelly McKee?"

Phillips' expression sagged. "Worse, Admiral. His father-in-law turned over Diana's trust fund to him, so now he just sits in his house and stares at the pictures of her on the wall." For an instant

Pacino was reminded of himself not an hour before, as he had mooned over his own wall hangings.

"You visit him?"

"Twice. He refuses to even talk about coming back to sea. I'm at a decision point. I can't hold the commanding officer's billet open on *Devilfish* forever. I have to put someone in to fill the slot, fill the void. It's starting to affect the crew."

"What about the XO?"

"Karen Petri? She's not ready for command at sea, not of a submarine."

"Bruce, I saw the disks. She did a damned good job taking the boat to sea when you scrambled *Devilfish* out of Norfolk."

"I'll think about it, sir. I don't know. First woman in command and all. She should go through the prospective commanding officer school and attack simulator trial like everyone else. Like I did."

"Maybe so, Bruce. Maybe so. I didn't mean to give you rudder orders on that. Still, you might consider giving her credit for the run she made to the South Atlantic. She was pretty solid. You could send a new XO out to *Devilfish* for an interim period, let her take acting CO until Kelly comes back." Pacino held his hand up. "I know, it's your call. Still, think about it." He shook Phillips' hand and said goodbye, realizing that he felt about the young admiral the way Donchez and O'Shaughnessy must have felt about him, a mixture of affection, desire to protect the younger man's career, to promote him and encourage his success. Life had come full circle.

He turned to Colleen.

"When's this boondoggle on Phillip's ship?" she asked, smiling.

"July 23," Pacino said. "Why, you got a date?"

Her face fell. "Actually, I do. I'm testifying before Congress that whole week. Cyclops Systems and the fiscal year 2020 plan."

"Damn."

"Oh yeah, don't look too broken up about it," Colleen teased. "A week at sea in the tropics with all those hostesses pouring drinks with little umbrellas in them. It'll be real tough."

"Oh shut up, woman," Pacino said, smiling.

In the Chief of Naval Operations' anteroom, Admiral Bruce Phillips waved to Joanna Stoddard. "Mind if I use the phone?" She waved him on.

With a few clicks on the computer screen Phillips patched himself into his opposite number at Naval Personnel, Admiral David Meeks.

"Dave, it's me. Listen, no time to explain. I need an executive officer for the *Devilfish*."

"What happened to Petri?" Meeks' fleshy face asked.

"We're making her acting captain, but she needs a second-in-command."

"What about McKee?"

"Let's see what happens. If he comes back, the *Devilfish* is his. If there's no sign of him in a year, the ship is Petri's."

"A year? Long time to keep the old girl waiting."

"Petri's tough. She can handle it. I don't think

she'd have it any other way. She was tight with McKee."

"Maybe she should talk to him."

Phillips paused. "Not a bad idea. Phillips out." He clicked off, waved to Stoddard, and hurried to his staff truck waiting at the VIP portal.

9

The confession I wrote has given me a new direction. I have found freedom not just in the experience of being outside the walls of my prison, but in writing, in the expression of what is inside my head. I wish that I had discovered this decades ago. It is a very liberating feeling, putting down on paper what is inside, thoughts that find no expression or meaning unless they are committed to handwriting. Or in this case, to a magnetic bubble memory.

Rafael gave me an amazing and strange device, a portable computer the size and weight of an old-fashioned magazine. If I write across its surface with a plastic pen, the words go into the device's memory and can be recalled in lines of perfect script or, if desired, in my own handwriting. A click on a software button identifies grammatical errors, spelling errors, suggestions for where to break a paragraph. I never push the button. This is a diary. What good is it if it has the grammatical cadence of the machine? So I have decided to start this journal today, Wednesday the 24th of June. I will write until my hand cramps. Then perhaps I will dictate into the machine and watch it transcribe the words in my handwriting. It is truly amazing!

Today seems to be the most eventful day since

Rafael came to my prison cell three weeks ago. I must say I have cultivated a tremendous respect for him, for his enormous appetite for knowledge, for the fact that he is swollen with wisdom. Wisdom in an earthy sense, but also wisdom about people, a knowledge of the human tendencies that goes far beyond my own, and up until I met Rafael, I thought that as an admiral, I had a better grasp on the human mind than anyone I knew. Rafael has proved me wrong in many ways. He knows machines as well as people, and to listen to him explain international politics is like hearing a chess master describe a basic move. It is all so simple to Rafael, but then Rafael is pure genius.

There is another miraculous quality to Rafael. Until I saw it in action I never liked this quality in a man. The quality of which I speak is what Rafael calls "salesmanship." It is almost what I used to call leadership, but it is more. It is a quality of persuasiveness, an attractiveness of personality, the showing of genuine interest and caring in the subject of the selling, and the results of this salesmanship are remarkable. It is as if Rafael has a sort of empathy with his clients, as if he can see into their hearts and determine not just what they want, but what they need. And he sells them. On the way from the prison we made a stop in Libya, where he met with the head of state. The meeting was more of a social call, or so it seemed to me, but Rafael laid the groundwork for a future series of meetings to try to sell a new idea, something exotic and economically out of reach for the present. But Rafael, when we left, was given a warm hug by the Libyan president and an invitation back. I cannot describe how he does it, but what Rafael wants (to sell consulting services) soon becomes what the customer wants, as if they suddenly become lonely at the thought of not having Rafael there to help them.

I have tried over the last few weeks to learn more about Rafael. He is a walking contradiction. At the same time he is warm to his clients, yet to me he is a closed book. I know nothing of his childhood, where he is from, who his parents were, why he lives in Florence, or what brought him to his career, not even how he made so much money to start this particular branch of business. But what I know of him is that he is successful, in business and with his transactions with others.

I have been given to understand something of a new project Rafael has begun. It is a project that has already cost him tens of millions of dollars over the last four years, begun even before his campaign to get me out of prison. All I know about it is that it involves equipment, and the equipment is somehow connected with undersea sabotage, or as Rafael puts it, the projection of power in an advantageous direction.

Beyond that, Rafael has only told me to wait. At this point I remain uncertain about what I mean to his company. So far I have not contributed much beyond the credentials of having designed the Omega-class submarine. It is painful to call it the Kaliningrad, *so now I refer to it by the name Rafael has called it. I sit in the meetings and listen and learn, and to date Rafael seems happy with that. So I am learning while growing rich. It certainly beats sitting in a prison cell. Which reminds me of something else. We arrived here in the Hindu Republic of India this morning on the Falcon jet. Rafael had arranged for us to land at the Indian Air Force Base immediately next to the presidential palace. When we touched down, several aides of Prime Minister Nipun Patel guided us to our quarters in the palace, telling us that Nipun's wife was seriously ill, that Patel would not meet with us until later.*

"Let's get this over with," Patel said. He stood, his shoulders slumped, and followed his aide, General Prahvin, out the door to the stairs. Down below, through three archways supported by deeply stained wood columns, was the glow of candlelight from the dining room. A long table crowded with plates of food and goblets of drink was the center of the room, with four chairs arranged at one end. Cushions littered the floor, each occupied by a woman more beautiful than the next. Patel walked to the seat at the end of the table and stood behind it. Two women led in the consultants, the Russian looking uncertain behind slightly glassy eyes, Rafael's face crinkling into a smile of pleasure as he came closer.

"Mr. Prime Minister," he said. "Thank you so much for taking your time to see us." A cloud of concern crossed his face. "But I've heard about your wife's illness, and I am so sorry. If you wish we can certainly postpone this meeting till later."

Patel dipped his head, shaking Rafael's hand. "It is not a problem," he said quietly.

"We'll eat with you and then see how you feel, Mr. Prime Minister. I can see now this is a bad time for you. I must apologize. I didn't realize the seriousness." Rafael looked embarrassed. "It's just that we found a way that we can economically ruin the Saudi Arabian Consolidated Republics and help you dominate the world oil market. But perhaps we should save this for later, because you'll need to make some very key decisions."

Patel's face had grown dark, but then at the end he burst into a smile. "Rafael, your magic works for everyone but me. I can see the wires, you know."

Rafael smiled too. "Maybe a year ago you'd be correct. But today"—he put his hands wide apart, palms up—"we have more work to do than merely selling you on an idea or trying to get you to sign a purchase order. We have something, something important, something that solves your problems. We stumbled upon the idea three years ago, but it was a concept without a customer. Now the world is different."

They both knew what he meant. Nipun Patel had come to power in India fifteen years ago after a bloody revolution, executing thousands of political enemies and establishing himself in charge of a group of parlimentary puppets.

Three years after the revolution, he had invaded Red China during the First Civil War, but by its end had been pushed back to the prewar border. Two years ago, during Red and White China's Second Civil War, he had fought the same border skirmish, invading Red China when it was busy in the middle of a battle with the Whites to the east, but this time he won, taking territory deep into Red China, carving a respectable half-moon-shaped chunk of territory north of continental India.

Sixteen months ago, Indian engineers had discovered a massive deposit of oil in the central plains of the new territory. Immediately India had approached British petroleum engineering and construction companies to help them build a fast-track giant refinery, a 1,200-kilometer pipeline, and an oil-loading port on India's east coast. Eight months ago India had ordered a twenty-ship fleet of oil supertankers from the Japanese, slated for delivery three months from now. In two months the refinery would be started up. If it came to capacity on the British timeline, it would begin pumping crude oil down the pipeline in three months.

Patel sat back, accepting the glass of wine poured by the serving girl with the silk blouse, the fabric at her arms so full it dragged on the tablecloth.

"What is your proposal?" Patel asked.

Rafael said, "India could be a giant in a few years if the oil is produced. That assumes that India will hold onto the territory, and I understand you have taken steps to assure that Red China won't be back. But it also assumes the Saudis will not pull any tricks. Simple tricks like lowering the price of oil. Or bombing your refinery being constructed at the Shaala oil fields, or the pipeline, or perhaps the oil-loading complex. Or bombing all three of them.

"If the Saudis are held at bay, India will be richer than the Argentineans, richer than the Saudis. You can accomplish your goals for this country. But we

came here not to be cheerleaders for your oil fields
or your rise to economic power. We're here to
show you a plan that can hasten that rise. India
can go to the very top of the food chain, and she
can do it by stepping on the faces of the Saudis.
What I'm about to show you is strictly confidential,
you understand, for your eyes and General Prahvin's only. I know your servants are beautiful and
heavily screened for security, but your lovely
friends do not, as they say in the West, have a need
to know."

Patel clapped his hands twice, and the room
emptied except for him, Prahvin, and the two consultants. "You said something about ruining the
Saudis. About cornering the oil market. And about
a concept without a customer, until now."

"I'm sorry," Rafael said. "My mind wanders
under the influence of this marvelous wine. It's excellent." He took a sip, then looked into Patel's
eyes. "This is what we have." Rafael withdrew his
computer pad from his coat pocket and set it on
the table. As he spoke, a three-dimensional image
materialized above the table—a blue, brown, green,
and white ball slowly rotating, lit up as if glowing
from within. The ball was about half a meter in
diameter. Patel stared at it, never before having
seen one of the 3D projections, but controlling his
face so as not to appear naive. He noticed Prahvin's
jaw had dropped, and the second consultant also
looked astonished just for a moment before re-
gaining his previous impassivity. Patel looked at the
ball, the white color clearing, the blue now revealed
to be oceans, the brown and green continents, the

ball's rotation slowly stopping so that the Saudi Arabian peninsula materialized facing toward Patel. The peninsula grew, the rest of the globe disappearing, so that there was a curving map hanging in the space between Rafael and Patel. General Prahvin had stood up behind Patel's shoulder to get a better look.

"The oil produced inside the Saudi Arabian Consolidated Republics is exported by sea primarily through the southern seaways. Fifty percent flows through the Gulf of Aden, twenty-five percent through the Gulf of Oman, twenty percent through the Mediterranean, five percent through the Iranian pipeline.

"Here on the western seaway, the Red Sea and Gulf of Aden, there is a place where the seaway becomes very tight, making the channel a sort of hourglass. We call this a 'choke point.' The constricted choke point is at the corner of Saudi Arabia and Africa, called Bab el-Mandeb. It is eighteen kilometers wide. The supertanker deep channel is only five kilometers wide. Every side is vulnerable as it passes through here. One of our patented undersea systems placed here would be able to target every tanker coming through the gulf, fish in a barrel.

"Now, look at the eastern seaway. The Persian Gulf gives way to the Gulf of Oman through another choke point here at the Strait of Hormuz. The waterway is wider, but the ship channel restricts to about fifteen kilometers. Again, one of our marine systems puts all the traffic on the bottom.

"The Med traffic mostly originates from the terminal at Beirut. The outbound shipping lanes fan out slightly, but another one of our systems about a hundred and fifty clicks off Lebanon takes care of the bulk of the shipping.

"Our plan is very simple. We will sink every oil tanker passing fully loaded through the Persian Gulf and the Gulf of Oman. Once the first few dozen sink, no one else will want to take their ships in to withdraw oil—it'll be a bad-luck undertaking. The oil tankers will instead line up at your oil terminal, and soon you will rule the oil market."

Rafael sat back in his seat and took another sip of wine, then looked over at Patel, awaiting a response. Patel's eyes gave away nothing, and no one moved to ask a question, so he continued.

"You're wondering if I'm insane. You're wondering, if every ship exploded in the choke points at the Gulf of Hormuz and Bab el-Mandeb, why wouldn't a foreign navy come by and get rid of what's blowing up the ships? Your mind is turning from the what to the how. Let us not too hastily leave the what. First, agree with me, if you will, Nipun, that if we were somehow able to sink the shipping coming out of the Saudi peninsula, it would prove most advantageous to your country."

"Of course it would."

"And have you any questions about the desirability of putting a blockade around the Saudis?"

"I am assuming, my friend, that you have devised a plan which, in your own mind, is feasible and sinks the ships in these choke points, as you call them. In the near term it might help my cause. But you are exactly right. One day after the first ship sinks, the Royal Navy or the Americans are there with patrol boats and gunships, and they destroy whatever you're using on these ships. Lasers or whatever high-tech gizmo you've dreamed up to do this."

"No foreign power will find out what is going on. You see, all the oil tankers will pass through these choke points, but they will not sink until they are far at sea. We've devised a method that can sink any ship we want to sink, in such a way that no one is the wiser. There will be no survivors. And the shipowners and the world's oil customers will be at your feet, begging you to fill them up. It will seem like 1974 all over again, except that instead of a group of Saudi oilmen, the profiteer will be you!" Rafael raised his glass and looked at the men in the room. "To India and the future oil dynasty!" He drained his glass with a flourish.

Patel and Prahvin continued to stare at him, as did the other consultant, the Russian, Novskoyy. The floating map of the Middle East faded, winking out. Patel crossed his hands over his chest.

"You'd better get to the how very quickly, my friend, or this meeting is over. I have never been a fan of science fiction. Or in this case, fantasy."

"My plan is certainly unproven. But here's my proposal. You know my terms and conditions. The easy payment plan. Eighty percent cash up front, twenty percent retention on completion to your satisfaction. We'll need one hundred and fifty million dollars if you order within the next two weeks. My Crédit Suisse account number is on my card—it's the same as the phone number. A hundred and fifty million takes down every ship coming out of the Saudi peninsula for the next six months. I can show you a demonstration that can firm up your belief, but the demonstration will be expensive for me, even though it will be no obligation to you. But if I conduct a demonstration of this system adequate to convince you, the price will go up. Five hundred million dollars after the successful demonstration. Part of that will be to recover the expenses of the demonstration, part because the value of the product has increased, part to line my pockets, and part just to punish you for not believing in me." Rafael smiled and held out his glass.

"This demonstration. What does it propose to show me and how will it eliminate my doubts?"

Rafael turned his computer back on and looked up at Patel.

"Pick a newspaper you trust. Any one."

Patel blinked. "London *Daily News*."

"I would have gone with the *New York Times,* but that's fine." He turned the computer so Patel could see the display. A few software clicks, and the Internet London *Daily News* came up.

"And why exactly am I looking at the paper?"

"Look for something related to the U.S. military."

"Is it this one, 'U.S. Navy Plans Love Boat Cruise'?"

"Click on that."

Patel looked at the computer for a few minutes, reading about the plans for the Navy's leadership to have a stand-down retreat on a cruise ship to the Caribbean.

"This will be your demonstration? You're going to use one of your gadgets on a cruise ship?"

"That's right."

"That's not much of a demonstration. It's a cruise ship. How hard can that be to sink?" Patel was growing annoyed.

"Read on. If it's like the *New York Times* article it will mention that there are some tight security measures."

Patel read. " 'The Public Affairs Office of the Pentagon issued a statement that security would be ensured by a small flotilla of cruisers, destroyers, and frigates, as well as a submarine, to guarantee the safety of the liner's passage.' "

"That will be our demonstration. The article may not have mentioned that the cruise ship is leaving from Norfolk, one of the most highly guarded and secure naval bases on the U.S. East Coast. And in the demonstration, we won't just knock out the cruise ship, we'll take down the escort vessels as well. Do you have any preference as to whether the escorts sink first or the cruise ship?"

"Cruise ship first," Patel said. "Then, when the escorts are alerted, make them go down one at a time."

Refael nodded seriously. "One at a time. Perfect. When you read about it in the *Daily News,* you'll owe us the eighty percent down payment on the five hundred million U.S. dollars."

"No. This is how it will be," Patel said, his voice as casual as it was before. He sat back in his chair,

stifling a yawn. "The price won't be five hundred
mil. I am being robbed at one fifty. You do the
demonstration, we'll pay twenty million, you start
your Saudi operation in six weeks, and after the
first fifty ships are sunk, we'll pay you a hundred
million. The next fifty ships, another hundred million. After that, I doubt there will be any more
shipping in the channel, but if there is, two million
a ship."

Rafael frowned. "I understand what you're driving at, Mr. Prime Minister. You want results with
minimal risk. I would propose the same if I were
sitting in your seat. Let me ask you if I can follow
the spirit of your request, in a fashion that will
allow me to survive financially." As he said this
last, Rafael had leaned far forward toward Patel,
looking into his eyes, the skin at the corners of his
eyes crinkling earnestly. "We'll take a wire transfer
now for twenty million. Once that clears, Mr. Novskoyy and I will leave and conduct the demonstration. At the successful completion of the
demonstration your people will wire-transfer fifty
million. Once the wire transfer is complete, we
commence the Saudi operation, on your timetable."

Patel nodded, yawning into his fist. "The terms
are acceptable. But I want one more thing. How
are you going to do this? Don't answer—I want
Mr. Novskoyy to take the question."

Rafael looked at Novskoyy, smiling slightly. Patel
noticed the older Russian man cough into his hand.

"Well, Mr. Prime Minister, it will work like this."
Novskoyy's voice was deep and commanding, Patel
thought. He reminded himself to ask Rafael to pro-

vide the Russian's résumé. "We have several new systems that have recently become operational. We'll stage them at the choke points, and they will target the merchant oil tankers."

"Systems," Patel prompted. "Submarines? Divers? An underwater shelter?"

"I've been asked not to go into deep specifics at this point, sir, not without being in an absolutely secure location. Even then, we would need to evaluate anyone who would come in contact with the data as a possible security risk. I'm afraid that even though you are paying our bills—and you know how much we appreciate that, sir—you yourself would have to undergo security screening. And it would not pass our internal protocol, Mr. Prime Minister, because one requirement to be admitted to the database is the need to know. And, sir—"

Patel held up his hand. "No, no, you're right, I don't need to know. I'll leave it like this for now. Perhaps after the demonstration you could show me your technology."

Rafael smiled. "After we sink so much shipping and hold off further commerce to the Saudi peninsula to the extent that you're broke, then I'll personally give you a tour of how we succeeded. Contingent, of course, on your payment of the final invoice."

Patel rose, yawning again. "General Prahvin, wire-transfer twenty million dollars to Mr. Rafael's account. Rafael will give you the account number. Thank you for your time, Rafael, and yours also, Mr. Novskoyy. After the wire transfer is complete, you are free to stay as long as you like and sample our hospitality."

"Thanks, but no," Rafael said. "We've got work to attend to. The demonstration is in a few short weeks."

"The general will attend you. Forgive me if I leave you to retire. It has been a long day."

Rafael bowed his head, offered his best wishes for Sonja Patel, and followed the general to the offices, Novskoyy following.

10

Rafael refused to say a word until the Falcon was over the ocean, waving Novskoyy off with a raised palm. Finally, when they had cleared Indian airspace, Novskoyy looked over at Rafael, who wiped his brow and smiled.

"Close call," was all he said.

"What do you mean?" Novskoyy asked.

Rafael laughed, choking, coughing, then took a drink of French sparkling water. "I couldn't believe how you handled that question. 'We have several new systems that have recently become operational. We'll stage them at the choke points, and they will target the merchant oil tankers.' And then you have the balls to tell him he doesn't have the goddamn security clearance to know any more! I didn't know whether to hug you or hit you, you Russian son of a bitch. But we got the order!" With that, Rafael reached into a silver ice bucket and withdrew a bottle of champagne, popping off its cork with a flourish.

A week before, Novskoyy would have glared at Rafael, but tonight, with all that had happened, he just smiled, a strange expression for him. He took the champagne and sipped it, the strange taste of the bubbling wine foreign to him, yet as it hit his insides, he felt immediately happier.

"Thank you, Rafael," he said.

"I made a huge mistake in not briefing you in depth," Rafael said after draining his glass. "But, my friend, I made a good hire when I signed you on. You, sir, are a genius. The fact that your plan thirteen years ago failed is amazing—whoever opposed you must have been quite a man. But even though your delivery was off, and the content of your little speech was bogus, you did very well. I couldn't have handled it better myself. Well done."

"So, since you did not brief me before, are you going to brief me now?" Novskoyy asked.

"There's nothing to brief you on."

"What do you mean?"

Rafael poured another glass for himself and topped off Novskoyy's glass. "I mean there's nothing to tell you. There's no system, no submarine, no undersea shelter, no mobile mines. Nothing."

"What? You did that just to fleece the Indian Prime Minister of twenty million dollars?"

"Oh no. Patel's reach is very far. His secret police have assassinated people in Africa, Asia, even downtown London. Stealing from Patel would be suicide. Besides, I want to visit him again when this is all over. His comfort women are the best. There's one I want to steal away from him to work for me. Sort of my personal comfort woman."

"In my country we called that a wife," Novskoyy said, his eyes glazing over, remembering the woman who had come to his room and used her fabulous mouth on him. He forced his mind back to the present. "So, if we have no system or way of sinking these merchant ships going into the Saudi waterways, what did we just do?"

"We made a sale."

"Of what?"

"Of what we sold, of course. Look, we found out what Patel is willing to pay to sink this American cruise ship with all the U.S. Navy muckety-mucks onboard as well as the shipping out of the Saudi channels. So, now we find a way to deliver. Or, more accurately, *you* find a way to deliver. That's what you're here for. You're the technical brainpower. I'm just the sales rep."

Novskoyy felt his heart stop. "You mean, we are starting from scratch, and within three weeks we have to come up with a system to penetrate the American defenses around that cruise ship? And sink her escorts? Twenty-one days?" Novskoyy felt his face flush. "And then sink the merchant traffic leaving the Saudi Arabian peninsula?"

"Relax, Al. You're a genius at this stuff. You can do it."

Novskoyy looked at Rafael through narrowed eyes, putting down his glass.

"Well, Al, you didn't think this was all sales meetings and counting our money, did you?"

"I never knew," Novskoyy said. "Because you never told me. You never tell me anything. If I'm going to be a partner to you, like you said, you'd better start sharing some information with me right now and stop this damn nonsense about what you do and what I do. And drop the superior attitude. If I were still commanding the Northern Fleet, I would have you shot, you bastard." Novskoyy's accent had grown deep as he became upset.

"You're right, you're right," Rafael said. "I was just doing exactly what you had said out of instinct. That stuff about security. How did I know you were a good security risk?"

"Well, dammit, now you know." Novskoyy stared out the window, completely overwrought.

"At least I got you to curse," Rafael said, smiling slightly. "I was beginning to wonder if you were human. Now I know that too."

"And meanwhile, I have twenty-one days to build some sort of weapon system that can neutralize the Saudi shipping. Do you have any damn idea how long it took to design and build the *Kaliningrad*? A decade! Ten years of my life, spending every day devoted to it! And now you expect me to come up with an undersea system that will sink a flotilla guarding a cruise ship and the cruise ship itself in less than three weeks?" Novskoyy fumed, breathing heavily. "Turn this plane around. We are going back to Russia."

"What?"

"Take me back to the prison. I quit."

Rafael looked at Novskoyy in shock for just a moment, then seemed to reach a level of understanding. "I don't expect you to do this alone, you know," he said. "Example. Have you been reading up on recent history in the computer newsfiles?"

"Yes," Novskoyy answered belligerently.

"Then you'll know that two years ago, six advanced-technology Japanese Rising Sun–class nuclear submarines suddenly disappeared during their sea trials. And suddenly they became the property of Red China. Did it ever occur to you to ask how that became possible?"

"Yes."

"I'll tell you how it became possible. A submersible designed by my staff engineers was delivered to the Red Chinese. Its demonstration run hijacked a Korean nuclear submarine while the Korean was submerged and going twenty knots."

Novskoyy stared. "Really?"

"Really. And do you know how long it took to build?"

"No. How long?"

"Ten days. Ten twenty-four-hour, intense, five-hundred-men-in-the-shop-working-around-the-clock-and-drinking-coffee-and-popping-amphetamines days. But we did it. And the Reds asked for a dozen more. We netted half a billion on that job. We're just doing the same thing again, except with a different country. We're not selling smoke and mirrors, we're selling a track record."

"Wait a minute. You built a submersible capable of stealing a nuclear submarine while the ship was submerged and making way?"

"We did. It worked quite well, in fact. But don't go thinking we can do it again to steal a supersub to do our job in Saudi waters. Standard procedure in every navy that runs nuclear subs now is to lock the hatches while at sea. We've become a victim of our own success."

"How did you do this? Who is the chief design engineer? The chief construction engineer? Who are these men?"

"You'll find out soon enough. The brains in charge of the operation is the managing director of da Vinci Maritime, our sister company. The MD is a former Chinese national named Suhkhula. Now listen, I haven't been briefed, but I understand that Suhkhula has something on the drawing board, ready for a prototype test. I'd notified da Vinci Maritime a few months ago that this system would need to happen. The Maritime people are on the case, and Suhkhula is managing the effort, just as with the Red Chinese submersibles. I'd wanted to introduce you in person, but I've got another sales call."

"Another one? What now?"

"Libya. Then Korea, then Red China. I'm going to talk to the political command structure to see if they're interested in seeing a demonstration of the system you're going to come up with. And then see if we can find a way to sell them the same service. If I can sell the demonstration alone to two of the three, we could gross another twenty or thirty million. If you have fifty million financing your system, I daresay you and Suhkhula should be able to construct a prototype that can do the demonstration. While you are shipping the prototype, the shop can be working on production of the second and third units."

"Get me to this shop. Get me to your man Sookoo-lah or whatever his name is. We've got to go now, right goddamn now," Novskoyy said, stress making his voice waver just slightly. He stared down at the floor of the jet. Rafael looked closely at him.

"You can do this?"

"I guess I will have to."

"There's more I have to tell you."

"More? I must tell you—I just cannot wait."

"Hang in there, Al. When I said there was no system, I was testing your reaction. The good news is that Suhkhula already has designed a system for sinking the Saudi oil tankers. That problem was solved a month ago."

"And how were you going to do that?"

"Suhkhula will show you. It involves biological systems."

"Biosystems? Great," Novskoyy said, his disgust plain.

"It's the demonstration of the American cruise ship sinking that is somewhat beyond our present capacities. And that's what I'm going to need you to concentrate on."

"Your biosystems. If they're good enough to conquer the Saudi shipping, maybe they can work against the American cruise ship."

"Ask Suhkhula. Maybe you're right. Computer," Rafael said to the aircraft piloting system, "new destination. Milano."

The computer's voice answered as the wingtip dipped, the plane turning northwest.

The Mercedes limousine pulled up to a giant finger of glass and steel, towering eighty stories high over the center of the city. Part of the building elongated into a slicing edge, the "prow" of the skyscraper pointing due south. Two-story-tall, red-lit letters spelled DA VINCI MARITIME.

Alexi Novskoyy climbed slowly out of the limo
and stood on the marble sidewalk, staring up at the
black sheer wall of the structure high over his head,
then around him at the other buildings in the design district. Gliding automobiles whispered by, not
a one emitting exhaust smoke, not a one making an
engine noise or tire sounds, and not a one having a
driver or even a steering wheel. Crowds hustled
around him, tall, beautiful women in strangely designed clothing, men wearing suits as strange as
the ones Rafael wore. Novskoyy smelled something
from a nearby restaurant, and he realized he was
hungry. Behind him the Mercedes had pulled silently away, leaving him alone for the first time
since he'd left the prison.

He felt a light touch on his forearm, and looked
down to see long fingers on his sleeve, polished
fingernails, a gold ring. He followed the fingers
up the slim suit-jacketed arm of a woman with dark
olive-colored skin. He looked up and saw the face
of a stunning Chinese woman, with elegant almond-
shaped eyes curving upward, strong cheekbones, a
round, sensuous mouth. Her hair was gleaming
black, cut sharply just above her shoulders, the hair
flipping upward at the ends. She wore a black suit
with a short skirt and a long jacket over a cream
blouse, a strand of subdued black pearls at her
throat. She was a head shorter than the Russian,
and her legs were long and slim and toned, her
muscles as defined as a mountain climber's. He saw
that she had extended her hand to him. He took
it, feeling the smoothness of her skin, the warmth
of it electric. Novskoyy realized he had stopped

breathing, and when he realized why, he felt his face burn. She was the key to a lock in his mind, an archetype, a deeply desired dream. He brushed the idea off, reminded himself of his task, and brought himself back to the moment.

"Admiral," the woman said in melodic Chinese-accented English. "I am honored to meet you. I am Suhkhula, managing director, chief designer, and design project director of da Vinci Maritime, S.A. Welcome to Milan."

Novskoyy stared at her, trying to find his voice. "*You* are Suhkhula?" He swore to himself. Again Rafael had sandbagged him, not telling him that da Vinci Maritime's managing director was a woman. He tried to regain his composure and stop staring at her. He bent slightly at the waist. "Alexi Novskoyy. I am happy to make your acquaintance. I am sorry, your name, Sook-hoo-la? Is that correct?"

She smiled. "Yes, Suhkhula. The accent falls on the last syllable. My father said he made the name up, but it is an ancient name, from a mistress of an emperor three thousand years ago. Come in. We've got a lot of work to do."

Novskoyy followed her up the marble stairs into the cavernous entrance foyer of the building and into an elevator that rose swiftly to the seventy-eighth floor.

Suhkhula's office occupied the acute angle of the building, the prow, two entire walls of the room three-meter-tall plate glass. Novskoyy was far from relaxed enough to sink into the leather couch against one of the windows, but the choice was that or a deep leather chair. He chose the couch and accepted a cup of espresso from the elegant Chinese woman, her body graceful and lithe, her black suit jacket twirling as she spun to sit in the chair on the other side of the coffee table. Novskoyy took a sip of the strong brew, the heat of it burning his tongue.

"I was thinking," he said. "I spent some time reviewing the computer files of the work da Vinci Maritime did for the Navy of the Ukraine. The Severodvinsk submarine projects of the last three years have been amazing. The ship has exactly what we need to execute the operation against the American cruise ship and her escorts." Suhkhula frowned, but Novskoyy continued, "It has deception devices, making itself sound like biologics, a school of shrimp; even its active sonar pulse shape is the sound of a whale groan or shrimp clicking. It has an ultrahigh-resolution littoral water navigation sonar for sneaking into shallow ports. And best of all, it has the Barrakuda model mobile mines. They catch up to the target surface ship, and instead of detonating, they attach themselves to the hull. And when programmed, they detonate, taking a ship down far away from the harbor where the attack was executed. So the work is done. All we have to do is deploy the systems." Novskoyy leaned back in his chair, pleased with his plan.

"Admiral?" Suhkhula put her slim index finger into the air. "There's something you should know."

"Um," Novskoyy said, hesitating. "Could you not call me Admiral? I want to be known as Al. It's more . . . normal."

"Fine, Al. You need to stop talking and start listening." Her voice was iron.

Novskoyy blinked, confused, thinking Suhkhula was supposed to be his subordinate as the design project director. A slight flush of anger came to his face, joining the flush of his deepening interest in Suhkhula as a woman. Which he insisted on ascribing to his long prison term.

"Forget mechanical systems. Forget submarines. Forget metal mines with solid explosives. And forget anything metal with air inside it."

"Why? What are you talking about?"

"The new antisubmarine systems out there, the ones used by the Royal Navy and the Americans, can detect man-made objects a hundred kilometers away."

"No, they can't," Novskoyy said, confident from his years of reading physics journals.

"Have you heard of acoustic daylight imaging?"

"What?"

"Acoustic daylight, Al. Sonar is gone. Acoustic daylight is in. The newer navies use flat sensors that detect sound the way the retina of your eye detects light. The background noise of the ocean surrounds a ship in the ocean, and another man-made ship blocks the sound waves or bends them or focuses them, just as an object in daylight bends or blocks light waves. And just as your retina perceives the change in the light field as an object, the flat panels see the change in the acoustic noise field as an object. Now you know the physics of acoustic daylight. It's not high-technology hearing, it's high-technology sight. And anything that has a density different from water shows up like an ink stain on a white shirt. Like a steel submarine with metal mobile mines."

Novskoyy's jaw dropped. "Just like that? A sonar system that can see? And you know this for a fact?"

"We know it for a fact. Let me see your computer."

He handed it over. She clicked through the software and gave it back. There were twenty websites describing acoustic daylight. He hit a few of them, finding immediately that Suhkhula was correct. His face sagged. He made her wait while he read the details. The room was silent for some twenty minutes.

"This changes everything. If the Royal Navy and the Americans have this, they could see us coming."

"Exactly. We even tried to design countermeasures to the acoustic daylight technology for the Severodvinsk modifications. We've got a system that makes the image from a Severodvinsk sub look like an indistinct shape, a school of fish. Trouble is, it shows up as a huge school of fish. It would arouse suspicion. Welcome to the new era in undersea technology."

"So, what do we do now?" he asked.

"Come with me," she said.

It took an electronic card key for the elevator to stop at the forty-third floor. When the door rolled open, Novskoyy found himself in a high bay area crowded with the sort of crawl-through mazes and tunnels typically found in a children's amusement area. Suhkhula stood next to him. For the first time in hours he forgot the woman, no longer smelling her perfume, no longer sensing her nearness, no longer wondering how she would look without her suit. Immediately in front of him was a chimpanzee wearing a surgical hairnet.

Making the scene surreal was that the animal bowed deeply at the waist. As he did, Novskoyy noticed a wire resembling a stereo speaker cord coming out of his skull. A bandage covered the spot where the cord entered. He straightened up and held out his paw to Novskoyy. When Novskoyy stared at him dumbly, the chimp reached over for Novskoyy's palm and shook it. Then he turned to a small table, picked up a box of cigarettes, withdrew one, and lit it, puffing smoke at the ceiling.

Novskoyy turned to Suhkhula, an eyebrow raised.

The chimp tamped out the cigarette and motioned them to follow him. Novskoyy followed Suhkhula and the animal behind the jungle gyms and puzzles to a dimly lit alcove where a large horizontal cylindrical glass or plastic tank filled with blue liquid lay surrounded by equipment consoles. Inside the tank a man in a pressure suit floated, his arms and legs limpy drifting in the liquid. His head was inside a bulky equipment box, the box crowded with hoses and cables.

"The chimpanzee is being controlled by the man in the tank. The cord going into the chimp's skull is a signal wire terminating deep within the animal's brain. The other end goes to the console, which is an interface computer feeding the animal signals from the human controller. The controller, a senior engineer and designer named Emil Toricelli, also has had a surgical alteration to accept the interface module of the computer in several lobes of his brain, and the interface connection ties him into the console computer. The controller and the consoles can make the monkey do anything physically possible for the animal. Give the chimp an order."

Novskoyy was fascinated. He had read about advances in brain surgery, but nothing like this.

"Run in place," he said to the chimp.

The chimpanzee immediately began running in place.

"Smile," Novskoyy said.

The monkey grinned.

"Jump up and down." The chimp obeyed. Novskoyy smirked. "Now stop. Go over and give Suhkhula a kiss."

Amazingly, the Chinese woman went to one knee and allowed the creature to smack her on the lips. She touched its face, then stood, a sad look on her face.

"Come with me," she said. They walked back to the elevator and returned to her office. Novskoyy sensed that there was something wrong. The idea of mental control of a lower mammal seemed so strange to Novskoyy that he barely noticed the change in Suhkhula's mood. Back in her office, he paced the room, trying to connect her previous speech with the chimp, and finally realizing how upset she seemed to be.

"What's the matter?" he asked her, still in a state of wonder about human control of an animal.

"The experiment," she said. "I love animals, all animals."

"And? It doesn't seem to hurt the chimp."

"It hurts him, all right," she said. "When the cord is connected, the personality of the animal lingers in the background, with the consciousness of the controller pushing it aside. But when the cord is disconnected at the end of the event or trial or mission, the animal dies. It dies in horrible agony, as if its brain were set on fire. I can barely talk about it."

Suhkhula looked down at the carpet for a moment while Novskoyy looked at her, unable to repress his attraction to her.

"Are you okay?" he asked.

"I'm fine," she said. "I feel like an idiot, but I've just always had this thing about animals. I can't stand to see them hurt. But this research is necessary for what you're doing."

"Why?"

"Because the only way we will be able to defeat acoustic daylight imaging sets is with biological systems."

"You're going to use the monkey to sink the ships coming out of Saudi Arabia?"

Suhkhula stared at him, then broke into a smile. "No, not quite. Dolphins."

"Oh, God," Novskoyy said in disgust. "Not this. I spent uncountable wasted hours in briefings about dolphin combat systems in my Northern Fleet days. It's ridiculous."

"That was obviously before we could control their motions with the central nervous system extender."

"It doesn't matter," Novskoyy said flatly. "A dolphin, no matter how well trained, no matter even if it is controlled as that monkey was, can't act as a combat system. They've got no hands, no way to manipulate things. Even if dolphins don't show up on acoustic daylight—"

"Oh, they show up, all right, but they are detected as dolphins and disregarded."

"Fine. They attract no attention on acoustic daylight sonar sets, but their mines would."

"No, Al. We'll use SG-1 explosives."

"And that means what, exactly?"

"Acoustic daylight sees metal objects and air-filled objects immediately. Any difference in density causes ocean noise to bounce or focus. But an object with the same density as water—that is, the same specific gravity—is invisible when viewed with acoustic daylight. Specific gravity is the ratio of a substance's density to the density of water. So SG-1 means the same density as water. We've got explosives that have the same weight and density as water, and we'll use them to blow up the ships. The SG-1 explosives would be enclosed in a polymer bag placed on the hull of the target ship. The polymeric material of the SG-1 bag is itself the same density as water, yet watertight for short periods of time. It encases and encloses the SG-1 liquid explosive until the explosive is detonated."

"And this explosive—what is it and how much does it take to kill a ship?"

"Do you know what happens when sodium comes into contact with water?"

"Unfortunately. The early Soviet nuclear reactors for navy service were sodium-cooled. The liquid sodium is a metal, and it has excellent thermal conductivity—ideal for transferring heat from a nuclear reactor, but explosive in contact with water. In one ship we had a leak of sodium to the bilges, which had a few hundred gallons of seawater in them—a gross procedural violation, but the dewatering pump was out of commission and the level alarms in the bilge were broken. The leaking sodium exploded in contact with the seawater, and the hull was breached. The ship sank and took down all hands with it. And ever since we've eliminated sodium in naval service. And that's what I know about sodium. But then, sodium is dense, which takes us back to the beginning."

"We've managed to perfect a chemical solution of sodium salts and a chemical precursor to peroxide. When a bag of binary catalyst—also near the specific gravity of water—is released into the liquid, it causes the sodium salt to react and form elemental sodium, and at the same time it causes the peroxide precursor to react and form liquid hydrogen peroxide. A second catalyst in the catalyst bag causes the polymer walls of the container to soften and dissolve. The failing walls of the container allow seawater inside, which in contact with sodium metal causes the sodium to react rapidly—an explosion, if you will—to form sodium hydroxide, and the detonating sodium acts as a fuse for the peroxide, which explodes a few milliseconds later."

He smiled at her. "Just one objection." Her guard went up. "It's just that SG-1 has the same specific gravity as water, and water weighs a ton for every cubic meter. I'm guessing you'd put about fifty cubic meters of SG-1 under a cruise ship hull. And a dolphin can't haul one ton, much less fifty. He'd die before he pulled a bag of SG-1 liquid from the bottom to a ship. It's too much."

"Maybe it's easier to show you than to tell you," Suhkhula said. "But I'm tired, and the virtual-reality-display rig is at my apartment. I worked this out after-hours, because there's something a little strange about me. I can work around the clock, but when I finally get tired, I have to go to bed immediately. I literally collapse. So I've taken to leaving the office when the sun goes down and continuing my work at home." She checked her watch. "It's eight now. If I order out, by the time we get to my place the food will be there. We'll eat dinner and have a glass of wine, and I'll show you the VR demonstration."

"You have put a lot of thought into this," he said, his voice intentionally soft. "I am sorry I seemed skeptical back there. I am amazed and gratified. I think you are a genius." He dropped his eyes for a second, looking up to find her staring at him, a vulnerable look on her face.

"We knew we'd have to do something like this after the last product stopped selling," she said, ignoring the compliment, but seeming embarrassed. "But the acoustic daylight sensors have put us at a standstill. And biologists and surgeons and animal behaviorists are not only expensive, but generally principled. They get annoyed at using animals for weapons research."

"So do you." By that time Suhkhula had shut the door to the office and walked with Novskoyy down the hallway. She was so close her shoulder rubbed his arm as they walked to the elevator. As they entered the elevator, he stole a glance at her profile. Her hair framed her face, her cheekbones magnificent, her exotic Chinese bone structure making her face somewhat flat, but the effect was sexually enticing. Her arms were slim, her shoulders muscular, her breasts small but upturned, the swell of her hips smooth, the shape of her backside so achingly perfect that all he could think about was cupping her buttock in his hand. He realized he was almost panting in desire when he noticed her looking at him.

"—egg rolls?"

"Excuse me, Suhkhula?"

"You seem distracted suddenly, Al."

"I must admit to you, I've never really worked with a woman before. Never anyone as brilliant or articulate or beautiful as you. It is . . . a difficult adjustment."

She smiled, her face lighting up. "And you've been in prison for a dozen years. That's always been a sexual fantasy of mine, getting a man fresh out of a prison cell. Don't worry, Al. I'll take very good care of you."

Alexi Novskoyy very nearly choked.

11

Novskoyy thought it would be difficult to concentrate once they reached Suhkhula's flat, as he was practically drowning in hormones he hadn't felt since decades before, but the apartment was about as romantic a setting as a warehouse. Suhkhula lived in a penthouse loft over a converted factory. The space was open and cavernous, but filled with so much clutter that it gave Novskoyy an immediate headache. Inside the entrance door was a huge wraparound desk with several computer stations set up in a semicircle. On the other side of the arrangement was a large black egg-shaped object, wires and devices coming out of it and connecting it to the computers on the desk. Beyond that was a small table near a kitchenette. On the far side of the huge room, near the windows, a large bed lay with the bedclothes rumpled and untidy. A pile of clothes littered the floor.

"I know it's a wreck," she said, slipping a glass of cabernet into Novskoyy's hand. "But it's cleaner than it looks." Her tone grew serious. "Step into the virtual-reality eggshell, Al. Then put on the eyepiece."

He climbed into the enclosure, which was the size of a powder room, through an opening in the bottom half, with a low overhead, forcing him to crouch down. Once inside, he was in darkness, compounded when the opening hatch rolled down. A voice came from above, amplified and deep, Suhkhula's voice, but the circuitry making her sound like a god. "Put the headset on, Al. Then you'll be able to see."

He reached out in the darkness and found a bar wrapped in padded leather. A headset hung on it, attached to a coiled cord. He strapped it on. Immediately he found himself suspended a thousand meters over a body of water, with sandy beaches on either side. He gasped in shock at the three-dimensional reality of it. A giggle from the sound system.

"Realistic, isn't it?" she asked. "This is the choke point at the Gulf of Hormuz." The view lowered, the water coming closer until he was perhaps fifty meters over the strait. Below him was a detailed view of a gigantic ship, the wake looking as real as if captured on videodisk, the ship likewise, the detail depicted down to the rust spots on the handrails. "To your right is a VLCC, for very large crude carrier, a supertanker. This will be our target. Below you to your left is a cargo/utility ship at anchor, the one colored red. This belongs to da Vinci." The view continued to change as his point of view plunged under the water and moved toward the bottom of the red cargo vessel. As he looked up at it from underwater, he noticed that the hull had a square opening in it, and that there were waves within the opening illuminated by bright interior floodlights. A disturbance was going on in the interior of the cargo ship, a dark shape blocking the light.

"Our guided dolphin is in the water here at our cargo vessel. Can you see him?"

"I see him. He's got a line or a cable in his teeth."

"There's a cable reel inside the hold of our cargo ship. The end of it is a polymer anchor with a plastic shock absorber."

Novskoyy watched in fascination as the dolphin swam with the cable underwater to the underside of the heavily loaded deep-draft supertanker, the VLCC. His view seemed to follow the dolphin, as if he were swimming after it. The dolphin reached the supertanker, the simulation real all the way to the sight of the supertanker's huge brass screws rotating far aft, even the deep bass noise of them thrashing in the water. The dolphin came under the midsection of the tanker carrying the plastic anchor in its mouth, then maneuvered to the hull of the giant ship, attaching the cable. Once it checked that the cable was secure, the dolphin returned to the cargo ship, following the cable that had paid out from a reel in the square opening. The view followed the dolphin up to the cargo ship, where it took another cable and repeated the routine, swimming rapidly from the cargo ship to the VLCC, anchoring the cable, and returning.

The dolphin then disappeared from view, and the hold of the cargo ship disgorged a large spherical bag that splashed into the water, then sank slowly.

"That's a bag of SG-1 liquid explosive," Suhkhula's supernatural-sounding voice narrated. "The bag is propelled along the cable by a cable trolley."

Novskoyy watched as one bag after another was moved to the supertanker.

"And as you can see, the bags are all anchored to the underside of the tanker. Let's light it off. The catalyst is in a small canister attached to the cable trolley. It also contains the detonator. The unit is on a timer."

The dolphin swam away, as if alarmed, while Novskoyy's three-dimensional view remained under the broad hull of the supertanker.

"Let's shift to slow motion and key in the mode to color chemical indication."

Novskoyy watched as the canister of catalyst was released, a brown dyelike liquid flowing like a stain in the bag, and the brown cloud caused the liquid around it to turn red. Novskoyy realized the red was not solid, but small particles of red dust. The brown faded, while the liquid in contact with what remained of the brown dye turned blue, until the bag was completely blue liquid suspending red dust particles.

"Freeze frame. Here the red particles are elemental sodium metal grains. The blue represents hydrogen peroxide. Slow motion."

The walls of the bag began to dissolve before Novskoyy's eyes, and as they did, a brilliant flash grew from the bag, exploding into a ten-meter-wide fireball, which expanded in slow motion, the sound around him mimicking an explosion in slow motion. His view was obscured by the explosion for a time, but when the whitish-orange fireball dissipated, the

hull of the tanker was ripped open in a jagged hole
reaching far up into the oil hold.

"The simulation has made the oil invisible, or
else the black leakage would prevent you from
seeing the gash in the ship. Stop simulation. In real
circumstances it is possible that the oil could catch
on fire as well, if there is a partially filled hold with
air inside. Or if the explosion ruptures the hull to
the upper decks and admits air, the oil and air in
the region of the fireball will definitely add to the
power of the explosion."

"Beautiful," was all Novskoyy could say, awe in-
flecting his voice.

"We worked very hard on this," Suhkhula said.

"You did a superb job. I am overwhelmed. By
your work. And by you." Novskoyy held his breath.
There was only silence. He felt a pain in his stomach as if he'd been punched, her silence a rejection.
But when the images in the eggshell went dark and
the door rolled up, Novskoyy blinked, first from
the light from the flat, then from disbelief. Standing
in front of him was Suhkhula.

She was naked, looking up at him with eyes that
seemed almost liquid, a slow smile coming to her
lips, an instant passing before one came to his. He
stepped close to her, picked her up, and carried
her to the bed.

12

When I woke up, she was gone.

The sun came in through the open blinds of a
window by the bed. I opened my eyes to chaos.
Bedclothes were tied in knots on the bed, clothes
were piled on the floor, dishes from last evening's
Chinese food littered the table outside of the sleeping
alcove. But worst of all was the emptiness. She was
gone. I felt the pillows for a note, but there was
nothing.

At first I sat up in the rumpled satin sheets, my
head pounding. I put my feet on the cool floor-
boards and ran my hand through my hair. Directly
in front of me was the suitcase given me by Rafael.
I had completely forgotten my things yesterday when
Suhkhula had first brought me to her apartment. I
found the bathroom, a huge affair done in marble
and gold fixtures. After I donned the Italian suit that
Rafael and I had shopped for, I walked to the elevator and went down. I stepped out into the heat of
the morning. There was a black Mercedes sedan at
the curb. I craned my neck to seek a taxicab, then
suddenly the door of the sedan glided open.

A computer voice said, "Good morning, Mr.
Novskoyy." I looked around, embarrassed at my
confusion, and I ducked into the car. The door shut,

the car gliding off to whisk me away to the da Vinci Maritime skyscraper, or so I guessed. When I sat back, a panel in the interior rolled open to reveal a fresh cup of espresso. I took it, mumbling, "Spasiba," then remembering it was a computer I was talking to. As I finished, the car's door rolled open to reveal the elegant front entranceway to da Vinci Maritime.

A young man waited by the door, greeting me with the same graciousness I'd experienced from the employees the day before, except today he seemed grim. I was reminded of the time I was arrested, the faces of the First Chief Directorate guards wearing the same dark expressions. The clerk led me to the elevator and asked me to follow him to a conference room.

As the door to the conference room opened, several shouts reverberated off the marble walls of the corridor, some in English, some in Italian. I could hear Suhkhula's voice, but I could not make out her words. I walked in and saw the engineers and directors of da Vinci Maritime screaming at each other. Instinctively I ducked as a coffee cup sailed by my face, flying across the room and shattering on the cherry wood of the wall panels. At that, Suhkhula's voice rang out through the room, fury at top volume, her tone penetrating to the very marrow of my bones, and the noise stopped. I looked at her, but her expression held little more than recognition. There was no tenderness there, no acknowledgment of our time together the previous evening.

"Good morning, Al," she said, her voice as impersonal as a hotel room. "You should be in on the

headline for the day. Toricelli is dead." She looked at me as if the name would have some meaning.

"Toricelli," I said, prompting her.

"The program manager who was directing the chimp in the mammalian control lab yesterday."

"What happened?"

"The surgery was performed yesterday late afternoon to remove the control port from his brain. After surgery his brain swelled. Apparently it was catastrophic—his brain functions went flat. He was brain-dead. They disconnected him from the respirator. He breathed on his own for a while but then crashed. A few minutes later he was gone." At the last words her eyes filled up, but she didn't look away or hold her hands to her eyes or do any of a hundred gestures that most women would do while weeping, at least the women that I know about.

I stood there and looked at her. I didn't want to give away my thoughts to the others in the conference room, or even to Suhkhula. Had it been a one-night stand for her? Did I mean nothing to her? I had to work with her for the next months as the undersea mammal systems project developed.

"I am sorry to hear that, and I offer my condolences to you, to all of you here. This should not have happened, and we will investigate immediately. Suhkhula, does Rafael know?"

"I informed him this morning. He's on his way. He said he wanted an immediate meeting with you. Meanwhile, I will show you to your office."

Without another word, Suhkhula led me down the corridor to the elevator. She did not say a word as the cab climbed from the fortieth floor to the sev-

enty-eighth. She led me to the end of the hallway approaching the corner of the building opposite her office in the "prow." A double door of mahogany came open as we approached it. Inside was a plush outer office, a male secretary at a wide polished cherry table working at a pad computer. A second set of doors opened, leading to a room with plate-glass windows on two sides framing the building's corner. The view below was as spectacular as it was from Suhkhula's office. The furniture was stark and functional: a large conference table, a desk the size of a limousine, a row of television widescreens. The only gesture toward comfort was two deep chairs with a cherry table between them facing the windows.

Still silent, Suhkhula went to a recessed sideboard and opened a panel that displayed several decanters and a row of glasses. She chose a bottle with a tan liquid in it and poured ten or fifteen cc's into one of the glasses, then drained it in a gulp. She repeated the action, draining a second, then motioned to me. I waved off the offer, amazed that someone could drink before eight in the morning. I looked over at her, and now she was crying openly, wiping tears from her eyes, her shoulders shaking. I went over to her and pulled her to me, and she seemed to surrender into my chest, becoming suddenly small, a crying child. I tried to soothe her with words, but she said nothing. Finally she sniffed, wiping her face with a tissue she'd produced from her purse.

"I'm okay," she said. "But the program is obviously canceled."

"So it would seem," was all I could think of to say. *"Were you close to him?"*

She nodded. *"I hired him, I trained him, I spent years with him. He was like a little brother to me. I can't believe he's dead."*

I held her for a long time, until the secretary walked in. *"Mr. Rafael is here, sir. He wants to see you in the conference room."*

I broke away from Suhkhula, then returned to kiss her on the cheek, a new tear wetting my lower lip. *"I am so sorry,"* I said, then turned and left.

Rafael smiled in genuine pleasure as Alexi Novskoyy entered the room, his hand swooping in to meet Novskoyy's hand—a salesman's handshake—but the hand then pulling Novskoyy in close, the other hand wrapping around Novskoyy's back, Rafael pulling him into a bear hug.

"Come, sit," Rafael said warmly. A large platter of pastries lay on the table, a gleaming coffee service next to it, two steaming cups of espresso at adjacent chairs.

Novskoyy looked at Rafael, who had begun eating a pastry. Novskoyy took the opportunity to speak. "You heard about Toricelli."

Rafael shrugged. "I heard."

"From what I understand from Suhkhula, this is extremely bad news. Toricelli was a key designer of the systems for mammalian control. And if this disaster happens every time we unplug from mammal control, we will not have many volunteers to direct the dolphins."

Rafael waved as he stuffed the last bite of the

pastry into his mouth. "I know," he said. He wiped his hands and mouth on a napkin, then grabbed another pastry. "You should try these," he said, his mouth full. "They're the city's best. Maybe Europe's best, at least outside Paris. Mmmm."

"So," Novskoyy said. "What do you think? The program would seem to have crashed."

Something was up, Novskoyy realized. Rafael did not display the slightest sense of grief or shock, at either Toricelli's death or the end of the program.

"Let me give you some pieces of information that up to now you have not had," Rafael said calmly. "Number one, Toricelli was a problem. We found out that he had spoken to a potential competitor of ours. Although nothing became of it, we later found out he was setting up his own consulting firm, exporting electronic information through an Internet connection. We had to get rid of him. It seemed most logical to do that when he was undergoing a delicate procedure like disconnection of the communication port. It *is* major surgery, after all. Brain surgery. Nothing to take lightly. Now, that's not to say it's unsafe. It's as safe as a ride in a baby carriage. But you know what the doctors say. Anything can happen during surgery. And last night, what happened was our way of firing an employee without integrity."

The idea that Rafael would have a wayward employee killed did not shock Novskoyy. It was perhaps odd that this had happened in the West, but at home such thinking was routine. On more than one occasion he himself had been forced to worry about the integrity of the organization first and the life of an individual second. In a way, that Rafael had done this gave Novskoyy a strange sense of confidence. Rafael cared enough about the company to take care of a bad apple. It showed Rafael's commitment and sense of responsibility.

Novskoyy sat back in his chair. "I understand. But Suhkhula—did she know about this?"

"No, not at all. She and Toricelli were close. She was a mentor to him, grooming him to replace her someday so that she could rise in the organization. And I don't fault her for this, but Suhkhula would not take the reality behind this news well. It is necessary to shield her from the more gritty aspects of running an organization such as this." Rafael paused to take a sip of the expresso. "Now it is your task to continue your test with the mammalian control technology. Do you think it can work?"

Novskoyy stood, starting to talk as he paced the room near the windows. "Suhkhula has me convinced. I believe it will work against the oil tankers. Against warships at their high speeds, I have my doubts. And there's a problem I haven't brought before Suhkhula, and that is that submarines with anechoic tiles—stealth antisonar coatings—will not accept a cable suction device. And a dolphin would not be able to cut through the coating and return to attach the cable to the exact spot working against a submarine's high speed of advance."

"So what are your thoughts?"

"The original plan before Toricelli died was to test this on our test tramp steamer, which is pulling into Port Lauderdale, Florida. In the early morning of Sunday, July 1, the dolphin under test was going

to attach SG-1 explosives to the test vessel, blow it
up, and then try to do a test on the underhull of a
visiting Royal Navy Astute-class submarine. We
were going to see how this coating reacts to a cable
suction device."

"Just get the pre-Toricelli plan back on track and
back on schedule. But remember, if it proves less
than successful, we have only until the 23rd before
the American cruise ship departs Norfolk Harbor.
That's not much time."

Novskoyy stopped his pacing and looked over
at Rafael. "I am not hopeful. Suhkhula thinks her
biological systems are the ultimate, but I have my
doubts. For that reason I've decided to be the controller of the dolphin to do the testing on July 1."

"No. It's dangerous. Your medical records don't
support such a decision. You've had angina, and
this will stress your body. Leave this to others."

"After Toricelli, you're going to have trouble
finding volunteers. Besides, if we're going to go up
against a flotilla of American warships, I want to
make damn sure that this will work."

"Fine. Let Suhkhula do it."

"We can't. She is the brains of this plan. So far,
I am only just coming onstream. If it doesn't work
with me, Suhkhula goes on."

"No, you're vital to the plan, and—"

"I'm doing the test. I've decided."

Rafael sighed. "Okay. But if you have doubts,
what's your backup plan?"

Novskoyy sat down opposite Rafael, leaning far
over the table and staring intently into Rafael's
eyes. "I've been through the files on the modifica-

tions that da Vinci Maritime did on the Ukrainian Severodvinsk-class submarines. The Severodvinsk submarine may be old, but it is incredible, more advanced than anything on my drawing board when the Omega-class subs sailed. It has a quiet-running torpedo with unprecedented range. It has mobile mines that can attach to a ship hull and wait to detonate until the ship is out of the area. It has a periscope that doesn't penetrate the pressure hull, with an optronics package in the rudder pod that can see the surface when the ship is hovering down to a depth of five hundred meters. It has its seawater cooling system suction valves on the top of the hull so the ship can rest on the bottom without fouling the condensers. It has a high-frequency, high-resolution three-dimensional environmental sonar for approaching littoral waters, so it can drive right into a harbor without danger of ripping open the hull on the rocks, and without being detected. And the broadband active sonar your people designed pings with a pulse that sounds like a school of shrimp, even to the ears of a marine biologist— active sonar, Rafael, that sounds like fish! And it has countermeasures against acoustic daylight imaging, the biologics generators, making the ship in open ocean appear like a school of shrimp in addition to sounding like one. And beyond that, we can sneak it to sea easily, since you sold Ukraine the hull decoy. The satellites and spies will believe the ship is in a drydock, while the real vessel is in the cave pens, and the new entrance to the sub pens is underwater—we can get the ship to sea without anyone knowing, provided we quarantine the crew.

If we put a Severodvinsk in the water of Norfolk Harbor, we can torpedo the cruise ship and her escorts and escape without being detected. It is perfect."

Rafael stared at Novskoyy for some time. "It sounds like you've worked this all out."

"Of course, I don't want the world knowing we are deploying a Ukrainian submarine. So, to get the Severodvinsk to sea quietly, we pull the hull decoy into the drydock and start working on it— the Americans will believe it is under construction and will have their guard down—while we kidnap the crew and captain and detain them, perhaps aboard the real Severodvinsk in the underground cavern of the submarine pen, and when we're ready, I'll board her and she will leave by the underwater tunnel exit. We could make the transatlantic crossing in twelve days and take a day to slowly make our way into Port Norfolk. It will be like taking candy from a baby."

"You've put a lot of thought into your contingency plan, Al. I like it."

"Well, you hired me for a reason. Suhkhula is brilliant, but she is down in her details as a scientist and she cannot see the big picture of planning a war operation. Whereas that is my specialty."

Rafael smiled. "I couldn't have said it better myself. Good luck, my friend. Call me immediately after your Port Lauderdale test."

Rafael left Novskoyy in the conference room. Novskoyy stood at the window, thinking about Suhkhula and the Severodvinsk submarines.

13

The world consisted of only two things. A loud ringing in his mind, and the assault of an electrical coppery taste where his mouth used to be.

He felt nausea, then pain, an aching in his back, a throbbing in his head—he had a head now, when before he did not—and then a sense of vertigo, as if he were floating, tumbling upside down.

There was a rushing noise, like that of river rapids, but then he began to understand that the noise was the slipstream of a jet. He was inside an airplane. He tried to feel his body, his back, and could sense the light touch of a soft mattress. Circulation returned to his limbs with pins and needles. He tried to sit up, but a rush of vertigo hit him. The world spun sickeningly around him, and a wave of nausea washed through his stomach. There was something wrong with his head. It felt strange. He moved his hand up slowly to his forehead. He encountered a heavy bandage wrapped around his eyes and the back of his skull. When he touched it, a sharp pain shot through his head and neck.

Someone spoke to him, the sound of it very strange. The voice was low in pitch. A second voice, higher-pitched, melodic. And as if he had retained the sounds, playing them over and over in his mind, he finally began to understand them.

"Well, Al, finally you've decided to wake up from your extended nap." Rafael, he thought.

"Do not try to move, Al. You will feel much better soon. Can you hear me?" Suhkhula.

"I . . . hear." His tongue was rubber in his mouth, dry and cottony.

"Do you remember anything?" Rafael again.

"They put the helmet on me. There was a checklist. Then drugs. That is all. Am I injured?"

"No, Al." Suhkhula's voice was soft in his ear. Her fingers picked up his hand, stirring a strong emotion. "You are fine."

"Bandage?" he asked.

"The surgery was done to remove the termination to the biosystem. We'll trade it for a smaller bandage this evening."

"What happened?"

Suhkhula answered first. "The dolphin was killed in the blast. We were worried about what would happen to you when you came to, but the doctors promised that aside from leaving your memories on the dolphin, you would recover fully. How do you feel? Do you remember anything?"

Novskoyy grimaced. "What *happened*?"

"You did great, Al," Rafael said. "You blew our tanker to hell. But the submarine was a problem. And somehow your dolphin lost its bearings and didn't return to the boat. We had no time. The liquid explosives blew up and vaporized you, or at least the dolphin you were operating."

Feeling was starting to return to his mouth and

limbs. The vertigo was receding. "I want to sit up and see you. Can you remove the bandage?"

In a few minutes he was looking at Rafael and Suhkhula. Both of them were dressed impeccably, but they had black circles under their eyes, lines defining their frowning foreheads, as if they'd been up for days. He looked down at his bed, noticing that he was wearing a hospital robe. Outside the aircraft's windows, the sky was black.

"Submarine," Novskoyy's voice croaked, prodding Rafael. "The British sub."

"Right. The cables wouldn't attach. The sound-absorbing tiles are too spongy. This is a serious setback. It means the liquid explosives can't be used to attack a submarine guarding the American cruise ship task force. But if that were the only problem, we'd go ahead with it and leave the submarine alone, have our demonstration, pocket the money, and execute the Saudi plan. But that's not going to do it." Rafael rubbed his eyes, the first time Novskoyy had ever seen him appear uncertain.

"Why not? We will attack the cruise ship and leave the submarine alone. Our demonstration is done for Nipun, and we take the equipment to the Persian Gulf and make even more money."

"It won't wash. Listen, back in Milan they've cranked this scenario into a political scenario analysis program on our DynaCorp Frame 180. The simulation revealed that the American government would perceive this as a terrorist attack rather than a military one. It's the cruise ship, with all the admirals on board. It changes the response completely. The fact that the guarding submarine survives means its acoustic daylight imaging sonar system's electronic history files will be examined in detail. And once they go back over it, they'll piece together the dolphin, the liquid explosives, the nearby dolphin system host cargo ship. We'll be ten minutes into the Saudi part of the operation before the U.S. Navy comes for us."

Novskoyy's headache was coming back. "Let me get this straight. We cannot use the dolphins and the SG-1 explosives on the cruise ship and the escort ships because your video game says the American authorities will put the puzzle together. They will be led to the Saudi operation, shut it down, and put us behind bars. That is it?"

"That's it. Isn't that enough?"

Novskoyy was silent. He was aware that it wouldn't matter what he said. Rafael had his opinion, and it would not change, and Rafael owned the business. Despite his skepticism, he needed to move the conversation on.

"For the sake of argument, let us assume that your little computer game convinces me. Where does that take you?"

"It takes us to Plan B, the one you yourself suggested before we even introduced you to the biological program."

"What are you talking about?"

"A Ukrainian Project 885 Severodvinsk-class submarine is taken covertly to sea and inserted into Port Norfolk with a load of mobile plasma-tipped mines. When the cruise ship *Princess Dragon* departs with the American Navy's brass, we attack it with the mines. About the time it's blowing up, and its escorts as well, the Severodvinsk returns to a western Atlantic hold position, where the second half of its mission begins."

"What about the acoustic daylight imaging of the American Navy?"

"That system isn't much good in a harbor, Al," Suhkhula said. He could smell the light scent of her perfume, the fragrance reminding him of their night together, but that seemed like it belonged to another lifetime. "I should have listened to you the first time."

"But what about the mobile mines? Won't they make noise and be detected?"

"Very short run-to-attach," Rafael said.

"But they attach magnetically. They will have the same problems with the sub hull the dolphin must have had with the British submarine."

"You'll hit the SSNX with torpedoes. Plasma units. The sinking of the American task force will not be connected to the loss of the Saudi oil carriers. The modes of sinking will be too different."

"But one thing I didn't think about was—why a Ukrainian submarine? Why not Russian? Or one we could borrow without the need to go through a foreign government?"

"This is all working out perfectly for us, Al. We fulfill our promise to Nipun in India by sinking the U.S. Navy cruise ship with the American brass on board, and collect our windfall. We put the dolphin system in the water in Saudi Arabian waters and put in place the blockade, again collecting even more of Nipun's money. Suhkhula will be going to the Persian Gulf to handle that, assuming we make our next sale."

"What sale?"

"We're going to the Ukraine now to see President Vladimir Dolovietz. We will sell him on the benefits of sinking the American cruise ship. It'll be perfect for him. He's got an operation going down in the South Atlantic they don't want the American Navy interfering with. Two South American countries are going to be duking it out, and Dolovietz is selling his services to one of them."

"I am beginning to have my doubts, Rafael. What happens in your simulation about the use of plasma mobile mines from a bottom-of-the-bay Ukrainian submarine, easily detected on acoustic daylight sonar?"

"The simulation says that if not for the U.S. SSNX acoustic-daylight-capable submarine, the Severodvinsk would succeed. But the American SSNX would cut her in half, which is why we would want to ambush it. There can be no telltale history disks on the SSNX, and all the escort warships will be on the bottom. There will be nothing left of the task force except some wreckage on the bottom."

Novskoyy closed his eyes, nodding.

Rafael continued, "So if the Severodvinsk can ambush the American task force, we all make money. All the operations succeed—the cruise ship demonstration, the South Atlantic Ukrainian work, and our Saudi plan. It will be a very big year for da Vinci Enterprises."

"Why did you say there was a reason I was going?"

"You're the preeminent submarine expert. You'll be there to make sure the SSNX submarine doesn't interfere with our operation. And to make sure the backwoods Ukrainian submarine commander does it right."

BOOK III
Vepr

14

The jangling of the phone was so loud and sudden that he punched it, startled from a deep sleep. The phone crashed across the floor, bouncing and banging. He jumped from the bed, heart pounding, and followed the noise. Finally his fingers closed around the heavy plastic handset, but the phone line was dead. The cord had been disconnected from the wall. He squatted there in the middle of the floor, staring stupidly into the dimness of the room.

He scratched his head and stood, carrying the phone back to the nightstand. He clicked on the lamp, plugged the phone back into the wall, and sat on the bed. The old clock on the wall, his great-grandfather's, ticked solemnly, the hands both pointing at the three, in the wee hours of Sunday morning. Beside him a young woman lay buried beneath a feather comforter and several pillows. For a long moment he looked at his wife, smiling. He'd been married for three years to Martinique, the daughter of an old family friend, a woman he'd known since she took her first steps. The prospect of being away from her was not a happy thought. In a few moments the phone would ring again, and odds were that it would mean that leaving her would be sooner rather than later.

On cue, the phone rang again. This time he answered it.

"Grachev," he growled, his voice hoarse from the previous evening's drinking. Last night they'd celebrated his wife's thirtieth birthday.

"There's a car waiting out front," a familiar voice said, resonant with authority. The man at the other end was alert as if it were midmorning instead of the wee hours. "You have four minutes to be in it." The connection clicked as the caller hung up.

Pavel Grachev blinked and put the phone down. Walking to the curtained window, he drew it aside, scanning up and down the street of brownstone houses in the seaside section of Balaklava, fifteen kilometers from Sevastopol's city limits. The view of an idling Volvo and its exhaust cloud was partially obscured by the line of trees out front.

"To hell with four minutes," Grachev muttered, walking to the bathroom. Staring back at him from the mirror was a hungover man of thirty-six, extremely tall, so thin as to seem gaunt, his height mostly in his thighs. His thin blond hair was spiked from sleep, his jaw coarse with gray stubble running from his sideburns past his hollow cheeks to his square chin and down to his chest. His skin was pale, almost porcelain. His face was narrow, his cheekbones prominent. His eyebrows were so lightly blond that they seemed to be missing, as did his eyelashes, his bloodshot eyes a faded blue the color of stonewashed denim. The face in the mirror looked haggard, washed-out, the lightness of his hair and skin making him look as if he'd lived in a cave away from sunlight all his life, which was not too far from the truth. His teeth were one feature he had no complaints about, their even whiteness straight out of a toothpaste ad. Once he'd shaved and showered, he would look older than he was, but more healthy than the mirror would allow for now.

He ran the shower water to hot, stepped in, then finished with the water at the full cold setting, nearly jumping out of the shower enclosure. After a fast shave he tried to brush the hangover out of his mouth, without much luck. He dressed in the dark, left Martinique a note, and kissed her, looking over her sleeping face, her hair covering her eyes, her long auburn locks half-hidden under the hood of the sweatsuit. She moaned. He kissed her again and silently shut the door, walking down the hall to the nursery, where young Pavel was sleeping. When he came into the dark room, Pavel was standing in his crib, his small fingers gripping the bars, smiling up at Grachev.

"Hi, Daddy," he said happily. "Up?"

"Morning, sailor," Grachev said, ruffling the youth's hair and picking him up. Pavel's body was light and warm as he carted him to the changing table. He changed the boy's diaper and buttoned him back into his sleepsuit.

"Daddy play?" The lad's voice was high-pitched, his pronunciation still in the experimental phase.

"No, son. Daddy has to go to town."

"Oh," the two-year-old said. "Getting toy?"

Grachev laughed. "No, young warrior. Not today. Maybe next time."

"Not go, Daddy. Stay."

"Go back to sleep, son."

The youth yawned and obediently lay down, shutting his eyes. Grachev leaned over the railing of the crib and kissed him, lingering at the door, reluctant to leave, finally walking away down the stairs to the entrance. Briefcase and hat in hand, he sank into the back of the Volvo. It took twenty minutes to reach Admiralty Square in the center of Sevastopol.

Grachev climbed slowly out of the limo and put on his cap. He walked past the granite columns of the entryway, past the four sets of security guards, flashing his computer chip badge, through the security surveillance foyer, and finally into the stainless-steel-paneled elevator car. The car, controlled by the security sentries, had no buttons. The elevator plunged downward, deep into the bedrock, finally opening to a reception area done in marble and cherry. A lovely blond girl in a tight-fitting sweater sat behind the desk, as alert as her boss had sounded.

"Hello, Karina. Admiral's in, I presume?"

"Conference room one, Captain Grachev." She smiled at him, her full red lips parting to reveal large white teeth. "You'll be wanting Colombian coffee, sir?"

"Coffee," Grachev said. "And a very tall bottle of water."

"And two aspirin? You look a little, well, not yourself."

"That would be great," he said. "You'll make a wonderful wife someday."

"I know." She smiled again, staring at him a bit too long. He smirked and walked past her desk.

The cherry-paneled walls of the passageway led to the large heavy door of the conference room, where Admiral Yuri Kolov sat in one of the high-backed leather chairs, staring at a handheld computer display. He stood up and smiled when he saw Grachev.

Grachev saluted the balding older man and reached out to shake his hand. Kolov's handshake was a vise grip, and he pulled Grachev into a bear hug, slapping his back. The two men went back twenty years, to when Kolov had been a mere captain-lieutenant in Ukraine's Black Sea Fleet in the first years after the Russian Republic closed up shop. Kolov, against his will, had been volunteered for a program to speak at the local schools about the fledgling Ukrainian submarine program. Grachev, a restless sixteen-year-old student with poor grades, had been enthralled by Kolov's stories of the sea. The danger, the camaraderie, the thrill of undersea combat. He had approached the naval officer after the speech. Their talk began a lifetime friendship.

In later visits, Kolov explained to Grachev how the Ukrainian Navy had been the inheritor of a large blue-water fleet when the Russian Republic left it behind. They had no idea of what to do with it, and with little training and nonexistent operating funds. There were only eight nuclear submarines back then, but the admirals on staff had ambitious plans to expand the flotilla. When Grachev made the decision to join the Ukrainian Navy, Kolov had

celebrated with him, and after Grachev graduated
from the Sevastopol Naval Institute, Kolov had
sworn him in as an officer.

Since then Grachev had risen in the ranks, in
parallel with Kolov's career, until the year that
Kolov had taken command of the submarine force.
Grachev had waited through that year, expecting
to assume command of a submarine despite his
youth, but after a hard life of training, nothing
seemed to happen. Then on Grachev's thirty-sixth
birthday, the week after Kolov had been Grachev's
best man at his wedding, Grachev visited Kolov's
office. There on the desk was an envelope with the
seal of the Ukrainian Navy, a shield depicting a
missile roaring from the sea, a dolphin leaping up
around it, the shield's background two crossed ceremonial sabers. The envelope's inscription read:
"Official Orders / To be Opened by Recipient
Only / Captain Second Rank Pavel I. Grachev /
Navy of the Ukraine / Black Sea Fleet."

Grachev looked up, uncertain.

"Go ahead," Kolov said. "Open it." But Grachev had known. The envelope contained orders to
take command of K-898, the Black Sea Fleet's
brand-new Project 885/Severodvinsk-class submarine *Vepr*—Russian for "boar."

Grachev had reported a week later to the Kola
Peninsula, to the city of Severomorsk in the northern Russian Republic, training on the systems of
the Russian-built Project 885/Severodvinsk-class
submarine, along with his prospective crew. They'd
returned after six months, Grachev finding Martinique pregnant and miserable. Since then he had

grown into his command, Martinique had become a mother, and young Pavel had come. Grachev realized, as he shook Kolov's hand at half past three on a Saturday morning, that he was happy, that this was what he'd always hoped his adult life would turn out to be.

"Admiral. Good to see you. Even at this hour on a Sunday. I suppose you'll be telling me what's going on?"

Kolov's smile faded as he waved the younger officer to a seat.

"We're going to have company in a few minutes. Two visitors to President Dolovietz's office left Kiev about the time I called you at your house, and—"

"Kiev's three hours away."

"They've got a corporate jet."

"Fine. And who are these people?"

"Consultants from a firm named da Vinci. Same people who did the submarine pen conversion, with the underwater egress tunnel. They did the Project 885 drydock hull decoy, and they did the design and installation of the Antay sensor and the Shchuka system."

Grachev lifted an eyebrow. *Vepr* had been placed in the drydock earlier in the year to have her tail-mounted sonar pod removed, to be replaced by the Antay sensor, an optronics device that resembled the sonar pod but could float to the surface on a cable like a buoy and record visual light spectrum images, a sort of buoy-mounted periscope. The Shchuka system was a large sonar array that was deployed from a torpedo tube. It had an inflatable foil device using the revolutionary acoustic daylight physics. Both systems had seemed a waste to Grachev, since neither one could be used while moving—the ship would have to be bottomed out or hovering for either unit to work, and when did that ever happen? The sonar pod was one thing, but taking away one of Grachev's torpedo tubes was unforgivable. He had secret thoughts of jettisoning the Shchuka device once they cleared restricted waters on the next mission, but he made sure Kolov didn't hear about those ideas.

"Where is the drydock decoy?"

"At the old submarine piers, tied up where we used to dock *Vepr* before the submarine pens were completed this month. We even have the hatches open, and sailors and officers going to and from the hull. From the outside, it is practically indistinguishable from the real *Vepr*."

Grachev laughed. "Do the pier workers know it's a decoy? It couldn't fool me."

"They say mothers can tell their twins apart, but no one else can. As long as none of the workers tries to enter a hatch, that decoy hull *is* a Project 885 submarine."

"Hell of a lot of trouble to go to for the sake of security."

"Anyway, the consultants will be here any minute. I thought I'd tell you something first. The mission you were slated for—the sortie with the fleet to the South Pacific—is canceled. You're going to Hampton Roads."

"Off Virginia? The U.S. East Coast?"

"Right."

"What's that mean to the mission to the South Atlantic? And who's going in our place? Not that bastard Dmitri and his *Tigr*. That boat may be a Project 885 but it's a bucket of bolts, and Dmitri's in worse shape."

"Not your concern. The consultants are coming to brief you, Pavel, and it's classified most secret. And before they get here, you need to know one of them will be going to sea with you."

"A rider? From a consulting company?"

The phone on the side table rang. Kolov answered it, listened, and put it down. "They're here." He stood, Grachev standing as well.

Karina escorted in two men and a woman. One of the men had a large frame and a beard running to gray. He had animated and intelligent eyes and wore an expensively tailored charcoal-gray suit. The second man was much thinner, with an athlete's build, a craggy, hollow-cheeked face beneath a mop of graying hair, piercing eyes, and a stiff—almost military—carriage. He wore an Armani double-breasted suit. The woman was a stunning Chinese dressed in a black suit with a tight skirt. Introductions went around the room.

The one named Rafael smiled. "Pleased to meet you finally, Captain Grachev. I have the good fortune of knowing who you are. Unfortunately, so does the intelligence network of the U.S. armed forces. That's why you're here."

"It is?"

"Captain Grachev, at da Vinci Consulting we have our fingers in a lot of pies. Electronic intelligence is one of them. We were doing some contract

work for your government when we found we were
hearing a lot of information about your submarine.
What concerns us, and your President, is that the
British and Americans will know the instant that
your *Vepr* deploys. They know not only when it
leaves, but where it is going, its mission, weapon
loadout, and more."

Grachev looked frustrated. "How can that be?"

"I'll prove it to you." Rafael handed a disk to
Kolov, who put it in.

Grachev watched in shock. For the next five minutes he watched a pornographic movie, several men
with two women, but the background of the discussion was about the *Vepr,* when it would sail for a
torpedo exercise. One of the men Grachev recognized as the machinery division warrant officer. He
bit his lip, wondering how he'd look the man in the
eye now. The disk would seem to prove Rafael's
case. Eventually, Rafael turned it off, but not before one of the women asked one of the men—a
sonarman who had since left the ship—how the
ship's sonar worked, and he had begun to tell her
things that were classified secret. Grachev could
feel his face flushing in anger.

"This is unacceptable," Grachev growled. "I will
have a very painful meeting with my crew."

Rafael waved off his demonstration. "Don't
bother, Captain. Those women work for us—as I
said, we have our hands in a lot of pies, and one
of the things we market is intelligence. We're under
contract for a number of projects, but one of ours
was to see if we could find out *Vepr*'s next mission.
But before you go out to abuse your crew, you

should be aware that we—and the foreign intelligence services—get most of their information from the ship's commander. My regards to your pretty wife on her thirtieth, by the way."

"What—?"

"This is where the best information comes from." Rafael switched disks. Grachev watched himself walk in the door of his own house. An embrace with his wife, and the usual husband-wife chatter about their days. When Grachev told his wife about his ship's plans to leave in a week to go join the remaining vessels of the fleet for a deployment to the South Atlantic, even telling her how little he thought of the plan to support Argentina's invasion of Uruguay, Rafael stopped the disk.

Grachev's face was a dark thundercloud as he stood up from the conference table. Admiral Kolov waved him back to his seat.

"Relax, Pavel," he said. "If they have this on you, imagine what they've got on me."

"Sir, these bastards have invaded my home. They've—"

"This is the original disk," Rafael said, pulling it from the machine and handing it to Grachev. "It's the only disk. It was reviewed only by our computer, which identified keywords programmed in and flagged them for review. Otherwise we'd have to spend countless hours reviewing footage. The only footage we've seen is what I just showed, and this was the first time I've seen it—I only heard the audio at the computer's flag. And this was the only item the computer came up with. I would not presume to spy on you outside of this demonstration, Captain. And in case you're wondering, the surveillance equipment was installed for a period of only two days, immediately after you were given orders and an operation briefing on the South Atlantic."

"Fine," Grachev said, the top of his scalp sweating. "Is that what you came here for, to show me the security leaks of my ship, and to embarrass me?"

"Hold on," Kolov said, his hand on Grachev's shoulder. "There's more to listen to."

"More?"

For the first time the Chinese woman spoke, her odd pronunciation of Russian lilting and melodic.

"We have spent five years establishing a capability in electronic interception. Cel phone calls, microwave computer links, UHF and VHF military radio signals. We have interception stations in key places bringing in data at an enormous rate. Our computers have been sifting through the harvest and correlating the desired intelligence."

The speech must have been practiced, Grachev thought, the Chinese woman stumbling through the Russian phrases.

"Wonderful for you," Grachev said, although his tone was not as severe as it had been moments before. Kolov was holding up a finger, so Grachev fell silent.

"And for you," Suhkhula replied. "Our harvest has shown that the U.S. intelligence agencies are fully aware of the planned sortie of the *Vepr* to the South Atlantic. They know that Monday, July 30, at four in the morning Eastern European time, you will depart, make for Gibraltar at fifty clicks, and intercept the surface fleet three hundred kilometers southwest of Brest, France. They know that rendez-vous will take place Friday, August 3, at fourteen hundred hours GMT, or thirteen hundred hours local time."

Grachev tried to keep his face impassive, but his own eyes were bugging out in astonishment. This detailed information was revealed only at his and Kolov's level, and it had never been the subject of any discussions with Martinique.

"How exactly do you know that? Did President Dolovietz tell you that?" Grachev could not keep from asking, but the Chinese woman had fallen silent.

"I can see I'll have to prove it to you." Rafael smiled. "Take a look at this." He handed Grachev his pad computer, a flat-panel display the size of a sheet of paper. "Click through to Friday's files."

Grachev maneuvered through the software to the files from Friday, June 29, 2018. There was a message from Kolov to him, giving him his sailing orders for Monday, July 30. It was in the proper format and looked like the message he remembered. Still, it was something Dolovietz could have given up.

"You are not convinced. Take a look at the next file."

Grachev clicked it. It was a video file, and after a moment it started, two screens flashing up on the display. On the left was a man he recognized, the admiral in command of the American Navy, but whose name eluded him. The man on the right was an olive-skinned man in a Navy uniform. The admiral was wearing a sweatshirt reading NAVY 90. The

background was a kitchen done in cedar plank paneling. A date stamp on the bottom of the file read
06/30/18 SATURDAY 15:34 GMT 10:34 EDT. The day after
Kolov's sailing order message.

"Morning, Paully," the admiral's image said. "I
was just heading out to the sailboat."

"Engine still giving you trouble?"

"Pulling off the starboard cylinder head today."

"Need any help?"

"Nah. Think of it as therapy."

"I think I need to find something to calm me
down. Especially after what Number Four came
up with."

"Let's go secure in five minutes."

"I'll call you back."

The screen went black, a blinking series of numbers counting down from ten seconds to zero. The
split screen display returned, the admiral's kitchen
background gone, the walls of an office behind him.
The other man's background had not changed. The
speech pattern was warbling and oddly delayed
from the movement of the lips of the speakers, as
if they were viewing an old movie that had come
out of synchronization, the obvious effect of the
secure video encryption. The admiral spoke first.

"What do you have? I'm set up to receive."

"On your screen now."

A third screen came up, this one showing Kolov's
message inside the body of a forwarding message
from a Mason Daniels IV to Rear Admiral Paul
White, the subject line reading UKRAINE INTERCEP-
TION 062918.

"National Security Agency comes through again,"

the second man said. Grachev assumed he was the addressee, Paul White.

"Daniels is on the case," the sweatshirt-clad admiral commented. "And the Severodvinsk submarine shoves off Monday, July 30, and forms up with the Black Sea Fleet. So it begins."

"Right after we get back from our cruise. We'll have to spend some time after hours going over this. So much for getting away from it all."

"Actually, Paully, this might work out. It'll put all our best minds on the problem. We can have relaxed meetings with our staff and plan our strategy."

"Any chance this is a deception from Ukraine, sir? To throw us off and make us show our hand?"

"Always possible, Paully. But if that were the case, Number Four would give us an indication. I think we have to assume it's real. The Black Sea Fleet submarine admiral has no reason to think we're reading his mail."

"Kolov," White said. "Sharp cookie."

"We have anything on the captain of the Severodvinsk?"

"Just what we had from the prostitute Number Four put at their first officer's bachelor party. He's a captain second rank, promotion pending to first rank, name's Pavel Grachev. He seems a straight arrow, didn't participate in the hanky-panky—he's got a young wife and a two-year-old at home—just drank and talked to his men in the other room. He can sock down the vodka, but that's not unusual. In his mid-thirties. Seems a little young to command a Severodvinsk top-of-the-line sub. He could be connected, one of Kolov's handpicked guys."

"Does Number Four have him covered?"

"He's under surveillance around the clock. We'll know when the Severodvinsk is ready to go—he'll walk out his front door with a duffel bag and a kiss to the wife. By the way, where's Colleen?"

"Getting ready to testify before Congress."

Rafael broke in. "The rest is personal chatter. And as you can see, they know every time Captain Grachev blows his nose."

"Which is why you're here, pulled out of your house in the wee hours, Pavel," Kolov said to Grachev. "Prepare yourself, my friend. I have some hard news for you." Grachev looked over, an eyebrow lifted. "You won't be going back to your flat. You're going to the submarine pens. From there K-898 *Vepr* will get underway, about two hours from now, with the sea scramble plan, through the underwater egress tunnel, reactor dead cold iron, on the battery, until you are below a hundred meters. You'll start the plant and exit Bosporus, then Dardanelles, then Gibraltar, and make way at attack speed on an indirect course along the Newfoundland coast for Hampton Roads, Virginia, U.S.A. There you will execute a covert mission, which you will be given details on after you sail. Any questions?"

"Questions? About a thousand. But the details will be given to me after I sail."

"Yes. In addition, Mr. Novskoyy will be riding *Vepr.* He will advise you on the ship's military systems and the intelligence harvest from the Americans. You are to offer him every courtesy."

Grachev's face stiffened. He would speak privately to Kolov about that. He didn't need any consultants to tell him how to fight his submarine.

"Very well, Admiral," was all he said. "Why is that such hard news, by the way?"

Kolov glanced uneasily at Rafael. "Perhaps Mr. Rafael should address that point."

"Captain Grachev, on Monday afternoon, July 2, in the middle of the Black Sea, you will be dead. So will your crew."

The briefing got worse and worse, Grachev thought. His head was beginning to hurt again from the hangover. He took a pull from his spring water bottle and stared at Rafael.

"Not really, of course," Rafael continued. "You see, by Monday you and *Vepr* will be long gone, but the decoy *Vepr* will put to sea Monday morning. It has been outfitted with an operational diesel engine and control surfaces. It can make ten knots on its own power, even submerge on its battery under computer control. Shortly after the computer takes it down, it will sink with great fanfare, a black box buoy rising to the surface and transmitting the last images from inside the submarine before it sank. Admiral Kolov's rescue operation will start that evening. Monday's evening news will carry word that the Navy of the Ukraine is calling the sinking accidental and ruling that *Vepr* went down with all hands. Friday, July 6, the memorial service will be held."

"The families will know the real truth, of course," Grachev said, his voice deep and menacing, his stomach filling with bile at the thought of Martinique at a memorial service for him when he

was actually still alive at sea. What would this do
to young Pavel?

"No," Rafael said. "The families, for all they
know, will be widows and orphans. The news cameras of the world will film their tears, the best way
to cloak *Vepr*'s departure. It is vital to keep the
Vepr plan secret—"

Rafael wasn't prepared for the specter of Grachev
coming across the table at him, and Kolov was not
quick enough to stop the young submarine commander from grabbing the consultant's Indian silk tie
hard enough to strangle him, Grachev's other hand
forcing Rafael's forehead all the way down to the
wood surface of the table, Rafael's large hands paw-
ing the air fruitlessly trying to get free.

"My wife and son will know the truth," Grachev
spat, "or else *Vepr* goes nowhere."

Kolov pulled Grachev away. Rafael gasped for
breath, while Novskoyy glared at both of them,
Suhkhula staring wide-eyed.

"My apologies, Mr. Rafael. I'd like to take a
moment alone with Captain Grachev, if you don't
mind." Kolov's voice was iron, his face beet-red,
his hands clenched around Grachev's shoulders.
Rafael, breathing heavily, his eyes bugging out,
nodded and went out with Novskoyy and Suhkhula.
The door shut solidly behind them.

"What the hell are you doing?" Kolov bellowed.
"Don't you realize those people have the ear of
the President? What will you do when Dolovietz
calls me and tells me to lock you up? Don't you
get it, Pavel? You're being sent on the mission of
the century, and if you're good, you'll come back.

Your ship will protect the operation to the South
Atlantic. We won't be able to do this without you.
If you go on the mission with the *Vepr,* you'll come
back to medals and brass bands and Martinique. If
you go to jail, there will be nothing but disgrace.
Have I not taught you anything over the last
twenty years?"

Grachev stared at the floor. "I'm sorry, sir. This
is a hard thing, as you said."

"Don't apologize to me, you fool. Apologize to
those consultants out there, and dammit, you make
damn sure you make Novskoyy feel welcome
aboard *Vepr.*"

"That's what I want to talk to you about. Why
am I taking a consultant? I can fight that ship better
than any other man alive."

"Which is why you're in command of her, Pavel.
Novskoyy goes because he will give you your final
mission orders at sea, and he will have responsibility for the overall mission."

"What 'overall mission'?"

"It is not for you to worry about, not now. All
you should worry about now is getting *Vepr* to sea.
These are your orders, and they come directly from
Dolovietz himself. They are waiting for you in your
computer in writing. If you value your career, you'll
do as I say. Now when the consultants come back
in, you kiss their asses as you've never kissed
asses before."

Grachev straightened his tie. "Sir, it's what I
do best."

Kolov suppressed a laugh and opened the door.

15

Captain Second Rank Pavel Grachev moved his officer's cap far back on his head. His blond hair fell out for a second before he moved the cap back down so that the bill was low over his eyes. He glanced down at his watch, yawning. It was half past four in the morning.

"Good morning, sir," said the first officer, Captain Second Rank Mykhailo Svyatoslov, in his phlegm-laced voice. Svyatoslov was Grachev's age, but could not look more different. He was an ethnic Ukrainian, olive-skinned, dark-haired, tall, and huge in girth. Unlikely as it might have seemed, Svyatoslov was the descendant of a Ukrainian duke who had fought and won a war against the nation of Danube in the year 967, one of the founding fathers of the Navy of the Ukraine, and a regal portrait of him hung in the Sevastopol Naval Institute. Svyatoslov was a newlywed, married that month to a slim petite blond girl who was a friend of Martinque's.

On board *Vepr,* Svyatoslov was entirely different from his hard-drinking and carousing shore persona. At sea he was the most professional officer Grachev had served with. He trained the officers relentlessly, part mentor, part drill instructor. He knew more about the Project 885 submarine than her designers, having been at the Sevmash State Center for Atomic Submarine Construction, Shipyard 402, in Severodvinsk in northern Russia from the day the first plates of low-magnetic carbon steel had rolled into the railyard until the *Vepr*'s maiden voyage and initial dive to maximum operating depth. When he first arrived at the shipyard, the submarine *Vepr* was being built for the Russian Northern Fleet, and her name had been *Admiral Chebanenko*. Much had happened in the six years since Svyatoslov reported as a lieutenant in the Russian Republic Navy. The *Admiral Chebanenko* had been sold to the Navy of the Ukraine a year into her construction, the name immediately changed to *Vepr* at the insistence of then Lieutenant Svyatoslov, who thought the "boar" name suited her from the epithets of the shipyard workers, who had been calling her an "export pig" ever since the rumor surfaced that she would be sold.

But more than a receptacle of knowledge, Svyatoslov was a fountain of energy, working through most of every night at sea preparing for the next day's drills and tactics. He was plugged into the pulse of the ship like no first officer Grachev had ever known, himself included. Perhaps the only problem with Svyatoslov's competence was that he had become so valuable as a first officer that he would likely be delayed getting a command himself.

"Good morning, Mr. First. Did Fleet Security wake you out of a sound sleep or pull you out of a waterfront bar?" Grachev was often sarcastic to the rotund first officer, and the first officer would usually respond in kind, which was not the typical military relationship between commander and second-in-command, but it seemed to suit them.

"Bar, of course, Captain. I was doing shots with a few visiting officers from the Royal Navy. I was only halfway through drinking them under the table."

Grachev thought about Rafael's briefing, and how easy it would be to get information about the sailing date of the submarine from people like Svyatoslov. He might be an excellent navy officer, but he was a definite security risk. But then, as Rafael had demonstrated, so was Grachev himself.

"Did they tell you why you were to be brought in?"

"Nothing, sir. I am hoping they don't give you a report on me. My behavior was somewhat lacking."

"Did you strike a guard?"

"No. I might have pushed one or two a little."

Grachev suppressed a smile. His first officer was not a shrinking violet, and who would want a submarine officer who was?

The two men fell silent, both holding on to the aluminum handrails inside the clamminess of the cavernous submarine pens carved out of a seaside mountain a few miles to the north of Sevastopol on the Crimean Peninsula. The above-water portion of the cavern was about fifty meters from the waterline to the reinforced concrete of the overhead, although it did not seem roomy inside, crowded as it was from platforms and handrails, electrical cable gantries, cranes, manlift equipment, twelve-meter-tall welding machines, and a nest of large-bore hoses carrying cooling water, reactor fresh water, potable water, distilled water, lubrication oil, amines, liquid nitrogen, liquid oxygen, and liquid helium for the superconductor coils of the high-efficiency motors. The submarine pen structure was a feat of civil engineering, constructed by workers with secret clearances, taking five years from groundbreaking to commissioning.

The platform where Svyatoslov and Grachev stood overlooked the single bay of the cavern where the view was relatively clear, at an elevation of forty meters over the deck far below. The floor level was obscured by gloom from the stark shadows made by the sodium and halogen floodlights. Far to the left, a large steel door rumbled in a loud boom that resounded through the cavern, the two panels separating and coming open very slowly, only darkness in between.

"Status of the crew, Mr. First?" Grachev asked, not looking at Svyatoslov.

"When Fleet Security so amiably pulled me in, they told me they'd let the men sleep for a few hours, than haul them in too. Probably about the time the ship is at water-level depth they'll be assembled in the crew briefing room. Waiting for you to tell them what's going on."

"It's not often that the entire crew of a submarine gets pulled out of hearth and home at five in the morning on Sunday."

"More like never, Captain. Are we going to the South Atlantic early?" He pulled out a silver cigarette box, produced a cigarette and a matching silver lighter, and lit the smoke, his hands trembling.

Grachev considered warning him about the prohibition on smoking, but knew Svyatoslov would ignore him.

Instead he let Svyatoslov's question hang in the air for a moment, finally deciding that there would be no crew briefing until *Vepr* was submerged. Kolov would be going to extreme trouble to cover the tracks of the ship's sortie, and it wouldn't make much sense to allow a base worker to overhear a rumor about their mission.

"I'll tell you later."

The two doors continued to open on the adjacent bay, and it took another ten minutes for them to open fully. Grachev stood and watched, content to exchange telegraphic sentences with Svyatoslov until he could see the nose of the giant vessel protrude from the opening. Slowly the submarine *Vepr* came into view.

Grachev looked down on her, his face taking on the lines of a man in love. She was long, 111 meters, and 12 meters in beam. She drew 8,200 tons fully submerged. Her bow was a perfect elliptical bullet nose, the transition to full cylinder marking the forward edge of the fin. The tapered forward-leaning conning tower was without a single sharp edge or straight plane. The aft end of it gently faired back into the hull, and the emergency diesel exhaust plenum led from far aft to the fin, making the trailing edge of the fin seem to extend another third ship length aft. The hull was smoothly cylindrical far aft to the tail of the turbine compartment, and the aft portion tapered to a sharp cone at the propulsor, where the rudder came into view. The surface of the upper rudder plane was high over the hull; the lower one beneath the hull was smaller but shaped similarly. Elevator planes protruded out the port and starboard sides of the hull. At the top of the rudder was an elongated teardrop shape, fully two meters in diameter and four meters long. It was the Antay optronics pod, for use when the ship was hovering deep and the captain needed to see the surface. The ship was a flat black color, the color of the sonar absorbent tiles. As the tail of the ship came through the opening, the steel doors began to close. The ship halted there in front of him, the hull resting on huge steel saddles on a massive metal table, which Grachev knew would soon descend, lowering the ship into the entranceway of the egress tunnel.

The hull was fabricated of five-centimeter-thick low-magnetic steel. The ship had been designed around the KPM-II pressurized water reactor producing over four hundred megawatts thermal. The steam plant put out 65,000 horsepower at the single-shafted propulsor, a series of water turbine blades enclosed by a hydrodynamic shroud. *Vepr* had four torpedo tubes 650 millimeters in diameter and two 533 millimeters. They were able to launch Berkut wake-homing torpedoes against surface targets, Bora acoustic antisubmarine torpedoes, Bora II antisubmarine plasma-tipped torpedoes, and the plasma-tipped Barrakuda mobile mines. The ship was capable of carrying thirty large-bore weapons and an additional eight small-bore units. In the forward ballast tank the vessel had eight vertical-launch tubes for cruise missiles, the current plasma-tipped

SS-NX-28 and the conventional SS-N-26. The tubes could also carry the Azov unmanned aerial vehicle for surveillance, able to let the ship spy on the entire over-the-horizon picture without the help of an overhead spy satellite.

The ship was a miraculous modern weapon system. She could fight a war at sea that could change the shape of a map—which was her current mission. She could sail into foreign ports and eavesdrop on cel phones and UHF circuits. She was a submerged battle cruiser, the most advanced war machine ever built.

The ship had begun to settle lower into the bay. Tremendous threaded columns turned at the four corners of the platform, driven by twenty-thousand-horsepower oil-enclosed motors. As the hull moved slowly downward, the steel platform below the saddles disappeared into black brackish water. Within a minute the lower curve of the cylindrical hull submerged.

Svyatoslov returned, Grachev so lost in thought he'd not noticed his absence. He pressed a cup of steaming coffee into Grachev's hands.

"Thanks. Any word on the men?"

"Yessir. They were brought in a few minutes ago. Crew lounge."

Grachev looked over. Svyatoslov was rubbing his eyes. "Maybe you should take a pill for that headache," Grachev said, his own hangover almost gone.

"I did, Captain. I don't suppose you know how long we'll be gone?"

"Why, Mykhailo? Anything wrong?"

"Nothing major, sir. Just, I was thinking perhaps it's time to settle down and get serious with Irina. She wants me to be home more, stop drinking with the boys, maybe have a baby. What worries me is, I think I'm ready to do that."

Grachev turned and stared. "You? You, of all people?"

Svyatoslov flushed, staring at his shoes. "I see you and Martinique. You're so happy. She seems to have made you . . . complete."

Grachev clapped his first officer on the shoulder. "I'll give you some useful advice on that once we clear restricted waters. Come on. *Vepr* is almost down to her submerged draft mark. Let's get the men aboard."

Grachev and Svyatoslov walked around the platforms and catwalks to the opposite side from the observation gallery. A gantryway extended horizontally from the steel structure to the top of the hull. It was anchored to a motorized mechanism that kept it horizontal while the vessel sank slowly into the water of the slip. Grachev made his way across the spongy hull tiles to the forward hatch, a meter-diameter circle of steel. Its cool and slightly oily surface was so polished that it was silvery. Grachev descended into the relative gloom of the forward airlock. The lower hatch led to the polished stainless-steel handrails of a ladder that hit bottom in a passageway sheathed in light gray plastic laminate resembling the interior of a cross-continental train compartment. The three doors around the ladder led to the offices of the department heads, and the passageway went aft to the steep stairs to the control compartment.

"Mr. First, I'm going to do a ship inspection. But now that you're aboard, there's something you need to know, and that is we have some bad news for Tenukha and Zakharov," Grachev said, naming the navigator and chief mechanical officer. "They'll be giving up their stateroom and sleeping in the two empty bunks of the warrant officers' quarters so we can give their room to the rider we're taking with us."

"Who is he?"

"Consultant. From the wonderful people who built this egress tunnel and some of the added-on feature systems of this ship."

"Fine, sir. I'll be the greeting party if he shows early, and if Tenukha comes aboard before the rider, he can show our guest around."

"I'll take a turn through control first. While I do that, clear out the rider's stateroom."

"If I might ask, Captain, what is the rider here for?"

"Boils down to a joyride. More on that later, Mr. First."

Grachev looked up the ladderway to the control compartment above him. The compartment was an ovoid of titanium supported on steel foundations and tied into the upper level of the first compartment by a short stairway through another hatch. The compartment protruded up into the envelope of the fin. Its egg shape had been designed to allow it to take full operating-depth submergence pressure. Its connections to the main hull—the electrical umbilicals, control wiring, fiber-optic cables, ventilation ducts, electronics cooling water and cooling helium—could all be disconnected in the event of an emergency. The structural steel foundations and the fin itself were filled with explosive bolts and rocket propellant charges so that the entire control compartment could become an escape pod. Grachev did not approve, since the design cramped the interior of the control room. Plus the escape pod design seemed almost a lack of commitment to the mission, a sort of ejection seat for the captain. Many times he had been tempted not to sign the work orders pertaining to the maintenance of the control compartment's connections, the explosive bolts and explosive charges, but had always decided to be faithful to the ship's designer's intent, whether or not he would have designed the ship that way himself.

Grachev stepped up the ladder two rungs at a time, emerging through the hatchway. The control compartment's lights were dim, the room silent, not even the air vents blowing. The ship was completely shut down, because its reactor would not be started up until it was far beneath the waves. Kolov's orders had specifically stated that no orbiting infrared detectors could be allowed to see the heat of the reactor vessel.

The compartment was a network of subcompartments, several booths lining the port and starboard sides. The four on the starboard side were display cubicles for the officers manning the three-dimensional attack computers. The four on the port side were devoted to weapons-control computer interfaces. A sunken well in the room's center was the periscope station. The one on the port side was the conventional optical unit, connected to the periscope unit in the fin with fiber optics. The starboard unit was tied into either the Antay buoy sensor or the optronics periscope, a nonvisual light-spectrum sensor.

The forward bulkhead held the ship-control station and the computer station for control of the ballast and diving systems, as well as the navigation interface and the communication computer station. Aft of the periscope well was a single compartmented area, the sensor cubicle, where the sonar system, the Antay sensor outputs, and the Shchuka systems were analyzed and displayed. At the forward end of the periscope well was a console station with a deep leather chair, which the deck officer would man during normal steaming or the captain during battlestations. The console's displays repeated the other key displays from the room's areas—target analysis, ship control, sensor display, weapons control, navigation, and communication. A small cubbyhole in the aft port corner was Grachev's sea cabin, a small booth barely larger than the narrow cot inside, for use when he did not want to leave the control compartment for his stateroom.

Satisfied that all was in place, Grachev returned to the first compartment and descended the steep stairway to the middle level, where the computer systems were housed in a separate, environmentally enclosed subcompartment. Entry was allowed only through the forward airlock, and only then by one of the computer officers or warrant officers wearing a clean-room environmental suit. Adjacent to it was another locked subcompartment, the battery enclosure. The huge, heavy cells provided ten times the power density of the first-generation lead-acid storage cells initially installed in the ship before she had a drydock overhaul to get the new computer control system. Aft of both subcompartments was the torpedo room, where all thirty-six large-bore and small-bore weapons were housed in racks. The computer controlled their insertion into the six torpedo tubes canted far outward. There was barely enough room to pass through a central catwalk to a stairway to the lower level, where the hotel facilities were set up, his stateroom at the bulkhead to the second compartment on the starboard side, Svyatoslov's on the port side. Forward of their staterooms were the staterooms of the department heads, the staterooms of the junior officers, the warrant officers' stateroom, and the noncommissioned quarters. Between the warrant and noncom quarters, the common head was located, a row of showers, toilet stalls, and sinks packed into a narrow room. Forward of the noncom quarters, extending across the beam of the ship, was the messroom and galley, which served also as the movie screening room, chess room, officers' conference room, and a lounge where the officers could relax.

Grachev stepped through the hatchway to the second compartment, a short space between the first and third, where the electronics for the reactor and steam systems were housed, as well as several tanks and a small machinery room. A single hatch-

way on the middle level led through a hatch to the
shielded tunnel through the third compartment—
the reactor compartment, which was never occupied because of its high radioactivity. The fourth
compartment was the turbine room, housing the
emergency diesel generator on the middle deck at
the exit of the shielded tunnel, with its sulfurous
stink of diesel oil, lube oil and diesel exhaust. A
ladder led up to the upper level, to the cleanest
engine room Grachev had ever been in. Lagged
large-diameter steam pipes threaded through the
compartment to the turbine generators that powered the electrical grid for ship's service and farther
aft to the DC propulsion turbine generators, massive three-deck-tall turbine casings taking every
kilowatt of thermal energy out of the high-pressure
saturated steam and driving two high-horsepower
liquid-helium-supercooled direct-current generators
tied electrically into the direct-current oil-enclosed
propulsion motor located outside the pressure hull
just forward of the rudder and elevator planes in
the aft ballast tanks. At the aft end of the room
Grachev took a ladder to the middle level, home
of the freshwater heat exchangers and the nuclear
control room and motor control center, to another
ladder down to the condenser and pump level. The
hydraulic systems and environmental control systems were housed here, including the oxygen generator, carbon dioxide scrubber, and hydrocarbon
burner. The liquid helium plant was forward beneath the diesel room. Grachev made a quick inspection of the helium system and went up a ladder

back to the tunnel. He made his way back to the control compartment.

Svyatoslov was standing behind the commander's console, where he'd tuned the flat-panel display on the console center to a video camera mounted on the observation deck they'd abandoned. The video display showed the ship being held at the normal surface waterline. All that was needed now was Grachev's report that the ship was ready to be submerged.

Alexi Novskoyy stepped onto the spongy-tiled deck of the submarine. He glanced at the surface of it, curving dangerously downward to the black water far below. A pungent, familiar smell came from inside the hull, bringing back memories of the past. Novskoyy stepped to the first rung of the ladder to the interior of the airlock, moved his feet to the outside of the rungs, and slid smoothly down to the bottom step-off. It had been too long, he thought, as the old feeling of being at sea returned to him. It would be a good mission.

Novskoyy walked to the stateroom he would be using on the run. It had the same light gray paneling that the entrance passageway had, the seams of the doors and cabinets done in stainless steel. The room was little more than a box three meters square and less than three meters tall. The door led to the central passageway of the lower level. On the bulkhead with the door, there was a small sink and mirror, with hooks to hang uniforms and hanging mesh bags for laundry. The forward bulkhead had two fold-out desks with two steel chairs, neither of them appearing comfortable. The aft bulkhead was filled with cabinets and cubbyholes, all of them flush with the surface of the bulkhead. The bulkhead opposite the door had two railroad-compartment-style bunks, both of them behind individual heavy curtains, with interior cubbyholes and reading lights. A display by the bunks showed the ship's course, speed, and depth. The course read 220 degrees; the speed read 0, as did the depth.

Someone rapped suddenly on the door. Novskoyy opened it. Lieutenant Tenukha stood there.

"Yes, sir. The captain sends his regards and respectfully invites you to the control compartment to see the submergence evolution. I'll take you if you wish."

Novskoyy smiled at the youngster. "I will get unpacked first, Mr. Tenukha. Please thank the captain for me and tell him, if the invitation stands, I will find my way there myself."

Tenukha handed over a data disk. "This is a visitor briefing file. It has maps of the ship. You need to wear this," he said, handing over a small black object. "Radiation dosimetry, worn on the belt. And please mind the warning signs. At frame 107, the third compartment, no visitors are allowed. That's the reactor and engineering areas. The computer cleanroom is locked out, as is the battery compartment, and the captain prefers you enter the torpedo room only with an escort. Other than that, the ship is yours. We hope you enjoy the trip." The young officer withdrew.

"I feel as if I were on a Black Sea cruise," Novskoyy muttered to himself. "Let's see what's in these cubbyholes."

Grachev cradled the handset against his shoulder. The circuit was an internal sub pen communication intercom plugged into a dataport connection umbilical on the ship's flank near one of the steel support saddles of the platform. Once they were outside the egress tunnel at the mouth of the cave, the dataport would be disconnected and the ship would divorce from the platform. Until then they had data, voice, and video to and from the control room of the sub pens.

"*Vepr* is rigged for sea. Ballast tank vents are open, all hatches shut, divorce from external power complete, battery supplying all ship's loads."

The voice in his ear acknowledged, and the connection clicked off. Grachev hung up the handset in the overhead above the commander's console and stood with his hands on the handrails of the periscope well.

The display showed the ship beginning to vanish into the oily blackness of the sub pen water. He watched as the top of the hull slipped under the water. Foam bubbled up in the slip water from the air that remained in their ballast tanks. Then the fin started to go, until only the top half of it was left, and then it too came down to the level of the water. The intercom buzzed. Grachev picked it up.

"All systems nominal," he said. The ship was not flooding, and the tunnel egress could proceed.

The ship continued to sink deeper, until the top of the fin vanished into the water, only a foamy

ring of small waves marking where she'd been. Svyatoslov clicked the display to show the view from
the fin camera, a viewing port designed for maximum operating depth, but usually used only at shallow depths. The tunnel would be illuminated with
floodlights while they exited, so that they could see
their progress.

Grachev waited, hearing the deep bass whirring
of the egress tunnel's platform as it lowered the
ship farther into the two-hundred-meter depth of
the egress tunnel. The ship's hull vanished far beneath the surface of the bay where they had been.
It took some fifteen minutes for the ship to reach
the bottom of the pit. When it did, the deck vibrated just slightly, then was jarred again as the
saddled platform began to carry *Vepr* out the half-
kilometer-long submerged tunnel to the Black Sea.
The velocity out the tunnel was much faster than
the vertical trip, taking no more than ten minutes.
At the end of the platform's track the ship would
come to a halt, which they would know from the
sudden deceleration. While Grachev waited for it,
Svyatoslov ordered the ship's electronic battle suite
started up, then got on the phone to the nuclear
control room aft to tell them to prepare to start
the reactor. The next ten minutes seemed to take
an hour. Grachev checked his watch frequently,
knowing that the battery endurance during an amp-
hour-eating reactor startup would be minimal.

Finally the ship jumped as the saddle platform
stopped.

"Urgent message marked for commanding officer's eyes only in on the cable datalink, sir," Svya-

toslov said, standing aft of the communication panel, to the right of Grachev's commander's console. They were still connected by the datalink to the saddle platform, and from there to the sub pens' communication center.

"I'll get it here," Grachev said, signing into his radio account system. He scanned it, beginning to frown. It was from Kolov, telling him that any direction from the consultant should be regarded as if coming from Kolov himself.

"Trouble, sir?" Svyatoslov asked.

"I think so. Kolov says the consultant has a blank check. We have to follow his orders."

"This guy know anything about submarines?"

Grachev looked up when he heard bootsteps on the ladderway to the control compartment, which emerged on the forward starboard corner.

"Permission to lay to control?" a deep-timbered voice asked. The consultant named Novskoyy.

"Enter control," Grachev said, looking up at Novskoyy.

"Hello, Captain Grachev. Thank you for having me aboard your fine ship," Novskoyy said. To Grachev the speech sounded rehearsed. "It seems shipshape and clean. My compliments."

Grachev was not sure how to proceed. He would be damned if he'd let this civilian think he was in control of the ship, yet any failure of hospitality would not be well received by Kolov or the President.

"Thanks," he said. "My first officer, Captain Second Rank Mykhailo Svyatoslov. You've already met Navigator Tenukha, who will be in the ship-control cubicle when we are ready to make way."

"What is the status of divorcing from the egress platform?"

"We're two minutes from the end of the tunnel. We'll divorce from the dataport, blow variable ballast, then hover while we start the reactor from the battery."

"No," Novskoyy said. "First we use the Shchuka system to see if there is anyone here. We don't want to be followed out."

"If that's the case, the Shchuka system will need to wait while we start the reactor."

"No. It must be listening while we are dead quiet—no reactor power until Shchuka indicates we are alone on the seafloor."

"That puts additional amp-hours on my battery, Mr. Novskoyy. You have any justification for this request?" Grachev made sure his tone was stern, and he labeled Novskoyy's command a "request." To blindly follow this man would lead to trouble. Odd that something about him seemed familiar, and that his English seemed to have shadows of a Moscow accent.

But Novskoyy seemed unsurprised. "To an outside observer, we might be indistinguishable from the egress platform. This could be a mere test of the system. But before you lift off the platform, it is vital that you self-delouse. It is possible a Royal Navy, American, or French unit could be bottomed out and observing the cave mouth. If you are cranking up pumps and blowing down steam headers, you will make noise. A covert shadowing submarine would hear that."

"At ten minutes of Shchuka processing time on the acoustic daylight frequencies, this will cost me thirty minutes," Grachev said, his voice intentionally gravelly. He punched some variable software keys on the display of his central console. "At our battery discharge rate, that will make it impossible to start up the reactor. Any other ideas, Novskoyy?"

The consultant frowned. "Deploy it for five minutes instead of ten. Then jettison it."

Grachev's face grew hot. He wondered if it had turned red. "We have only four Shchuka pods. We cut one loose, we're down to three."

"You will only need three. One here, one at Gibraltar, one in Norfolk Harbor. That leaves you with one in reserve."

So Novskoyy did know the mission. And on the face of it, what he said did make some sense. Yet Grachev perceived that he was in a power struggle for the ship, and damned if he'd let this consultant take the ship from him.

"It's unusual. I'll confer with my fleet commander," Grachev said, standing. "Mr. First, get me Kolov, and patch him through to my stateroom." Grachev stepped past Novskoyy, keeping his face neutral as if the man were not there, and walked down the ladderway to his stateroom.

The stateroom was a combination sea cabin and office, the entrance opening into a conference room, a long oak table going diagonally through the space, ending in a large oak desk. The six chairs around the table were ergonomic and elegant leather Swedish-design swivel chairs. The walls were paneled in walnut, the wood taken from an ancient Ukrainian three-masted schooner's captain's cabin. The forward bulkhead had a curtained opening leading to the stateroom, a simple bed set into the corner with a reading lamp and a computer display able to show the view of any of the ship-wide monitoring cameras and any data the captain would demand on the ship's location or speed, depth, and course. Grachev tapped on the computer display at the small desk, ordering the software to video him into Kolov's office.

Karina put him right through. Kolov smiled warmly.

"Pavel. You should be almost ready to disconnect from the egress tunnel. I'm glad you called. I was having a message sent to you about the consultant."

"That's why I'm calling," Grachev said, frowning. "This civilian Novskoyy is trying to give me rudder orders. He just told me to do a Shchuka system delouse while on the battery when my main priority is getting the reactor started up. By the time I'm done playing with the goddamn Shchuka toy these bastards designed, I'll be cold dead iron on the bottom of the Black Sea, blocking your ten-billion-ruble egress tunnel. Request permission to tell him to fuck himself."

Kolov laughed. "Permission granted, Pavel, except when you're done, you'll have to apologize and do as he says. He's a vendor of intelligence information, not all of it at our disposal."

"How can that be? He's under contract to Dolovietz to provide intelligence. I'll tell him to goddamn well provide it."

"There's a reason we're conducting the operation this way, Pavel. Number one, no one ashore, not even me, is to know what's in Novskoyy's detailed plan. That protects you from our being compromised or penetrated. Up to a certain point, you have to trust Novskoyy. Do as he says. If he imperils ship safety or mission effectiveness, you are the captain. It's your call and your responsibility. But as to the nuts and bolts, if you accommodate Novskoyy without getting killed, that's also your mission. It's not an easy thing, Captain Grachev." Kolov glared at the screen. "If it were we wouldn't need men of your talent to do this."

Grachev sighed to himself. "Very good, sir. Sorry to bother you."

"Good luck, Pavel. Come home safe."

The video winked out, the image of Svyatoslov replacing Kolov, the first officer phoning him from control.

"Sir, the ship is stopped at the departure plane of the egress system."

"I'm on my way."

16

Captain Second Rank Pavel Grachev waited until it was a half hour after sunset on the second day out of port, Monday, July 2, to come up to mast broach depth. As he raised the starboard optronics mast, the ship was crawling at twelve clicks at a keel depth of seventy meters, the deck's angle sloped three degrees up. The optronics mast rose over the top of the fin by some four meters, reaching for the sea above. As the ship penetrated the shallow warm-water layer at sixty-five meters, the mast's infrared, visual light spectrum, and blue laser seekers did a full upper hemispherical search at maximum sensitivity, attempting to help the captain avoid collision.

In a few hours *Vepr* would be so close to the shipping lanes coming out of the Bosporus Strait that an approach to mast broach depth would reveal several dozen surface ships in to the strait from the Mediterranean to the Black Sea, most of it merchant shipping. But tonight there was nothing showing up on the unit, the shipping still far over the horizon.

Satisfied that there were no dangers overhead, Grachev ordered the ship shallow. The upward tilt increased to fifteen degrees. The mast penetrated the sea, the waves rolling toward the view. The low-light enhancer made the surface, flooded with bright moonlight, look as if it were noon. The mast had binocular lenses, allowing Grachev to peer out of it much as out of a conventional periscope. The eyepieces restricted the amount of data displayed to the human observer, but the Second Captain—the shipwide computer control system—had access to all the data available from the surface. If there were an approaching surface ship that the watch officer failed to notice, the Second Captain's annunciator alarms would jar the man's attention.

"Mr. Zakharov, take the scope and patch the satellite UHF video frequencies to the captain's stateroom's video. Lock it out of the crew mess, though."

If Zakharov thought the order odd, he didn't show it.

"Yes, sir. Right away."

"Low power on the horizon, optic module trained to the bow."

"I have the scope, sir."

Grachev glanced at Svyatoslov, motioning toward the stairs down to the first compartment. Svyatoslov blinked, nodding almost imperceptibly, and followed the captain down the steep stairs. The two men said nothing until Grachev's stateroom suite door was shut and bolted.

"Bring it up on BBC," Grachev ordered. The first officer flicked the channel to the news block, ignored SNN, and tuned to BBC One. The scene was Sevastopol, depicting people emerging from the admiralty building, most of them crying or hiding their faces, a few officials dodging the cameras and microphones of the press. It was surreal to see the building he worked in twice a week on an international news program, particularly one with breaking news.

". . . sinking of the Navy of the Ukraine's nuclear submarine *Vepr* in what admiralty officials have admitted to be the worst maritime disaster in modern naval history. Admiral Yuri Kolov, when asked to comment, promised to issue a statement later in the day. We go live now to the press room of the Ukrainian Navy's admiralty . . ."

"We're dead, man," Svyatoslov smirked, shaking his head.

The scene shifted to the press room of the admiralty, the background cream-colored curtains, the emblem of the Navy of the Ukraine behind the podium, the omnipresent shield with the missile and the leaping dolphin, the crossed sabers, and at the podium Yuri Kolov, eyes swollen and bloodshot, his face frozen in a frown.

A knock came at the door while Kolov was fooling with his notes.

Svyatoslov cracked the door open. Al Novskoyy stood outside. "May I come in? I heard the video is on."

Grachev glared at Novskoyy. At the crew briefing, Novskoyy hadn't said a word. It had been left to Grachev what to tell the men, whether to let them in on the "security plan" of sinking the *Vepr* decoy. Grachev had made the decision that the crew should know as little as possible. Not that they were incapable of handling the information, but it would lower their performance. In the end, Grachev had frowned sternly at the men, told them that their sortie was an emergency, and that their orders would be coming in later, when they were in position.

"When will we know what this mission is all about?" Grachev asked.

"I am authorized to give you navigation waypoints once we transit Gibraltar and enter the Atlantic," Novskoyy said, propping one boot on the bulkhead. "Even then, they will be an indirect way to reach our operational area. Believe me, Captain Grachev, I am maintaining your philosophy—the more you know, the more you worry. When the time comes, I will tell all. Until then, enjoy the trip."

Grachev grimaced, annoyed that he didn't know his own mission, but able to keep his peace. His eyes returned to the screen as Kolov opened his mouth.

"This afternoon," Kolov's gravelly voice said, so low Svyatoslov had to crank the volume, "the Navy of the Ukraine's front-line submarine *Vepr* went down in the deep water of the Black Sea. Shortly before she passed through her crush depth, the hull ejected what we call a 'black box buoy,' which contained a data log of her last hour submerged. The buoy was recovered this evening and replayed aboard the salvage ship *Tucha*. The buoy's transcript has not been fully analyzed, but in the few hours we have had it available to us, we have made the preliminary determination—"

"Come on, Uncle Yuri, get to the point," Svyatoslov muttered.

"Shut up," Grachev said, annoyed.

"—ship suffered a brittle fracture of the monel seawater piping going to the ship's port condenser. This pipe is subject to full sea pressure and is sixty centimeters in diameter, so flooding through this piping would be catastrophic even if not stopped within seconds. The ship normally has a hull closure valve able to isolate the piping system from sea pressure and stop the flooding. We believe the valve shut and stopped the flooding but then drifted back open. The flooding had shorted out the control circuits to the hydraulic systems that operated the hull closure valves, allowing the hull valve to reopen and restart the flooding, and also caused the stern of the vessel to be heavy, angling the ship upward. The condenser seawater piping rupture, the massive flooding, and the shorting of several major electrical systems resulted in the loss of the nuclear reactor, and with it, all propulsion capabilities. At a time when the ship was extremely heavy aft, with no power, and with the flooding restarting, the crew activated explosive charges in the ballast tanks, which we call the emergency deballasting system. The purpose of this system was to—"

"God, even describing our premature deaths, Uncle Yuri is boring."

"Knock it off, Mr. First. This is serious."

"—as much weight as possible, allowing the submarine to ascend to the surface in spite of the increased weight of the water in the fourth compartment. We believe there was a third failure in this accident, after the pipe shear and the closure valve coming back open. The deballasting charges in the aft ballast tanks, instead of detonating and generating high-pressure gas forcing out ballast water in the tanks to lighten the ship, caused a structural failure in the metal of the hull of the ballast tank itself. The explosive charge's gas generation went to waste as the gas leaked out the ruptured ballast tank. The *Vepr,* now heavy aft with continued flooding, lost her forward momentum and began traveling backward toward her maximum operating depth. We believe that she was traveling at a speed of approximately sixty clicks as she penetrated the plane of her crush depth. The fourth compartment, the turbine room, was already equalized to sea pressure from the flood, but the third, second, and first compartments imploded catastrophically from the pressure. The hull of the *Vepr* hit the rocky bottom and broke apart."

Kolov's voice croaked at the last word. He struggled visibly for control, wiping his eyes. Finally he looked up from his statement.

"I am sorry, ladies and gentlemen. The crew of the *Vepr* were all friends of mine, old comrades, handpicked and trained over decades. I will continue with the statement."

"Please," Svyatoslov said. Grachev just glared at him. Novskoyy's face was blank.

"The Severodvinsk class of attack submarine, the modified flight, is designed with a detachable control compartment which may function as an escape pod. The fourth and final failure of the ship came at this point as the explosive bolts of the sail blew off over the control compartment, as they were supposed to. The structural connections all properly disengaged or blew off as required. However, one set of cable connectors did not sever on the escape signal but remained connected. The twelve three-centimeter-wide cables were enough to keep the control compartment from separating from the main hull in time, and the ending of the data log is marked by the impiosion of the control compartment."

Kolov sniffed. The press room was dead silent except for the clicking of digital still cameras.

"We have a disk of the final moments of the submarine's loss, which was recorded into the black box buoy. I requested that this record be sealed in consideration of the families. I was met by a representative of the *Vepr*'s next of kin, the commanding officer's wife, Martinique Grachev, who requested the control compartment recording be played so that the families might know the whole truth, however unpleasant, and the request was specific that it be played for the members of the press. I have the permission of President Dolovietz to show this disk. Members of the press corps, please forgive me if I step out of the room while it is played. I have seen it once. Once is enough."

Kolov stepped away from the platform, and Karina, dressed in a long black dress, her flashy makeup gone, her eyes puffy and pink, her face swollen, took Kolov's place and activated the controls to the flat-screen video display.

"This should be interesting," Svyatoslov said, his voice acid. "Hard to see how this will be faked.

Martinique and Irina will know. There's no way actors will be able to carry the day with our wives. Or with our families, or even with our friends."

"No?" Novskoyy asked. "You remember the Severodvinsk training simulator back in April? When the battlestations crew was asked to fight a simulated flooding of the control compartment? We taped it."

Grachev was turning to stare at Novskoyy when he saw himself and Svyatoslov in the control compartment mockup last April, struggling desperately to fight the flooding, their grins of exasperation— some of the drill actually making them laugh at the absurdity of trying to survive—looking like desperate grimaces on screen, the disk taken out of context, changing the picture from what it was, a lighthearted drill in a "Disney World" simulator machine where the crews all failed to beat the flooding computer but at least improved their ability to think in a half-flooded compartment, to what it appeared to be, twelve men in the final moments of struggling for their lives.

They watched the video until a wall of water washed across the lens, knocking the view half sideways, and all that could be heard was muffled screams. Most disturbing was the scream in his own voice, shouting "Oh, God!" And in the stateroom, the color came to his face. The voice was truly his, but the words had been taken from an evening of passion he'd had with his wife, the night that his house had been bugged by the da Vinci consultants. They'd obviously lied to Kolov when they'd said they hadn't listened other than to see if he had discussed the sub's mission. The other screams were taken the same way. Svyatoslov's dying words seemed to be "Goddamn *Vepr*," which had actually probably been said to his own wife in frustration with the ship.

There was a final rushing noise of water and the disk went to static.

"Turn it off," Grachev ordered. He could stand no more.

The video scene winked out. Grachev reached for the intercom phone. "Deck Officer, depart mast broach depth for one hundred meters, forty clicks, advise of shipping at the channel approach." He waited for Zakharov's acknowledgment, then put the phone down, blinking hard, his eyes scratchy.

"You were correct not to share this with the crew," Novskoyy said, his own eyes haunted as he stood. "Excuse me, Captain." He shut the door behind himself.

Grachev looked at Svyatoslov. "You okay, Mykhailo?"

"I don't think so, Captain." He sniffed, staring at the deck. "Why would Kolov do this? What could be so goddamn important that they want to torture our families like this? And us?"

"I don't know, Mykhailo, I don't know. I'm not sure I want to know. It could only get worse. Go on, Mr. First. Take a shower. A long, hot hotel shower. Then get to control. We've got about five hundred surface ships to avoid hitting on the way out of the strait. We've got to have our war faces on for the men. We owe them that."

Mykhailo Svyatoslov, deflated, seeming half his

normal size, nodded silently and shuffled out of the room. Grachev glanced at the dark video display, remembering. He sat at his desk and began dictating to his handheld computer, starting a letter to Martinique. Before they got to their operation area, he would upload it to the black box buoy, so that she would know what had happened, and more importantly, how he felt about her, in case life were to imitate art.

Ten o'clock Eastern European time was three in the afternoon in Alexandria, Virginia, where Admiral Michael Pacino sat on the front three inches of the leather couch facing the display screen, where the control-room video of the Ukrainian submarine *Vepr* had just played.

"Mute the sound, Paully," Pacino said to Paul White, sitting on the chair beside the couch.

"I can barely believe it," White said. "An escape pod control room, shipwide computer control, constantly monitoring video systems, and they still sink and die from a pipe rupture."

"The greatest design in the world goes nowhere without even greater maintenance," Pacino said absently. "They didn't die from a pipe rupture, or from the deballast system problem, or from the cable connectors not disconnecting. They died from bad maintenance. Any one or even two failures at the same time, and *Vepr* would have sailed on."

White was silent for a moment, watching the families mourning the crew of the ill-fated submarine. "Any chance this isn't real? A cover-up for *Vepr* so that she can sneak into the Atlantic?"

"Hard to imagine why they'd do that, Paully," Pacino pronounced. "It looked pretty real to me."

"A little too convincing."

"Come on, Paully. If you want, ask Number Four at NSA to analyze the video. Look for a chart with the wrong ocean, chronometer with the wrong time—or a watch that isn't synchronized with the bulkhead clock, or discontinuities with the soundtrack. If the Ukrainians altered the video, they must have left fingerprints."

"I'll get on it, sir."

"Meanwhile, I don't think we need to trouble the *Piranha* anymore. You can tell Bruce Phillips to bring her home."

White nodded and left. The last remaining Seawolf-class submarine, *Piranha,* had been lurking in the Atlantic west of Gibraltar waiting for the *Vepr* to outchop the Mediterranean, on her way to join up with the Black Sea Fleet in the Atlantic, but Bruce Phillips' *Piranha* had been on station for months, her crew were exhausted, the boat was overdue for a dry-dock overhaul, and keeping her on patrol no longer seemed to make sense.

BOOK IV

Stand-down

17

Martinique,

It is our twenty-second full day at sea, and I feel so distant from you. You and our son, Pavel. I miss you and everything about you. The way you look at me, the curl of your hair, the color of your eyes when you look at little Pavelyvich, the shape of your breasts as you lean over the sink to wash your hair. I miss the sounds of you sleeping, the warmth of your body on the bed next to me. I miss your voice, your laughter, and the love you give me.

Perhaps most of all I miss your mind, darling, the way you see things I don't and cut straight through to any issue. I wish you could be here with me, I'd love to know your impression of our rider, Consultant Novskoyy.

Since we set sail, Novskoyy has been my shadow, except for the briefing I gave the crew. The one time I needed him, there in front of the men demanding to know why they'd been kidnapped in the middle of the night, he was not there. And although I resented him at first, I find now a certain familiarity about him. He is a Muscovite White Russian, his accent thick to my ears. Tall, craggy, older, late fifties or early sixties, with a deep voice and a quick manner. Toward people he has a commanding atti-

tude—not quite superior, just as if when he issues commands, it never would cross his mind that anyone would disagree with them. And he is as technically expert as I or even Mykhailo, although there were details about the ship—the active quieting system for one—that he knew nothing of, but caught up on quickly. Almost as if he were the ship's original designer, coming back for a cruise after many of the new systems were added on. Yet he does not carry himself as an engineer or a scientist, but as a military man. I have asked him if he is ex-navy, but he never answers or even seems to hear the question. He insists upon remaining a mystery.

And yet he spends most of his time with me and Mykhailo, as if we were birds of a feather. It is all I can do to break away from him long enough to write you these words. Since he first stepped aboard, he has mellowed toward us, or perhaps we have become more understanding of him. Either way, we get along, play chess, discuss the submarine and her capabilities, lean over the Second Captain navigation display plot and look at our past course. Novskoyy—Al, as he prefers to be called—will not divulge our orders, or even navigation waypoints beyond the next one. We approach chart coordinate M, and Novskoyy hands me a slip of paper with the latitude and longitude of the next waypoint, coordinate N, and the speed of advance he wants to make good. He insists that the navigation chart be displayed only to the three of us, that none of the officers know. So far I have obliged him.

I do not know how much of this record will be censored, how much will make its way to you. If all goes well, this file will be deleted, never to be read by anyone. But if the censors pass this, and if you find a map file that shows where these strange-sounding places are, I will tell you that the course Novskoyy has laid in has taken us northward to the coastline of Labrador, Canada, and then down just deeper than the North American continental shelf past Nova Scotia, past the coastlines of the American states of Maine and Massachusetts, along New York's Long Island, bisecting the shipping lanes to New York, and southward past the New Jersey shore, and the Delaware-Maryland-Virginia peninsula to the entrance to the great bay, the Chesapeake. The entrance to the Chesapeake is called Hampton Roads, and the city to the south of the opening is called Virginia Beach, which changes to the city of Norfolk just inside the bay. You have heard me mention Norfolk before, my love, as the home of the world's most powerful navy. And even though the Americans lost over half of their battle fleets in the war of the East China Sea and the Japanese blockade, what remains is frightening in the number and in the individual capability of each ship.

Last night, Sunday, Novskoyy ordered me to enter the Hampton Roads traffic separation scheme, which was to the west by some 150 kilometers. I do not know if you realize how significant that is. First, he has ordered me to penetrate the sovereign waters of another country, inside their twelve-nautical-mile limit. Second, the entrance to Hampton Roads is overrun with shipping traffic. Worse, if possible, than Gibraltar. Perhaps that was his intention, to have the closely spaced ships—like trucks on a high-

*way—mask our acoustic signature. Although with
the Second Captain engaged in active quieting mode,
for every pure tone we put into the sea from rotating
machinery, the ship's hull hydrophones put out an
identical tone exactly phase-shifted by one-half
wavelength, which cancels out the noise completely.*
Vepr *would be quieter than a hole in the ocean if
not for the flow noise around the skin of the ship—
minimized by going slow—and transient noises, like
dropping a pan on the floor of the galley, which are
minimized by crew discipline, since whoever makes
a noise detected by the Second Captain scrubs the
bathrooms that day. It seems to work. But my mind
is wandering. Entering Norfolk Harbor, with a water
depth of scarcely fifteen meters, is a dangerous
thing, amounting to breaking and entering a house.
If the Americans, with all their naval might, with
their antisubmarine systems, detect us, they will be
entirely justified in shooting us with intent to kill.
Just another reason to write you this letter. Never
before have I put this ship in such a magnitude of
danger.*

*Our three-dimensional high-frequency secure
littoral bottom-sounding sonar mapped out the
bottom contours of the approach to the Chesapeake Bay Bridge-Tunnel, where water depth is barely
enough to keep the top of the fin submerged. There
on the partly sandy, partly rocky bay floor I bottomed the submarine, using the thrusters for maneuvering, and using the seawater cooling water suction
valves mounted on the top of the hull to avoid fouling the seawater systems with sediment. I shut down
the propulsion turbines, further quieting the ship,*

and then the port electrical turbine and rigged the ship for hostile sea quieting. The vessel is a ghost ship now, bottomed out not far from the Bay Bridge-Tunnel, the Antay sensor periscope raised beside several abandoned wood pilings. No one would suspect a hostile submarine to be hiding here, but if they came looking for it and found us, it would be over.

God knows—or I should say only Novskoyy knows—what we are doing here. Every few minutes I feel a need to peer out the Antay sensor and make sure no one has discovered us. The sensor view is constantly playing on my stateroom video displays. The reality is that if we are caught, there will be no way to escape stealthily or quickly. I am hoping that soon, perhaps by sunrise this morning, Monday the 23rd, Novskoyy will tell me what my ship is doing here.

I am anxious to do whatever it is I am supposed to do and get out of here, whether it is spying, taking soil samples, or perhaps even letting Novskoyy out the forward airlock so he can go on some odd mission of sabotage. Until then, all I can do is wait, and by writing you, have you waiting here next to me.

I send good thoughts to you and to young Pavely-vich. Give him a kiss for me, and tell him his daddy loves him.

And I love you, dearest Martinique. Please, never forget me, never forget us.
Pavel

Michael Pacino threw his arm across the bed, feeling the warmth of Colleen's body on the deep mattress in the darkness well before dawn. He pulled her closer, feeling her against his chest. He found her mouth and kissed her, his mouth reaching past her teeth, and finding her tongue, her tongue rough, rougher than before, and there was hair on her lip, and he opened an eye and stared into the smiling face of his black lab, Jackson.

"Bleah!" he spat, sitting up in the king-size bed in the top loft of the Annapolis timber-frame house overlooking the water of the Severn River and the breathtaking view of the Naval Academy. The property, surrounded by water on three sides, was accordingly nicknamed Pacino Peninsula by the Pentagon admirals and generals who gathered here every second weekend for keggers and football parties and barbecues. He looked over at the bed, realizing that only he and Jackson were there, then remembered with disappointment that Colleen was gone, in D.C. to testify before the Armed Services Committee about the Cyclops battlecontrol system. He yawned and looked at the clock, the digits reading 3:15, a few minutes before the alarm he had set. He stood as Jackson jumped off the bed and wagged his tail, ready to go on their usual six-mile jog through Annapolis and the grounds of the Academy.

"Not today, buddy," Pacino said. "You're staying with Lucille. I'm gone for a week." He rubbed the dog's head. "Yes, Daddy's going to sea for a week."

He took a shower, donned his tropical white uniform, and grabbed his bag and his briefcase. His driver, Marla, drank coffee in the kitchen with a bleary-eyed Lucille, the young housekeeper hired by Colleen. He greeted them both, grabbed his coffee, and walked with Marla to the Lincoln truck. Security prevented him from using one of the new drive-by-wire software-controlled limousines, so Marla drove the updated shiny black utility vehicle, with bumper flags flying four gold stars in a blue field, the new emblem of the Department of the Navy on the doors. He stared at it for a moment, thinking it seemed like just yesterday his doors had read "Unified Submarine Command." He shrugged at the absurd speed of the passage of time and ducked into the truck.

Once they had pulled onto Route 50, cruising toward the Beltway at a leisurely 140 mph, he clicked on his WritePad computer. The print was blurry, and he pulled out half-frame reading glasses from his briefcase to scan through his messages. A video e-mail from Colleen taken from her hotel room came on. His pretty wife was dark Irish, a female version of her father, Fleet Admiral Dick O'Shaughnessy. She smiled at him from the suite, saying she wished she'd stayed at the Annapolis house and commuted in, but her staff was holed up in the Watergate, working late into the night during the testimony. There was no hope of an early wrap, she said, but she was hoping to join him in the Caribbean if the schedule held. In the meantime, she cautioned, he was to keep away from the hostesses. A kiss blown to the camera, and her image winked out.

The rest of the e-mails were not as light. Pacino clicked into the security-clearance module of the computer where several Release Twelve messages awaited him. One intelligence briefing highlighted the ominous developments in Sevastopol. During the night two more destroyers of the Ukraine's Black Sea Fleet had started their engines. The two that had warmed up their engine rooms two days before looked ready to put to sea. Apparently the mourning over the loss of the Ukrainian submarine had not canceled the plans of the fleet.

The day and night before, the aircraft carrier *Admiral Kuznetsov* had been surrounded by ten cranes lifting dozens of pallets of supplies onto the deck high above the pier. The satellite photographs were chilling. The supplies weren't just parts for the ship or the aircraft. Most of them were food. *Admiral Kuznetsov* wasn't just upgrading her readiness, she was getting ready to go to sea in the immediate future. The infrared scans were alert for her nuclear reactor to be started up within hours.

Naval Intelligence was also keeping a close eye on the submarines at the piers, but there seemed to be little activity. Probably the entire flotilla was grounded for a maintenance review, Pacino figured, which would mean the surface force would be unguarded when it sailed to the South Atlantic. He made a mental note to himself to see if NSA could confirm any communications coming out of the Ukraine about a submarine maintenance standdown.

But other than the quiet of the sub force, it was obvious that the Black Sea Fleet would be at sea by next week on a combat mission.

Pacino took off the glasses, staring at the darkness of Washington, nearing the southern curve of the Beltway before it crossed the Potomac. This was it, he thought. He had wondered if his tenure as Chief of Naval Operations would span a world crisis. It made him wonder—was that what he wanted? A war? Or would he rather retire in peace during a dead watch? But was that really for him—a four-year stint as the commanding admiral of the Navy, spent pushing paper, fighting only peacetime political skirmishes with the politicians and the other services? Or would he command a service at war, as his predecessors had? Was it now his turn? And again, was that what he wanted? He was nearing 50. In a half century of walking the earth, would this be his destiny, to fight and kill his fellow man? Why now, now that he was in command, the ultimate command for a naval officer, was he having doubts?

Despite the chilling nature of the messages, it was hard for Pacino to imagine that the Ukrainians were the enemy. There was an innocence to them. They had none of the menace of the Soviets, who had ruled half the globe when Pacino had been the executive officer of the *Cheyenne*. They had none of the anger of the United Islamic Front of God, the determination to exterminate the infidels of the other half of the world. They didn't even have the eye of the tiger that the Red Chinese had had when they crossed the line to push the White Chinese into the East China Sea, firebombing 35 cities to ashes and hitting the border with dozens of infantry and mechanized divisions. These people were just the Ukrainians, inheritors of a massive war fleet with no mission, their recently elected young president having made the mistake of putting the fleet up for rent, willing to allow them to perform a mercenary mission for the highest bidder, willing to let his constituents' sons and daughters fight a combat mission for the purpose of invoicing a foreign nation in U.S. dollars. The world was making less sense, Pacino thought. And if this were to be the enemy, a rent-a-fleet, that Pacino had spent his life training to fight, then there was absurdity in the script. Could he get himself and his forces whipped into a frenzy to fight the military equivalent of a paid-by-the-hour security guard? He sighed, turning off the computer.

There was still something eerie and chilling in the atmosphere today, he thought. He could feel none of the excitement and anticipation he had expected at the prospect of taking his senior officers on a cruise to the Caribbean for a week on a luxury liner. There was a restlessness inside him, a disquiet. There was something deeply wrong. Something was coming, and coming soon. Coming for him. He could not put his finger on it, and somehow he doubted it had anything to do with the Ukraine or the feuding states of Argentina and Uruguay. This was something else. For a moment he was glad that Colleen had not come with him.

He was startled by the last thought. This was insane, he thought. He simply had to relax. This matter of thinking there was some dark force out there, some lurking evil, was an unhealthy sign. His Navy and his career had never been better. The only threat on the world scene was a mercenary fleet, which could be defeated by a single U.S. submarine, as Kelly McKee had demonstrated. If Pacino were honest with himself, this was turning into the best time in his life. A half century of struggle and bitterness, and finally his life was rewarding. And he had spent so much time in the wars of his life that when blessed peace came, he couldn't recognize it. There was no danger, no evil out there waiting for him, he told himself. He was simply experiencing the post-combat jitters of a radar operator looking at a blank screen, the absence of a threat seemingly ominous after fighting so many of them.

There was no threat, he told himself again. There was nothing to be worried about. He looked out the window as the sun climbed over the horizon. The staff truck had reached the gate to Norfolk Naval Base, where an honor guard stood at attention on either side of the road. The base commander was obviously aware of the arrival of the Chief of Naval Operations. The truck arrived at the pier, the door opening. The pier was almost deserted. Pacino's arrival was timed to put him onboard the cruise ship long before the senior officers arrived so that he could greet them as the host of this week's stand-down.

The next hour was spent shaking hands, clapping shoulders, and schmoozing with the officers of the naval security task force that would escort out the *Princess Dragon*. Once on the ship, he took a few minutes in his stateroom suite, which was huge even by luxury liner standards. He unpacked and met his aide, fighter pilot Lieutenant Commander

Eve Cavalla, and walked down five decks to the
wide receiving lobby where the companionway extended to the pier. Eve had arranged a cocktail
party here to greet the arriving senior officers. For
the moment there was nothing to do but wait for
his men to arrive.

Pacino drank a cup of coffee with Eve Cavalla,
watching as Admiral Bruce Phillips made his entrance down on the pier. Marching with him was a
phalanx of submarine officers clad in formal service
dress whites, with high collars, gold buttons, and
full medals. Pacino tried not to laugh at his stunt.
This was practically a vacation trip, and Phillips
was marching in like the brigade commander at the
Academy, missing only his ceremonial sword—but
wait, Pacino thought, looking closer, realizing that
Phillips and his honor guard *did* have their swords,
marching with them drawn at their shoulders. He
shook his head, watching as Phillips did a column
right and marched in front of his platoon up the
gangway to the top, executed a left face, rendered
a sword salute to the American flag aft, then did a
right face back to Pacino and gave him a sword
salute, Phillips' eyes squinting in a war face. Pacino
saluted back.

"Permission to come aboard, *sir,*" Phillips
barked.

"Granted, Admiral," Pacino replied, amused. It
took a few minutes for Phillips and his men in
"choker" whites, to get aboard with all the sword
salutes, but eventually they had sheathed the weapons and were knocking back drinks at the bar with

the Hawaiian-shirted pilots and the black-shoe officers of the surface fleet.

Kelly McKee walked slowly down the fishing bridge, the wind blowing the hair off his face. His cheekbones burned in the harsh July sunlight and the force of the wind and salt spray. The fishing pier extended toward the harbor, perpendicular to the Chesapeake Bay Bridge-Tunnel near the first tunnel that dived beneath Thimble Shoals Channel, the seaway leading from the piers of Norfolk Naval Station and the Norfolk International Terminal to the unrestricted waters of the Atlantic Ocean. The channel was a ruler-straight line with lit buoys on either side, resembling a runway when viewed at night from the bridge of a nuclear submarine.

He hadn't expected to come here. He didn't know why he had come. For the last month— could it really be that long since Diana died?—he had been wandering inside the house, missing her, waiting for the front door to open, for Diana to come bouncing back in. He stared at her pictures. He opened dusty forgotten photo albums and sat in the easy chair, remembering. He played the old disks of their honeymoon. He would put his face in her pillow and smell her. Over the course of the month, her scent had worn off the house, leaving nothingness. All he could do was spray her perfume into the air, but eventually that ran out.

He visited the gravesite. She had wanted to be buried at a cemetery near the church where they'd been married, and for the last month he had witnessed the grave change. At first, it was a hump of earth covered with artificial turf under a tent. A few days later, the tent was gone and the soil had been compacted flat, the turf mat disappearing. A few days later, fresh sod was placed on the top of the raw earth, the sod's seams naked. Weeks later, he could barely tell that the grass had been new sod, the seams having vanished. Every visit he brought roses, her favorite. And when he would bend down to lay the roses at the head of the grave, he remembered the first time he'd brought her the flowers. And the last. And every time in between.

He had ordered the granite headstone the week after she died. It had been promised for the one-year anniversary of her death, at least until he had visited the stone mason and doubled the price. It would be here inside another month, or so they'd promised.

When he wasn't wandering the house seeking a talisman of Diana or at her grave, he would scan the channels of the television, going through all two thousand of them silently, the unit muted, the house silent. He barely ate. Going to the grocery store was an exercise in buying the things Diana had liked.

There were visitors at first. His father-in-law, George Marchese, had come in his Lexus, wearing a suit costing three months of McKee's salary. He clapped McKee on the shoulder, told him that he had set up Diana's trust fund for McKee, then sat with him looking at photo albums. On a later visit, they'd visited the grave together. There were few words, and McKee knew Marchese was uncomfortable. There was no third visit.

His friends from the old days, Academy class-mates, stopped by. It was as if they were visiting him in prison, sitting on the other side of a glass barrier. His friends from the boat came over, Karen Petri first, then the engineer, navigator, artificial intelligence officer, weapons officer, main propulsion assistant, radiation controls officer. It was so odd that these men still seemed so associated with their functions, just as Karen was his executive officer first, his friend second. Their visits were strained. Last week the phone rang, a voice saying simply, "green alert." It was the sensor officer, giving him the traditional signal that they would arrive at a moment's notice to drink his beer and empty his refrigerator. Except that they didn't rely on his beer stock, they brought three cases of their own, and hamburger meat and buns and charcoal, and within a few minutes there was a party roaring through his house, his officers' wives and girlfriends spending more time talking to him than the men did, the girls offering condolences, asking him what his plans were. And they seemed to share his silence when he said there were no plans. One of them asked if he was going to return to the ship. He said he'd left the Navy a month ago.

Bruce Phillips came very week. Every week he brought a bottle of Jack Daniel's. Every week they sat on the deck drinking, not saying much. Bruce reminded him that the captain's slot on the *Devilfish* was reserved for him, but McKee just looked down, silent.

The night before, a knock had come at the door as the sun was going down. He answered, wearing

jeans and a golf shirt, catching a glimpse of himself
in Diana's hallway mirror. His face looked even
thinner than it had when he returned from the
South Atlantic. His hair had grown out, now covering his ears, his bangs hanging into his eyes. At
first his beard had grown, but it itched and reminded him of wearing a beard at sea, and he had
shaved ever since. When he opened the door,
Karen Petri was there, her brown eyes looking at
him in liquid sympathy. She was holding a bottle
of merlot. She said little, just pouring for the two
of them. At one point she told him the captain's
billet was still open for him. As with Phillips, he'd
remained silent, shaking his head.

When the wine was gone, McKee was nodding
in exhaustion. Petri walked him to his bedroom.
She stood him by the bed and pulled his clothes
off, stripping him completely naked. She put him
into the bed and sat on the bedcovers, looking
deeply into his eyes, her hand stroking his face. He
barely noticed; the wine had made him drowsy.

"Shut your eyes, Kelly," she'd whispered. He
had felt her kiss on his forehead, and then the light
clicked off and she was gone.

The sun came up in the morning, his signal to
rise whether he was tired or not, hungover or not.
He had taken to jogging to the beach and back,
the pain of the exercise a release from the pain of
missing Diana. After a shower he sat in front of
the television widescreen and drank coffee, clicking
through the channels, until by some miracle he
found himself looking at the image of the *Devilfish*.
He stared at it, then at Karen Petri, resplendent in

her starched service dress khakis, being interviewed by a reporter. He turned up the sound, but by then the picture had shifted to a helicopter view of the ships of Norfolk Naval Base.

"—a flotilla of surface vessels tasked with guarding the cruise ship *Princess Dragon* as the entire upper echelon of the Navy goes to sea this afternoon for a week of what Admiral Michael Pacino calls 'stand-down.' "

The story went on to describe the coming voyage. McKee tried to forget about it, and was barely conscious of starting the car and driving to the Bay Bridge-Tunnel, then pulling off to the fishing pier on the inland side. Around his neck were the binoculars his wardroom had given him as a present for his thirty-eighth birthday. He stood there leaning against the stainless-steel handrails, staring inland, looking for the hulls of ships approaching from over the horizon.

18

Above on the surface, the waters of the Chesapeake Bay were glassy smooth, the sun high in the sky on the late morning of July 23. Captain Second Rank Pavel Grachev pressed his face to the number one periscope, using the optical unit instead of the Antay sensor, wanting to see the actual surface above. The bay was quiet, with nothing visible on the water's surface save a floating barge in the distance. Its crane was doing construction on a row of concrete piles for the replacement lanes of the new bridge. The workers were concentrating on their craft, and no one noticed the pole sticking out of the water three kilometers east.

"Captain?" a voice in his ear asked. It was Zakharov, the deck officer.

"Yes," he answered, not taking his eyes off the periscope lens.

"The first officer sends his respects and requests your presence in your stateroom suite for an early lunch with him and Mr. Novskoyy, sir."

"Very good. Take the scope, low power, on the horizon, two two zero degrees true."

"I have the scope, sir."

Grachev wiped the sweat from his eye sockets and walked as quietly as he could down the steep ladder to the first compartment, emerging into the centerline passageway of the lower level. The smells of lunch being cooked made him suddenly hungry, even at this early hour. He had changed the ship's chronometer to accord with local time when they'd penetrated the traffic-separation scheme of Hampton Roads so that they would instinctively know when the surface was in bright daylight and when it was dark. The change from Eastern European time was a seven-hour difference, and he had felt jet-lagged for two days. When he opened the door to his stateroom suite, the smell of the stew became stronger. Novskoyy and Svyatoslov looked up at him as he shut the door behind himself.

He took his seat at the head of the table and filled his bowl with the rabbit stew with its thick gravy. Svyatoslov passed him a basket with heavy biscuits, then a plate of butter. He spread his linen napkin over his lap and buttered a biscuit, taking his first bite of the stew. It was excellent, hot and spicy the way Martinique made it. The taste made him miss her.

"Anything new topside?" Svyatoslov asked between bites.

"Nothing. It's a nice sunny summer day. We should be fishing."

"This would taste good on a picnic table, eh, Captain?"

Novskoyy pushed his bowl away and wiped his mouth, saying nothing. When Grachev and Svyatoslov had finished, Grachev buzzed the steward, the dishes were swept away, and he poured from a carafe of coffee that the cook had made especially for him.

"It is time I told you about the mission," Novskoyy said.

Grachev put his cup down and glanced at Svyatoslov. "Then I suppose it is time we heard."

"It is not a pleasant situation. This afternoon the American Navy of Norfolk will put several ships to sea. It will be a small task force. The order of battle consists of two destroyers, the *Tom Clancy* and the *Christie Whitman*. Following them will be an Aegis II–class cruiser, the *Admiral Hyman Rickover*. There will be a submarine screening the task force, the USS *Devilfish,* an SSNX-class nuclear fast-attack sub with acoustic daylight imaging capability. And then, finally, the cruise ship *Princess Dragon*. The warships will be escorting out and providing security for the cruise ship, because it is going to sea with an unusual cargo—the entire contingent of ranking admirals and senior line officers of the U.S. Navy. They are sailing to the Caribbean for a week. The purpose of their trip is a retreat, a 'stand-down' as they are calling it, for the senior officers to put their heads together about the future of their navy."

Grachev stared into Novskoyy's eyes. "And that is important because . . ." His voice trailed off, an attempt to prompt the consultant.

"*Vepr* will torpedo the submarine and deploy two Barrakuda mobile mines against each of the surface warships, then four Barrakuda mines against the cruise ship."

Grachev calmly took a sip of coffee while staring

over the rim at Novskoyy. "Let me get this straight. You want us to ambush not only warships, but an unprotected civilian cruise ship, which according to you is full of naval officers from the senior ranks of the American Navy."

"The Americans plan to attack the fleet sailing to Argentina. We are launching a preemptive strike." Novskoyy held up a disk. "Your Admiral sent a disk. Maybe you will find it worth watching." He laid it on the table and abruptly walked out.

Grachev looked at Svyataslov. "What the hell. Let's check it out."

Grachev brought up the video unit and plugged in the disk. It showed Kolov's office, the admiral appearing exactly as he had just before Grachev left him at the admiralty building.

"Pavel. I'm sorry I can't talk to you live, but transmitting from where you are now would not be advisable. I gave Novskoyy this disk in case you decided the mission smelled fishy. I told him that you almost certainly would. My submarine commanders are men, not monsters. They, particularly you, Pavel, would not take kindly to instructions to commit war crimes such as sinking hospital ships or unarmed cruise ships, especially if those orders came from outside the normal chain of command. So here I am, trying to tell you your orders. All I can do is explain your mission, Pavel. I can't carry it out for you.

"As you know, President Dolovietz has hired some of the most brilliant consultants in Europe, or the world for that matter, in da Vinci consulting. Among their talents is the ability to intercept communications. E-mails. Video uplinks. Phone calls. You saw what they did to your house. Well, they did not confine their work to monitoring Ukrainian security. They have spent considerable resources attempting on behalf of the Ukraine to eavesdrop on the U.S. military and the U.S. government, on communications concerning Ukrainian security.

"You might as well know what they found out. In a moment I will roll the tape that da Vinci intercepted. It is a bit too detailed to be a forgery. Watch these excerpts and I will continue my address to you at the end."

The disk image changed. The hull of the American SSNX submarine *Devilfish* appeared in the background. A dark-haired woman in a khaki uniform walked across the gangway. The view shifted to the inside, where the dark-haired woman, obviously the captain of the submarine, spoke to the men in the control room. Subtitles appeared at the bottom of the screen to translate her words. A chronometer rolling with the date and time showed that the video had been taken six weeks before. The scene shifted, the camera view, from the fin of the sub, depicting a helicopter. A dark-haired man was lowered to the hull and pulled inside. The video clip then rushed from scene to scene—the tactical brief with the officers, the run southward to intercept the mock Ukrainian surface fleet, the rendezvous with the fleet and the submarine captain's attack, the appearance of the mock Severodvinsk submarine and its sinking, and the outrunning of the Severodvinsk's torpedo. The clip ended after the final scene of the video conference between the sub captain and his commanding admirals.

Grachev and Svyatoslov exchanged looks. The first officer's face had turned white. Kolov's face came back on the display.

"Pavel, I'm back. As you can see, the Americans have plans for the battle fleet headed to the South Atlantic as well as the Severodvinsk escort submarine, which would have been you.

"Your mission today is to sink the cruise ship carrying the brains of the U.S. Navy so that they can't plan an attack on our fleet, and then to withdraw farther into the Atlantic and sink anyone who comes looking for you, until it is safe to come back home, all to safeguard the fleet operation in the South Atlantic. It is certainly not palatable to contemplate sinking an unarmed cruise ship. I too would have my doubts. But know this—these are the men who would kill Ukrainians, by the tens of thousands, without a blink. What did the American sub commander say—'These orders come to me from the President of the United States?' Something about how he swore an oath of obedience. Well, Pavel, so did you. And so did I. I urge you to follow your orders, Pavel."

"And now comes the hardest part of this little speech, Pavel. It is this. If you decide not to follow these orders, you won't be returning from this mission. You are already dead, so the sinking of the submarine *Vepr* will not be newsworthy. I have something to show you."

Kolov held up his handheld computer, the video zooming in to see the image, an Internet newsfile,

dated August 1, 2018—a week and a half in the
future. The headline was VEPR CREW RESCUED,
under it a subtitle reading, "Unidentified crewmembers picked up by tramp steamer, treated in a
hospital in Greece, sub commander awakens from
coma and tells tale."

"This is how we planned to bring you back to
the Ukraine, to avoid giving your families heart
attacks when you walk into your houses. You got
out of the control compartment after all, but suffered exposure waiting on the surface, until a rust-
bucket freighter picked you up, but the language
barrier and the state of your health kept the Greek
crew from repatriating you until you could be
treated in Athens. You fly home to a hero's
welcome."

Kolov let that sink in, then frowned. "But if you
do not accept the mission, Novskoyy has orders to
sink the ship. The self-destruct charges in the ballast tanks have been changed from molecular explosives to plasma. There will be nothing left of
Vepr bigger than your pinky finger if they detonate.
This mission is so sensitive, and compromise of it
could so thoroughly embarrass the Ukraine, that
this could be no other way."

Kolov swallowed, a sad look coming to his face.
"I know you, Pavel, and I know what you are
thinking. You want to find a way out of this. You
have been confronted with the reality of this world,
that morality is not always the rule of the day, that
sometimes we do things we are not proud of, that
we labor on through a world of unfairness. And I
know if you were here you'd storm into my office

and drop a letter on my desk. I wish it were that simple.

"You have my apologies for putting you in this miserable situation, Pavel. I wish it could be any other way. We were going to task the *Tigr* with this mission instead of your *Vepr,* but you are the best, Pavel. Only you will have the guts and the brains to come home from this mission. So do your work and come home, Pavel." Kolov waved the computer. "The headlines await you."

The video clip ended abruptly. Grachev stared at the screen, knowing that Svyatoslov was staring at him. Grachev frowned at Svyatoslov and said, "I'm not stupid. I know when I'm boxed in."

19

Twenty nautical miles west of the Chesapeake Bay Bridge-Tunnel, the long fingers of the piers of Norfolk Naval Base pointed west, tucked behind a corner of land that sheltered them along with the sprawling complex of Norfolk International Terminal, where a half-dozen roll-on/roll-off cargo ships were docked beside an equal number of supertankers. The piers of the naval base were as full as Karen Petri had seen them. The aircraft carrier *John Paul Jones* lay tied up at the farthest pier north from the berth of the USS *Devilfish*. The submarine piers around the wide black hull of the SSNX-class ship were filled with older Los Angeles–class submarines next to the empty berth of the one remaining Seawolf-class submarine, the highly decorated USS *Piranha*, now on patrol somewhere in the Atlantic. While the brass of the Navy took their stand-down, the fleet was taking its own rest, with the exception of the Bush-class destroyers *Christie Whitman* and *Tom Clancy*. The Aegis II–class nuclear-powered cruiser *Admiral Hyman Rickover*, which neared the tonnage of a World War II battleship, had joined the destroyers on the afternoon's sortie to provide security for the cruise ship.

Commander Karen Petri had watched the surface

ships get underway from a spot on the pier north of her submarine. The destroyers had done impressive back-full/ahead-flank maneuvers. One second they were tied up to the piers with their flags hanging slack. The next they burst into motion, both ships sounding loud and long blasts on their horns while pulling simultaneously backward into the channel. Even their surface search radar dishes rotated together in perfect synchronization as the ships maneuvered ahead and turned together. They shrank in the distance, growing dark gray in the haze as they neared the turning point. They left behind the Elizabeth River Channel of Norfolk Harbor and entered Thimble Shoals Channel on the long approach to the gap in the Chesapeake Bay Bridge-Tunnel.

As they moved out of sight, the *Rickover* made its pier departure maneuver, and if the destroyer underway had been impressive, the mobilization of the *Rickover* was positively thrilling. An ear-shattering blast from the ship's horn resounded across the water. The massive ship with its symmetrical tall pyramidal superstructure backed astern into the channel with astonishing acceleration. The flags flew toward the bow from the wind of its rearward passage, and when the vessel was a ship length into the channel, the sound of it vibrating was heard over the water, the ship drawing to a halt as sudden as its backward motion. It sat there suspended in the channel for a bare instant, then rushed ahead, its bow pointed directly at the concrete pier it had just left. In what seemed certain catastrophe, the ship neared the razor-sharp pier, but then in the

final moment responded to the rudder. The bow
came around, the amidships portion of the cruiser
sliding by the concrete pier and leaving it behind.
It accelerated ahead of its white boiling wake. The
flags now blew straight out from their masts toward
the stern as the ship grew distant, then majestically
rotated to show its full elegant profile and sailed
beyond view.

Petri sighed, knowing the departure of the *Devil-fish* would have none of the fanfare and glamour
of the surface ship underway. As she turned, she
saw the two tugboats tied up at the submarine's
bow and stern, there to pull her away from the pier
gently. The ship was barely able to maneuver close
to the pier, which would rip open her fiberglass
nose cone. Petri had been the executive officer of
a cruiser of the same class as the *Admiral Hyman
Rickover,* and she realized she missed the thrill of
a back-full/ahead-flank underway. If she had stayed
with the surface force, she would be a captain now,
a commanding officer. Not just an acting captain,
but a *real* captain.

She turned to look at the hull of the *Devilfish,*
her nostalgia and envy for the cruiser vaporizing.
In an odd way, this ship had a way of pulling feel-ings from deep inside her, making her much more
attached to it than she had ever been to any of her
previous ships. She might not be *Devilfish*'s perma-nent captain, but she couldn't love the ship any
more than she did. The hull was a deep black, the
surface of her shiny from the sharklike foam skin
covering the steel, an anechoic coating, to absorb
rather than reflect the pings of active sonar and

trapping noise from the inside of the ship, making the ship a stealth vessel, at least to the kind of sensors still prevalent in most of the combat navies of the world. Her conning tower, her sail, was much different from the vertical fins of the other submarines at the pier. *Devilfish*'s was a teardrop, the same kind of sail that the Russians had built in decades past, the fin leaning far forward, streamlined over every surface. Otherwise, the hull was an unremarkably shaped fat cigar, the width of her so great that the skin where she penetrated the water was gently sloped. The nose surface curved into the water forward, the stern curving more slowly into the black murky water of the slip aft. There was a stretch of water, then the rudder towering out of the water, seemingly unconnected to the rest of the sub. On top of the tall rudder was an oblong teardrop-shaped pod resembling a wing tank on an airplane, housing several sonar systems. Less than 10 percent of the ship was visible from the surface, her bowplanes and tail section lurking underwater, out of view.

Forward of the sail a large hatch was latched open. Two hatches were open aft of the sail. The lines were singled up to the deck cleats, the long gantry holding the shore-power cables reaching over the stern. The cables were now disconnected, the cable gantry slowly withdrawing toward the pier. Petri walked to the end of the pier, studying the current and water level. On the deck of the submarine, two officers dressed like her in short-sleeved khakis climbed from the hatch aft of the sail, then walked toward her over the gangway. The stiff one, Acting Executive Officer Paul Manderson, so far had seemed to be the strong, silent type. If he had objections to working for a female captain—an acting captain at that—he kept them to himself. Manderson and the other officer, Dietz, were talking to each other in tones Petri couldn't hear. They came up to her and saluted. She returned the salute. Manderson spoke first.

"Afternoon, ma'am. The ship is ready in all respects to get underway. All department heads have signed off on the pre-underway checklist. No major discrepancies."

Except we're missing our captain, she thought.

"Very well, XO," she said in a clipped voice. She turned to Artificial Intelligence Officer Bryan Dietz. "Officer of the Deck, your report?"

"Yes, Captain," Dietz said quietly. "The reactor is in the power range with a normal full-power lineup running two slow-speed reactor circulation pumps port, two starboard. Propulsion is on the main motor, spinning the propulsion turbine generators with power shunted to the idle resistor bank, ready to answer all bells. Cyclops battlecontrol system is nominal with neural network online and self-checks in continuous mode. Torpedo room is secure with all weapons in cold shutdown, all tubes rigged for Defcon three. Navigation fix is onboard from the GPS NavSat, confirmed on commercial channels. Ship's inertial navigation is nominal and tracking. The security scuba swim is complete and signed off, no suspicious or unusual objects detected on the hull. Maneuvering watch is stationed. All lines are singled up. We've received this message from Unified Submarine Command granting permission to get underway." Dietz handed Petri his WritePad computer for her signature. "Tugs are tied up fore and aft, forward unit bow to bow and aft unit bow to beam. Track is laid out of Norfolk. PIM is loaded into Cyclops." Dietz took a breath. "Request to raise and lower masts as necessary. Request to rotate and radiate on the radar. Request to remove the gangway. And request permission to get underway, ma'am."

Petri wrote her name in the WritePad's signature block. He voice was deep and authoritative:

"Officer of the Deck, raise and lower masts as necessary. Rotate and radiate." She lifted an eyebrow. "Wait on removing the gangway and getting underway, Off'sa'deck, until we're all aboard, if you don't mind."

"Raise and lower, rotate and radiate, Off'sa'deck, aye." Dietz snapped to attention, whipped Petri a salute, and spun on his heel to the ship, Manderson following.

Petri looked around at the pier one last time, then climbed onto the gangway and across the black water of the slip to the hull of the ship, her black combat boots squishing softly into the sharkskin coating.

"*Devilfish,* arriving!" rang out over the pier, the announcement that the commanding officer had come aboard. She felt a momentary pang at missing Kelly McKee, but swallowed hard and walked to the sail, where a temporary chain ladder hung from the bridge cockpit.

"Captain to the bridge!" she yelled, climbing the

rungs carefully to the top of the sail. Over the bridge coaming she could see Dietz wearing a khaki jacket and binoculars, his petty officer lookout behind him along with another petty officer phone talker. Petri climbed over the coaming, noticing that the men kept their eyes averted as she hoisted her long legs over the bulkhead. She stood on the grating leading below to the forward compartment upper level, then stepped the four steps up the flying bridge, which was just three temporary stainless-steel handrails bolted to the top of the sail. From here Petri was twelve meters above the water of the slip, a tall crow's-nest vantage point overlooking the harbor. To the right, on the other side of the cruiser berths, the cruise ship could be seen getting ready to depart. The *Princess Dragon* would proceed down the channel with *Devilfish* bringing up the rear.

"Officer of the Deck, remove the gangway," Petri commanded, accepting binoculars and a handheld VHF radio from the lookout. She put the binoculars to her eyes and looked northward to see the aircraft carrier piers, where the tugboats were swarming around the hull of the USS *John Paul Jones*. *Jones* would be putting to sea last, several hours after *Devilfish* steamed past. Once in unrestricted waters, with the carrier air group's F/A-18s, F-22s, and F-45s, the cruise ship with the brass embarked would be as secure as a baby in its mother's arms.

A crane on the pier rumbled with diesel-engine growls as it pulled the gangway up and off the hull.

When it was gone, Petri could almost feel the pull of the sea on the deck beneath her boots.

"Officer of the Deck," she said, feeling her heart pounding in excitement, "get underway."

"Get underway, Officer of the Deck, aye, Captain." Dietz said it as if she'd asked him to pass the salt and he was simply handing it over. He hoisted a bullhorn to his mouth and announced to the deckhands, "Take in line one! Take in three! Take in four, five, and six!"

Petri watched as the deckhands hustled over the deck, pulling the heavy Manila lines tossed over by the seamen from the tender ship working at the massive bollards on the pier. The lines were coiled on the deck and packed into line lockers, open cubbyholes in the hull with heavy hatches. Finally all lines but number two were aboard. The diesels of the tug engines came to life, their loud roaring making normal conversation impossible. Dietz looked at his watch, glanced at his WritePad computer's chart display, and hoisted the bullhorn again, one of his hands on a lever resembling the throttle of a steam engine.

"Take in line two!" he commanded the deck. When the line was disconnected from the bollard, he turned to the lookout, who had climbed to the flying bridge next to Petri to hoist the flags on Dietz's command, and shouted, "Shift colors!" *Devilfish* was officially underway. The lookout up on top of the sail next to Petri hoisted the Stars and Stripes on a three-meter tall stainless-steel flagpole, the flag slack in the calm of the afternoon. Next to the American flag, the lookout raised the

flag of the Unified Submarine Force, the pirate flag
with the force's motto in Gothic script. A half second after ordering the flags raised, Dietz pulled the
lever in the forward bulkhead of the cockpit, and
the ship's horn emitted a painfully loud booming
blast, the horn sounding for a full eight seconds.
While the horn sounded, the ship drifted slightly
away from the pier. The horn stopped, and Dietz
said into a VHF radio, "Forward tug back one
third. Aft tug back one third." The tugs' engines
roared, pulling the eight-thousand-ton submarine
away from the pier at dead slow. The black water
of the slip gradually opened up between the hull
and the pier.

"Forward tug all stop. Aft tug all stop," Dietz
called into the VHF radio, stopping the units now
that the ship was off the pier. "Helm, all ahead one
third, right full rudder," he said into the bridge
communication box's microphone. The reply rang
out loudly in the cramped cockpit: "All ahead one
third, right full rudder, Bridge, Helm, aye, throttle
to ahead one third, rpm rising to three zero. Ship
is at ahead one third, my rudder is right full."

Dietz replied casually, "Very well, Helm." The
tug engines quieted back to idle as *Devilfish* moved
slowly ahead, the water of the slip churning up
slightly on either side of the fat black hull.

"Bridge, Helm, rudder is right full, no course
given."

"Steady zero zero five," Dietz said. He leaned
out over the cockpit coaming, making sure the rudder was turning right, then pulled his head back in
and glanced down at his chart, then up at the scen-

ery. The pier behind them began to rotate until the ship came around to the north. The deck vibrated underneath Petri's boots, a motion of pure power, a deeply satisfying sensation.

"Are we missing anyone?" Pacino asked Paully White. They were hurrying down a passageway from his stateroom on the way to the continuation of the arrival party for the officers.

"I'm afraid so, Admiral. I just got off the phone with NavSea staff. There was a fatality in the shipyard at Electric Boat at the DynaCorp New Construction Facility. Apparently a shipyard worker was welding on the hull plates of the *Virginia* and forgot he was standing on a scaffold. He walked off the platform and fell over fifty feet to his death."

Pacino stopped short. "Oh, no. Where's Captain Patton?"

Captain Jonathan George S. Patton IV had commanded the SSNX-class submarine *Devilfish* on her maiden voyage out of the building ways during the East China Sea conflict. The ship had sunk six hijacked Japanese Rising Sun–class subs, and had suffered a catastrophic torpedo room fire during the battle. When she'd been patched up, Patton had been put in charge of new construction of the NSSN class. Now that it was officially out of the prototype stage, he was supervising the construction of the NSSN-class submarine *Virginia,* the follow-on to the *Devilfish.* Patton and Pacino had had a recent discussion about Patton's unhappiness with his station in life. Patton had never said it, but Pacino knew Patton felt that he, not Bruce Phillips,

should have been given command of the Unified
Submarine Command. Pacino had chosen Phillips,
with whom he'd had a longer history, going back
to the Japanese blockade days. Patton was next in
line, his heroism earning him the Navy Cross in
Operation *White Hope,* but his experience was just
a hairsbreadth short of what Phillips brought to the
table. Unfortunately, Patton felt so strongly about
it that Pacino feared he'd resign.

Pacino knew Patton would take the shipyard
worker's death particularly hard, and he asked,
"Where was John?"

"He was in his limo on the way down," White
replied. "He got the call, turned around, and went
back to Electric Boat. He said he wanted to see
the family."

"He wouldn't feel right coming on our little vacation, not after that happened."

"Exactly, Admiral."

"We got everyone else?"

"We're missing your Annapolis roommate,
Sean Murphy."

"Sean called me before. He won't be coming."

"What's going on?" White asked, not as discreet
as he should have been.

"Let's just say it's a personal thing," Pacino said.
"He can't make it right now." In fact, Murphy had
lung cancer. After going into remission a few years
before, it was back now, in full force. His wife and
children wanted him to go in for chemotherapy,
but he wasn't sure. One thing he was sure of was
that he did not have the strength to make this
cruise.

Pacino bit his lip. Terminal cancer at age fifty, after everything Sean Murphy had lived through. It seemed far less than fair. If Pacino could have given his old Academy roommate ten years of his own life, he would have gladly done it.

Pacino tried to turn his mind away from the dismal events striking his two friends and forced himself to smile as they returned to the amidships reception hall at the companionway and began to greet his officers. Soon the enthusiasm he showed became genuine. The company of these fine men cheered him up. He accepted one of Phillips' recommended Anchor Steams, marveling at the cooperation of the weather. When it was time, the sun high overhead as the afternoon approached, the officers climbed to the bridge to watch the civilian crew get the ship underway.

20

Once again Pavel Grachev strapped himself into the seat of the command console in the forward part of the periscope well, adjusting his headset. "Attention to orders," he said on the circuit. On the aux seven display, twelve windows showing the faces of his tactical watch officers depicted his men concentrating on their own displays, where the image of his face was shown.

"We are being ordered to attack a surface action group leaving Port Norfolk on the way to the Atlantic, and from there farther south. There will be three surface warships and one submarine escorting out the high-value unit, a white-painted cruise ship called the *Princess Dragon*. Our orders, confirmed today by Captain Second Rank Svyatoslov and me, are to destroy the task force."

Grachev let this sink in, then continued, "The cruise ship, our main target, has aboard her the entire cadre of U.S. Navy senior officers. The purpose of their sortie is to take the ship to calm tropical waters where they can plan a mission of destruction against the Black Sea Fleet of the Navy of the Ukraine. You have all been briefed on the mission of our fleet to the South Atlantic. Apparently the Americans have found out about it. Our fleet commander has given us orders to execute a decapitation assault on the American Navy's leadership. The theory is that if they are dead, our mission to the South Atlantic will have the time to succeed."

He turned to Svyatoslov. "Mr. First, line up Shchuka system unit four for immediate launch."

"Yessir."

Within ten minutes, the Shchuka unit had lifted off from the torpedo tube, streaming its data wire. It drifted to the bay bottom, anchored itself to the silty soil, and inflated its foil hydraphone-surfaced balloon. A few seconds later, data streamed into the Second Captain's battlecontrol system.

"Sir," Svyatoslov reported, "Shchuka unit four is on the bay bottom and active. The Second Captain has the battlespace on three-dimensional virtual reality."

"Very good," Grachev said. "Line up large-bore tubes one through four for Barrakuda mobile mine launches, data wires connected."

"Yessir," Svyatoslov replied. "Barrakuda units one through four loading now."

It would take a few minutes for the units to get into the tubes and have their cables connected to the tube breech doors, and then a few more minutes for the tube doors to shut and the tubes to flood with seawater while the mines' power units warmed up, the onboard ring laser inertial navigators stabilizing. Grachev could take this time to unstrap from his command console and go to the VR booth on the starboard side, but he decided to re-

main at the command console and let the first officer guide in the mines.

Soon Svyatoslov's voice rang in Grachev's headset: "Sir, Barrakuda units one through four are
ready for launch."

"Very good, Mr. First. Take VR zero. When the
battlespace is ready, and only on my orders, you
will take out units one through four and target the
outbound warships, one for each destroyer and two
for the cruiser. When you have them launched, prepare to load tubes one and two with Barrakuda
units five and six for the cruise ship and tubes three
and four with Bora II antisubmarine torpedoes."

There was a resource bottleneck problem here,
Grachev thought. While the ship was wire-guiding
the mobile mines, the tubes had to remain dedicated to the mines connected to the ship by their
data wires, which meant the tubes could not be
reused for the next round of mines or torpedoes.
Grachev had intentionally targeted the warships
first, thinking that anything could happen before
the cruise ship passed the Chesapeake Bay
Bridge-Tunnel.

"Yessir. Taking station in VR zero."

There was nothing to do now but wait for the
American task force to exit the bay. Grachev
scanned the acoustic daylight images of the
Shchuka unit four. He pulled a set of virtual-reality
goggles from the side of the console and slipped
them on, seeing the bay around him as if he were
submerged in a bathing suit thirty meters below
the calm surface. The VR system at the command
console was poor compared to the startling reality

of the VR cubicles, but Grachev preferred to serve his watch here.

A few hours, Grachev promised himself. In a few hours all this would be over.

The captain of the *Princess Dragon* looked amused but war-weary as he took the giant vessel out, using her thrusters to maneuver off the pier, then backing down without tugs, turning swiftly on a single point in the river in spite of the strength of the current, and moving ahead as the ship's six massive gas turbine engines throttled up, her twin screws kicking up a white wake aft.

Pacino could feel the ship roll as they took the first turn, but otherwise the deck of the *Princess Dragon* was as steady as the floor of the Hyatt Hotel. He watched as they moved down the seaway. The wind of their passage picked up, wanting to steal his officer's hat. The sounds and smells of the sea seemed to reach into him, erasing all his previous troubles. Here, at sea, with his senior officers and an ice-cold bottle of Anchor Steam, there were no enemies, no Ukrainians, no dark forces.

He would remember this day his entire life, he thought.

Devilfish picked up speed as they fell in behind the broad gleaming white stern of the cruise ship. Petri smiled to herself as several of the senior officers waved to her. The *Princess Dragon* made the turn eastward into the Chesapeake, the submarine slicing through the massive cruise vessel's wake. The scrubby pines on their right masked their view of the runways of Norfolk Naval Air Station.

"Bridge, Navigator," the speaker rasped. "Mark the turn to zero three five."

"Helm, Bridge, right full rudder, steady course zero three five," Dietz ordered, his voice still casual, again craning his neck over the bridge coaming to check the swing of the rudder.

The world rotated around the ship as the rudder turned them, and the Bridge-Tunnel of Interstate 64 became visible.

"Bridge, helm, rudder is right full, passing zero two five, ten degrees from ordered course."

Dietz acknowledged, hoisting binoculars to his eyes, scanning the channel. He turned to look at Petri, who was stepping back down into the cramped cockpit.

"Rig the flying bridge for dive," she ordered Dietz, "and take it up to fifteen knots."

"Lookout, rig flying bridge for dive. Helm, Bridge, all ahead standard."

The water at the bow rose slowly up over the nose cone, climbing steadily up the hull until the foredeck from the sail lip to the bow was completely underwater. The bow wave began to get louder below them, a low-pitched growling in a duet with the noise of the wind. The Interstate 64 tunnel was approaching. A few miles beyond, the tall, boxy stern of the cruise ship could be seen lumbering down the channel. Behind them the twin periscopes were rotating furiously, Judison's men taking visual navigation fixes.

"Bridge, Navigator, hold you fifty yards right of

center of channel. Recommend steer zero three four.
Request to raise the radar mast, rotate and radiate."

Dietz spoke quietly into the bridge microphone,
Petri listening closely. "Helm, Bridge, steer zero
three four, raise the radar mast."

The speaker barked a reply while a noise behind
them marked the raising of the radar mast high
over the other masts.

Beyond, the Interstate 64 Bridge-Tunnel, the
pricey shore property of Ocean View steadily
passed. The water ahead was glassy smooth, the
afternoon sun glaring off the water. The navigator
had them turn to course east, aiming for the Chesapeake Bay Bridge-Tunnel and the start of the
Thimble Shoals Channel. Three huge supertankers
were cruising inbound, all of them loaded to the
gunwales with Saudi crude.

The cruise ship had sped up in front of them,
the distance now four miles. Petri called for a speed
increase to twenty-five knots. Dietz ordered ahead
flank, and the noise of the bow wave roaring over
the hull and the wind howling in their ears was like
music to Petri. At the bow, several dolphins began
to jump in the foam of the bow wave, leaping
ahead, splashing into the water, and then vanishing.
Petri smiled at the dolphins, the submarine's good-
luck charm, and scanned the waters ahead with
her binoculars.

The lines of the I-64 bridge ahead extended
across their track except where the tunnel made it
disappear. They passed over the bridge and continued on, the sea and scenery continuing to pass
astern. She could see the arching span of the Ches-

apeake Bay Bridge-Tunnel at the horizon, marking
the entrance to the Atlantic. Petri called down for
coffee, and when it came was content to drink the
strong brew and enjoy the sweeping beauty of the
Chesapeake Bay.

On the Chesapeake Bay Bridge-Tunnel fishing pier,
a vendor called Kelly McKee out of his reverie,
offering him a hot dog. McKee dropped his binoculars and accepted it, paying from a wad of bills in
his pocket. When he returned to his vigil, the first
ships were well in sight, two gray sleek destroyers,
then an Aegis cruiser, plowing the seaway in
straight lines. The radars on the high masts of the
destroyers rotated slowly, and large flags from the
tall masts flapped in the slipstream of their passage.
In the binoculars McKee could see the men on
deck, serious officers on the bridge wings and inside
the windows of the bridge. The cruiser behind the
destroyer was still gray in the haze of distance, lumbering slowly down the seaway. Two miles behind
the cruiser a bright white hull appeared, which
must be the cruise ship, McKee thought.

   McKee watched the cruise ship as it slowly made
its way toward him. As it grew he realized it was the
biggest cruise liner he had ever seen, all superstructure above the waterline, the boxiness of her tapered
at the bow and stern. McKee turned his eyes upward,
and on the promenade deck was a row of men distin-
guished from the others, who wore Hawaiian shirts
and shorts—these men wore starched tropical white
uniforms with gold shoulderboards. Flag officers. Admirals. He couldn't make out who they were, nor did

he want to raise the binoculars to his eyes. At that moment he decided to turn his back on the ship and walk back to the car.

He never saw the admirals sending a junior officer running to the bridge, or the result of that action—the dipping of the cruise ship's American flag, an ancient seagoing gesture of respect.

When the *Princess Dragon* neared the first tunnel of the Chesapeake Bay Bridge-Tunnel, Pacino thought he saw Kelly McKee standing on the fishing pier, and immediately he sent his aide to the bridge to order the captain to dip the flag. Just as the vessel passed through the gap, the flag was dipped, but by then Kelly McKee had turned and was walking back to his car.

Pacino watched him helplessly, wondering what he could do to make the man return to his life, then remembering how he himself had gone into shock and mourning when his first command, the old fast attack submarine *Devilfish,* had gone down in the Arctic Ocean. How he had left the Navy and taught at the Academy and tried to forget, but a part of him would never forget. Once a man is a submarine commander, there is no turning back. Just as an astronaut will always have that one defining experience in his life of having gone into space, so would a sub skipper always have that one period in his life of being the ultimate dictator at sea.

Kelly McKee would be back, Pacino realized, just as he himself had come back. The moment would find him. And until that moment, Pacino would have to wait and do his job, which today was drinking beer and getting a tan going to sea on a sinfully luxurious cruise ship surrounded by his friends.

"Like it, sir?" Phillips' voice said in Pacino's ear.

"Nope." Pacino paused. "I love it." He clinked his bottle against Phillips'. "But you're in deep trouble with me, Admiral. You should have thought of this years ago, dammit." Pacino smiled.

"Admiral, I'll *take* that fuckin' hit," Phillips said, the traditional submariner's response to unfair criticism from an inspection team.

Pacino stared out to sea as they passed the ships at anchor, watched as two dolphins splashed at their bow wave, and basked in the feel of the sun and the wind.

"Sir, we have the task force on Shchuka sensors two and three," Computer Systems Officer Lieutenant Gezlev Katmonov reported from the virtual-reality cubicle behind Svyatoslov's. Katmonov was a talented youth, but looked like he'd been pulled out of his high school classes just that morning.

"Very good. Mr. First, you have the targets?"

"Destroyers approaching the gap in the Bay Bridge-Tunnel now. I have the forward unit out of the gap, the western unit about five hundred meters behind, coming toward the gap."

"Shoot Barrakuda unit one in swimout mode."

"Unit one away," Svyatoslov reported.

Grachev strapped on the VR goggles and leaned back in his command seat. The view was like looking through a porthole, but what his goggles were tuned to was the seeker camera/nonvisible light sensor/blue laser seeker in the nose cone of the

Barrakuda mobile mine. Within a heartbeat the hole vanished. The mine's turbine engine started burning its oxidized liquid fuel and leaving the tube. The view opened up to the bay around him, which looked as though it were moving slowly, perhaps walking speed. Off in the distance Grachev could see the hull of the first destroyer as Svyatoslov guided the unit in.

"Ready for Barrakuda unit two sir," Svyatoslov reported. "Mr. Lynski will guide it out."

"Very good. Shoot when ready."

The second mobile mine left the ship, guided by Warrant Officer Lynski in VR cubicle two. By pushing a software button on his aux one display, Grachev could toggle his view between unit one and unit two. As he watched, the slow-moving mines placed themselves in the paths of the oncoming destroyer hulls. The hulls grew huge overhead, dwarfing the mobile mines. The hull of the first destroyer passed directly overhead, and the mine drove upward and connected itself to the hull. Then as it shut down its propulsor, the electromagnet held the unit to the metal of the hull long enough for two welding arms to protrude from its body and spot-weld the unit directly to the destroyer, while a secondary chemical system emitted the two components of a strong epoxy glue, supergluing the two bodies together. The first Barrakuda turned off the electromagnets permanently, conserving power for the unit's computer and warhead-detonator circuit.

"Unit one is attached, Captain."

"Very good. Set the detonator for coordinate

alpha plus the time delay assigned and disconnect the wire."

Coordinate alpha was a position about eighty kilometers east of the coastline. The ring laser inertial navigator would count off the latitude and longitude until coordinate alpha was reached, and then start a time counter. The timing was planned so the cruise ship would explode first.

"Shutting down one, reloading with unit five."

The second Barrakuda unit connected itself to the hull of the second destroyer. Soon Svyatoslov's men had put two Barrakudas on the cruiser and two on the cruise ship. All tubes were disconnected from the mobile mine guidance wires and reloaded with Bora II torpedoes for the attack on the submarine.

Grachev reconfigured the console to examine the view out the Antay sensor, protruding a mere half meter from the smooth bay water. As he watched the massive cruise ship drove by in the gap of the Chesapeake Bay Bridge-Tunnel, dipping its flag momentarily, then raising it. That was odd, Grachev thought, shrugging and settling back. With their mines laid, there was nothing to do but wait to see if they detonated on schedule.

"Sir?" Svyatoslov asked. "What about the submarine?"

The sub was just approaching the gap in the bridge-tunnel. Grachev watched its image in display zero. It was beautiful, with a Russian-style sweptback sail and a pod on the rudder far aft.

"What about it?"

"When will you be attacking it?"

"Later. I'll let you know."

21

"Penny for your thoughts, Admiral."

Pacino was leaning over the windswept railing on the starboard side of the promenade deck, squinting against the sun's shimmer off the short lazy waves of the Atlantic thirty miles out of Norfolk Harbor, the hotels and skyline of Virginia Beach slowly fading astern. Young Lieutenant Commander Eve Cavalla had joined him, having lost her tropical white uniform for a skirt and a silk blouse, her long auburn hair taken out of the usual ponytail and combed out, falling to her shoulders and blowing off her face in the wind, highlights shimmering in the redness of her hair. Her glasses were gone, contacts and Ray·Bans taking their place. Pacino glanced over at her, a sad smile coming to his face.

"I was just thinking about the last time I saw this view. It was the final time I took *Seawolf* to sea as her captain," he said, his voice trailing off.

"And?" she prompted, cocking her head to look at her boss's face.

"It was during the war. The big one, World War III. We had sat out the whole thing, *Seawolf* sitting high and dry in the dry dock, getting the original Vortex tubes shoved into her. The Battle of Iran was going down about then, and all I could do was sit there wearing a hard hat in the yard, watching my ship get torn apart."

He stopped again, taking a beer from the waiter, Eve taking a glass of wine.

"You got called to sea?"

"I keep forgetting," Pacino said. "It was so highly classified that it never made it into the newspapers. Or the history books." He laughed, a self-mocking noise. " 'Seawolf Wins World War III, Sub's Skipper a Hero.' "

"So, what did happen?" Eve had pushed the Ray·Bans up into her bangs, the bright green of her eyes staring into his.

"Oh, hell, Eve, it was a long time ago and it doesn't matter anyway. I've got to change."

He left her there staring at him, half angry, half astonished. Inside his stateroom he pulled off his uniform, taking a moment to look at his Navy Cross, the one Donchez, the former Chief of Naval Operations had given him for the mission that lost the *Seawolf.* Somehow the decoration was supposed to compensate him for the loss, he thought.

He knew he had to shake off this sudden melancholy somehow. He hung up his uniform and donned his tropical vacation clothes, hoping they would lighten his mood. But it was no use. Without Colleen here, he was half of himself. He looked in the mirror, bit his lip, smoothing his windblown white hair, and left the stateroom. When he emerged back onto the promenade deck, he could see that Eve had left their spot on the railing and had found a pilot friend; the two of them were deeply involved in a conversation. Pacino manned the rail, staring out to sea, although Cavalla looked over at him once, smiling at him.

"Better be careful, sir," a whiny voice said in his ear.

Pacino looked up at Rear Admiral Paully White, his Vice CNO and old friend from the Japanese and Red Chinese wars. White was a few years older than Pacino, a few inches shorter, a few pounds heavier, but with a full head of hair as black as when he'd been a teenager. The pounds had arrived when he'd quit smoking, but in the last year White had become an exercise fanatic, as habit-bound with that as he'd been with cigarettes, but he fought the fact that now he could taste his food. White was from the Kensington area of Philadelphia and spoke with an accent as thick as any Pacino had ever heard. When he'd first met White the accent had been a severe irritant, but they had become fast friends, and today that whining speech was musical.

"Why's that, Paully?"

"Cavalla has her eye on you."

"That's absurd. I'm married." Pacino's tone was peeved. "She's twenty-five years younger than me. And . . . I'm married."

"And she's not. And the way she was looking at you. Like a tiger looks at a steak."

"Paully."

"Nice day, ain't it, sir?" White changed the subject as if it had never been raised.

"Beautiful."

"Absolut and orange juice, please, and another

Anchor for the Big Boss," he said to the waiter. "Don't it just make you wish we'd left behind the phones and the radios and the computers?"

"Yeah. But any particular reason you mention that?"

White scowled in worry, looking left and right to make sure they were alone.

"Oh, yeah. You'd better put your warrior's hat on for a minute, sir. The *Admiral Kuznetsov* put to sea a half hour ago. The Ukrainians are doing this thing, they're really going to do it. The situation is going just the way our simulation went."

Pacino nodded, thinking.

"Any intelligence on the Ukrainian Black Sea Fleet submarine force?"

"Nothing, sir. The subs are cold iron ever since the *Vepr* went down."

"They've got to be grounded."

"It'd be nice to know instead of guessing, though, Admiral."

"We should talk to Number Four at NSA." Number Four was their friend Mason "Jack" Daniels IV, the National Security Agency Director. "Daniels should be able to set up a better harvest of naval base communications. We need to know what they're up to."

"I'll see if Number Four can come up on video tonight."

Pacino thought. They had a light schedule that day, the first day at sea devoted to relaxation. The first seminars weren't scheduled until Tuesday morning, tomorrow.

"Okay, see what you can do."

White left without a word, leaving Pacino staring out to sea. They had left Norfolk far behind, the only thing around them the sea and the sky and the three surface warships escorting them out, now at various distances and bearings from the cruise ship, screening her as if she were an aircraft carrier. A few miles astern the new SSNX-class submarine *Devilfish* could barely be made out, visible more from her white wake than from her superstructure. A seagull swooped by. At the bow a single dolphin jumped next to the bow wave. Pacino smiled. It was impossible to worry with the seascape around him. A contentment filled him for a moment, and he didn't ascribe it to the beer or the sea, but simply enjoyed it.

"Did you want to do a voice-over in the chopper?"

The cameraman shouted at her and into his boom microphone, his voice scratchy and full of static on her Mickey Mouse headset.

"No," she shouted back. "I'll do it in the sound studio. All this noise makes it hard to hear my own voice, and if I can't hear myself I sound like a moron."

Victoria Cronkite shook her long brunette hair, wanting it off her shoulder while she concentrated. She was a segment producer and news special reporter for Satellite News Network. She'd traveled down from Washington to Norfolk to capture the departure of the U.S. Navy's boondoggle to the Caribbean on a cruise ship, the most flagrant waste of taxpayers' money she had ever witnessed. She would not be reporting daily, since the cruise was not significant enough to make it into the nightly news. Her executive producer had instead told her to cover the entire course of the "stand-down." Then a segment report on *Correspondence: Confidential* would be perfect to expose this racket for what it was. So she would do the voice-over later.

She looked over at Doug, who was shouting something.

"What?"

"Vicky, do the voice-over up here anyway. It will sound more dramatic inside the chopper. You know, 'We're here two thousand feet over the American convoy which is not bringing a big stick to advance U.S. foreign policy, but a big suitcase full of bathing suits and Hawaiian shirts.' It'll sound more immediate than a sterilized version from the sound stage."

"Okay, fine. But you know I can't modulate my own voice up here. If I sound like a Mongoloid, we're erasing tape and starting over again, even if we have to pipe in phony helicopter noises."

Doug laughed over the intercom. "Ready to roll in three, two, one."

Immediately Cronkite's voice changed to that of a seasoned veteran reporter, the one she mockingly called her TV voice.

"This is Victoria Cronkite reporting for SNN news, and as you can see from here above the waters of Hampton Roads, five ships of a U.S. Navy task force are departing Norfolk Harbor for a secret mission. The ships of the force include the front-line destroyers *Tom Clancy* and *Christie Whitman* as well as the massive nuclear missile cruiser

USS *Hyman Rickover,* with the SSNX submarine *Devilfish* bringing up the rear. But, you might ask, what is this confidential mission? What are these ships doing on today's highly classified sortie?"

She went on like that for some moments more as the cruise ship approached the Chesapeake Bay Bridge-Tunnel.

The first Barrakuda mobile mine had attached itself to the hull of the cruise ship about a third of a ship length from the bow, some five meters behind the location of the ship's bridge, the navigation control center. The weld had held steady since the unit's electromagnets had turned off, and the seawater-environment epoxy had solidified.

The mine waited patiently, its only power going to the ring laser inertial navigation system and the onboard computer, which clicked off the time and watched the ship's position. When the navigation module indicated the ship was eighty kilometers southeast of Norfolk, the unit looked to its time delay setting for the correct interval after the eighty-kilometer point. The read-only memory indicated a time delay of zero, which made it time to activate the arming device.

The arming module came to life on the orders of the central processor, doing the silicon equivalent of a morning yawn in its full series of self-checks. Immediately after a report of satisfactory, the central processor ordered the unit to detonate the low-explosive charges at the forward and after ends of the mine.

During a single ten-microsecond interval the forward and after low explosives received intense electrical signals. The resistive effect caused their temperatures to soar until combustion began, the ignition of the thumb-sized charges constrained by thick forged casings fore and aft, the flame front and blast effect propagating toward the center toward a dual metal disk called the fail-safe plate, which was normally arranged to be a closed door, but which had been rotated to align two centimeter-diameter holes with the butt end of the low-explosive charges on the action of the arming circuit. The holes led to a passageway to the intermediate explosives, slightly larger charges with five times the explosive power of the low explosives, but much less sensitive, requiring much more than a small electrical signal to explode.

The flame fronts from the low-explosive charges ignited the secondary explosives, which were each the size of a soda can, and like the low-explosive charges, constrained on all sides but one by thick forgings, so that their blast effect was directed toward the warhead center, where the high-explosive charges lay waiting and inert.

The high explosives were shaped charges, arranged in a chevron so that their detonation would focus most of their blast effect in a single direction, both detonating in a synchronized explosion and focusing their energy on the warhead center.

The pulsing hammer impact of the high-explosive charges each blew a cone of plutonium from the warhead ends to a waiting doughnut of plutonium in the center of the warhead. The plutonium was blown into a single dense sphere, beginning the fusion explosion trigger of the plasma warhead. The plutonium sphere was not so different from what it had been before the high-explosive detonation, the same mass, but three chunks of the mass had been blown together into a single ball, and that had extreme significance to a nuclear physicist, because the surface area of the plutonium had suddenly decreased, leaving much less space available for neutrons formed by plutonium fissions to escape into space. Instead, the background level of fissions caused the neutrons to remain mostly inside the sphere of plutonium, causing more fissions, which led to more neutrons, which caused even more fissions and an explosion of neutrons, until the nuclear chain reaction spiraled in a runaway. The fission bomb converted the mass energy of the plutonium to thermal energy as the plutonium temperature soared from twenty degrees Centigrade to two hundred to two thousand to twenty thousand and beyond. In the igniting energy of the fission trigger, bags of heavy water, deuterium, joined in. The nuclei of the heavy deuterium fused together to form lighter helium, the whole less than the sum of its parts, and what mass was no longer present converted to pure energy. The deuterium was fused entirely to helium while the plutonium atoms fissioned into fragments. The temperatures at the center of the warhead roared up to two million degrees, then to twenty million.

The warhead so far had progressed from being a high-explosive bomb to an atom bomb to a hydrogen bomb. Had its design stopped there, the resulting explosion would have caused a mile-wide

mushroom cloud and radioactive fallout, the nightmare of the previous century.

But just as the hydrogen bomb had piggy-backed
on the fission bomb to become even more destruc-
tive, the plasma bomb was built using a fusion-
bomb trigger. A host of substances lying waiting
between deuterium canisters added to fury of the
nuclear fire. The fusion bomb's explosion diameter
was scarcely a half meter, the soaring temperatures
activating what the physicists called "star dust." Its
effects had been discovered in the high-energy col-
liders built in the early twenty-first century and put
to use before the end of the first decade, its result
the confinement of the massive energy of the nuclear explosion in a small volume, the thermal energy of it focused within itself, held within a rapidly
generated and incredibly powerful magnetic field
instead of propagating outward in the explosion of
a hydrogen bomb. The same energy of the nuclear
detonation held within the genie's bottle of the
magnetic field caused the mass contained inside to
continue to soar in temperature, past a hundred
million to two hundred million degrees, so hot that
the atoms' electrons flashed off into space, followed
by a piercing wave of gamma radiation. The incredibly hot plasma, a cubic meter sliced out of the
bottom level of Hell, glowed there in the space
coordinates of what had once been the innocent
underbelly of a pleasure cruise ship.

The accords of the first decades of the new century had outlawed fission and fusion bombs, taking
them off the shelves of the militaries of the world,
until the nuclear physicists demonstrated the first

plasma warhead at the famous DynaCorp Labs in Los Alamos, New Mexico. Placed inside a mock building in a mock city, the plasma warhead showed how much the technology had further tamed the atom. Instead of the explosion flattening the city to ruins, the plasma detonation had confined all the unfocused thermal energy within one room of the building, carving a perfect sphere in the concrete walls before bringing down the building and only the target building, the effect solely one of temperature and missing the horrors of wide-pattern radioactivity and blast effect that had led to the condemnation of nuclear weapons in the first place. As the demonstration showed, the plasma bomb was unlike its father and grandfather, the atom bomb and hydrogen bomb, both weapons of mass destruction. It was a surgical incendiary device. Within months, conventional weapons were replaced with plasma warheads on the cruise missiles and laser-guided bombs of the U.S. military.

The first use of a plasma warhead in a full-scale military test had been in the Bahamas submarine test range, where then-Captain Michael Pacino witnessed its underwater detonation in the warhead of a Vortex missile, in the early days of World War III against the United Islamic Front.

The first use in warfare had come weeks later as Pacino targeted the UIF supersub in the Labrador Sea even as his USS *Seawolf* blew apart from the detonations of the Nagasaki torpedoes, the plasma Vortex detonation taking out the dictator of the entire United Islamic Front of God, which then sued for peace in an early end to the conflict while the Labrador Sea incident remained cloaked under the veil of a top secret classification.

The second use had come during Operation *Enlightened Curtain,* when Pacino, then a rear admiral, had targeted Japanese Destiny II–class submarines with plasma-tipped Vortex Mod Bravo missiles, putting almost all of them on the bottom of the Pacific.

The third use had come in the Chinese Second Civil War, when Red China executed its massive sneak attack on White China, employing plasma warheads in firebombing of Shanghai and Hong Kong, and in the same war against the American rescue Rapid Deployment Force—Operation *White Hope*—when stolen Japanese technology had been turned on the Americans, the stolen subs then targeting the advancing American surface fleet with plasma-tipped torpedoes. It was Vice Admiral Pacino's counterattack with plasma-tipped Vortex Mod Bravo and Charlie missiles that had won the battle.

Some would later say that perhaps it was fate that the ship carrying Admiral Michael Pacino, the first man to use a plasma warhead in anger, came under the surface-of-the-sun-glow attack of a plasma mobile mine.

But whether it was fate or irony or coincidence, the plasma front grew upward into the hull of the *Princess Dragon* and ignited it into a scene from Dante's *Inferno,* and in time, the result of the plasma detonation would become only smoking fires and smoldering debris on the sea.

Admiral Michael Pacino was looking down at the water washing aft along the cruise ship's hull, enjoying the hypnotic effect of the wake, when it happened.

At first there was the flash. The sea around the amidships portion of the ship changed from dark blue with whitecaps to burning red. Pacino's eyes widened in astonishment as the red glow burst out from their hull and traveled through the water outward, forming a giant circle around the ship. The next thing he noticed was that everything else had frozen. The waves, the wind, the very passage of time. A seagull flying some ten feet away from him had come to a stop, not budging an inch from where it flew next to the ship. With dismay Pacino recognized what was happening. It was not that time had stopped or slowed; it was that he had just been hit with a surge of adrenaline.

The red glow had pulsed outward about a half ship length around the vessel, calming from its earlier stark bright red to a glowing pale orange, but as the color faded, something changed. What a moment before had been the glowing surface of the water now became white as the sea around them burst into foam. The foam ignited into a rising cloud of white, as if he had found himself next to the nozzles of a rocket pointed upward.

As the white explosion of foam happened, Pacino dimly realized that there was no sound. This freakish event was completely silent. If there had been a sound, perhaps it had made him deaf. But there was no time to ponder that thought. The seagull was slowly being blown upward by the blast of white from the sea around them, rising and flipping, his wings breaking in the violence of the gusher.

Pacino felt the deck roll to port, five degrees, then ten, the railing now on an uphill angle. He had a moment to peer down over the side, and felt as if he'd peeked through a window into Hell itself. Where there had been ocean before was now a fireball, flames boiling up in an orange-and-black cloud that was rising slowly along the hull. He pulled back in time to watch the fireball blow upward past the railing where he had just had his head.

He realized he was slowly falling toward the deck, probably blown by the shock wave of whatever the rising explosion was. He was facing aft now, falling slowly and watching stunned as something happened to the hull. Before his eyes it opened up along a fault line in the deck. The ship split in half, the after portion rolling away from him to starboard, the forward section to port. He could see the insides of the aft portion of the ship, the deck below, people inside, being tossed like dice on a crap table, but their bodies tumbling in slow motion.

Ahead of him he could see several people on the deck, bouncing slowly as they hit. A woman in a short silk skirt slammed into the side of a bulkhead, her legs flying, her head hitting the wall. Blood burst out and something else, something gray and oozing—her brain. She came to rest with one hand smashed behind her back, her legs spread, one broken, and her head laid open against the wall, painting a pattern on what had been a white surface. Except what before had been a bulkhead, a vertical wall, was now seemingly below him, becoming a floor under him, as Pacino realized the ship was rolling.

All this time there hadn't been a sound, not until this very moment, when all the violent energy of the explosion hit his ears at once, as if someone had suddenly turned a firehose on each ear full force.

By then the aft hull had spun so far relative to Pacino's forward hull that he caught a glimpse of the blue of the hull paint, then where it turned black, then the scorched metal of what must have been the keel itself. But the instant after that the smoke rolled through the grisly field of Pacino's vision, the flames and rolling black clouds of smoke now pulling his horizon in close, and he could see no more than ten or twelve feet in any direction.

An instant later, finally, he smashed into the deck. The impact with the polished wood of the deck somehow kicked him back into normal time, with all the horror that came with it. Two bodies flew over him and smashed with ungodly force into the same bulkhead that the woman had hit, their broken bodies adding to the gore of her broken frame. Pacino skidded hard along the deck into the pileup, smashing his head into a rib cage. His vision became blurred, and a sickening feeling came to his stomach, not just from the horrible burning smell or the feel of three dead bodies, but at the motion of the hull sailing sideways. The deck was becoming a wall while the bulkhead was now solid beneath him, a new deck, but even that changed as the wood deck continued to roll over his head. Then he was staring up at the deck rail where he had stood not seconds before, the sky peeking out between gaps in the black smoke rolling up from the wreckage of the cruise ship. But even as Pacino stared up at the railing, he could see the sky moving in the spaces between the rails. The hull was rolling still, and the deck was tilting over so far as to become more of a ceiling. The sky disappeared from between the rails, only smoke visible, until there was a splash, the railing smashing into the sea.

For the railing to go into the water meant that the forward hull had rolled so far that it was completely capsizing. But if that were true, Pacino tried to reason, he should be underwater. Instinctively his lungs filled with a smoky breath of air, and as if in answer to his thought, a crashing wave of black seawater hit him like a fist. Underwater, the noise of the flames and explosions changed to a deeper bass. But there was something else going on with his ears—they were pounding on his skull. Pressure. He was being taken deep, and his ears were popping. He had to get out, a screaming voice in his head shrieked.

Holding his breath, he pumped his arms madly, kicking his feet, trying to get away from the bulkhead. As panic began to nibble at the edge of his thoughts, he felt the railing with his hands and the wood of the deck with his head, and without further thought he hand-over-handed the railing, kicking himself over it, knowing that if he failed to get on the other side of the railing the ship would take him down with it. He cleared the railing, swimming in darkness.

He realized his eyes were closed, and he forced

himself to open them. If he swam the wrong direction he would drown. By the way his ears had popped, he could be fifty or a hundred or 150 feet underwater by now, and the only thing that would save him would be a mad rush for the surface.

When he opened his eyes, he could see nothing. The effect of the darkness and the horrifying sounds of the rolling explosions in the deep was hideous, and he felt fear fighting the logical part of his thoughts, struggling for control.

Then the explosions came, lighting up the world around him in a frightful and eerie glow. Over to his left, just for an instant, he could see the giant hull of the ship sinking, upside down, the ripped portion amidships angled downward, the bow pointing mournfully up to the surface, and Pacino had the merest impression of the waves high overhead. The ship was so huge that the forward fragment of it was distant in the haze of the water, but he was looking far up at it, its exhaust stack pointed downward. He had to be two hundred feet deep, and the lit-up hull fifty feet to his left was sucking him downward. He didn't know what was worse—seeing that huge misshapen hull in the ghastly light of an explosion, seeing how frighteningly deep he was, or not seeing it when the light of the explosion went out as soon as it had come, a lightning flash.

Suddenly Pacino was as frightened as a child in the grip of a nightmare. He wanted to scream in fear, and his eyes felt odd, as if even under the seawater he was crying. It came to him then that this was how he would meet his end, this is how he would die. He had always wondered what the last moment would be like. And even though he had emergency-blown through thick ice from the crippled *Devilfish,* and escaped the broken hull of the *Seawolf,* and been pulled from the wreckage of the USS *Ronald Reagan* a week after crashing onto her deck in the flames of a fighter jet accident, he had never before felt a finality nagging at him as he did now. Suddenly he saw all the past scrapes with death, saw them for what they were, something that would make him tougher, and saw this for what it was—his end. With that thought a flaming rage burst out of him, and he made a decision, that he would live. He bit his lip until he could feel the blood, and he aimed for the surface and swam with every ounce of energy left in his frame.

He swam for where he could remember the waves being, pumping his legs, pulling his arms. The crushing force on his chest was intense, the depth squeezing him. His ears felt as if they'd ruptured from the explosions or the pressure. He swam upward for what seemed like several minutes, his air running out. He wondered if he was fighting the rush of downward water from the sinking of the ship, and whether he had gotten vertigo when the light of the underwater explosion had gone out, and was no longer swimming upward. The pressure should have eased on his lungs and ears by now, he thought. It would soon be too late to matter. He had perhaps only another sixty seconds of endurance left.

He swam, counting his strokes. Count to sixty, he commanded himself. Pumping his legs and arms, counting, he reached forty, then fifty, soon sixty, with no sign of getting close to the surface. He kept on, seventy, eighty, ninety. He was becoming exhausted. His legs could barely move, his arms were lead. He couldn't hold his head up. He tried to keep his eyes open, to find the surface, but there was nothing but blackness. And his air was out. He couldn't fight the impulse to breathe any longer, even though he knew he was underwater. He knew the second he took in water he'd panic and it would be over. But there was nothing more he could do.

All the anger of a few moments before had evaporated into his exhaustion. He felt as if he were ninety-eight years old, and with the physical fatigue came resignation. There was nothing he could do to save himself, and perhaps this was meant to be, this was his answer, his destiny.

He tried as hard as he could to stop it, but nothing helped. His body was on automatic now. His mouth opened and his lungs pulled, and water came crashing in. With it came a furious panic like nothing he'd ever experienced. He pumped his arms and legs, thrashing, mindless, blackness growing at the edges. The awful shrieking horror of the pain in his chest felt as if he were being ripped open by a giant rusted fishhook, but mercifully the part of his mind that felt pain was shrinking, receding. The black tunnel of his mind began to eat away at the light. Just like a television screen going dark and shrinking to a single point of light, so did his rational mind fade, the smallest kernel of it all that was left in a sea of blackness, until even the tiny light went slowly out, and miraculously he could hear voices, dimly at first, then louder, more distinctly, but the voices were not from this world—they were the voices of his father and Dick Donchez and the crew of his old *Devilfish* and the dead men from the *Seawolf,* but they weren't dead anymore, and he could see his father, see him as if he were standing right there in front of him, and he was young, as he was when Pacino was very small, and he looked so big, so tall, as he had when Pacino was a boy, and he wore a robe so dazzlingly white that it almost hurt Pacino's eyes.

He felt his father's arms go around him, his voice soothing, an inner peace arriving with his father's touch, Then there was a young and vigorous Dick Donchez on the other side of him, and they were walking with him and carrying him and he could hear himself saying his father's name and hear his father's laughter. He called Donchez's name and Dick laughed back, and it was then that he knew that he had arrived somewhere, that he had reached a destination, a better place, and the heaviness, the sadness, that he had carried with him for so many years since *Devilfish* went down was finally lifted.

22

Victoria Cronkite, who had been looking at the cruise ship while recording whatever came to her—knowing she would do a heavy edit back at the studio— suddenly stopped in midsentence as the water around the hull of the cruise ship strangely became blood-red. The red spread in a heartbeat to a ship length away from the vessel while Cronkite stared dumbstruck, her mind trying to make sense of the red ring. But as soon as the red came it vanished, and the sea around the ship erupted into a white explosion, as if a nuke had gone off under the hull. The water blasted upward in a huge jagged pattern surrounding the ship. The hull of the beautiful cruise ship became invisible for a split second, and then visible again but surrounded on all sides by a ball of violent orange flames. The fireball rose in a huge mushroom cloud, the black top of it rolling slowly up to where their helicopter was.

It was then that she heard the sound of a cannon firing in her ears, a deafening detonation that seemed to have made her hearing vanish. It was replaced by a rushing noise that drowned out the chopping of the rotors, like a river rapids, but even more violent.

The helicopter jumped forty feet in the air and then sank a hundred, rocking violently. Cronkite ripped the Mickey Mouse ears off and stared out the window, trying to see over Doug's camera. There below them the *Princess Dragon* was barely visible in the smoke and flames, but Cronkite could make out the hull ripping in half, the bow rolling to the left, the stern to the right and capsizing, but where blue hull should be only a scorched jagged blackness. The stern soon vanished into the water. The surface was now covered with flames from fuel or the remains of the burning explosion. The bow section took longer to go under, the stack exploding, then the superstructure continuing to roll until the hull appeared, also black and scorched, but this part of the ship sinking much faster.

"Did you keep the camera on that?" Her voice sounded barely audible in the noise of the chopper and the rolling explosions, now calming slowly, but her hearing was half lost.

"I got it all!" Doug shouted. "Do a real-time commentary! We'll be live with the tape rolling. Give me fifteen seconds."

Cronkite looked out over the boiling sea where a cruise ship bigger than one of the World Trade Center towers had exploded and sunk in less than sixty seconds. But as she began to think about what to say, the warships escorting the task force to sea—all of which had turned quickly around to come to the rescue—exploded in the same sort of eerie sequence, Doug's camera capturing it all.

The explosions shook the bridge of the *Devilfish* a few seconds after the blinding flash erupted from where the cruise ship had been.

Captain Karen Petri was looking aft, trying to see if the aircraft carrier was leaving Hampton Roads, when the first flash lit up the sky behind her. Its glow reflected off the masts and antennae reaching out of the sail. The exclamations of the officer of the deck and lookouts were drowned out by the shock wave, a pulsing roar strong enough to be felt deep in the chest. Before Petri's stunned eyes the cruise ship disappeared in a fireball that ascended to the sky. When the smoke of the mushroom cloud cleared after some minutes, the ship could again be seen, but it looked nothing like it had before the explosion. Petri's jaw dropped as the giant ship broke in half and capsized so fast that within a few seconds it seemed to be pulled under as if by a clawing hand from the deep.

She was about to order the ship to close the distance to the dying vessel, to see if they could help the survivors, when the destroyers exploded, one after the other. The same roaring sound wave knocked them against the bridge coaming, coming in a double hammer blow, and mushroom clouds marked the former positions of the destroyers. The only thing recognizable in Petri's binoculars was the transom name of the second ship in line, the block letters spelling USS TOM CLANCY, visible for a split second before the stern vanished in the cloud of black smoke. When the smoke cleared, there was nothing left.

"I have the conn. All ahead flank!" Petri said on instinct, grabbing the bridge-box microphone out of Dietz's hand and yelling into it. "Mark the bearing to the cruise ship."

"Bearing one zero five," the navigator's shaking voice said.

"Helm, Captain, steer one zero five," Petri commanded. The clearing smoke at the bearing to the cruise ship was some two thousand yards ahead, a nautical mile. She would be there in two minutes at thirty knots.

Up ahead, the massive profile of the USS *Admiral Hyman Rickover* could be seen as it turned to render assistance. As it came around to the west, the flash burned Petri's eyes as it too exploded into a spectacular fireball and began to sink.

Dietz stared open-mouthed at the grisly scenario. Petri didn't know what force had allowed her head to be clear while those of the men around her were in fog, but she prayed a silent prayer of thanks, and drove the ship on toward the wreckage of the *Princess Dragon*.

Fleet Admiral Richard O'Shaughnessy, the Chairman of the Joint Chiefs of Staff, looked up at the supersonic bomber high overhead. The aircraft had flown in to Andrews Air Force Base for his inspection. General Nick Nickers, U.S. Army, and Air Force chief General Paul Gugliamo stood next to O'Shaughnessy, proudly explaining the significance of the jet. They were about to escort him onboard when four Lincoln staff trucks came roaring down the strip toward them, all of them flat black with flashing beacons on top.

Nickers craned his neck to look, his eyebrows rising over his aviators sunglasses. Gugliamo stepped out in front of the other general officers, trying to find out what was going on. The trucks were going at least a hundred miles an hour down the runway, only braking at the last minute, skidding to a halt just in front of the bomber. Before the trucks stopped, the doors of all four opened and commandos rushed out, machine guns in their hands, bandoleers of grenades on their fatigues. The commander held a MAC-12 machine pistol in one hand, an Uzi in the other. The three officers were surrounded by the commandos within one second of the trucks' arrival.

"Code seven," was all the commando leader said, seizing O'Shaughnessy by the arm and hurling him into one of the trucks. The older officer banged his shoulder on one of the other commandos entering from the other side. Four doors slammed and the wheels screeched as they accelerated. The other officers were in two other trucks, each going a different direction. O'Shaughnessy removed his cap and glared at the commando in the front seat.

"What's going on?"

"Security code seven is all I'm authorized to report, Admiral, until we have you in the NMCC bunker."

Code seven meant little to the JCS chief, who knew it only as a dimly recalled security emergency involving the top ranks of the military, a contingency plan practiced in earnest by the security troops charged with the physical security of general officers, but scoffed at by the general officers themselves, men who had fought wars and feared no terrorists' bullets. O'Shaughnessy waited, his lips narrowed in a furious grimace, until the truck came to a halt at a Sea Serpent CH-88D command helicopter. The black-clad commandos hustled him into the chopper. The rotors throttled up, and the wheels came off the pavement even before the hatch shut.

"What's going on?" O'Shaughnessy asked one of his captors. The senior man, a Navy commander, produced a WritePad computer. A few clicks of the software admitted the admiral to the SNN website, where a video clip was playing in one window as text news scrolled next to it, another window showing a news reporter speaking about the tragedy at sea. O'Shaughnessy froze as the images played on the screen.

"So this is why you grabbed me."

"We're not sure how widespread the attack is, sir," the commander said. "But anyone over the rank of brigadier general is assumed to be a target and brought to the code one point of security. We're taking you to the Crystal City bunker outside of D.C."

"No. I'm not going to any bunker. Take me to the Pentagon."

"Sorry, Admiral, that's impossible. Washington is not a good place to be right now. The Pentagon is considered unsecure, sir. With an attack like this on the senior officers of the Navy, we must presume the Pentagon is a secondary target. It's been evacuated except for NMCC and a Joint Special Warfare guard team, and the flag is being shifted to the NorVa Bunker, the underground National Military Command Center in Crystal City."

"Goddammit, I said no. If the Pentagon is ruled

out, take me to the White House, and don't give me any more nonsense, Commander, or I'll fly this chopper myself. You read me?" O'Shaughnessy hadn't had to throw his weight around since the Battle of Iran, and felt out of practice, but the maneuver worked.

"Major! You heard the admiral! White House South Lawn, now!"

The aircraft banked steeply as the Marine pilot flew them north toward the Beltway. There was relative silence in the aircraft for a few moments, until O'Shaughnessy addressed the SEAL commander again.

"What's the status of informing the President about this?"

"Secretary of War Masters was with her when this happened, sir. The press secretary came in and informed them."

O'Shaughnessy was silent for a moment, watching the awful replay of the sinking of the *Princess Dragon*. Men, his men, were dying right before his eyes, one of them his own son-in-law, and he thought about his daughter, Colleen.

"I wonder how she's taking the news," O'-Shaughnessy said aloud. The commander shook his head, thinking the admiral was speaking about President Warner.

The hearing room was huge and intimidating. A long horseshoe-shaped elevated table faced the witness table. The high-backed leather chairs were occupied by the senior senators and representatives of the Armed Services Committee, listening while she read her statement about the Cyclops Battlespace Control System, now into its fortieth page.

Colleen Pacino paused to take a sip of water while the committee chairman, National Party Senator Arlen Ridge of Pennsylvania, held up a hand to her. A Navy lieutenant aide had hurried into the room to whisper into Ridge's ear. Colleen Pacino cocked her head, staring at the exchange, beginning to think it looked serious. Ridge was glancing at her in between staring at his table while the aide spoke. The aide put a WritePad down in front of Ridge, who looked at it for a moment, his skin going ashen.

"Um, we're going to adjourn for the day," Ridge said, his voice oddly elevated. "Ms. Pacino, could I speak to you, please?"

The room was emptying around her as she made her way to the table, the aides and congressmen filing out.

"Colleen, it's about your husband," Ridge said quietly, turning the screen of the WritePad facedown on the table.

Colleen O'Shaughnessy Pacino, raised by a Seal officer and as tough as her father had ever been, by his own admission, gave Ridge an iron-hard look.

"Let me see the screen," she said in a low, threatening tone, the same voice her father would have used on a disobedient subordinate.

"Colleen, I think it best if—"

"Give me the computer."

Ridge slid it over to her, his lined face grandfatherly as he watched her expression change, silent tears flooding her eyes and spilling onto her face, her fist pressed to her mouth.

"Oh my God," was all she could say, her voice trembling.

Midshipman Third Class Anthony Pacino slouched in one of the seats in Michelson Hall's "Yankee Stadium," the bowl-shaped room half full of third class midshipmen, newly advanced from plebes when the seniors, the firsties, graduated a few weeks before. The briefing was being held on the upcoming third class cruise, this contingent of the U.S. Naval Academy class of 2021 going to the Mediterranean aboard the surface ships of the Unified Surface Command. Pacino's group would be airlifted to the USS *George Washington,* a nuclear aircraft carrier on deployment with the Fifth Surface Action Group.

As the lieutenant commander droned on about the logistics of the cruise, Pacino slouched even farther into the seat, his eyes half shut, boredom and lack of sleep making the briefing unbearable. The evening before had been one of the first times that young Pacino had been granted liberty in the town of Annapolis, having been under restriction since six weeks before, thanks to his failing conduct grades. It wasn't that he had done one terrible thing, but a whole range of them. He'd gone "over the wall" with a group of his classmates during Dead Week before finals, a common experience in which midshipmen would disregard the regulations and make an escape to town, where a diner named Chick's stayed open all night catering to such adventures. And although the experience of escaping the walls of the Academy was common, it was also a Class-A offense, serious enough to merit being considered for dismissal. Pacino had quoted John Paul Jones as he got his friends together, saying, "Gentlemen, he who will not risk cannot win," and they'd donned jeans and gone out the basement locker-room window.

They'd had a large Chick's breakfast at three in the morning, relishing the feeling of forbidden freedom, then attempted to sneak back into the Academy, but Pacino had had the bad fortune of rushing by Admiral Murphy himself, the commanding admiral—the Superintendent—out walking his Dalmatian during the wee hours, obviously suffering from insomnia. Pacino, trapped, had slowed to a walk, trying to maintain his composure, and said, "Good evening, sir," as if strolling the grounds at three in the morning was normal. But by then it was too late. Pacino's face, with its shadow of his famous father's countenance, coupled with his frequent rubs with authority, made him immediately recognizable—in addition to the fact that Murphy and Pacino's father went way back to their own Annapolis days. Despite the fact that the admiral was a family friend, Pacino was keenly aware that his father had given instructions that young Pacino was to receive no favoritism. For just a second, Pacino wondered if the old man would simply let him go, but then Murphy ordered him to halt. The recrimination, however, didn't come, as the older man chatted amiably with him for a moment, talking about the puppy. Pacino even sank to one knee and petted the dog while getting his face licked. He said good-bye to the admiral, shaking the Supe's hand, then hurrying back to Bancroft Hall, thinking he'd been given grace and finally scraped by without being punished, that Murphy had given him amnesty—that is, until he found three first-class midshipmen, seniors, in his room, all of them wearing bathrobes and dark expressions of anger.

"You're class-A'd, Pacino," the company commander had snarled at him, putting him back on restriction. The punishment had finally come to an end yesterday at noon, allowing Pacino to go out legally into town, where he sat at Riordan's, ordered a Harp, and talked with his friends until the delicious blonde sat down next to him. Her name was Helen, and she seemed interested in him, even kissing him as they parted at closing time. The memory of her kiss and her face drifted lazily across Pacino's mind as the excruciating briefing rolled slowly on in the hot academic hall, luring him closer to an in-class nap.

Pacino's features were soft and feminine, his lips full and perfectly shaped, his face graced with his father's prominent cheekbones, but his mother's softer nose and elegant blue eyes. He had even inherited her lighter hair, which was straight and longer than Navy regulations allowed. He was taller than average, yet nowhere near the towering height of his father. He was barely aware of the room around him when he felt the hand of an officer on his shoulder. Startled and guilty, he sat up immediately in his seat, wishing he'd been more vigilant. Sleeping during a military briefing was punishable

by several weeks of restriction, which during cruise
would be harsh, restricting him to the ship while
the others went on liberty in the foreign ports. He
couldn't believe that he was in trouble yet *again,*
the horrible thought coming to him that he could
well be approaching the last straw.

"Mister Pacino," the lieutenant said. Pacino
gulped. At the Academy, first class midshipmen
were like gods, and officers like this lieutenant were
celestial beings. "The Superintendent wants to see
you. Now."

This was it. Pacino's mediocre grades and military conduct failures were catching up to him, he
thought. Not even his father would be able to help
him now, and what would Dad say when he heard
that his son had been dismissed from Annapolis?
Pacino followed the lieutenant out of the room,
being stared at by the others, while a Marine Corps
second lieutenant whispered in the ear of the
briefing officer, but Pacino barely noticed. The walk
to Leahy Hall seemed to take forever, the tropical-
white-clad lieutenant grim, the march seeming like
a trip to the gallows.

The Superintendent's office was on the first floor,
occupying most of the building. A cherry-paneled
outer office was busy with aides and secretaries.
Pacino was too anxious to notice much until the
huge wooden doors opened and he found himself in
the room with Vice Admiral Sean Murphy. Pacino
walked in slowly, his shoulders slumped, his heart
racing, wondering how he would explain this to his
father. He looked up at Murphy's face, the lines at
the admiral's eyes crinkling into crow's-feet. The

old man's expression was gentle, however, and perhaps a little sad. Could it be that Murphy was going to ask him to leave? Pacino felt the contents of his stomach turn in anxiety. Murphy emerged from behind a desk the size of a small boat and clapped him on the shoulder, his dry hand shaking Pacino's. Pacino stared into Murphy's dull blue eyes, confused.

"Sit down, son," Murphy's hoarse voice said.

"Yessir," Pacino said, his knees bending, sitting on the front three inches of the chair, the seat barely taking his weight. Murphy leaned against the overhang of the desk.

"I'm afraid I have some hard news for you, Anthony. The stand-down cruise ship your father was on has been attacked. Some kind of terrorist thing, we think, and the TV news is saying there were no survivors. We may have to face the fact that your dad is dead. I'm so sorry, son, I'm so sorry. . . ."

But Anthony Michael Pacino couldn't hear the words anymore. Tears began streaking down his cheeks, his head in his hands, the sounds of someone crying the only sound, Pacino realizing dully that the sound was coming from him.

23

"All stop," Petri commanded. The submarine glided slowly to a halt in the sea. Around them the water was on fire and the smoke from the flames made it almost impossible to breathe.

"Break out the OBA's," she commanded the officer of the deck. Oxygen breathing apparatus rigs were rubber lungs with chemical oxygen generators, which when lit off would fill with oxygen. It was a lightweight alternative to carrying heavy scuba-type air packs for firefighting. "Rig for surface and open all hatches. Get the deck manned. I'm calling 'man overboard' until we've picked up every body floating out here."

"Yes, ma'am," Dietz muttered.

"And we *will* recover every single casualty onboard, is that clear?"

"Yes, ma'am."

"And Dietz?"

"Ma'am?"

"Snap the fuck out of it. Get hold of yourself. We've got a job to do."

Over the next hour, the deck crew, wearing OBAs over life vests and safety harnesses, pulled in one dead body after another. Some of them were horribly mangled; some looked as if they were only sleeping. As they were pulled up on the hull, the medic, Chief Corpsman Richard Keiths, examined them to see if they were alive. He listened to their chests, peered into their eyes, and occasionally looked up at the sail, shaking his head. A news helicopter flew overhead, filming the scene, the only noise other than the shouting on deck. A second and third chopper joined them, then two Coast Guard cutters and three V-55 Sea Witch search-and-rescue tiltrotor aircraft. The coasties concentrated on the destroyer and cruiser graves while *Devilfish* completed the harvest of bodies from the cruise ship.

Petri slowly drove the ship in decreasing-radius circles, pulling the bodies from the ocean. The pitifully small number of them put a lump in her throat. There had been over thirteen hundred senior and midgrade officers on board the *Princess Dragon* when she went down, over forty admirals, and they had pulled less than a hundred casualties from the flaming seas. Of those pulled up onto the hull, only nineteen were clinging to life, and those had been hoisted aboard the tiltrotors for medevac to Portsmouth Naval Hospital. The dead were carried below. Eventually, the wind picked up and the fires died down, along with the smoke, leaving only an acrid stench and acres of floating debris, but no more corpses. Finally Petri ordered the deck rigged for dive, and the body-laden ship turned around to return to Norfolk.

As if in a nightmare, she lowered herself down the bridge hatch, walking over the deck plates of the upper level to the crew's mess. The tables were unbolted and cleared away, the bodies in blankets on the deck, the room a makeshift morgue. The burning smell invaded her nostrils, making her want to choke. She bent to one knee at each body and uncovered the corpse, trying to see if she could identify any of them. One by one she undraped them. The third corpse made her gasp—the boss, Admiral Phillips himself, his face gray, a deep gash across his throat half decapitating him. The fourth body was another admiral, still in uniform, the nametag reading PAUL WHITE. The next was someone looking vaguely familiar, a man whose lower body had been blown off—Vice Admiral David "Sugar" Kane, the former captain of the *Phoenix*. The admirals must have been on the promenade deck, Petri figured, accounting for the high body count of brass they'd recovered.

Petri slowly covered Kane's face and lifted the blanket off another corpse, and found herself staring at the tanned, lifeless face of the Chief of Naval Operations, Admiral Michael Pacino. Or, she corrected herself, the former Chief of Naval Operations. She reached her hand out to touch his forehead tenderly as if taking the temperature of a beloved child, wondering who had done this evil.

The man who had been Michael Pacino was surrounded by a light, a whiteness so bright that it should have made his eyes ache, but instead it was a beautiful glow. A strangely familiar feeling of warmth and joy coursed through him as he looked at his father and Richard Donchez. But they stopped smiling at him as if something serious had occurred to them at the same time. Without opening his mouth to speak, his father addressed him.

Son, you have to go back.

"No," Pacino said. "I can't. I'll never go back. I want to be here. With you and Dick. I want to be in this place."

It is not your time, my son. And there are things you have to do.

"No, Dad, there's nothing more to do. I've done everything I could."

No, my son.

The new, bright, joyful world evaporated instantly.

Obviously, it had just been a dream all along.

Commander Karen Petri's hand touched the flesh of Admiral Pacino's forehead, and to her astonishment it was warm. An eyelid of the corpse twitched, just slightly but definitely.

"Corpsman!" Petri shouted. "Chief Keiths! One of the men is alive! Get an ambu kit in here now!"

Keiths leaped from the door on the other side of the passageway, a bag in his hand. Petri was already sprinting to the control room.

Within five minutes, a Coast Guard search-and-rescue V-55 tiltrotor hovered over the hull of the *Devilfish,* pulling up one last figure in a full body sling. The wings rotated to the full horizontal as the aircraft picked up speed, accelerating toward Norfolk Naval Air Station.

Katrina Murphy was forty-six and looked fifteen years younger. Her blond hair was wavy and long,

and her body was toned from constant workouts.
Her sky-blue eyes swept across the entranceway as
Sean opened the door and limped into the foyer,
barely able to stand on his own. She rushed to him
and held him up. He pointed at his study adjacent
to the hallway, and she pulled him in and gently
put him down on his favorite leather chair, then
rushed to get him some water. When she returned,
he was sweating. She pulled off his jacket and loos-
ened his tie.

"Thanks," he said.

"How's Tony?"

"He took the news hard," Murphy said in his
gravelly voice. "Hell, we all did. Patch was the hub
of the Navy. Without him I don't know where I'd
be. In a Chinese prison somewhere, or an un-
marked Beijing grave. I can't believe he's gone."

She rubbed his back for several moments, and
when she stopped she realized he'd fallen asleep.
After summoning the help and having them put
him to bed, she went into the den to watch the
news reports, the channels all covering the sinking
of the *Princess Dragon*. She was busy thanking
heaven that Sean hadn't gone to sea on the doomed
cruise ship when the front doorbell rang. She let
one of the stewards get it. Probably a delivery, she
thought. But then her steward led in a big man
with a handlebar mustache. He wore an Army uniform with five stars on his epaulettes and a nametag
reading NICKERS. He pulled off his hat, stuck it
under his arm, introduced himself, and spoke
slowly.

"Ma'am, I'm here to take Admiral Murphy to

the White House. He's now the acting Chief of Naval Operations, and the President wants him there now."

"He won't be going," Katrina said. "Find someone else."

Nickers stared at her. "Um, ma'am, the next-highest-ranking naval officer in active duty is only a captain."

"Fine," Katrina said. "Tell the President she can promote that guy. Sean's staying here. He's too sick to be—"

In the entranceway Murphy appeared, wearing his service dress khakis, weaving slightly on his feet as he leaned on a cane.

"Let's go, General," he said.

"Sean!"

"Warner needs me," he said. "And I'll be back in a few hours."

General Nickers grabbed Murphy's briefcase and walked the admiral to the Army staff car, looking over his shoulder at the admiral's quarters.

"You said something inaccurate back there," he said.

"What do you mean, General?"

"Nick. Call me Nick. You said you'd be back in a few hours. You won't. Admiral, we are at war with whoever did this act of terrorism on the high seas. You're the Chief of Naval Operations now, and you're running the show."

Murphy nodded, slowly sinking into the back-seat. As the limo rolled, he glanced at the house, where Katrina could be seen peering through the window.

"Tell me again why you failed to shoot the American SSNX submarine."

Novskoyy's voice was harsh and accusing, but his eyes were expressionless and black.

"Oh, the hell with you, Novskoyy," Grachev said, smiling, his tone light. "This was not a 'failure' and you know it. I printed this down for you after the last time you asked that question."

Grachev slid his handheld computer across his stateroom table to Novskoyy. Novskoyy didn't look at it but kept glaring at Grachev. Grachev moved over and picked up the computer and put it right in front of Novskoyy's eyes, undaunted by the consultant's attitude. "As you can plainly *see* here, Novskoyy, this is a shot pulled down from Shchuka sensor four. You do remember we shot the Shchuka, don't you?"

"Go on, Captain," Novskoyy said.

"The large oblong object in the right lower portion of the screen is us. We're very photogenic, don't you think? But good God, we do stand out. The contrast is startling, even to the naked human eye, without a computer enhancement. If someone with acoustic daylight imaging had been looking, we would have been in hot water."

Novskoyy dropped his eyes to the table.

"Ah-hah!" Grachev grinned. "You *are* listening. So, if you can listen, perhaps you can reason, too, even if you are a consultant. And if you can reason, maybe you can agree with me what would happen if the SSNX—with its acoustic daylight imaging capability—were to happen by, mad as hell and spoiling for a fight. Would it be your consulting opinion that perhaps it was wise to sneak out of the bay while the SSNX was picking up survivors?"

"Captain, you had a perfect opportunity while the sub was in the middle of the explosions, with her sonar gear half deaf from plasma blasts. Four, five wake-homing Berkut torpedoes, or half as many Bora IIs, and the SSNX would be dust on the sea. Instead you devoted your energies to sneaking away like a thief in the night." Novskoyy's voice was resigned, tired.

Grachev clapped the older man on the shoulder. "Good, glad you finally see things my way. We will set up on the SSNX as it leaves Port Norfolk, which it is bound to do any time—"

"Why do you think that, sir?" Svyatoslov asked.

"Because, Mr. First, the remainder of the American Navy's leadership—probably some retired admirals reactivated or whoever couldn't make the cruise trip because of a death in the family or gall bladder surgery—now suspect a submarine attack. They'll send the SSNX out to find us."

"Maybe," Svyatoslov said. "Maybe they'll send her with some 688 Improved subs and a group of sub-hunting destroyers and helicopters."

"Maybe an armada. Mr. First, Mr. Novskoyy, I'm going to get some sleep," Grachev said, almost jovially. "If you'll excuse me, gentlemen."

The men walked out. Grachev got undressed and climbed under his bedsheets as Monday, July 23, became Tuesday, July 24. He stared at the overhead in the dark room for some time. Tomorrow, or even in the next hours, the American vengeance would come, righteous and furious and deadly.

He would have to command the ship beyond her limits, because the SSNX submarine was coming after him, of that he could be sure. In the next few days one of them would be sent to the bottom of the sea.

Grachev yawned, stretched, and shut his eyes. His breathing became slow and deep as he fell into a dreamless sleep.

BOOK V

VaCapes

24

Jonathan George S. Patton IV had been awake for forty-six hours by the time the V-44 Bullfrog tiltrotor vertical-takeoff turboprop landed in his front yard, waking his startled neighbors. Patton hung up his WritePad videophone with one hand and grabbed his bag with the other. Outside the front door, the huge rotors of the aircraft barely slowed. The wind of the great machine whipped the trees, even making his truck bounce on its shocks. Marcy was looking at him, half angry and half afraid.

"I know you have to go," she shouted against the hurricane wind of the rotors, her hair blowing into her face. "But please be careful. You are all I have."

Patton looked at her, his expression hard, but a lump forming in his throat, knowing her words would echo in his mind until the next time he saw her. He frowned harder, the carved planes of his face even more harsh, his diesel-oil-black hair blowing in the wind as he put his cap on, the scrambled-egg brim low over his eyes.

"Good-bye, honey," he said, unable to say more, knowing his voice would crack. "I'll call you."

Lame parting words, he knew, but she would understand. By then he was ten steps out the door, grabbing his officer's cap as it almost flew off his head, running for the airplane.

The three men inside, all wearing crash helmets, waved salutes at him and pulled him in.

"Good morning, Admiral!" one called.

It sounded strange to Patton's ears, that it was morning—after 2 a.m.—and that the crewman had called him 'Admiral' when he was a mere captain, the four gold braid stripes on the shoulderboards of his service dress khaki uniform jacket proof that he was far short of being an admiral. He nodded to the men and took a seat as the aircraft lifted off vertically, then trembled violently as the wings tilted level, then climbed to the southwest. As the Connecticut coastline faded behind them, Patton's WritePad's annunciator alarm beeped. He opened up the software and paged his way in.

```
240658ZJUL2018
IMMEDIATE
FM          COM NAV PERS COM, WASHINGTON,
            DC
TO          J.G.S. PATTON IV, CAPTAIN, U.S. NAVY
SUBJ        OFFICIAL ORDERS
UNCLASS
//BT//
```

1. (U) REPORT IMMEDIATELY FOR DUTY USUB-COM HEADQUARTERS NORFOLK VA AND AS-SUME PERMANENT COMMAND OF UNIFIED SUBMARINE COMMAND.

2. (U) YOU ARE HEREBY FROCKED TO THE RANK OF 0–8 REAR ADMIRAL. PERMANENT RANK TO FOLLOW PENDING CONGRES-SIONAL CONFIRMATION.

3. (U) CONGRATULATIONS. FAIR WINDS AND
   FOLLOWING SEAS.
4. (U) CAPTAIN C.B. MCDONNE, USNR, SENDS.
   //BT//

So, Patton thought, the V-44 crew knew.

"Sir," the pilot called from the cockpit. "Admiral Murphy sent this." He handed back a brown interoffice envelope.

When Patton opened it, an envelope fell out along with two shoulderboards, both of them gold overlaid with gold braid anchors and two stars. Inside the envelope were two collar emblems—silver double stars—and a note, which read, *John, sorry you made flag rank without the party or the photographer or the brass band, but never has our nation been so in need of your talent and especially your courage. I'm deeply honored to have you as my commander of the Unified Submarine Command. And now we have work to do. I will meet you at your new headquarters. Sean Murphy, CNO.*

So that's how it happens, he thought glumly. The goal of a lifetime, the position he'd wanted since he was a midshipman at the Academy, and when it came, he got it by default, by the death of literally everyone who outranked him.

But if the way he had attained the rank and station of ComUSubCom was depressing, his feelings about it were drowned out by his grief at the disaster at sea yesterday afternoon. The entire brass, all of them gone, including his mentor, Michael Pacino, and his rival, Bruce Phillips, his friends, and comrades of the battles of the past five years.

Patton had been made famous in the Japanese blockade as captain of the submarine USS *Tucson* when he had counterattacked the Japanese submarine wolfpack that had just torpedoed the USS *Lincoln* carrier battle group. Two of the enemy subs sank and the third popped to the surface, quiet and inert. Patton's sudden idea to board the surfaced Japanese Destiny nuclear submarine had led to his fame as his officer of the deck filmed him boarding from the periscope camera, his acetylene torch cutting into the hatch, his face a mask of anger as he stepped into the enemy sub with a MAC–11 automatic machine pistol in one hand. That film clip had played worldwide, the Navy's logo practically changing to Patton in his at-sea coveralls with the American flag patches on the sleeves as he forced his way into the Destiny. A photo landed on the cover of *Time Newsfile* with the title DAGGER-IN-THE-TEETH COURAGE: CDR. JOHN PATTON.

He'd gone from *Tucson* to the USS *Annapolis,* one of the newest and most recently modernized 688I submarines, screening the armada invasion force heading to the coast of White China on the day after Red China jumped across the line in a full-scale war. The *Annapolis* had taken a near hit from a plasma torpedo, and he should have been consigned to a watery grave with the rest of his crew, but Senior Chief Byron DeMeers had found him and pulled him out of the vessel, and he and DeMeers had floated in a life raft. Again, the press had made him an icon for courage incarnate after he took command of the USS *Devilfish* and pressed the assault against the Red Chinese subs.

He had gone on from the victory in the East China Sea to be put in charge of the Navy's NSSN program, the new attack submarine transitioning from the prototype SSNX to the production run of the class, beginning with SSN-780, the USS *Virginia.*

And now here he was, on the way to his new headquarters, his first duty to avenge the deaths of his comrades. So be it, he thought.

The pilot turned around and looked at him snapping on his new shoulderboards.

"Looks good, Admiral. Looks like you've always worn them." He smiled. "We got you something for the occasion, sir. After the *Princess Dragon* went down, we were going to use this at our memorial service, but I think it would be better luck if I gave it to you to celebrate your stars."

He handed back a bottle of Jack Daniel's. Patton stared at it for a moment, the obvious coming to him.

"Hand me back some cups—paper, plastic, thermos cups, whatever," Patton said. The copilot handed back a stack of conical paper cups from the bulkhead-mounted water cooler, looking at Patton as if he'd gone mad.

"Drink up, everybody," Patton said, his voice clipped and harsh as he poured four generous measures of the bourbon for the flight crew and himself. "A toast, gentlemen. To our operation to find the bastards who sank *Princess Dragon.* May they burn in hell for eternity."

The flight crew took the cups but looked at him sheepishly.

"Um, sir, we can't drink this in flight. You know that."

"Why not?" Patton demanded, an odd confidence blowing into his soul.

"Well, for starters, Navy Regs."

"Fuck Navy Regs," Patton said. "Admiral's orders. Bottoms up."

"Aye aye, sir," the copilot said. "To the sinking of the bastards who sank *Princess Dragon.*"

"Hear, hear." The copilot and flight engineer tipped their cups, then, shaking his head, the pilot.

Patton downed the bourbon, balling the cup up and tossing it in the corner, then dropping the bottle next to his briefcase. He leaned against the window and shut his eyes, knowing he needed to sleep, even if it was for just an hour. As he began to feel himself drift off, he thought he heard the pilot say something to the copilot.

"Can you believe that? Drinking in flight?"

The copilot answered immediately.

"You heard the admiral. Fuck the Regs. That's why they call him Blood and Guts Patton. Ballsiest fucking naval officer since Nelson himself walked the earth. I feel sorry for those bastards who plugged the cruise ship. They don't know who the hell they're dealing with. But they will soon."

"I think you're right," the pilot said. "Washington Center, this is Navy Foxtrot Zero Two at flight level three three zero," he continued, official business returning to the cockpit.

And John Patton, Rear Admiral, United States Navy, Commander Unified Submarine Command, smiled for the first time in a month as he fell into a deep sleep.

25

Lieutenant Commander Karen Petri walked down the passageway of the headquarters building of the Unified Submarine Command as fast as she could, trying to remain dignified. She was dressed in service dress whites, the uniform with a highly starched tunic with huge gold buttons and a high choker collar. Her shoulderboards bore two broad gold stripes with a narrow gold stripe in between. Her left breast was adorned with full medals, her Battle of Iran Expeditionary Medal the highest-ranking of those she'd earned in her World War III service as executive officer on the *Port Royal*. But even more vital to her was the gold pin above the row of medals, the submariner's dolphins. Beneath the tunic, which narrowed at her waist and came down below her hips, was the black leather belt of her officers' sword, only the hook and straps coming out a small slit on the left side. The hook held the black sheath of the sword, the scabbard facing rearward, the handle pointing forward.

She had been delayed by the 0800 colors ceremony, the slow raising of the American flag while the bugle blared into the postdawn sunshine. The huge flag had gone to the top of the mast and then descended to half-mast. The nation was mourning the loss of the *Princess Dragon* and the accompanying task force. The flag of the Unified Submarine Command joined the Stars and Stripes at half-mast. The USubCom emblem was a Jolly Roger pirate flag, its skull leering dangerously above crossed bones, the Gothic script above reading "Deep Silent Fast Deadly" and below that "Unified Submarine Command," the flag rumored to have been designed personally by former CNO and past ComUSubCom, Michael Pacino, the man who'd been transferred to Portsmouth Naval Hospital from the deck of the *Devilfish* yesterday afternoon.

When the bugle stopped, Petri dropped her salute, wondering if this would be the last time she'd salute the American flag in the uniform of a naval officer. This morning's session was likely to take away her submarine dolphins and her sword for dismally failing at her duty to protect the surface ships from a subsurface threat. Odds were she would walk out of the headquarters building a civilian.

Finally she arrived at the massive oak door of conference room one on the zero deck of the HQ building. A quick check of her watch showed it to be 0807, July 24, almost thirteen minutes late. Her orders had required her to be here before eight so that the new admirals could arrive after her. For some reason, even though she knew her career was already over, her lateness distressed her, making her feel that she lacked competence even in these small details. Last night, after *Devilfish* had come in and tossed over the lines, the investigation crew from HQ had arrived, demanding computer records of the attack, downloading the files from the Cyclops battlecontrol computer, taking her officers into rooms and interviewing them under video cameras as if they were police suspects.

She had left the ship at one in the morning, arriving home to her empty suburban two-story house. Taped to her front door was a note in Kelly McKee's handwriting, reading, *Karen, Please call me as soon as you get home, Kelly,* but she was too exhausted and figured that the note had been there for hours and McKee was probably long asleep by now. She had sat watching the news forlornly, the coverage of the *Princess Dragon*'s sinking captured by a news helicopter. Finally she stopped torturing herself and went to sleep, alternately too hot and too cold, the sheets twisting over her sweat-soaked body.

She knocked three times on the door, and a peeved voice called, "Come." The voice sounded familiar. When she cracked the door open, she began to understand why. Inside the room was a green-felt-covered T-shaped table. Two men rose when she came in. The one on the left was a grizzled older blond-haired admiral she didn't know. A brass name plate in front of his seat read ADM. S. MURPHY CNO. The man on the right was the one whose voice was familiar, John Patton. Patton was no longer a commander, or even a four-striper, but now wore the two stars of flag rank, and his brass name plate read REAR ADM. J. PATTON COMUSUBCOM. Patton had obviously been put into Bruce Phillips' chair.

The green table's end, covered with a felt tablecloth just as legend had it when an officer's sword was to be broken, had a single wood witness chair.

"Board of Inquiry number two zero one eight tack zero one two is now in session, Admirals Murphy and Patton standing in judgment," the older admiral said as he banged a gavel. His voice was sickly, sounding much more gentle than Patton's had, which, she thought, might be an even worse sign than Patton's harshness.

"Raise your right hand," Admiral Patton commanded, his voice a hammer blow. He continued, swearing her in. She repeated the oath, her stomach flooding with bile, her mouth tasting like battery acid.

"Be seated, Commander," Murphy said. "Please state your name and position for the record."

She took off her cap and unstrapped her sword, keeping it on her lap. She stared at the men and the lens of the video camera between them and said, "Karen Elizabeth Petri, lieutenant commander, United States Navy, acting commanding officer of the SSNX-class submarine USS *Devilfish,* hull number SSNX-1." She was amazed that her voice was level, with just a trace of a tremor that probably only she could hear.

All hope vanished as Patton spat out a single question: "What happened out there?"

Over the next twenty minutes she gave her statement, the words flowing as if she had rehearsed for days, even though she had scarcely devoted an instant's thought to what she'd say at this moment. Her story continued to the point she'd found Pacino alive, to his medevac and the docking of the *Devilfish* in port that night.

When she finished, Murphy ordered them all to stand. "Board of Inquiry is hereby concluded," he said, banging his gavel.

"Commander," Patton said, "please wait outside for a few minutes."

Petri put her cap on, strapped on her sword, and saluted the admirals, stepping to the door and shutting it behind her.

In the passageway there was an uncomfortable wood bench. Petri ignored it, pacing the hallway as the low voices inside the hearing room buzzed. *Just get this over with,* Petri thought, *so I can get started with a new life and put this nightmare behind me.*

"Your recommendation, Admiral?" Murphy asked, leaning back in his chair.

"There was nothing she could do, sir," Patton said, in his clipped habitual speech pattern. "You saw the display readouts yourself. There was nothing there. The Cyclops didn't detect anything above threshold. Neither did the operators, and they were all at max alertness—the audio tapes showed that—and the OOD and Petri were as on their game as we could ever expect. Sir, she runs the tightest ship I've ever seen, maybe too tight. Her crew love her, they'd walk through fire for her, and she and McKee trained them better than any captain I've ever known. I heard about Petri months ago, and it's all true. We can't trash her, Admiral. Other than Kelly McKee himself, she's the best there is."

"What about that anomaly by the Bay Bridge-

Tunnel? The spot on the acoustic daylight record? A possible submarine?"

"I saw it, sir. Admiral, I've spent hours at the VR consoles of the Cyclops—that was my ship once—and I can tell you, a return like that could come from a rock or a piece of construction debris from the cofferdams the marine construction company left on the bottom. And there were no rotating machinery sounds, barely even a thermal trace. Could it have been a diesel boat hiding in the silt? Maybe. But the task force went down miles and miles away from the bridge. I'm guessing they were hit by mobile mines, which could have been laid days or weeks before and floated, just waiting for the task force. And you saw the Cyclops output at the sinking scene."

Patton grimaced. The acoustic daylight showed the sinking broken hull of the cruise ship in extreme detail as it plunged to the bottom in three major pieces, the stack sheering off as the hull went deeper and became lost in the bottom.

"They were alone. There wasn't a soul out there with them. Whatever took down that task force, it wasn't something the *Devilfish* could have stopped. Petri's clean, sir."

"I agree." Murphy looked out the window for a moment. "What do you think of the FBI Counterterrorist Group's theory?"

"Haven't heard it."

"I'll send you an e-mail. They suggested a bomb planted by terrorists."

"Of course. They're the counterterrorist squad. Keeps them in business."

"The case does seem compelling."

"No, it doesn't," Patton said. "We sweep the underhulls of ships for bombs before they leave. All four of those ships were examined by divers within minutes of their departure, and to get a bomb under a hull while the ship is moving would take a diver-propelled vehicle that *Devilfish* would have seen."

"So, maybe the bombs were placed in the bilges or voids in the frames from the inside."

"Bullshit. The ships were tied up at the Navy base under the highest security. The cruise ship was swept for weapons, also immediately before departure. We need to remember the explosives were plasma. No way a terrorist got on four or five plasma warheads without leaving a wide swath."

"So what was it? A torpedo attack?"

"More likely mobile mines. Very tough to detect. They don't move, they linger on the bottom, a ship sails by, and they pop up and stick to the hull."

"Well, wouldn't that be detected by the *Devilfish*?"

"Maybe. Probably. Or maybe not. Hell, sir, I don't know. Obviously nothing showed up on the Cyclops system. But my best guess is still mobile mines."

"So why didn't *Devilfish* go down?"

"Two possible reasons. She's got a sharkskin anechoic antisonar coating. Nothing sticks to it, not even barnacles. A mobile mine would fall back to the bottom, even an electromagnetic one."

"True. What's the other reason?"

"*Devilfish* would have seen a close mobile mine

or the launch platform. These mines might even have been set before the SSNX rounded the bend into Thimble Shoals."

Murphy considered Patton's statement. "Okay. I'll buy it. But will the President?"

"There's only one man who's ever had her ear. Pacino."

"I'll talk to her. But meanwhile, what happens now?"

"If you accept my recommendation, I'm sending Petri and *Devilfish* back to sea, to the Virginia Capes Op Area to do a full Cyclops scan. I'll leave her out there in VaCapes for a month if I have to, but I'll wager my dolphins she won't find anything."

"Are you putting *Devilfish* to sea with Petri in command, or are you going to talk to McKee about coming back?"

"I went to his house early this morning, sir, after we left the O-club." They'd parted at the front porch of the officers' club at five in the morning after drinking coffee and getting acquainted for a few hours, discussing their options for the actions they'd need to do in the upcoming days and weeks.

"You did? What did he say?"

"He said he's out of the Navy. Said Petri's *Devilfish*'s skipper now, and he'll never go back to sea, not even on a sailboat. He's finished. He all but threw his sword at me when I left."

"Poor bastard," Murphy said. "Did you read about what happened to him?"

"Yessir. He looks pretty bad, Admiral, hadn't

shaved or cut his hair in a month, eyes bloodshot. I think he was half drunk at four in the morning."

"I'll stop by after I see Patch Pacino," Murphy said.

"Leave him alone, Admiral. He needs time."

Murphy nodded, then turned the conversation back to the VaCapes sanitation mission. "Any other assets we've got that can help *Devilfish* in the VaCapes?"

"I took a look at that, sir. It comes down to acoustic daylight imaging, and short of the Virginia-class NSSN, the only ship in the fleet with the capability is *Devilfish*. If we supplement her with the Yo-Yo remote acoustic daylight sensors, she'll be able to cover the entire VaCapes by herself, limited only by her computer processing and the endurance of the crew."

"What about the *Virginia*?" Murphy asked. "How close is she to being able to sail?"

Patton lit up, as if he had been asked to talk about his child. "Her mechanicals are done with the exception of ship-alts on the port torpedo tube banks and a problem with the turbine rotor on the port main engine that's been repaired—so she's got two large hull cuts being sealed up. Her computer's in and tested with the old software, the latest SSNX version from the old Cyclops system aboard the *Devilfish*, but putting her to sea like that would be like making you wear your son's clothes—they keep you covered but they don't fit. And you'd look funny." Murphy snorted at that. "The *Virginia*'s computer system is supposed to be miles ahead of SSNX's, a revolutionary approach to a three-

dimensional display of the battlespace, using a downlink from the Predator unmanned aerial vehicle and
the Yo-Yo acoustic daylight pods—the ones
dropped by P-5 Pegasus patrol planes—a satellite
downlink from the CombatStar satellite, with wire
inputs from the Mark 8 and Mark 5 Sharkeye systems and the new Mark 23 Bloodhound unmanned
underwater vehicle. The software integrates everything in real time—all of it—and displays it for the
crew in a virtual-reality system allowing them to
'fly' around the battlespace. It's so real that most
test subjects threw up from motion sickness when
they emerged from virtual reality. We thought we
had it fixed, we loaded it aboard, and it performed
beautifully until it came to running the Doberman
ATT system and downlinking the CombatStar and
Yo-Yo acoustic pod inputs. Those two modules
failed miserably—we offloaded both subroutines
for more debugging."

"ATT? Doberman?"

"Mark 17 antitorpedo torpedo ATT system,
called the Doberman, I guess, because it's an attack
dog for incoming torpedoes. The counterfire solution for situations where we get shot at by an
enemy sub. Right now only a hell of a computer
can guide the unit, and no onboard computer has
the processing speed or power to handle the job.
It's like trying to knock down a bullet with another
bullet, and even the technology from the antiballis-
tic missile systems didn't work—they've had to start
with a clean sheet of paper. Besides which, the old
SSNX version of Cyclops isn't up to the task of the

Doberman's guidance processor. So the computer system is flawed."

"That's it? The NSSN is ready to go to sea with a slightly degraded combat system except for closing some hull cuts?"

"Well, there is one other problem. It has only the precommissioning crew and no weapons, because the computer problems are expected to take a year or more to debug. If I had a week I could button up her hull cuts and put her in the water with the amputated software, her precommissioning crew—a bunch of kids without any training—some Vortex Mod Delta missiles, and a few Alert/Acute torpedoes, but that would be reckless. Why take the risks when I've got *Devilfish* sitting in Norfolk with a hot reactor and an operational battlecontrol system and a crack crew?"

"Just asking, John." Murphy stood, painfully slowly, pushing on his cane. Patton tried to help him, but the CNO waved him off. "I'm going to Portsmouth Naval Hospital to check on Patch, then up to the White House to brief Warner, then back to the Pentagon."

"What's the latest on Patch Pacino, sir?"

Murphy shook his head. "There's a possibility he's brain-dead."

"Damned shame, sir. I owe that guy my life."

"Me too, John, me too." Murphy clapped him on the shoulder. "I'll send your respects. Call me tonight."

Murphy limped out of the door, seeing Lieutenant Commander Karen Petri standing off to the side, staring at him. On impulse he walked slowly up to her and took her hand. "Good luck out there, Commander," he said gently, shaking her hand as hard as he could, then turning to walk to the VIP portal. Petri stared after him, astonished.

When she turned she saw Admiral Patton looking at her.

"Sir?" she said.

"Get back to *Devilfish*," Patton said, his voice as clipped as it had been inside the chamber. "There will be an op order waiting for you. You'll be doing a max-scan search in the VaCapes Op Area for any possible submarine intruder that might be out there, and for any possible waiting mine systems. We'll be supplementing you with Mark 12 Yo-Yo pods from P-5 Pegasus patrol planes. I want that area scoured, sifted, searched, sanitized, and sealed, and I want *you* to be the one to do it. Got it?"

Petri frowned at him, at rigid attention. "Yes, sir. Aye-aye, sir."

Patton nodded, frowning back. "Dismissed."

She saluted and watched him turn and hurry for the elevator bank. For a moment Petri felt like asking him what the official verdict had been, but realized it would have been a stupid question. She was five steps down the hall when she heard Patton's pointed voice behind her.

"And, Petri, one more thing."

She turned to face him. "Yes, Admiral?"

"On the way to your ship, stop by the uniform shop and buy yourself some full commander's shoulderboards. And a capital ship command pin. You're *Devilfish*'s permanent skipper. Sorry we can't have a change-of-command ceremony for you.

There's not much time these days for pomp and circumstance." His voice had become as gentle as it had been all day, yet still sounded somewhat acidic. Perhaps that's just how he was, Petri thought.

"Aye-aye, sir. Thank you, sir," she said, but Patton was already twenty steps away and around the corner.

26

"Attention all hands," Commander Karen Petri's voice boomed on the Circuit One PA system throughout the decks of the USS *Devilfish*. It was tied up to pier 27 with singled-up lines, shore power disconnected, and the reactor critical. The maneuvering watches were stationed and the deck crew was ready to uncoil the heavy lines from the cleats so that *Devilfish* could get underway in accordance with Op Order 2018-0724-TS-001, which had been downloaded to Petri's WritePad, and which read:

```
241537ZJUL2018
IMMEDIATE
FM         COMUSUBCOM, NORFORK VA
TO         USS DEVILFISH SSNX-1
SUBJ       OPORDER 2018-0724-TS-001
COPY       CNO, WASHINGTON DC
           COMUSURFCOM, NORFOLK VA
           COMUAIRCOM, NORFOLK VA
           SURFACE TASK FORCE 2018-07-02
TOP SECRET
//BT//
1. (C) USS DEVILFISH AUTHORIZED UNDERWAY
   1600Z, 1100 EDT.
2. (S) USS DEVILFISH TO SUBMERGE ASAP AT
```

EXIT THIMBLE SHOAL CHANNEL PER LITTO-
RAL WARFARE ATTACK PLAN 2017-1202 WITH
NO LESS THAN TWO (2) FATHOMS UNDER
KEEL.

3. (TS) FIRST MISSION PRIORITY IS SANITIZA-
TION OF NEAR WATERS OF NORFOLK HAR-
BOR FROM ANY HOSTILE SUBMERGED
CONTACT, SEARCH AREA TO INCLUDE ELIZA-
BETH RIVER, THIMBLE SHOAL CHANNEL,
NORFOLK TRAFFIC SEPARATION SCHEME,
WORKING OUTWARD TOWARD LIMITS OF VA-
CAPES OPAREA AS DELINEATED IN COMU-
SUBCOM OPPLAN 2200 REV 4 DATED 11/22/17.

4. (S) AREAS DESCRIBED IN PARA 3 ABOVE WILL
BE CLEARED OF SURFACE TRAFFIC BY SUR-
FACE TASK FORCE 2018-07-02 WITH MER-
CHANT AND NAVY SHIPPING HELD INSIDE
NORFOLK OPERATING BASE, LITTLE CREEK
AMPHIB BASE AND FIVE (5) MILES OUTSIDE
EASTERN BOUNDARY OF NORFOLK TRAFFIC
SEPARATION SCHEME.

5. (TS) RULES OF ENGAGEMENT: UPON DETEC-
TION OF ANY HOSTILE CONTACT, USS DEVIL-
FISH AUTHORIZED ANY REASONABLE
EMPLOYMENT OF SHIP'S WEAPONS AT DIS-
CRETION OF COMMANDING OFFICER TO DE-
STROY HOSTILE CONTACT.

6. (TS) UPON ENCOUNTER HOSTILE TRAFFIC
AND PRIOR TO ENGAGEMENT, USS DEVIL-
FISH MAY POP SLOT BUOY SIGNAL NUMBER
ONE (1) PER COMUSUBCON OPPLAN 2200
SAME REVISION. UPON COMPLETION OF EN-
GAGEMENT USS DEVILFISH SHALL CONTACT
COMUSUBCOM BY MOST EXPEDITIOUS MEANS

WITH SITREP TO FOLLOW. IN THE EVENT NO
HOSTILE TARGETS DETECTED, USS DEVIL-
FISH SHALL REPORT BY SLOT BUOY SITREP
AT TWELVE (12) HOUR INTERVALS.
7. (C) REMAIN UNDETECTED.
8. (C) GOOD HUNTING AND GODSPEED, KAREN.
9. (U) ADMIRAL J.G.S. PATTON IV SENDS.
//BT//

Weapons release would be at the discretion of
the commanding officer? Petri thought in wonder.
That was as much a blank check as a submarine
commander would ever get. She had never expected to see that in print. She stood on the periscope stand of the control room, the microphone
of the Circuit One coiling into the overhead above
the captain's plot table at the forward quadrant of
the railed-in platform. She continued with her
speech.

"As each of you knows, yesterday the cruise ship
Princess Dragon was destroyed a few miles outside
of Norfolk Harbor right under our noses. We never
saw anything coming, and that fact prompted the
board of inquiry each of us suffered yesterday."
And this morning, she thought. "As you may have
suspected, *Devilfish* has been given a clean bill of
health following the board of inquiry. We are being
sent to the shallow waters of Norfolk to screen and
sanitize the area from any possible threat, to see if
whatever sank *Princess Dragon* is still lurking there.
All watchstanders are to assume that as of right
now, this ship is at war." Petri paused to let that
sink in. "If we find a hostile contact, the rules of

engagement authorize us to shoot. And shoot we will. I expect every watchstander aboard to be at maximum readiness. We will be tossing over the lines in five minutes, and *Devilfish* will not be returning home until we have put whoever shot down *Princess Dragon* on the bottom." Again she paused. "A final note, crew. As of this morning I have been promoted to full commander and handed permanent command of the *Devilfish*. My only regret is that Kelly McKee has decided to leave the Navy. I want you all to know that I am deeply proud to go to sea with each one of you and to be your commanding officer. I propose we dedicate this run to Commander Kelly McKee and sail back home with an enemy submarine silhouette painted on our sail. That is all. Carry on."

On the bridge, Lieutenant Commander Bryan Dietz heard the speech coming over his headphones and whistled to himself. He glanced at Junior Officer of the Deck Toasty O'Neal. "Holy smokes. A wartime op order, Toasty," Dietz said. "You may see some action this run, youngster."

"Status of the Azov?" Captain Grachev called from the command console of the control compartment of the submarine *Vepr* some 165 kilometers to the southeast of Norfolk. The ship was resting on a rocky outcropping of Nags Head Majoris Ridge at a depth of 428 meters, a few kilometers from where the continental shelf plummeted deep to the Atlantic floor. The location of the bottoming was far enough from the Norfolk traffic-separation scheme to keep them out of sensor range of the SSNX

submarine, while being close enough that the exit
of Port Norfolk was at the extreme edge of the
range circle of the Bora II antisubmarine torpedoes, provided they were launched in low-speed
transit mode at shallow depth to maximize their
range.

The Azov that Grachev referred to was one of
four 53-centimeter canisters in the forward vertical
launch system tubes housing the Azov unmanned
aerial vehicle, a modified cruise missile that could
overfly a target area and downlink aerial intelligence. Its advantages were obvious—the ability to
acquire over-the-horizon targeting information
without relying on expensive and unreliable satellites. Its disadvantages were more subtle—a detected Azov could lead to *Vepr* being detected, or
at least the confirmation that a hostile submarine
was in the area, causing a massive antisubmarine
warfare hunt.

"Azov number one is warmed up now," Svyatoslov reported. "The datalink self-check is satisfactory. Request you raise the Antay pod."

"Nav, raise the Antay pod," Grachev ordered.
Far aft, the elongated teardrop-shaped pod detached from the top of the rudder and began to
float to the surface. A few moments later it penetrated the waves and looked skyward. Then it deployed the extremely high frequency radio
transmitter and receiver to uplink to and downlink
from the Azov. There would be two separate EHF
frequencies for uplink and downlink, so both tasks
could happen at once. The Azov's intelligence data
would be beamed down to the Antay pod's EHF

receiver antenna, and from there to the cable sinking to the deep, almost 450 meters straight down to the rudder of the *Vepr* and into the ship's command compartment, to be read by the sensor computer modules of the Second Captain.

"Antay's up," Navigator Tenukha reported from the sensor station aft. "We've got data. Partly cloudy topside, no aircraft in visual range."

"EHF antenna rigged out?"

"Antay camera shows a good rig-out, sir."

"Program readback from the number one Azov?"

"Number one Azov shows the initial flyout at being zero four zero with a shallow climbout angle of ten degrees until it reaches seven thousand meters, when it will turn west until it overflies Norfolk, then turns and does a pace pattern over the Chesapeake Bay and Hampton Roads."

"Mr. First," Grachev said into his headset. He was standing behind the command seat of his command console, too excited to sit. "Launch Azov unit one when you are ready."

Svyatoslov had manned sensor cubicle two in the aft starboard corner of the room. The cubicle was a cube one and a half meters on a side, not even big enough to stand in, but with the VR goggles on, reclined on a leather couch, Svyatoslov had no complaints. His vision was black, he was completely blind, but soon the Azov would be in the sky, giving him a virtual-reality look down at the world.

"Tube one coming open, Captain," Svyatoslov said into his boom mike. "Tube one membrane remains sealed. Gas generator arming sequence enabled, Second Captain has the countdown, request command enable now."

"Command enable entered," Grachev replied, keying in his password to his console, giving Svyatoslov and the Second Captain his permission to launch the Azov.

"Sir, system has captain's enable. Arming circuit in auto. Countdown to three, two, one, and *fire*!"

Thirty meters forward of the control compartment, at the base of vertical launch tube one, which was in the forward frames of the ballast tank, gas generator number one ignited. The gas generator was a small charge of solid rocket fuel ducted to a distilled-water reservoir. As the generator's charge lit off, the hot exhaust gases spewed into the reservoir, almost instantly vaporizing the water to high-temperature steam, suddenly pressurizing the bottom of the tube. The only thing between the steam and freedom was a heavy canister in the cylinder of the tube. Like the gases of an artillery shell at the breech of a cannon, the high-energy steam pushed hard on the bottom of the obstructing canister. Some of the steam escaped around the body of the waterproof casing and pressurized a plastic membrane stretched across the muzzle of the tube, rupturing it violently with steam that blew upward. Meanwhile the pressure at the bottom of the tube put four million Newtons of force on the bottom of the cylindrical missile canister, making it no different from a youngster's spitwad in a straw. The canister gathered speed quickly, taking less than a second to go from stationary in the snug tube to a hundred kilometers per hour out the muzzle of the tube. The canister slowed slightly as it rose—not in seawater, but in a massive bubble of escaping steam. The steam bubble began to cool in the deep water until it finally broached the surface above.

Halfway out of the water, the flanks of the canister were exposed to the morning sunlight. The canister's top blew off, the explosive bolts rupturing, and under the force of a small booster rocket charge, similar to the charges in a fighter jet's ejection seat, a canister within the canister blasted out and into the air. As the inner canister blew upward, it ruptured along twelve score lines. Explosive bolts detonated and hurled the formerly waterproof can in pieces away from the structure beneath.

What remained after the canister blew apart resembled a cruise missile in the fins-stowed state. Two large mid-fuselage wings were folded into the body, and three fins were folded at the bottom near the rocket's nozzle. After the canister surfaces fell away, the engine of the rocket ignited. The solid rocket fuel sent the rocket straight up for a distance of twenty meters as the nozzle gained control of the missile's attitude, then pitched the unit over so that it began climbing skyward at a shallow angle of ten degrees. The missile's wings remained tucked under its body, but the aft control surfaces sprang outward, acting like the feathers of an arrow. The missile continued climbing, reaching an altitude of forty meters over the sea. The radio transmitter in the nose cone of the missile came alive, transmitting the EHF "all-nominal" signal down to the seawater-blue Antay pod floating unobtrusively on the

short choppy waves of the Atlantic. The missile's
EHF receiver listened for a reply from the Antay
pod's antenna, but for the next second nothing was
heard. After another full second of rocket-powered
flight, it still received nothing back from the Antay
pod's transmitter.

The unit climbed another fifty meters and tried
another downlink, with the same results. And three
failed downlink attempts automatically started the
unit's self-destruct sequence. It rotated the aft fins
so that it changed course downward toward the
water, still under the solid rocket motor's full
thrust. Within three seconds it impacted the surface
of the water with a small splash. Hitting the water
at a speed of five hundred clicks was equivalent to
smashing into solid concrete. The wings and airframe immediately disintegrated, while the rocket
motor sheared off and spun helplessly into the
depths, eventually sputtering out. As the missile
body sank, a second self-destruct sequence kicked
in. Several explosive charges around the mid-body
detonated after a time delay of thirty seconds, en-
suring that no salvage diver would dredge up the
Azov. Within a few seconds after the completion
of the self-destruct sequence, little was left of the
unit bigger than a shoe box.

"What the hell happened?" Grachev demanded.

"Checking now, Captain," Svyatoslov reported
from sensor cubicle two. "We never had a downlink from the unit. Failure mode is either in the
EHF downlink or the uplink. If it's the downlink,
we can launch a second Azov and have a satisfac-

tory deployment. If it's the uplink, we could be out of luck."

"Goddamn," Grachev cursed. "Line up missile two. And for God's sake, Navigator, dammit, check the software switch lineup to the Antay pod and the EHF antenna. Let's go!"

"Yes, sir," Svyatoslov said. Grachev's outbursts were as familiar as the feel of his worn at-sea shoes. "Second Captain lining up tube two. Azov unit two self-check is satisfactory, unit airframe and propulsion system readbacks nominal, navigation flight plan readback nominal. We're ready for launch, sir."

"Fine, dammit. Navigator, report the damn status of the Antay pod."

"Same as before, Captain," Tenukha called. "Unit confirmed on the surface. Unit camera shows full rig-out of the EHF antenna. All circuits are showing full connectivity. We have continuity, Captain."

"I can see you are all scratching your heads over this," Grachev said, glaring briefly at Novskoyy, who stood next to the command console. "I want everyone to check their switch lineups, software switch lineups, self-check readbacks, and continuity checks. Go over it again. Now. Mr. First, report!"

The same report came back to Grachev as a few moments before. There was nothing he could do but launch a second ten-million-Euro Azov, without having found the flaw that blew up the first unit. The second unit could experience the same problem.

"Second Captain has the countdown, ten seconds, request command enable, sir."

"Command enable code entered," Grachev said again.

"And enable indicated at three, two, one, *fire!*"

Tube two's muzzle door opened, the membrane still sealing the cylindrical tube below.

Seconds later the number two gas generator ignited, the steam pressure blasting the canister out of the tube up into the depths of the sea. The canister rose to the surface, and the inner canister was blown skyward and exploded as the first one had. The missile rocket motor ignited, the fins snapped out, and the unit climbed to fifty meters and transmitted an all-nominal signal to the Antay EHF antenna below.

There was no reply. Another attempt at downlink, met once again with silence. A third unsuccessful attempt, and the missile dived for the sea.

Four hundred meters below, Captain Second Rank Pavel Grachev ripped off his headset and threw it to the deck.

The bridge cockpit, atop the sail of the USS *Devilfish,* was breezy in the wind of their fifteen-knot passage, and the sun, high overhead, was warming the air to the eighties. Salt spray climbed up the sail from the bow wave below as the bulbous nose of the submarine burrowed into the water. Inside the small cockpit of the leaned-back Russian-style teardrop shaped sail stood Bryan Dietz and Toasty O'Neal, and behind them, sitting up on the high coaming of the cockpit, was Captain Petri, wearing working khakis with a light khaki jacket, Ray·Bans covering her eyes, her binoculars around her neck. Petri felt a freedom she hadn't experienced in years. The vibrations of the ship beneath her climbed her spine and warmed her spirit, even if this was a wartime mission, or perhaps because it was.

The bridge communication box and the three officers' headsets squawked with Kiethan Judison's Houston accent: "Mark the turn to course zero eight five!"

"Helm, Bridge, right full rudder, steady course zero eight five," Toasty O'Neal called on his boom microphone as Dietz watched him.

Devilfish made the turn into the start of Thimble Shoals Channel. The buoys on either side made it look like a runway as the ship steamed down the seaway.

"What happened this time?"

"Captain, we've got the same answers as last time," Svyatoslov reported.

"Here's what we're going to do. Navigator, shut down the Antay pod, button it up, and pull it back down to the rudder and make sure it latches."

"But Captain—"

"Shut up, Mr. First. Navigator, execute!"

"Yessir, Antay pod shutdown sequence start, and the EHF antenna indicates rig-in. Antay door is shut, unit is rigged for full submergence. Cable reel is hot and rolling, Antay pod has departed the surface and coming down. Two minutes to stowed and latched position. Do you want me to call out cable length, sir?"

"Belay your reports, Nav," Grachev said, his eyes on his auxiliary readouts.

Eventually the pod came down to the top of the rudder and was captured, the system latching the pod to the rudder post.

"Antay pod stowed and latched, Captain."

"Very good," Grachev said. "Navigator, deploy the Antay pod to the surface."

"What are you doing?" Novskoyy asked.

"When in doubt, line up the systems again from scratch and push the button. If it doesn't work, we're into Plan B, which means we go into the bay shooting."

"That's a suicide mission at this point," Novskoyy mumbled quietly.

"Bingo, Al," Grachev said, equally quietly. "Your flair for the obvious rises to the surface once again." Then he practically screamed, "Navigator, your report, dammit!"

Fifteen minutes later, the Antay pod was again floating on the surface, the top hatch open, the ELF antenna protruding into the sun-drenched sea air.

"Captain," the navigator said. "Antay pod's on the surface, antenna door is open. Pod camera shows EHF antenna rigged out, EHF downlink and uplink continuity sat."

"Very good. Do an EHF transmit/receive test."

"Executing. We're getting reception of the transmitted signal, but that doesn't prove much, sir."

"Mr. First, you ready to ride a third time?"

"Yes, Captain."

"Good. Cross your fingers and launch Azov unit three, tube three, when you're ready. Command enable entered."

"Yes, sir, and Second Captain has the countdown at ten seconds. Five seconds, fingers crossed, sir, and two, one, *fire!*"

Azov unit three was blown out of the ship, rising in the cloud of steam. As twice before, the inner canister hurtled skyward and blew apart, and the folded winged missile started its rocket engine and climbed vertically for a fraction of a second as it arced over to its shallow climb angle. The downlink transmission to the Antay pod hit the ELF antenna, and this time the antenna returned the signal with a radio check uplink. The central processor of the unit was satisfied, and it continued the rocket-powered climb at a shallow angle.

"We got it! Unit three is airborne, all-nominal signal received! We have downlink, Captain!" the navigator reported.

A quick cheer rose up in the control compartment. Grachev growled, "Mr. First, you have a camera view?"

"Yes, Captain. I'm flying back here."

In the sensor cubicle, strapped into the leather couch, Svyatoslov had ordered the couch to rotate until he was hanging suspended in it, facing the deck. Had he taken off his virtual-reality goggles, he would have seen the eggshell-shaped black felt contour of the cubicle under the seat, along with the seat-mounting pedestal, not twenty centimeters from his face. That was a rather uninteresting sight, but with the VR goggles, Mykhailo Svyatoslov was flying as if he were riding the missile. The sea flashed below him in a rush of speed. The horizon extended with every meter of height the rocket gained. At the moment there was not much to see but ocean, but at the horizon on the left he began to see the first hint of a shoreline.

As the rocket thrust withered, the missile began to free-fall. Then the small jet engine aboard lit off, the wind of the missile's passage windmilling the compressor vanes and pressurizing the central combustion chamber annulus with high-temperature air that flowed aft through the windmilling turbine out the exhaust port. The rocket motor farther aft shut down, and sixteen explosive bolts detonated and jettisoned the rocket booster. The unit tumbled away, eventually making a small white splash on the surface of the sea far below.

Fuel was then injected into the combustion chamber and several spark plugs energized, igniting the fuel-air mixture and sending the temperatures and pressures in the combustion chamber soaring. The high-energy mix was ducted aft to the turbine, no longer freewheeling but zipping into high speed on its oiled journal bearings, driving the compressor at the nose end by a central shaft. As the turbine wound up, the shaft spun faster, spinning the compressor faster, sending combustion chamber pressures higher, until after another full second the jet engine was self-sustaining, and the thrust from the hot exhaust gases passed out the aft nozzle where the rocket booster had been.

The wings, up till now folded under the vehicle's belly, rotated outward. They looked fragile, like a glider's, but were constructed of a carbon-fiber composite full of radar-absorbing material. It took several seconds for the unit to stabilize its flight path with the wings deployed, but soon it was again flying arrow-straight, still climbing at a shallow ten-degree angle.

The Azov unmanned aerial vehicle continued climbing to the northeast on jet engine power, until it reached an altitude of seven thousand meters. High above the sea, it was able to look at the coastline of the United States far below. The unit turned to the west and began flying toward the mouth of the Chesapeake Bay and Hampton Roads.

High above the earth, Mykhailo Svyatoslov looked down on the beauty of the morning sun drenching the beaches of northern North Carolina and southern Virginia, the pointing finger of the Delaware-Maryland-Virginia peninsula jutting downward on the horizon, dim in the haze of distance, and he could clearly see the Chesapeake Bay Bridge-Tunnel extending across the mouth of the Chesapeake, the long line of it interrupted at the two tunnels where it dived under the surface to allow deep channels for deep-draft merchant ships and large naval vessels.

"Captain, still no contacts," Dietz reported. "Five miles from the Bay Bridge-Tunnel, ma'am."

"Off'sa'deck, bring her to all stop."

"Aye-aye, ma'am. Helm, Bridge, all stop. Sonar, Bridge, stopping."

"Bridge, Helm aye," the bridge communication box squawked.

"Bridge, Sonar aye," Cook said into their headsets.

The ship's bow wave calmed as 7,700 tons of nuclear submarine came to a halt in the middle of Thimble Shoals Channel.

"What's up, Skipper?" Dietz asked, looking at Petri with an odd look on his face.

She couldn't exactly say she had an odd feeling, so she put her binoculars up and scanned the horizon on all sides. "Tell sonar to conduct a multifrequency search, broadband, narrowband, acoustic daylight. Give them ten minutes."

"Aye, Captain," Dietz said, speaking into his boom mike.

Petri jumped down from the ledge of the top of the sail and joined the two officers in the cockpit. She picked up the WritePad chart computer, the display the size of a poster, able to display the chart of the bay even in bright sunlight. She scanned the chart, stabbing her finger at a point ten miles away, then paged through the software to display a window superimposed over the chart, the tactical signals for the surface task force. She picked up the UHF tactical Nestor satellite secure voice radio handset, an old-fashioned telephone handset done in red plastic, a transmit button set in the middle of the grip. She called to the control room in her boom mike, "Radio, Captain, is Nestor aligned?"

The answer came back from "Mr. Clean" himself, Senior Chief Morgan Henry: "Nestor's up and freqs are aligned."

"Very well, Radio."

She pulled off her headset and put the red telephone to her ear and spoke. "November uniform, this is tango sierra, over."

The speaker of the handset crashed into loud static. Petri adjusted the volume knob on the red panel under the forward lip of the sail. The static changed into a bleating tone as the computer's encryption of the incoming voice activated, the signals delayed by the encryption and decryption.

"Tango sierra, this is November uniform flag, read you five by, over."

She had just heard from the commander of the Navy surface task force holding off all merchant traffic at Norfolk. The commander of the task force, a Navy commander freshly frocked from lieutenant commander five hours earlier in the aftermath of the decapitation of the Navy's senior ranks, reported to Petri, who not only commanded the submarine *Devilish* but the surface action group, at least until the ship transited into the Va-Capes OpArea.

"November uniform, this is tango sierra. Immediate execute, break, go to Seven Eleven and pick up a case of Twinkies, break, over."

There was no levity on the circuit in the task group commander's reply. "Roger, understand execute Seven Eleven trip for a case of Twinkies, break, November uniform out."

Petri had just ordered the task group commander to shepherd the merchant traffic farther out to a point labeled T for Twinkie, where they would be safe from the unit she was about to launch down the channel.

"Off'sa'deck, in five minutes load a Mark 5 Shark-eye into tube one."

"Sharkeye tube one, aye, Captain."

She'd decided to hold the ship here and fire the unit down the channel, where it would drop an acoustic daylight sensor to the bay bottom exactly where she wanted it, extending the range of the sensors.

Dietz made the orders, then looked at Petri. "Wouldn't it be more effective to drop a Mark 12 Yo-Yo pod from a Pegasus, ma'am?"

"Yes, OOD, but I'm saving the Yo-Yos for deeper water. For what I want, a Mark 5 will do."

They waited, the hull stationary in the channel center, while sonar searched the bay and the torpedo chief loaded tube one with a Mark 5.

Twenty thousand feet above Petri's head, a tiny aircraft flew over. It was an eighth the size of a Cessna single-engine plane, with a radar signature smaller than the return from a seagull. As the unit looked down on the ship there in the channel, the signal from it downlinked in a narrow EHF beam to a receiver far distant, where it was received on the antenna of a floating pod and sent down a fiber-optic cable four hundred meters to the nuclear sub-marine *Vepr,* where a dozen officers scanned the crisp photographs of the sub lying in the channel, a perfect and juicy target.

27

"Sir, Bora II torpedoes loaded in large-bore tubes one through four," Weapons Warrant Officer Lynski reported from his weapons-control cubicle.

"Very well," Grachev replied, still standing behind his command console instead of inside VR console zero on the starboard side. Somehow he just felt claustrophobic trussed up inside the egg-shaped VR cubicle. He wanted to stand on the deck of his submarine's control compartment, cross his arms, watch his displays, and pace the room if he wanted. Perhaps, he thought, he was carrying the genes of a square-rigged sailing vessel's captain, happier pacing the deck in the wind and weather than wedged into a submarine's battlecontrol system's booth. "Connect weapons in tubes one through four to the Second Captain weapons-control system."

"Aye, Captain, bringing units one through four on-line now."

"Weapons Officer, flood tubes one through four."

"Flooding, sir."

"Open muzzle doors one through four."

"Opening muzzle doors. All units on-line, sir. Target?"

"Feed it in from Second Captain's downlinked location of the SSNX submarine, designate as target one."

"Aye, Captain."

"Program units one through four for slow-speed, shallow-depth run on the Second Captain navigational waypoints." Grachev's aux two display showed the chart of their position at the lower right and the opening of the Chesapeake Bay, with Thimble Shoals Channel at the upper left. The depth of the water was indicated by color contour, and the SSNX's position was fed in from the Azov orbiting undetected seven thousand meters above the target.

"All units programmed, sir. Request command enable plasma warheads."

"Command enabling units one through four," Grachev said, glancing at Novskoyy and typing into his console the captain's passwords to unlock the plasma detonators for all weapons.

"Enable keys onboard units one through four, Captain."

"Very good." Grachev removed his headset and rubbed his eyes, turning to Novskoyy. "You happy now, Al? We'll drive the Boras in and blow the SSNX to iron filings on the bottom of the bay, then withdraw farther east."

"Fine, but your orders are to keep anything from coming off the U.S. East Coast. That surface task force has capabilities that worry me. And they might detect the torpedoes on their transit."

"As long as you're worrying, why not worry about dropping dead in your boots from a heart attack?" The consultant was hopeless, Grachev decided, strapping his headset back on.

Novskoyy ignored the comment. "And you need to devote a tube to deploying the remaining Shchuka sensor. We need to have acoustic daylight capability in case we're approached by someone with the same capability."

"Fat chance, Al. The only warship with that capability is about to go down." Grachev spoke into his boom mike. "Attention to orders. We'll be shooting four Bora plasma torpedoes into the Chesapeake to target the SSNX, target one. Once she goes down, we'll haul in the Antay, self-destruct the Azov, and withdraw to open ocean. Firing interval one minute, to keep each torpedo from getting confused by the wake in front of it. All stations, report status."

Thirty seconds later, all four Bora torpedoes were ready for launch. Grachev nodded to himself. "Weapons Officer, tube one launch when ready."

"Aye, Captain, Second Captain has the countdown. Ten seconds, sir."

Bora unit one lay snugly in the seawater-flooded monel torpedo tube amidships. The electrical system was alive with energy from the onboard fuel cell, and the onboard computer—a somewhat less advanced version of the *Vepr*'s Second Captain—was fully awake and waiting calmly for the launch order. The trajectory to the target was programmed in. The sailing directions called for the torpedo to climb at a thirty-degree angle as soon as the propulsor was at full revolutions, to a depth of twenty

meters, then slow down to transit speed, a mere
eighty clicks, and drive north to a point due east
of the Norfolk traffic separation scheme, then turn
west and proceed toward the target. By then the
sub was sure to have come out of the bay, where
future intelligence would allow the torpedo to deploy on target.

The onboard processor received the countdown,
which was ticking past three seconds to one, the
signal for the torpedo to start its engine. The pressurized peroxide fuel tank loaded a solenoid valve
that opened to the combustion chamber. The chamber's spark ignited the self-oxidizing fuel to several
thousand degrees. The violently expanding gases
were ducted to the turbine and from there to the
water exhaust valve and into the tube. As the
countdown clicked down to zero, the turbine had
spun up to just short of a hundred rotations per
minute; at the same time the unit felt the pressure
building up from the water in the aft part of the
tube. As the pressure soared, a ball valve rotated
aft, loading the water in the tube with water at
one hundred atmospheres greater pressure than the
water outside the muzzle door. The force of the
pressure accelerated the five-ton torpedo out the
tube and into the water. The control cable spooled
out of the propulsor shroud, the thin wire connecting the torpedo to the tube in case the ship's Second Captain wanted to update the torpedo on the
new location of the target. The structure of the
tube zipped by the forward camera sensors.

The turbine spun past its idling speed of twelve
hundred RPM and throttled up as the solenoid V-

ball valve opened farther. The turbine inlet temperature and pressure increased. The turbine spun its output shaft linked to the counterrotating propulsor vanes. The thrust built up, accelerating the torpedo past ten clicks to twenty, thirty, forty. The weapon sped up during the climbout of the deep on the way to its transit depth of twenty meters. Then the unit leveled off, its speed stabilizing at eighty clicks as it headed north.

The unit drove on like that for some time, only the waves rolling past overhead, the water too deep to detect the bottom below, with nothing on either side, alone in the sea with the exception of the thrumming of its propulsor vanes and the rush of water on its flanks.

"Unit one away, Captain," Lynski reported.

"Very good. Get on the interval, Weps."

"Yes, sir, we're ready for tube two."

Over the next three minutes tubes two, three, and four were fired. Their Bora II torpedoes were hurtling out into the sea, their wires linking them to the *Vepr* below while the units zoomed northward, the wire reels in the torpedo tubes spinning as kilometer after kilometer of wire paid out of each.

"Time to turn, Weps?"

"At a speed of eighty clicks, we have ninety minutes to wait, Captain. The units will then turn west and sail toward the mouth of the Chesapeake."

"I suppose that's the problem with sitting so far away. Watchstanders, we have a wait in front of us, so everyone settle down, but remain at max alert status."

Grachev took off his headset and pushed his sweaty hair off his forehead. He stood and looked at Novskoyy, who was staring at him.

"What?"

"Nothing," the older man said.

"Want some coffee while we wait, Al? I've got the best beans this side of South America."

Novskoyy smiled, revealing the even teeth of a younger man. "I would like that."

Grachev nodded and keyed his console, ringing the galley below.

"Tango sierra, this is november uniform flag, over."

Petri picked up the red handset. "November uniform flag, this is tango sierra, over."

"Twinkies purchased, over."

The surface task force had moved its merchant ships out of the way of the Mark 5 Sharkeye.

"Roger," Petri said. "Tango sierra is letting out the dog, over."

"Roger, understand, letting out the dog, november uniform out."

"OOD, launch the Mark 5," Petri ordered.

"Launch the Mark 5, aye, ma'am. Coordinator, Off'sa'deck, shoot tube one."

"Standby," came over Petri's headset from the executive officer, Paul Manderson, in charge in the attack center on the middle level.

"Shoot," the weapons officer, Dick Van Dyne, said.

"Fire," Dietz commanded.

Even here, high above the deck of the submarine, the violent launch of a torpedo tube could be heard and felt. Petri scanned the water of the channel to see if she could see the torpedo-mounted Mark 5 blasting out of the amidships torpedo bank and running down the channel, but there was nothing but the blue-green bay water.

"Tube one fired electrically," Van Dyne's voice reported.

"Bridge, Sonar, own ship's unit, normal launch," Senior Chief Henry called.

The Mark 5 Sharkeye sailed down the channel, heading out at thirty knots to the opening of the bay, to a point ten miles east of the Chesapeake Bay Bridge-Tunnel, where it would deploy the Sharkeye acoustic daylight pod. Until it reached its destination, Petri would keep the ship here in mid-channel. This search would be damn thorough. There would be no boards of investigation to accuse her of missing anything.

"What's the SSNX doing?" Grachev asked, sipping his coffee next to Novskoyy.

Aft, in VR sensor cubicle number two, Captain Second Rank Mykhailo Svyatoslov flew at seven thousand meters above the Chesapeake, looking down at the surface warships escorting the merchant vessels southward, the submarine still in mid-channel, stopped.

Svyatoslov selected high power in his binocular vision, making the gyrostabilized view below expand until he seemed to be hanging suspended from the sky fifty meters above the sail of the submarine. He could see the three khaki-clad officers on top of the fin talking to each other, bent over a chart, looking down the channel.

"Sir, nothing. It's just sitting there."

"That's odd," Grachev mused. "I would have expected it to come screaming out of the bay looking for us."

"They may think their ships were sunk by terrorist bombs loaded aboard before they sailed. Maybe the SSNX is having trouble."

"No. If the SSNX was having problems, there would be tugboats coming to help it. And there are no tugboats. Plus the surface merchant traffic is being kept out of the area. That's suspicious. And a surface warship task force. Hey, Mr. First, what's the surface ship order of battle?"

"One Aegis II-class cruiser, three Bush-class ASW destroyers, three fast frigates."

"No chopper carrier. The destroyers, they got helicopters on deck?"

"Yes, all three, but the rotors are stowed."

"Hmm. Still nothing doing with the SSNX?"

"No, sir."

"Weapons Officer, turn the four Bora units to heading three zero zero, northwest," Grachev ordered.

"Sir, they could run low on fuel," Lynski said, sounding uncertain.

"I'll turn them early. We're going to cut the corner instead of coming in due west."

"Why?" Novskoyy asked.

"I have a feeling that if these units get detected, we'll want the surface group and the SSNX to think the launching point was east-southeast instead of south. They'll probably launch a hundred counter-measures down the bearing line."

Novskoyy nodded.

The Mark 5 Sharkeye slowed as the onboard ring laser inertial package indicated it was nearing the target area. The propulsor spun down until the unit was at bare steerageway, controlling its direction as it approached the sandy bottom at a depth of twenty fathoms, 120 feet. The body of the torpedo angled upward as it continued to slow, finally landing on the sand of the bottom.

The nose section split open, and ten basketball-shaped hydrophone sensors floated out of the unit. Each of the spheres had a different preset buoy-ancy and weight. All were tied to the torpedo body below and to each other by thread-thin wires. In the next seconds the spheres rose in the warm water, coming to rest at different depths. The linked spheres formed a single acoustic daylight array scanning the near ocean, ten miles east of the mouth of the Chesapeake. As the array came on-line, it first reported the positions of the group of surface ships overhead and to the south. It looked west and saw the Bay Bridge pilings. And off to the southwest, four high-speed incoming torpedoes.

Dutifully the Mark 5 Sharkeye sensors fed the data to the torpedo body below, to the central processor, which emotionlessly reported the data down the fiber-optic wire back to the torpedo room of the stationary *Devilfish,* and from there to the Cyclops battlecontrol computer, which read out in the control room where Paul Manderson, the XO, stood watching a flat display panel acoustic daylight image readout, and to the bridge repeater on the forward lip of the sail, where Dietz, O'Neal, and Petri all saw the data cascade into the display at the same time.

"Torpedo in the water!" Dietz sputtered. "No, four of them, bearing one zero two, range twenty nautical miles! Captain!"

"I see it," Petri called, her voice eerily calm. "Call it, OOD, and get us out of the bay, ahead flank."

Dietz shouted into his boom microphone, "I have the conn, Helm, Bridge, all ahead flank! Steer course zero eight five. All spaces, Bridge, multiple torpedoes in the water!"

"Bridge, Helm, throttling up to flank. Steer course zero eight five, Bridge, Helm, aye, RPM passing one zero zero, steady course zero eight five, reactor power eight zero percent."

The ship began to move, slowly at first, the bow wave building up, the deck beginning to tremble with the power of sixty thousand horses at the shaft.

"Belay reports, Helm." Dietz turned to Petri. "Captain, shouldn't we be heading *into* the bay? We'll be driving into four torpedoes."

"I'll tell you why, OOD. Sonar, Captain, classify incoming torpedoes."

"Bridge, Sonar, torpedoes are Russian Republic Bora series weapons, with ducted water-jet propulsors, making way at approximately forty knots, range extremely distant, outside forty thousand yards but with very distinct up-Doppler, all units definitely inbound."

"Sonar, Captain, can you distinguish if they are Bora I or Bora II weapons?"

"Captain, Sonar, Bora II."

Petri looked at Dietz, whose eyes had grown wide. "We have four plasma-tipped torpedoes on the way in, OOD. If we turn around, they'll follow us into Port Norfolk. They could wipe out downtown if they detonated at the waterfront. We'll take *Devilfish* to open ocean, distract the torpedoes, and draw them north. Meanwhile we'll put out our own counterfire. But first, rig the bridge for dive. As soon as we're clear of the Bay Bridge, pull the plug—we're going down. Got it?"

"Yes, ma'am," Dietz said, his eyes glassy with shock.

"Down ladder!" Petri shouted, opening the grating to the bridge access tunnel and lowering herself quickly down the accessway to the upper level of the operations compartment.

28

"Here's a development," Svyatoslov said.

"Go ahead," Grachev said as he put down his empty coffee cup.

"ASW choppers on the destroyer decks are getting ready for takeoff. The surface formation is breaking up. They're heading away from the merchant ships."

Grachev leaned in to squint at display zero in the center of the command console. He rolled the close-up lever to bring the view closer to the deck of one of the destroyers, where a crew was deploying the aircraft. Grachev shifted the view to a second destroyer, where a helicopter was taking off, nosing down so the rotor circle tilted.

"Three choppers airborne," Svyatoslov said. "Surface group is starting to spread out. The cruiser is falling in line behind the destroyers."

"Frigates?"

"Out ahead of the destroyers. They're in a random screen, moving southeast."

"SSNX?"

"That's odd. It's not going back into port. It's sped up, it's heading *outbound*. And it's going damn fast, Captain. I'm getting plumes of water from its bow."

"Could be submerging."

"It has all of five meters under the keel," the first officer sniffed.

"Looks like it's settling into the water."

"Mother of God, what is it doing?"

"I don't care, goddammit," Petri spat. "Take her the fuck down!"

"Aye-aye, Captain. Pilot, open the aft ballast tank vents. Maintain one fathom under the keel with the high-frequency bottom sounder, nonsecure mode."

"Sir, I can't keep up with it at this speed. I'll bottom out."

"Do your best. If it's between broaching the sail and scraping bottom, pop out the sail."

"Pilot, aye."

"This is the captain," Petri's voice boomed on the Circuit One. "We have four inbound Bora torpedoes, and it looks like they are programmed to come into the channel and find us. We're at the mouth of Thimble Shoals Channel now, and we're going to keep heading east. With any luck, the torpedoes will follow us and not continue into Norfolk Harbor. We'll be putting out Mark 58 torpedoes on the incoming bearing line."

Petri put up the microphone and stood at the periscope stand, looking down on the hastily assembled battlestations crew.

"Attention, fire-control team," she said. "I plan to put three Mark 58 Alert/Acute units down the bearing line to the incoming torpedoes. As long as we're whole, we'll put out a dozen Mark 58s." It might cost every crewmember of the submarine, but she had to get those plasma weapons away from the residential section of the bay. "Carry on."

"Sonar, Captain, do we have *anything* on the firing platform?"

"Captain, Sonar, no."

"OOD, status of the slot buoy." She'd ordered the ejection of a radio buoy with the simple message "*Devilfish* under torpedo attack this position."

"Slot buoy away, Captain."

"Tube status, Weps?"

"Tubes two through six dry-loaded with Mark 58s. Power connected, ring lasers warming up, gyros starting now."

"Watch them. Report when ready. I want an immediate launch when they're set."

The deck shook with the power of the main motor pushing them through the shallow water at 50.8 knots. For a moment Petri contemplated shifting to emergency flank, then decided against it. It was hard enough maintaining depth control with a flank bell on. The extra speed was not built into the bottom sounder's nonsecure littoral water evasion mode, and they could easily bottom out or broach at whatever the SSNX's top speed turned out to be at emergency flank.

She glanced at the chart, seeing that they'd exited the bay.

"Pilot, left one degree rudder, steady course zero four five." A larger rudder angle could send them into a snap roll, and the single degree would turn them on a dime at this speed.

"One degree, zero four five, aye, my rudder is left one degree."

Petri scanned the bottom sounder. The Cyclops interface showed there to be ten feet of water above the sail, about thirty feet below it. There would be one hell of a rooster tail above them, she thought, wondering if another news camera would be catching this.

"Sonar, Captain, torpedoes tracking us?"

"Conn, Sonar, yes."

"Dammit."

"Captain, units two through six warmed up and ready for launch. Request to flood tubes."

"Make tubes two through six ready in all respects. Report status."

"Aye, Captain," Van Dyne reported from the weapons interface panel. "Port bank flooded, flooding starboard bank. Port bank pressurized. Request to open port bank outer doors."

"Open port bank outer doors."

"Aye, Captain, port outer doors rotating open, ready to shoot two, four, and six."

"XO, you have three firing solutions entered?"

"Yes, ma'am," Manderson snapped in her headset. If only they had something they could launch against the incoming torpedoes, she thought. But shooting down an incoming torpedo would be like taking rifle aim at a quarterback's football toss from the highest row of the stadium.

"Range settings?"

"Mark 58 unit two, set to search at ten thousand yards. That's our safety unit. Unit four, fifteen thousand. Unit six, twenty thousand. Passive circlers with active-range sampling."

"Very well. Firing point procedures, tubes two, four, and six, linear salvo."

"Ship ready," Dietz reported.

"Weapon ready," Van Dyne said.

"Solution set," Manderson said.

"Tube two, shoot on generated bearing," Petri said. Ten minutes into her first submergence as the ship's captain, she was shooting.

"Set," from Manderson.

"Standby," Van Dyne said, keying the standby fixed function key.

"Shoot," Petri ordered.

"Fire!" Van Dyne said, hitting the fire fixed function key.

A quarter-second swish noise sounded, the prelude to the sudden BOOM of the torpedo firing ram venting its high-pressure air inboard. The deck jumped as if they were in a bus that had hit a speed bump at fifty per, and the eardrums of every crewmember took a closed-fisted blow as the ship's atmospheric pressure spiked from the air overpressure of the firing ram.

Two decks below, the Mark 58 Alert/Acute torpedo was ejected from the tube. Its engine started, reporting back by fiber-optic wire that all was normal.

"Conn, Sonar," Chief Cook's voice rang in Petri's ear. "Incoming torpedoes are getting closer. Still tracking, constant bearing at one six zero. Rough triangulation between own ship's acoustic daylight arrays and Mark 5 remote array puts first incoming torpedo at range four thousand yards."

"Sonar, Captain, ping active and confirm acoustic daylight range."

"Conn, Sonar, ping active aye."

A sudden *bing* noise rang out, the noise loud in the whisper-quiet control room.

"Conn, Sonar, we have a high Doppler return from the bearing to the torpedoes. Range shows three four zero zero yards."

"Captain aye," Petri said. With the first torpedo at that close a range, they would need to do something. "OOD, have we got room to put the torpedo directly astern and run northwest?"

"No, ma'am. We'll run aground in . . . five minutes."

Petri bit her lip. "Pilot, all ahead emergency flank."

"Emergency flank aye, Maneuvering, Control, emergency flank, report when ready. Captain, Maneuvering answers preparing for emergency flank bell."

Hurry the hell up, Petri thought.

The first of the Bora II torpedoes closed relentlessly on the retreating target. The ship's loud wake noise and propulsor cavitation at such a shallow depth gave it away. Fuel level was low but calculated to be well within requirements for putting the warhead on target.

The Bora II had increased speed to attack velocity, 125 kilometers per hour, against a target that was running at barely ninety-five. As the Bora drove on, the target became steadily closer. It was time to rotate the arming fail-safe plate and align the low-explosive charges with the intermediate explosives. The computer closed several interlock contacts in the ignition circuit to the heavy plasma warhead in the mid-body of the torpedo.

It would not be too much longer.

"Speed climbing to fifty-five knots, fifty-six, fifty-seven . . ."

"Belay the report, Pilot," Petri called. She needed to think. What would be the effect if she turned, hard, just as the torpedo was closing? The five-ton weapon was much more maneuverable than a 7,700-ton submarine. It would be like trying to outmaneuver a motorcycle from the wheel of a bus. Was there a chance that she could drive the *Devilfish* outside the search cone of the torpedo?

"Steady at sixty-four point nine knots, ma'am," the pilot reported.

"Very well," she said absently.

For the next three minutes, Petri pushed the watchsection to launch torpedoes four and six, the units away. She cut the wires and ordered the starboard tubes readied, but it would take a few moments to line up.

"OOD," Petri asked, "what's the bottom here?"

"Captain?"

"Mud, silt, clay, sand, or rocks?"

"Chart says sand, ma'am."

"Not good enough. Click through to the Hydrological Survey of 2017. Quick! I want the exact bottom conditions at a point a half mile directly in front of us! Diving Officer, mark sounding and sail clearance!"

"Ma'am, sounding five fathoms, sail clearance twenty-five feet."

"Take her down, to sounding two fathoms, and watch the bottom suction! We're taking her close!"

"Yes, ma'am, but we're at emergency flank. The bottom sounder won't keep up if there's an obstacle ahead."

"Keep her down. What buoyancy have you got?"

"Neutral within a hundred tons. We didn't get time to do a trim, Captain."

"Flood depth control one and two till they're full."

"Flooding depth control one and two, Pilot aye."

The ship, plowing ahead at almost sixty-five knots, nosed downward toward the bottom. On the other side of the conn platform Bryan Dietz's head sprouted droplets of sweat as he stroked the software keys of the WritePad computer.

"What is it?"

"Not there, yet, Skipper."

She'd never been called that, she thought strangely, her mind becoming unfocused in this moment of stress.

"Come on!"

"Almost, okay, I've got the survey, inserting the lat/long now."

"Come on, come on!"

"Sand, ma'am. Sand down to a depth of a hundred fifty feet!"

"Good. Pilot, maintain two fathoms under the keel."

"Pilot aye, two fathoms, ship's depth is one hundred feet, ma'am."

"Very well. Attention in the fire-control team. When the torpedo is close, within five hundred yards, I am going to take her into the sand of the bottom. We'll grind to a halt and with any luck bury ourselves in the sand and the torpedo will keep going. We will full-scram the reactor and deenergize the entire electric plant—vital and nonvital AC buses, the DC grid, all the way to the battery breaker. That will kill every piece of machinery aboard with the exception of Cyclops. OOD, check on Cyclops emergency cooling. Maneuvering, you got all that?"

"Conn, Maneuvering aye."

"OOD?"

"Cyclops emergency cooling is lined up, Captain."

"Very well. Sonar, Captain, range to incoming torpedo number one?"

"Seven hundred yards, but the range is very rough, ma'am."

It was now or never, Petri thought.

"Everyone grab a handhold!" She took a deep breath. "Pilot, take her down, one degree down angle on the ship! Maneuvering, Captain, on impact, insert a full scram and open all breakers! Pilot, if she bounces, you keep the down angle."

She felt like closing her eyes as tight as she could but realized she had to look steely-eyed and brave. How the hell, she wondered, had Kelly McKee done it? Then the hull hit the bottom at sixty-four knots.

*　　*　　*

"Where is the surface force headed? And the choppers?" Grachev asked the first officer.

"Heading down the bearing line to the torpedoes, southeast," Svyatoslov said, a laugh in his voice. "We've got them all fooled, Captain."

For now, Grachev thought. "Any threats close, anything at all?"

"Nothing, sir."

"Any sign of a detect of the Azov?"

"No, sir. We've escaped with the crown jewels."

"Can you pin down the location of the SSNX?"

"See the rooster tail? I've got it circled on your display."

A circle came up on display zero on the command console. A wake rising up from the sea where there was no boat.

"Amazing," Grachev said, stunned that he was winning.

One hundred eighty kilometers north-northeast of *Vepr*'s position the submarine *Devilfish* smashed into the sandy bottom at sixty-four knots. At that velocity the hard-packed sand made the hull skip like a rock, the rear of the ship rising higher than the bow. The reactor control rod mechanism spring releases opened as their inverter breakers tripped from the shock. The control rods were driven to core bottom by the powerful springs set into their mechanisms. The nuclear flux that had sustained the nuclear fissions dropped to a small fraction of its previous levels. As the plant scrammed, the electrical operator, strapped into his seat with his hands

on the breaker levers, managed to flip open three
breakers before he was thrown back into his seat
by the bounce.

The stern rising up higher than the bow with a
forward velocity now forty-eight knots sent the ship
diving for the sandy bottom again. This time the
nose-cone fiberglass dome disintegrated, shearing
off the spherical array of the BQQ-10 and denting
and slightly rupturing the forward ballast tank and
jarring the forward four vertical launch tubes off
their steel foundations. The wound of the ballast
tank acted as a shovel, and the rapidly approaching
sand piled up into the space and began to bury the
bow under a wave of sand. The accumulating sand
further slowed the vessel, and within two seconds,
with a negative g-force of over two gees, the submarine ground to a halt on the shallow bottom,
canted slightly over in a four-degree list.

Back aft in the maneuvering room, the unconscious
electrical operator had come to rest on his panel.
Behind him the engineering officer of the watch and
chief engineer, Todd Hendrickson, who had hung
from a handhold in the overhead until the ship
stopped, pulled the EO back from the electrical panel
and snapped open the remaining AC and DC breakers, killing the ship. The vessel became completely
inert except for the battle lanterns and the Cyclops
system, which was on emergency cooling for the next
twenty minutes. Beyond that, the computer system
would overheat and shut itself down.

In the control room, Karen Petri let go of the
overhead handhold she'd gripped, kicked almost
horizontal by the deceleration of the ship. The

room was now quiet except for the moaning whine of the Cyclops system's computer.

"Sonar?" she said into her boom microphone, but it was dead. She pulled it off and opened the curtain to Chief Cook's kingdom on the forward starboard corner of control. "Chief?"

"Still inbound," Cook said, his headset nowhere to be seen. The only light in sonar was the green glow from the display panels between the virtual-reality cubicles at either corner of the room. "If we're quiet we'll hear it with the naked ear."

"How's sonar?"

"Lost the sphere. Hull arrays are half functional. What's above the sand we must have kicked up. We lost the wires to the Mark 5."

Petri vanished, finding Dietz. "Any flooding?"

Dietz rubbed his head, his fingers coming back bloody from a wound on the top of his scalp. "We're switching phones, reports are coming in. Pilot?"

"No flooding, OOD."

The sound of the incoming torpedo came through the hull then. The noise was a high-pitched squeal that started to wind down as if the weapon were becoming uncertain. It drove by, slowing down by the second, but than its noise receded and vanished.

Petri glanced at Dietz, watching him start to smile.

"It's not over yet, OOD. This one's confused, and there are three more coming."

Dietz nodded, then looked above him into the overhead. Petri suddenly became aware that the surface was eighty-five feet over her head.

29

"Got a problem, Captain," Lynski said from his enclosure. Grachev stepped up to the sliding door leading to it.

"I'm right here. Go ahead."

"Big noise from the target, then it seemed to change in the torpedo seeker's field. We've got nothing in the first unit's seeker field."

"Very good, Weps. Mr. Navigator, change configuration, take manual control, and turn the torpedo around. Bring it back slow."

Tenukha spoke up from his cubicle. "Reconfigured. Second Captain has turned over control of torpedo one to me, and I'm at dead slow."

"Turn around," Grachev ordered.

"Turning now, three five zero. Course north, zero one zero, coming around, zero three zero, sir, fuel low-level alarm."

"Warhead armed, Nav?"

"Fully armed, sir."

"Course?"

"Around to the south, sir, creeping up. I have no passive and no narrowband."

"Ping active high-freq."

"Pinging now, sir."

"Get the nose camera up and the blue laser. Let's map out the contour."

"Driving back slowly. No Doppler on active returns. No large-field zero-Doppler return. Blue laser contour shows flat bottom. Low-low fuel-level alarm, Captain."

"How much time?"

"Twenty seconds, sir."

"What do you see?"

"Still nothing but flat sand. Rock outcropping several hundred meters south."

"Drive for it, Nav."

"Ten seconds, sir, turbine spooling down."

"Set it down on the bottom and take the unit to standby."

"Yessir, weapon slowing, slowing, bottom coming up, and unit is . . . in the sand. Velocity coming down, velocity zero. Torpedo is on the bottom and stopped, going to standby mode. Okay, we're in standby on unit one, wire continuity remains green."

"What are you doing?" Novskoyy asked.

Grachev held up a finger to silence him and kept talking to Tenukha. "Pick up unit two from the Second Captain."

"Yes, sir, unit two is in my control now. I'm about a kilometer south of the rock outcropping that unit one is north of."

"Fuel status?"

"Low, sir, approaching low-fuel alarm."

"Bring unit two up to the rock outcropping to the north, bare steerageway, and light the blue laser, the visual spot, and the nose camera."

"Blue laser, visual spotlight, and nose camera up. Should be on your displays, sir."

"Got it. Now, bring two in slow and low."

Grachev and Novskoyy both leaned over display zero, watching the visual display as the sand approached the torpedo. The featureless bottom came toward the camera at ten clicks.

"There it is, I see it," Grachev said, tapping the face of the display. In the display a large ridge protruded from the sand, half covered with sand. It had a ruler-straight shape on the upper right hump, almost exactly level. "Bring us around, circle it."

"Yessir, I've overdriven slightly, low fuel level. Coming around back to the south, low-low fuel level. I'm losing it."

"How far from that hump?"

"Five hundred meters, maybe six hundred."

"Set two down on the sand."

"Bringing two in."

"Distance?"

"Four hundred fifty meters. Unit two is in standby."

"Take three. Bring it in at walking speed. Get as close as you can."

"I'm too far away to see it, sir, and I've got a low-low fuel level. This unit's out. I've got to bring her down now. Unit three on the bottom, in standby. Distance twelve hundred meters."

"Too far. Bring four in as close as you can."

"Can't, sir. Four is out, too late to take four to standby. Turbine is stopped, fuel cell is empty. No sign of four."

"Continuity?"

"No readback on four, sir."

"Keep it lined up."

Grachev pulled off his headset and ran his hands through his hair, something he did when he was out of ideas.

"What now, Captain?" Novskoyy asked.

"I'm thinking. I can either detonate these warheads now or cut the wires and shoot more torpedoes. I can't do both. Either that thing in the sand is the SSNX, or it's an old sunken hull or a big piece of concrete or construction debris hauled off and dropped offshore. I can't confirm it as the SSNX. But if it is and it's playing possum, if I cut the wires it will get away clean. If I command-detonate the weapons, I fill the water with noise and bubbles. Any torpedoes launched after that would be blind."

"What if you set the plasma units off on a time delay, cut the wires, and launch four more torpedoes?"

"Can't. There's no time-delay capability. It would be an easy program module, but nobody thought of that when the Bora torpedo was designed."

"What about the overhead photographs? What did the Azov show?"

"Mr. First! You heard Mr. Novskoyy. What did your eyeballs show the SSNX position to be?"

"Sir, I was following the task force, but the cameras were still tracking to the north. If you roll back the disk to where the wake was before, it should track."

"What have you got on the surface force?"

"Antisub formation rolling at about forty clicks, now about twenty kilometers to the southeast of Port Norfolk. They're following the bearing line the torpedoes came in on."

"How far from us?"

"A hundred forty-five kilometers, bearing three four nine."

"They're opening range, then," Grachev mumbled to himself. "And not much of a threat anyway. Unless we give ourselves away."

"How would you do that?" Novskoyy asked.

"By lighting off four plasma warheads."

"You already have—the four torpedoes you shot. But nothing you do with those warheads gives away your position here."

"Hell with it. Second Captain, take the Azov intelligence on the SSNX and show the position tracking from moment of submergence to present time."

"Yes, Captain," the electronic voice acknowledged. "Now watch."

Grachev and Novskoyy leaned over the main display and watched the hull of the SSNX as it sank into the water at its maximum speed. Soon nothing but the fin showed, and after a few more minutes, just a rooster tail wake was showing. The wake continued, turning out of the bay and to the northeast, then subsided completely, the water calming to its previous state.

"There," Grachev said. "Right there the SSNX vanishes. It could have slowed down and turned or bottomed or changed direction."

"Which means it could be anywhere."

"No. The torpedoes were following it. First, let's take the visual data. Second Captain, bring up a chart and, based on SSNX maximum detected speed, from the position of visual loss, show the SSNX location circle growth with time, up to the present."

A chart appeared on display zero. The Second Captain pinpointed the location of the SSNX at the moment it was lost from the visual overhead view. A circle anchored on that location grew rapidly with time, soon spreading out all the way to the entrance to the Chesapeake Bay.

"Well, that's no help. Second Captain, based on the fact that the SSNX was running from four torpedoes, chart the probability distribution on the chart." Grachev turned to Novskoyy. "This should show the circle growth to be biased in the northern directions."

An ellipse appeared on the chart, the lower point of it anchored at the point where the SSNX went invisible and continued northeastward.

"Now, Second Captain, integrate the probability distribution with Bora torpedo intelligence to show where the SSNX track went after it went invisible." To Novskoyy: "Those torpedoes tracked the SSNX long after it and it's wake vanished from the surface."

The chart's probability ellipse narrowed, the point of invisibility no longer anchoring it. The ellipse collapsed and moved to the northeast, then vanished to a point that moved at almost 130 clicks in a line that was the continuation of the SSNX wake's previous track. The point continued northwest, then suddenly stopped. A new ellipse started and grew steadily northeast, but this time it was a fatter ellipse, as the starting point was now in open ocean, or at least closer to it.

"It could still be anywhere," Novskoyy complained.

"We don't have to worry about this segment from when it dropped off the Azov screen to here, where the torpedoes lost it. But it could be anywhere in here. And since the probability ellipse is going northeast, it's farther outside of our weapons range. If this submerged ridge isn't the SSNX lying and hiding on the bottom, then the SSNX is long gone."

"Which would mean we'd have to get closer and launch more torpedoes," Novskoyy said.

"Hold on a minute," Grachev said. "We've got the Azov airborne, and it's got another ten hours or so of endurance—"

"Ten hours and forty minutes, Captain," Svyatoslov interjected.

"So we can keep an eye on the bay with Mr. First's eyes. At least until it runs out of power. How long to sunset, Mr. First?"

"Another six hours. But I'll see the hull on infrared if it comes back after dark."

"We've got the rock outcropping or whatever it is surrounded with plasma warheads," Grachev said to himself, leaning over the command console, thinking hard. "I could shoot a Shchuka acoustic daylight sensor and confirm that ridge."

"You'd have to come off the bottom and get closer," Novskoyy said.

"That's no good. There's only one Shchuka sensor left. Watching the near ocean space here is useless. So we wait and let Mr. First scout for the return of the SSNX."

"What's your gut feeling on the rock outcropping? Is that the SSNX?"

"I don't know, Al. If I want to I can wake up three of the Bora torpedoes and command-detonate the plasma units, and I can synchronize the explosion to within a few milliseconds. I've got two to the north and one to the south. If that thing is the SSNX, I can rip it apart."

"And if you do that, with the plasma warheads that far away, will you kill the sub, or just hurt it?"

"Let me put it this way. If our hull were there, we'd expect to have three or more compartments rupture. It might even break the hull in half. That answer your question?"

Novskoyy rubbed his eyes. "How could the SSNX be there one minute and disappear the next?"

"By hitting the bottom," Grachev said. "That thing down there is probably it."

"But we don't know, and if you command-detonate the plasma warheads, all you might end up doing is blowing up a coral reef."

There was silence for several minutes.

"I'm going to my stateroom to shut my eyes," Novskoyy said.

"See you." Grachev leaned back over the command console and tried to think.

*　　*　　*

Petri's eyes roved the poorly lit and listing control room. "Chief Cook, what do you have on the torpedoes?"

"Two shut down to the north, one to the south, and—wait a minute—that's it, number four has shut down. We're all alone, at least as far as I can tell."

"Good. OOD, get the word to maneuvering to restart the reactor and place the electric plant in a full-power lineup." She pulled up the handset of a sound-powered phone and selected the radio room.

"Radio, Captain."

"Radio, ma'am," Senior Chief Henry's baritone replied.

"Bring a slot buoy and the coder."

"Right away."

"How long on the restart, Off'sa'deck?"

"Normal full in ten."

"Slot buoy," the radio chief said, plopping a baseball-bat-sized object on the aft chart table. The buoy was designed to be shot out of a signal ejector—a small torpedo tube—and float to the surface to transmit a radio message to the overhead satellite. "Coder," he said, producing something resembling an old-fashioned notebook computer.

Petri typed, "*Devilfish* evaded torpedoes by bottoming, location as follows—"

"Nav, report inertial nav's latitude and longitude."

Judison read it off while Petri continued typing: "Four incoming weapons shut down after *Devilfish* hit bottom. *Devilfish* damage from bottoming includes BQQ-10 spherical array. Widescan acoustic daylight arrays remain nominal. Currently restarting reactor to continue search. Will call for P-5 units with Mark 12 Yo-Yo pods at 1730 ZULU."

"Load it and shoot it, Senior," Petri ordered. "Off'sa'deck, status of the reactor?"

She was starting to feel herself again. Some measure of control had returned to her now that the incoming weapons had shut down.

"Ma'am, reactor's critical, warming up primary coolant loops, steaming the headers in one minute."

"Very well. Radio, Captain, status of the slot buoy launch?"

"We're loading it now."

Petri paced the conn platform, impatient to begin the search.

"Which unit has the most power remaining?" Novskoyy asked.

"Number three, but it's at extreme range," Grachev replied.

"If we awaken the sensors long enough to peek at the target, we'll be able to see if they're lying low."

"If we turn them back on, we'll burn power. We may not have the juice to command-detonate."

"Keep the two close-in units off, and use them for the command detonation. You can listen with number three."

"It might come up with nothing, and all we've done is lose a plasma warhead."

"Then you might as well just detonate them now.

You've got a microphone with a long wire right where the hull of the target is. You should use it."

"Navigator, bring up unit three in passive listen mode."

"Aye, Captain."

"Main engines are warm, ready to answer all bells."

"Attention in the fire-control team," Petri said. Her voice had climbed from its normal deep, authoritative timbre into a higher, scratchier tone. The sound of it gave her an anxious, heavy feeling in her abdomen. She clenched her jaw, commanding herself to control her fear. She coughed, hoping it would bring her voice back. "We're going to try to back out of the sand. My concern is making too much noise on the way out, so we'll go easy at first. Officer of the Deck, watch the inertial readout and call velocity. I want to know the instant we're moving." Her command voice had returned, at least for the moment. "Pilot, I have the conn. All back two thirds."

The deck began to tremble.

"Velocity zero," Dietz said. "Still stuck."

"Give it a second."

"Captain, backing at sixty RPM."

"Very well. Pilot, blow depth control one."

"Blowing one, ma'am."

"Ten-degree dive on the bowplanes, Pilot."

"No motion, Captain."

Petri waited, the deck still trembling but nothing further happening. She would need more power.

"Depth control one going dry, Captain."

"Blow depth control two."

"Blowing two."

"Very well." Petri waited, but other than the shaking of the ship, there was no result.

"OOD, do you have motion?"

"Nothing, Cap'n."

"Captain, depth control two dry, shutting down."

"Very well, Pilot. OOD?"

"Nothin'."

"Pilot, on my mark, we're going to bubble the aft ballast tanks with the EMBT blow system, but be ready to vent immediately."

"Yes, ma'am."

"Pilot, emergency blow aft, back full!"

"Blowing aft," the helm officer snapped, pulling up a stainless-steel handle while pulling the throttle lever back to the full detent, "back full—"

"We're moving! Point five per second, one point five, two feet per second—" Dietz shouted over the pilot.

Petri expelled the next order in one word: "Secure the blow! Vent aft! Flood depth control to the interlock!"

"Blow secured, venting aft main ballast tanks, flooding DCTs one and two."

"All stop."

"All stop, aye!"

"Three feet per second reverse, down angle on the ship two degrees," Dietz said.

"Full dive on the bowplanes!" Petri ordered. "All ahead standard."

"Two feet per second aft," Dietz called. "Point five, zero, ahead point five."

"Pilot, take charge of your bowplanes and make your depth one hundred feet, all ahead two thirds,

right five degrees rudder, steady course south. Off'-
sa'deck, secure at the inertial panel and take the
conn.''

"Energize unit three when you're ready, Nav,"
Grachev ordered, glancing at his watch.

"Aye, Captain. Command inserted, central processor is up, self-checking hydrophones, continuity
sat—"

"Fuel cell readout?" Grachev asked.

"Two minutes remaining with the unit online.
Should last for twenty hours at standby. Wait a
minute . . . Captain? I think we have something."

For the next three seconds Grachev piped the
hydrophone output into his headset, his eyes growing wide. "Warm up one and two and send the
signal to four also! Prepare all units for synchronized command detonation."

"Aye, sir," the navigator said, flashing his fingers
over his display in the virtual-reality cubicle. "Units
one and two processors coming online, no response
from four."

"Come on," Grachev said. The sounds in his
headset were clearly a rotating screw, air bubbles,
and scraping metal on sand.

"One, two, and three are up, sir."

"Command-detonate sequence, captain's code
reinserted."

"Second Captain has the units, and two, one,
mark."

The sounds of Grachev's headset—the propulsor
noise, air bubbles, flow noise, and scraping of
metal—vanished. Only silence remained.

*   *   *

The lengths of the thin fiber-optic wires on the ocean floor that linked the Bora II torpedoes to the torpedo tubes of the *Vepr* varied by as much as two thousand meters, but the total lengths of them from the termination inside the interface cabinets of the *Vepr*'s middle-level torpedo room to the terminations inside the torpedo bodies were identical to the tenth of a millimeter, which was vital because the optical signals generated by the *Vepr*'s Second Captain traveled at the speed of light, arriving simultaneously to the interface modules of the three plasma-tipped torpedoes. This activated the weapon processors to detonate the high-explosive triggers of the three warheads, which bloomed into plasma incandescence within milliseconds of each other.

Although the three warheads of the torpedoes were quite distant from each other, they formed a sharp triangle which contained the submarine USS *Devilfish*. And the American sub, the newest in the fleet, the pride of her designer, Admiral Michael Pacino, found itself in the center of a triple hammer blow of steel-shredding force. The overpressure of the shock waves of the three detonations hit the hull of the *Devilfish* in rapid succession. The first would have been bad enough to cripple her, scramming the reactor as the inverter breakers tripped open from the shock, the rods beginning to descend into the reactor core, the power level plummeting. The ship was jarred sideways, the sail taking the overpressure and making the ship heel over to port, exposing the top of the hull to the second and third shock waves, which arrived almost at the same time. The double impact was sufficient to rupture the HY180 high-tensile steel stretched between the I-section structural hoop frames along a compartment hull weld. The rupture further opened as the force of the plasma detonation pushed hard on both ends of the ship. The tremendous force broke the back of the submarine, and the ship came to rest on the sand of the bottom in the shape of a boomerang, the sail reaching horizontally to a new mountain of sand that had been scooped up from the bottom by the giant hands of the plasma blasts.

The rupture in the hull had occurred at the bottom of the reactor compartment, immediately flooding the space with seawater and stopping the beating heart of what had been one of the most powerful warships in history.

Bryan Dietz had no idea the submarine had just been smashed by three plasma explosion shock waves inside of two seconds. All he knew was that one second he was standing by the inertial readout repeater panel on the port side of the control room, feeling calm if not exactly safe and secure. The next two seconds of his life contained as much detail as entire years of his memory.

He was just turning his head to walk to the periscope stand and take the conn from Captain Petri and get the ship out of the shallows when the nightmare began. The room began a violent and sudden tilt. For just an instant his mind turned to the diving trainers at the sub training facility in Norfolk, which were mounted on hydraulic legs to give the feeling of severe angles, but never in the trainer had the deck ever flipped like this. It took less than a quarter second for the deck to be rotated a full ninety degrees. If the deck had plunged beneath his feet, leaving him literally hanging, it returned in an instant to smash him in the head. Its tiles were the next thing he saw as his field of view rotated forward, capturing the blur of the rotation of the room. The lights clicked out, and the consoles sputtered into darkness. He bounced on the surface below him, crashing down into it with his rear end, his legs flying out in front of him. The thing he'd fallen on had a strange shape to it—the inertial navigation console he'd been looking at moments before. Soon after that he hit his head again on the vertical surface beside him— the former deck, now a wall. A moment later he was tackled, the officer crashing past his head onto his shoulder and slamming him in the gut. The body of the man who'd hit him landed in his lap. Another body landed on the cabinets to his left, followed by the mighty impact of one of the navigation plotter tables as it slammed down to Dietz's left.

Only then did Dietz perceive the first sounds of the event. A rushing sound, a fire hose at full force, but worse, as if he'd put his head into the nozzle of an F-22 dual jet fighter as it lifted off at full afterburners. The noise was so loud and so violent that it existed for only a heartbeat. Either his eardrums ruptured or his brain was so overloaded with sensation that he could hear no more.

The next ticks of the clock happened in total darkness, mere impressions of falling objects— manuals, books, rulers, pencils, coffee cups, another body. The sound then returned, no longer a roaring but two explosions, one rapidly after the next. They were followed by another roaring sound, but this one different, closer and from his left, a howling whistle at first, then dying to a dim flowing sound, and then the screams of the men in the room. One of the shrieks was coming from his lap.

His hand had drifted down at that point, encountering a face, a head, long hair, and a dim part of his mind was at first surprised, then linked the long hair to the ship's captain. He shouted, "Captain! Captain?" His other hand joined his first as he tried to pull the captain off his lap. He wondered if he might be breaking her neck or paralyzing her, but he *had* to move. They might all be dying. He stood, trying to be careful not to step on her, pulling himself to his feet by something overhead, a piece of metal he couldn't identify, and he forced himself to think about where the control battle lantern was. When he was finally able to remember, he had to mentally rotate the room by ninety degrees, find the inertial panel at his feet, slippery with a liquid, and then put his hand into black space where the lantern should be. Finally he found it and clicked it to life. The spreading beam of it ended one nightmare and started another as Dietz looked around him at the wreckage of the room and began to comprehend how close to death he was.

The chief engineer and battlestations engineering officer of the watch, Lieutenant Commander Todd Hendrickson, instinctively reached out for a handhold in the maneuvering room in the upper level of the aft compartment. He looked up in time to see the reactor operator fly out of his seat and tumble to the door of the room. The RO blew through the heavy glass of the door and vanished, and the engineer realized that the deck was no longer horizontal but had become a wall.

While the glass door to the space was shattering, a sixteen-inch main steam pipe on the starboard side, pressurized on the inside to seven hundred pounds per square inch, ruptured, spilling the high-energy saturated steam into what had been the hull of the aft compartment. Within seconds, the steam generators depressurized into the aft compartment, filling the entire space with high-pressure, high-temperature steam, turning the entire space into a lethal pressure cooker.

Steam blasted into the maneuvering room from the man-sized hole in the heavy glass door left by the fall of the reactor operator. The next breath Hendrickson took was to form a scream that died in his throat as his heart stalled, the fluids in his body starting to froth, his blood boiling even as he stood there in his boots. His flesh turned lobster-red and then black.

Like Hendrickson, the other men in the compartment died before their first screams finished, their flesh roasted in mere seconds by the double-ended pipe sheer and the skyrocketing temperatures in the compartment. The aft compartment remained connected to the reactor compartment by the steel that had ruptured in the ship's central hemorrhage, which remained connected to the forward compartment. Running from one compartment to the other were thousands of cables, wires, and fiber-optic cables, including phone circuits, PA circuits, and sound-powered phone lines, which were always on, always transmitting.

A hundred feet southeast of Hendrickson's body, Lieutenant Commander Bryan Dietz stood staring at the room, only now realizing in his numbness that he was standing with one foot on the console of the ring laser inertial navigation cabinet and the other on Captain Petri's left leg. He stepped off and put out his hand slowly, dreamily, toward the command console. He found one of the sound-powered phones in time to hear one last echoing scream and the horrible rush of steam.

He looked down slowly at Commander Karen Petri, now visible in the light of the battle lantern. Her left coverall sleeve had been ripped half off, and there was a deep gash in her shoulder. Her face was marred by a black eye that was swelling shut, and a tooth was missing from the bottom row, but at least she was staring back at him, and she was alive. He pulled her to her feet, relief pouring into him that she stayed standing; she wasn't paralyzed as he'd feared. He starting speaking to her in a rush.

"Captain, I think we may have lost the aft compartment. Major steam leak if my ears are still working."

But Petri looked back at him stunned, her left eye no longer visible. She looked at him intensely, then said, "Dad? Daddy? Where are we?"

Dietz put one hand on Petri's shoulder and one on her waist and sat her down on the inertial cabinet, wondering what the hell to do next.

30

"Sir, loss of wire continuity units one through three."

It was a good sign, Grachev thought. All units must have detonated, or at least one had and its explosion had blown up the others. *Vepr* was too far from the explosions to hear it immediately. The sound waves had to travel through almost 180 kilometers of water before they'd be picked up by the ship's hydrophones.

"Good. Mr. First, give me a flyover at the Bora location."

Grachev waited. It took some time for the report to come. Grachev saw the output on his screen before he heard the first officer's report.

"Sir, we have three wide-diameter white foam splashes. Let me pipe in the audio."

The roaring sound came in over Grachev's headset from the sensors of the Azov.

"Keep it overhead. But keep an eye out over the horizon for what the surface force is doing."

"Captain, I've got the OTH, and from here I can see the surface ships have reversed course."

"The heat is off," Grachev said, pulling off his headset. "Nav, get a turnover from the first officer and maintain the Azov aloft. Crew, secure from

tactical stations and get some rest. Mr. First, join
Mr. Novskoyy and me in my stateroom, and have
the cook prepare a hot meal for the crew."

Bryan Dietz leaned over the chart table, which had
come to rest on top of the radio repeater console
on the port side of the USS *Devilfish*'s control
room, now the floor of the crippled ship. The
righting moment built into the ship would normally
never allow her to stay rolled over, Dietz thought.
They were either buried in sand, partially flooded,
or broken in half.

There was a hand protruding from the table with
an academy ring on one finger. Dietz rolled the
chart table off and found himself looking into the
startled eyes of the navigator, Kiethan Judison.

"You okay, Nav?"

"Never better," Judison groaned, staggering to
his feet. "Where's the skipper?"

"You're not going to like the answer," Dietz
said, but Judison didn't wait, finding Petri sitting
on the upper part of the inertial navigation binnacle
with her back leaned up against a bank of piping
that used to form the overhead. She was staring
steadily into the room with her right eye, her left
completely swollen shut in a dark shiner.

Judison leaned over her, looking into her right
eye, and then pulled open the flesh to see her left.
He turned to Dietz. "Pupils are different sizes.
That's not a good sign."

Dietz waved his arm around the room. "Try to
find a fucking good sign here, Nav."

There had been ten officers in the room when

the explosions had gone off. At this point Judison and Dietz were on their feet, Captain Petri and Dick Van Dyne were semiconscious, and Paul Manderson and David Dayne were covered with blood. Together Dietz and Judison went through the space, starting with Manderson and Dayne. Manderson's neck was broken, he wasn't breathing, and he had no pulse. Dayne had been spurting blood from a neck wound, and the bleeding had stopped on its own. He was not breathing, and his gray flesh was growing cold. Toasty O'Neal was lying on his left arm but seemed whole. Evans, Horner, and Daniels were breathing but unconscious. Daniels was turning white, possibly from internal bleeding. It had been a bad day throughout the control room, Dietz thought.

"You realize with the ship canted like this, the escape trunk won't work," Dietz said to Judison. "And neither will the emergency blow system. Even if it works and puts air in the ballast tanks, it might turn us upside down, and we'd be in worse trouble. Looks like we'll be waiting here for rescue."

"Listen," Judison said, his usual booming voice back to normal. "That escape trunk will work, even if it becomes a dumb airlock and we've gotta hold our breath while it floods. As long as the inner and outer hatches still work, we're in business. We've got to get everyone alive to the escape trunk. I'll go to the upper level and drag down the supply boys. You start on the middle level and lower level. Here," Judison said, handing Dietz a handheld

VHF radio from the navigation storage locker. "Channel one. Tell me what you've got."

Dietz picked up the slot buoy message coder from the wreckage on the navigation console. It seemed to work.

"We should send one of these before we start," he said. "It would be nice to have someone waiting for us. Especially if you're wrong about the escape trunk."

Easygoing Judison—never one to take offense— nodded. "Find a slot buoy in radio on your way to the lower level. Combination is K-L-E-M. Captain's initials. At least the former captain."

Dietz nodded, taking a wall-mounted battle lantern into his hand, tucking the slot buoy coder into his coveralls, and strapping the radio to his belt with the mike on his collar. "Radio check," he said into the mike.

"Good. Let's get out of here."

"It doesn't make much sense to stay," Grachev said to Svyatoslov while they waited for Novskoyy. "We've put down their only acoustic daylight platform and the only truly capable submarine. The surface forces are something to watch out for, but we could put them down too if we burn up all our weapons."

The door opened before the first officer could reply. Novskoyy came into the room and collapsed on a seat, pulling the plate of fish over and eating hungrily. Grachev was not hungry. Even the coffee tasted bad.

"Well," Grachev said. "Can we get out of here

now? Or do you have more bad news for these Norfolk bastards?"

"Aerial recon photos?" Novskoyy asked.

Svyatoslov reached for the remote and clicked one of the widescreens to life. He selected the Antay EHF receiver output pulled from the still-orbiting Azov unmanned aerial vehicle, being flown by the deck officer in the control compartment. The surface force could be seen driving northwestward, having spread out and slowed to search speed.

"Put the reticle on the coordinates of the torpedo detonation," Novskoyy said, taking a spoonful of soup.

Over the position of the three plasma detonations there was an oil slick and what looked like a truckload of floating debris.

"No rafts, no survivors." Svyatoslov stopped chewing and stared at the display.

"We killed her, from what I can see," Grachev said. "What's next?"

Novskoyy wiped his mouth and sat back. "We're finished here. We need to withdraw slowly and quietly to the southeast. Walking speed. I want us to go no faster than thirty clicks, and lay in a serpentine departure course. No one is to track us. Let's hurry and pull out before the search from the surface ships becomes more serious."

Grachev pushed his plates away, having eaten nothing. "And then what?"

"Take us to the equator at twenty-five degrees west longitude. We'll rendezvous with the Black Sea Fleet surface task force and screen them for the journey to Uruguay. Your ship is charged with delivering those ships safely to the beaches. Now that the American admirals and their acoustic day-light platform are gone, that mission should prove . . . routine.''

Grachev said nothing, waving the first officer out with his head, hurrying up the ladderway to the control compartment. Once there, he stepped be-hind his command console and issued a flurry of orders to the deck officer.

"Man tactical stations. Command-self-destruct the Azov and confirm it's down, then withdraw the Antay pod. Rig out the horizontal plane thrusters and bring up the idle turbines.''

Almost 150 kilometers north, the Azov un-manned aerial vehicle dived for the sea and disinte-grated on impact. Thirty seconds later, the self-destruct charges blew the remainder of the air-frame apart.

Four hundred meters overhead, the Antay pod's EHF antenna retracted, the door shutting over it, the pod watertight. Seconds later it vanished from the waves and began its trip deep, finally latching onto the top of *Vepr*'s rudder. By that time all turbines were online, and the horizontal plane thrusters started. The submarine lifted off the sand and rocks of the bottom and turned to the southeast.

Bryan Dietz climbed vertically up the ship-control console to where he could get a grip on the door to the systems booth, throwing it open so he could use the doorjamb as a ladder step. With the handle of the battle lantern held in his teeth, he hauled his wiry body up the side of the systems room to the central passageway forward, crawling on what used to be bulkheads. The door to the sonar room was open, Chief Cook hanging out of it. Dietz stood on the passageway bulkhead and tried to see if the chief was still breathing. He was; his head was bruised, but otherwise he seemed whole. Dietz pulled him out of the doorway and laid him on the woodgrain wall paneling, then craned his neck up into the space. One sonarman was conscious, his eyes as wide as quarters, in the corner and making whimpering noises. The other two were down but breathing.

"Come on," Dietz said to the conscious sonarman. "Give me a hand."

The sonarman didn't move, his eyes still huge. Dietz reached in to grab him, but he withdrew back into the space between the former deck and the bottom of the sonar flat-panel display console. And Dietz, having become more comfortable around computers than people, pursed his lips in disgust and pulled out of the sonar doorway and continued on a few feet to the door to radio. He keyed in the combination. The door fell away down into the darkened room.

Dietz found the bulkhead-mounted battle lantern and snapped it on. The inside was a mess. Several radio drawers had come out of their racks, severely injuring the two duty radiomen. Dietz climbed in and checked them, but they were covered with blood and cold. The nightmare was growing worse every second, he thought, grimly laying the younger of the two radiomen gently aside so he could get

into the storage locker. The inside was a cluttered
wreck, but Dietz found a functional slot buoy. One
last look at the room, and he climbed out and continued down the passageway past the door to the
ESM electronic surveillance measures room beneath him and to the computer room over his head.
He came to the stairwell. The ship's ladder's steep
steps turned onto their side seemed surreal in the
conical beam from the battle lantern.

"Dietz, you up?" his radio blared. Dietz turned
down the volume while stepping through the railing
of the stairwell to the lower level.

"Go, Nav," he said into the mike.

"Where are you?"

"Opening the hatch to the torpedo room compartment. It's heavy. Wait one."

Dietz shined the lantern into the porthole in the
face of the hatch to the torpedo room, praying that
none of the weapons had fallen off the racks or
leaked. A fire or contaminated atmosphere would
kill the survivors, and God knew they hardly
needed any more bad luck. The room looked clear.
Dietz put down the lantern and the slot buoy and
put his fingers on the latch, undogged the mechanism, and heaved against the fireproof hatch,
latching the heavy steel door vertically above his
head. He shined the beam inside the room, repeating his prayer for the integrity of the torpedo
fuel tanks. Things seemed relatively intact. Dietz
climbed in and shut the forward hatch after him,
redogging it in case a leak started while he was
inside.

The narrow catwalk through the room led between the rows of rack-stowed weapons, which seemed inert despite the roll of the ship. Carefully Dietz crawled over the torpedoes and kept scanning for a leak of self-oxidizing fuel. It took ten minutes to reach the aft bulkhead of the room, ten minutes of inching his way along the cold cylinder of one of the Mark 58 torpedoes. At the aft bulkhead he shut the hatch of the torpedo room behind him and emerged into the tilted-over auxiliary machinery room, the home of the emergency diesel and the hatch to the bottom of the escape chamber.

And immediately Dietz smelled something wrong. He turned to face forward, and saw the hatch of the battery compartment, a six-foot-tall enclosure built beneath the torpedo room. The hatch looked entirely normal, as normal as it could tilted ninety-five degrees from its usual state with only the light of the battle lantern illuminating it, except that something dripped slowly from the rounded square of the hatch. Dietz kept shining the light on the drip, keying the microphone of the VHF radio.

"Yo, Nav," he said, his voice steady but his heart in his throat, "we got a major problem down here in AMR One. I've got battery acid dripping out of the battery compartment. Give it a few minutes and it'll eat through the gasket, and once it hits the seawater and oil in the machinery bilges, we've got chlorine gas and hydrochloric acid. I don't need to tell you, that's damn bad for children and other living things."

"Roger, Dietz. How much time you think we have?" Judison's voice boomed.

"Grab an emergency air mask and set your watch, Nav. If we're not out of here in ten minutes, we won't be getting out of here. And, Nav?"

"Yeah, Dietz."

"If you have any ideas at all about how to get an unconscious person to hold his breath to get out the escape trunk, write them down and submit them for extra credit."

"I might have to take a gentleman's C on that one, Dietz."

"Right now I'd be ecstatic to get a C."

Dietz loaded the signal ejector and fired the radio buoy out horizontally, hoping the emergency CO_2 canister would work and that the unit wouldn't just hit a sandbank. When he'd hit the launch key, he shut the outer door, drained the tube, and opened the breech door. The tube was empty, so at least the buoy had left the ship.

That done, he began the trip back to control to help Judison get the others. This time he took the aft stairwell in the machinery room. Two trips through the torpedo room would be tempting fate.

"Sir, flash message down from the ComStar satellite, loaded into your WritePad," the radioman said.

Rear Admiral John Patton nodded, reaching into his bag for his WritePad while his staff truck bounced on the two-lane blacktop highway leading from the interstate to Portsmouth Naval Hospital, where he hoped to see Patch Pacino, who, rumor had it, was showing brain activity after all. Admiral Murphy had called and said he'd meet Patton in the hospital room. Patton clicked through his software, finding the message flashing on his queue.

241945ZJUL2018
FLASH FLASH FLASH FLASH FLASH FLASH
FM   USS DEVILFISH SSNX-1
TO   COMUSUBCOM
SUBJ   SOS
TOP SECRET
//BT//

1. (TS) USS DEVILFISH DOWN THIS POSITION. SINKING RESULT OF MULTIPLE PLASMA DETONATIONS.

2. (S) POSITION LATITUDE 37DEG47MIN36SEC NORTH/LONGITUDE 75DEG04MIN54SEC WEST/ DEPTH 112 FEET BOTTOMED.

3. (S) SHIP HEELED OVER 95 DEGREES MAKING ESCAPE TRUNK FUNCTION UNCERTAIN. TWENTY-SEVEN (27) INJURED AND UNCON- SCIOUS INCLUDING COMMANDING OFFICER, FORTY (40) CASUALTIES, TWO (2) MEN FOR- WARD OF FRAME 110 CONSCIOUS AND UNINJURED: NAVIGATOR AND ARTIFICIAL INTELLIGENCE OFFICER.

4. (S) DAMAGE ASSESSMENT: ALL POWER LOST. BATTERY COMPARTMENT LEAKING ACID. TORPEDOES SEEM INTACT. ATMOSPHERE BECOMING CONTAMINATED. REACTOR COM- PARTMENT BELIEVED FLOODED. NO CON- TACT WITH WATCHSTANDERS AFT OF FRAME 110.

5. (S) WITHIN TEN MINUTES OF THIS TRANS- MISSION FORWARD SURVIVORS WILL BE AT- TEMPTING EMERGENCY SUBMARINE ESCAPE.

6. (S) REQUEST IMMEDIATE SURFACE RESCUE
   AND AIRCRAFT MEDEVAC OF INJURED. IN AD-
   DITION REQUEST IMMEDIATE RESCUE FORCE
   TO ASSIST IN SURVEY OF AFT COMPARTMENT
   AND ASSISTANCE IN EVACUATION OF INJURED
   MEN AFT.

   //BT//

"Holy shit," Patton mumbled, reaching for a satellite secure voice handset.

It took forty-five minutes to haul the injured to the
lower hatch of the escape chamber, and by then the
battery-acid leak had become a steady drip. Dietz
glanced at it through his emergency air mask, knowing that hydrochloric acid would eat his lungs in seconds if he breathed in the gas. There would be only
minutes to get the two loads of survivors to the hatch.
The semiconscious and unconscious were given emergency masks and walked to a position at the base of
the hatchway. Judison would go up with the first load
and the emergency surface kit. Dietz would bring up
the second round.

Dietz and Judison manually pulled the lower hatch
of the escape trunk open. The heavy hatch opened
into the trunk with the hinge vertical in its 90-degree-
rolled position. The trunk was a large airlock designed to "lock out" up to nine Seals with full combat
gear and breathing apparatus at once. If the occu-
pants wore only lightweight Steinke hoods, it would
accommodate more than twice as many men. But
making it work in the horizontal instead of the vertical would be the trick, Dietz thought, with no power

and no hydraulics, and perhaps with no high-pressure air.

The two men lifted the injured and the unconscious into the trunk and fitted their Steinke hoods. The clear plastic hoods, covering the head and strapped onto the torso, were designed to be filled with high-pressure breathing air at the same pressure as the surrounding depth, so that as the swimmer ascended into shallower water with lower pressure, the excess air would spill out the bottom of the hood rather than overinflate the unit.

Finally all the hoods were on the survivors. Dietz plugged in the air hose and handed it to the navigator, then handed him the backpack survival package. As Dietz stepped to the hatch, he turned to look at Judison. The realization dawned in him that if something went wrong, this would be the last time they saw each other. The falling expression on the older man's face reflected that he, too, was coming to the same thought. The two had played poker together since their first days aboard back when Kelly McKee had taken command from the legendary John Patton. They had anchored the ship's softball team, played backfield on the *Devilfish* football squad. At that moment Dietz saw that if he gave the moment the slightest significance, he would bring down bad luck on both their heads.

He casually nodded at Judison, bringing the hatch off its seating surface by two inches, then called, "See you in a few, Kiethan." He pulled the hatch shut before the navigator could reply, spinning the dogging wheel hard. He tapped twice on the metal of the hatch and waited. Over the next incredibly slow

ten minutes, Judison filled the Steinke hoods of the
injured crewmen with air and flooded the trunk,
opening a valve to the sea and venting the air out.
In normal operation, the trunk would have had a
space of trapped air behind a vertical steel curtain so
that the upper hatch could be opened without the
space being completely underwater, but not so with
the trunk tilted over. Judison would have to completely submerge the interior, open the trunk upper
hatch, and maneuver the injured out the hatch. The
buoyancy of their hoods would send them to the surface above. When he was the last remaining, he was
supposed to shut the outer hatch and hear it click in
the latch. If he failed to accomplish that, if his own
Steinke hood's buoyancy carried him to the surface
before he was able to shut the hatch, Dietz and the
other men would never make it out alive.

Dietz stood there in the space, still wearing his
emergency breathing air mask, waiting for the trunk
outer hatch to shut. He heard the sound of the trunk
flooding, even the clunking noise of the upper hatch
opening, but for a long time there was silence. While
he waited those seemingly eternal minutes to see if
Judison would be able to shut the outer hatch, he
scanned the room and the remaining injured.

Captain Petri was out cold, leaning against the diesel engine's exhaust manifold. The others were lined
up next to her, the emergency breathing air masks
snaking through the space, plugged into each other
and to the manifold in what used to be the overhead.
Dietz looked over at the battery hatch, which was
now streaming battery acid into the bilges. A green
cloud was starting to form. He checked his watch,

knowing that if the chlorine gas and hydrochloric acid reached any significant concentration, it would defeat the seal of the breathing masks and destroy their lungs. They'd die horribly painful deaths before they ever reached the inside of the trunk.

Panic began to swell inside Dietz as he thought he smelled something inside his mask. A sharp pain stabbed his chest—the acid hitting his lungs—and he began to pound his battle lantern against the wall of the escape trunk, but there was no response. He tried to convince himself that Judison was already gone and had already shut the upper hatch, but he heard two knocks back.

"Hurry up!" Dietz shouted, his voice hoarse.

He could wait no more, he decided, and threw open the two valves of the trunk drain pipe. Seawater poured into the space. With the trunk tilted over, it would only drain halfway, but that should be enough if Judison had been able to shut the upper hatch.

Please, God let the Nav have shut the upper fucking hatch.

The trunk continued to drain, but Dietz could no longer wait. He undogged the inner hatch and tried to push it open, but it would not budge, because Dietz was pushing against a crushing wall of water, the three-foot depth of it exerting hundreds of pounds of force against the hatch. Only equalizing the pressure would allow him to overcome the weight of the water. That or fully draining the trunk. He watched the drain pipe, the water level in the space rising, now above Captain Petri's thighs; the other crewmembers submerged in the drainage and bilge water—and battery acid—up to their waists. Dietz pushed frantically, but the hatch still would not budge.

Fright was now crawling down his throat, and his motions became jerky, instinct taking over for conscious thought. He found a valve operating lever, a six-foot-long piece of three-eighths steel with an operating box wrench on the one end, a T-handle on the other, and tried to pry open the hatch just a fraction of an inch, fiercely pushing against the steel, but it wouldn't budge.

He was starting to scream in frustration when he felt a hand on his shoulder. He turned to see the face of Captain Petri. Her left eye was black and closed, but her good eye was squinting at him with an expression of anger. Her steely voice sounded distorted through her mask as she said, "Dietz! Knock it off and use this! We'll push together." In her other hand was a crowbar with a sharp flat claw tip. Dietz looked at her stupidly until she pushed her way past him and wedged the claw between the hatch and the seating surface.

"Hammer it in between with this," she shouted, pulling a heavy toolbox out of the water of the compartment. "No, just hold the crowbar!"

Dietz held the bar as she whacked it with the toolbox. Finally she tossed it, the heavy box splashing and vanishing in the black water outside the circle of the battle lantern.

"Now, help me pry," she commanded.

Dietz put both hands on the bar, glad to have his panic focused on this task, and he pushed harder than he could ever have imagined. He could actually see the thick crowbar beginning to bend with nothing happening to the hatch, until at last it opened a slim crack. The water inside the trunk came spraying violently out of the crack between the hatch and the seating surface. The firehose spray was strong enough to knock him off his feet if he hadn't been completely pumped with adrenaline. As the water came out he kept heaving against the bar, until eventually the water flow eased enough that Petri could open the hatch an inch. The water was spilling slowly now, and Dietz shoved hard one last time, the hatch coming fully open.

"Come on," he screamed, reaching for the first of the unconscious men. Man after man he put into the space, Petri helping him, until they were all inside. Dietz shut the drain valves, waved in Petri, and took one last look at the space. The water had risen to a few inches short of the bottom coaming of the escape trunk hatch, the water now lapping the battery hatch, but with the rising cloud of green a few seconds in this air would mean death. He grabbed the battle lantern and reached for his hose connection, ready to unplug as he looked up at Petri.

But she wasn't moving, just staring at the water around her waist.

"Captain, come on," he shouted. "We've got to go! The chlorine will kill us if we stay. Come on!"

But Petri lifted her head slowly and looked at him. There were tears streaming out of both eyes, and she had begun to shake. For a moment Dietz thought she must have been succumbing to the hydrochloric acid in the air, but there was something else going through her head.

"Captain! Come the fuck *on*!" he screamed again. But she shook her head.

"No," she said slowly, sadly. "You go. Get the men to the surface. I'm the captain. I lost this ship. I'm staying here. I'm going down with the *Devilfish*."

She said it with an air of finality and turned her back on Dietz. Her famous-last-words speech barely registered in his panic-stricken mind before the battery hatch blew open. Battery acid flooded the space, and the chlorine hissed up. Without conscious thought Dietz raised the battle lantern in his hand and swung it as hard as he could in a perfect softball homerun arc, connecting solidly with Petri's skull. The captain collapsed like a rag doll into the water of the flooded space. Dietz tossed the battle lantern into the escape trunk with one hand while grabbing Petri with the other, and before he knew it, the hatch was shut and dogged.

Dietz flooded the trunk while he pulled off the emergency masks of the injured and jammed lolling heads into Steinke hoods, then used the air hose to fill the hoods, Petri's second-to-last, his own last. Then he watched the water level rise. Claustrophobia grabbed him by the throat as the water level climbed high over his head. He shut the vent valve and swam to the latch of the outer hatch and shoved it mightily. He had expected it to be as hard as everything else had been that afternoon, but it flew open, almost expelling Dietz into the sea. He held on to the latch and forced himself back inside the trunk. He threw out the men one by one, their hoods shooting them to the surface.

Last came Petri. As he tossed her upward and out of the hatch, he mumbled to himself what the Circuit One PA system usually announced when the captain left: "*Devilfish* departing." Then he took a last peek into the trunk to make sure he hadn't forgotten anyone. When he saw that he was alone, he tapped twice on the hull with his academy ring and let go of the hatch.

He looked upward at the dim and diffuse light and blew his breath out, shouting, "Ho! Ho! Ho!" as they'd taught at the submarine escape blow-and-go training tank in Groton. The air in his lungs would blow up as he rose into the lower pressures of shallow water. High above his head he could start to see rays of light streaming down from the sunlight of the surface, and soon the bottoms of the waves could be made out. His body rocketed to the surface, driven by the balloon of his Steinke hood, and his entire upper body came roaring out of the water, only to splash back down, then bob in the waves. He pulled off the hood and ditched it. Looking around him, he felt Judison's arms pull him out of the water. A black survival raft was floating on the Atlantic. Dietz had only the merest impressions of the others inside, among them a passed-out Captain Petri.

Exhausted, half poisoned by the atmosphere of the machinery room, and more than half drowned, Dietz looked out at the horizon at the Aegis II–class cruiser hull. The American flag was visible even here, miles away, and a helicopter roared out of nowhere and turned to come back around and hover overhead. And Dietz, a lieutenant commander in the U.S. Navy and fifth in command of the submarine *Devilfish*, began to laugh and cry at the same time. Mucus from his nose and tears from his eyes ran down his face, and he didn't care.

Because in spite of everything that had happened to him that day, he was still alive.

BOOK VI

Hammerhead

31

Admiral Sean Murphy rose slowly to his feet as John Patton came out of the revolving door. Patton turned to his senior aide and chief of staff, Lieutenant Commander Byron DeMeers—formerly his sonar senior chief from his 688-class command days, but given a battlefield promotion last evening—and told him to wait in the entrance lobby of the Portsmouth Naval Hospital critical-care facility. Wait and man the communication circuits. Patton turned from DeMeers to Murphy, saluting and shaking the older man's hand.

"Admiral. I came as fast as I could," Patton said. "You heard the news?"

"Can't talk here, John," Murphy said, glancing over his shoulder. "I've got Patch's room under double quarantine for security. We can talk there."

"What about Colleen Pacino? Isn't she there?"

"She's cleared. She had to be—she won't let anyone in to see him without her presence. She runs the doctors around like they're plebes."

"Always liked her," Patton said.

The two men walked to the elevator and from there down a long hallway to intensive care. There was a separate wing, completely empty except for the armed Marine guards, what looked like an entire company of them. Their identification tags were checked, then they were ushered through metal detectors and escorted to a large room filled with medical equipment. They saw Colleen Pacino first, sitting in a deep chair. She rose to her feet as they came in. She was of medium height, a stunning brunette, wearing a slim-waisted suit. But she seemed washed out, as if she'd gone a week without sleep, which couldn't be too far from the truth. The admirals shook her hand.

"How is he?" Patton asked.

"He's good," she said, her tone forced. "He has excellent brain activity. They think he could come out of the coma anytime." She hesitated. "Would you two like to be alone with him? I could use a cup of coffee."

"Go ahead, Colleen," Murphy said, a father figure to the younger woman. "Take a break. We'll watch this old seadog for you, make sure he doesn't pinch any nurse's behinds."

"Thanks, Sean," she said, not smiling, sounding exhausted, and she withdrew. They went through a gap in the curtain, and there in the room's center, surrounded by hoses and tubes and wires, lay a pale old man in a hospital gown, his white hair spiked by sweat. Patton barely recognized him as Patch Pacino. His breath caught as he saw Pacino lying there so helpless and near death, and a huge lump formed in his throat.

"What do you think? Will he really wake up?" Patton managed to ask, feeling guilty about talking about his friend in front of him.

"They say so," Murphy said. "Somehow it makes

me feel better just to be here, even if he can't hear us yet."

"You guys went way back," Patton said.

"Patch was my roommate from plebe summer on. He made a career out of saving mine."

Patton nodded. A stretch of five minutes passed with Pacino unmoving. Patton glanced at his watch.

"So, sir, you did hear the news?" he asked Murphy.

"I just got off the phone with the President," Murphy said. "Choppers should be here within a half hour with the survivors."

"Two dozen of them. We lost almost a hundred more souls this afternoon, with the guys aft broiled by the steam leak."

"And you lost your number one warship," Murphy said. "Our only acoustic daylight platform."

"No, Admiral," Patton said, the lump in his throat gone now, his voice hot acid. "The NSSN, the USS *Virginia,* is on a crash program. You ever heard of a ship supe named Emmit Stephens?"

"Patch used to talk about him," Murphy said, glancing over at the submarine admiral. "Said he got *Seawolf* to sea in four days when it should have taken a month."

"He's working for me now. *Virginia* is getting a weapons loadout even as we speak. By tonight Electric Boat will be pushing the down button on the platform. By midnight she'll be starting up the reactor. This time tomorrow she'll be underway on nuclear power." Patton's jaw clenched. "This time next week the men who sank *Princess Dragon* and *Devilfish* will be on the bottom."

"*Devilfish,*" Pacino croaked slowly. Both men turned in astonishment.

Pacino's left eyelid was drooping markedly, but his eyes were otherwise clear. His lips were chapped, his tongue appearing slowly, tentatively on his lips. Within seconds nurses and doctors appeared, pushing the admirals aside, evaluating Pacino. They waited for several minutes until a doctor asked them to leave, just as Colleen returned. They tried to hustle her out also, to no avail.

Patton spent the next hour with the survivors of the *Devilfish* as they were brought in by helicopter. The ship's navigator, a lieutenant commander named Kiethan Judison, and the artificial intelligence officer, Lieutenant Commander Bryan Dietz, were the only two walking wounded. Patton had them wait in the chair area outside the emergency facility while he walked the ER with the attending physician, going from bed to bed, waiting outside the ER's operating room complex for four patients to come out. After a half hour, he found himself beside the bed of Commander Karen Petri. The woman looked as if she'd lost a fight against a gorilla. Her left eye was black and swollen shut, her face bruised, her lips fat from a facial impact, her skull wrapped in a plaster partial cast. One of her arms was splinted, and bandages wrapped her chest.

"Commander Petri," Patton whispered.

There was no reply. Patton left and went to the chair area, where Judison and Dietz were sitting.

Patton began with the same question he'd hit Petri with this morning, a lifetime ago.

"What the hell happened out there?"

Judison and Dietz calmly went through it for him. Patton nodded. He was standing to check on the wounded again and call for his chief of staff when he heard a voice behind him.

"John," Murphy said.

"Yes, sir," Patton said, turning toward the admiral.

"Patch is asking for you. You'd better hurry— I'll catch up in a few minutes."

Patton hurried to the elevator bank.

Kyle Liam Ellison "Kelly" McKee had been drinking since he'd left the fishing pier of the Bay Bridge-Tunnel thirty hours before, mostly Jack Daniel's. His bout had been interrupted just before sunrise when John Patton stopped over to talk to him. He'd droned on and on, but McKee had wobbled on his feet, unshaven, unshowered, and ready to throw up, nodding with mock intelligence as Patton said whatever he came to say, something about the cruise ship and a disaster. Finally Patton had taken him to his bathroom, washed him up, and put him into pajamas. He bodily lifted McKee onto the bed and turned off the light. Finally, the front door had clunked shut, leaving McKee in silence.

The sun rose, flooding the room with diffuse dreary daylight through the gauzy curtains Diana had put up, that McKee had always hated but now seemed to love, reminders of his wife. He sank into a half-sleep, at one point certain that the pile of pillows next to him was Diana, back from wherever she'd been, but after holding her and kissing her,

he finally realized it was only a down pillow, and
he fell back asleep.

When he opened his eyes again, the light of the
afternoon was fading. He walked downstairs to the
room that had been his study, where the photographs hung in dusty frames on the walls, where his
dead father and grandfather and great-grandfather
lived. He walked into the room and past the oil
painting of Diana to the central photograph on the
wall next to his desk, perhaps the family's most
famous, and he stood there staring at it, one minute
clicking into the next. He felt as if his ancestors in
the old photo had called him here, perhaps to
scream at him about how he'd destroyed his life.
He stepped away, just for a moment, just long
enough to take down Diana's oil painting and some
of the other photographs on the wall and pile them
in the corner. Just the men in his family remained
on the wall, staring at him, and as he continued to
stand there, something began to happen inside him.

Rear Admiral Jonathan George S. Patton IV skidded on the highly waxed floor outside Pacino's
room as he tried to slow down his jog from the
elevator. He grabbed the doorjamb and half-
vaulted into the room, eliciting the frowns of two
interns and the attending. He ignored them all as
he shoved past them and approached Pacino's bed.

The admiral's eyes were sunken in deep sockets
and surrounded by dark circles. A small tube bi-
sected his face, feeding oxygen to his nostrils. IV
needles snaked into his left arm; a sheet covered
the rest of him. Patton forced his lips to smile.

"You look great, Admiral. How do you feel?"

"You bullshitter," Pacino said slowly, his voice croaking and weak, his speech heavily slurred as if he'd just come from serious dental surgery, the sound of it making Patton's throat heavy again, one of Pacino's lips rising slightly as he struggled to smile. "I hope you're doing a better job running the Unified Submarine Command than you do reassuring patients."

Patton's smile became genuine at that moment, the next words from his mouth coming on their own. "Fuck you, Patch." And both of Pacino's lips rose, a grin on his face, but the effort of it seemed to exhaust him, and he shut his eyes.

"Sit down here and tell me everything, John," Pacino said. "Start with the moment the cruise ship blew apart."

Patton launched into the story while the light dimmed in the room and the sun set to the west outside Pacino's window, the floodlights of the hospital complex coming up as dusk became evening, and by the time it was fully dark, the story was finished. Patton turned in time to see Murphy come quietly into the room, obviously not wanting to disturb Pacino, but not wanting to miss out either. Patton waved Murphy in, and the CNO came over and squeezed Pacino's hand, then sat in the corner.

"So," Pacino said slowly. "Petri's hurt. *Devilfish* is on the bottom along with most of our senior officers and a surface task force. We never heard the saboteurs or the intruder submarine with our conventional sonars, and acoustic daylight didn't see anything until the torpedoes were inbound.

You think the firing ship was far over the horizon for both attacks, or that the cruise ship went down from mines. It sounds like any way you slice it, we are in big trouble, with an entire fleet bottled up for fear of a submarine attack we can't prevent or even detect."

"Hit the nail on the head, sir."

"And you have ideas on something you can do to get this guy."

"The NSSN, Admiral," Patton said. I've been working on the USS *Virginia* since I gave up command of the SSNX. If this had happened three months from now, *Virginia* would be ready, and we would have put this guy down."

"Or it would have sunk just like the SSNX. Look, John, this is coming down to stealth. The element of surprise. Whatever you do, you have to get the advantage of surprise back." Pacino began coughing then, and Colleen rushed over, holding his head and wiping his mouth.

"Just a few more minutes," she said to the admiral. Pacino continued on, waving a hand of acknowledgment at her.

"John, I don't know what to tell you, except find a way to surprise these men. And, John?"

"Yes, Admiral."

"Get McKee. Find him and put him on the NSSN. Get that ship into the Atlantic and tell McKee I said to come back with a broom hanging from the yardarm or don't come back at all."

A broom was the ancient Navy signal that the ship had done a clean sweep, sinking everything.

"Use handcuffs to get him on that sub if you

have to. He's the only sub commander who can do this for us."

Pacino began coughing again, Colleen imploring Patton with her eyes to leave. He touched Pacino's shoulder and his free hand, threw him a rigid salute, and said, "Get better, sir."

When he found Byron DeMeers, Patton spat a string of orders at him, among them the command to find Captain Kelly McKee.

"But he's just a commander," DeMeers said, looking up from his WritePad.

"Not anymore," Patton said. "He's got four stripes and the newest nuclear submarine in the fleet. He just doesn't know it yet."

The photograph in McKee's study had been taken on the aft deck of the fishing boat, a tourist special, with his eighty-eight-year-old great-grandfather Kyle standing proudly with a large sport fishing pole in one hand, his other on his son's shoulder, sixty-five-year old Liam McKee, who had his hand on the shoulder of thirty-seven-year-old Ellison—McKee's father—who in turn had his hand on the shoulder of eight-year-old Kelly McKee, who crouched down with his hand on the large corpse of a grimacing hammerhead shark. And the four generations of McKee men stared steely-eyed at the camera, victors over one of nature's most vicious beasts, a victory made even more significant by the fact that Kyle had served in the World War II submarine *Hammerhead*—the ship's battle flag tattooed on his forearm—while his grandson Ellison had served in the Cold War version, the Piranha-class nuclear submarine *Hammerhead,* SSN-663. The McKee between them, Liam, Kelly's grandfather, had forsaken submarines for Navy jets, having flown an F-4 over Vietnam before leaving the service in '67. As McKee stared at his dead ancestors, he could almost hear Diana's voice speaking to him. She'd always hated this photograph, thinking it had brainwashed her husband into following a Hemingway macho fantasy. But as he stood there, still shaky from yesterday's binge, her voice slowly hushed and the voices of the McKees swelled in his mind, and it was as if he could hear them, smell the cigar smoke of his grandfather, the Coors on his father's breath, and feel the sunshine on that day off the Florida Keys when the tour guide had held up the camera. McKee bowed his head and shut his eyes.

An hour later, McKee shaved off two weeks of beard and brushed his teeth. He opened his closet and found the service dress khaki uniform hanging there in plastic just the way it had been before the Wyoming vacation. He put it on, pinning on the ribbons and his dolphins—both taken from the crumpled uniform he'd thrown in the corner when he had returned from the South Atlantic—then snapping on his commander's shoulderboards.

The ringing of the doorbell startled him. He checked the clock on the wall: seven-fifteen. There were two state troopers on his porch and two cruisers in the driveway.

"Are you Captain Kelly McKee, sir?" one of the troopers asked.

"Commander. Commander McKee," he corrected him.

"You're coming with us, sir. Admiral Patton wants to see you."

At first McKee was about to insist that he could drive himself to the pier, but then reached to the crystal bowl by the door and withdrew his keys and wallet, took his Coach briefcase with his WritePad computer inside, and shut the door behind him.

He climbed into the front seat of the first cruiser, not saying a word until the car screeched to a halt at Oceana Naval Air Station in southeast Virginia Beach. McKee walked to the staff truck waiting on the other side of the guard shack, where a frowning muscular petty officer in a crackerjack uniform ushered him into the backseat. The truck sped down a road ending at a huge hangar, where a V-44 Bullfrog tiltrotor aircraft was just starting its huge rotors.

He got out and walked to the airplane, where he saw the stern carved face of John Patton, wearing the shoulderboards of a two-star admiral. Patton's eyes narrowed as McKee straightened and saluted, deciding to put on his own war face.

"Good evening, sir," he said crisply. "You sent for me?"

Patton's look of disapproval lightened, just slightly.

The V-44 Bullfrog landed vertically on the helipad of DynaCorp's Electric Boat New Construction Facility, Groton, Connecticut, shortly before ten. The rotors had barely begun to wind down when Admiral Patton and Captain Kelly McKee stepped out into the balmy air of the Connecticut coastline.

Inside the plane, Patton had told McKee what had happened to Karen Petri and his crew. McKee had been enraged. He asked several times about Karen's condition, shaking his head at the report of his dead former shipmates, the sinking of his former submarine. After staring out the window of the plane for a half hour, he had finally gotten around to asking Patton where they were going and what he was doing here.

Patton first reached into his briefcase and handed McKee two new shoulderboards, those of a full captain with four gold stripes, then produced a new solid gold capital ship command pin, a gleaming skull and crossbones set within the circle of the pin. The older man then handed over a sheet of paper, official orders from Commander Naval Personnel Command. McKee had looked at it by the light of the plane's dim reading lamp:

```
250235ZJUL2018
IMMEDIATE
FM         NAV PERS COM, WASHINGTON, DC
TO         K.L.E. MCKEE, COMMANDER, U.S. NAVY
SUBJ       OFFICIAL ORDERS
SECRET
//BT//
```

1. (S) REPORT IMMEDIATELY FOR DUTY DYNA-CORP NEWCON FACILITY GROTON CT AND TAKE PERMANENT COMMAND OF PRECOM-MISSIONING UNIT USS VIRGINIA, SSN-780.
2. (U) YOU ARE HEREBY FROCKED TO THE

RANK OF O-6 CAPTAIN. PERMANENT RANK TO
FOLLOW PENDING SELECTION BOARD
APPROVAL.
3. (U) CAPTAIN C.B. MCDONNE, USNR, SENDS.
//BT//

McKee was silent at first, pinning on the new
shoulderboards and the capital ship command pin
below his ribbons and his dolphins. But after that,
he still said nothing, and that surprised the admiral.
Finally Patton looked at him and asked, "Well?"

"Well what?"

"Don't you have anything to say about being
handed command of the NSSN? Or have any curiosity at all about what your mission will be?"

"As far as what the mission is, I assume I'm
being sent to track down the hostile submarine.
Correct?"

"Bingo. But what about the *Virginia*?"

"*Virginia*?" McKee said in disgust. "You named
a fast attack submarine *Virginia*? What's that all
about? *Virginia* is a battleship name. Or a cruiser
name. Or a ballistic missile sub's name. I'm not
going to sea in an attack sub named goddamn *Virginia*. You're going to have to do much better
than that."

Patton's voice sounded peeved. "What the hell
are you talking about? It's been named *Virginia* for
four years. The whole program is based on this
name."

"It's a stupid name," McKee repeated. "It's not
the name of a combat submarine, and I'm not taking command of it with that name."

Patton's face remained locked in a dark frown. His arms crossed over his ribbon-covered chest.

"Just for the sake of argument, McKee, what would *you* name the ship?"

"A name with a real tradition in the fast attack business. The USS *Hammerhead*."

"*Hammerhead,* huh?" Patton said, frowning. He seemed to come to a decision. "And that's it, that's your only beef?"

"I didn't say that. What did you load me up with?"

Patton sighed. "NSSN carries twenty-six room-stowed weapons. We gave you twenty Mark 58 Alert/Acute torpedoes, two Mark 23 Bloodhound underwater surveillance vehicles, and four Mark 17 Doberman ATTs—don't ask, I'll tell you about them in a minute—with the vertical launch system loaded out with two Mark 5 Sharkeye sensors, two mark 94 Predator unmanned aerial vehicles, and eight Vortex Mod Delta antiship underwater missiles."

"Crew?"

"We've got a full precommissioning unit—"

"Not good enough. Get Kiethan Judison up here—he's the XO. And get Bryan Dietz here, too. He'll be the navigator. I want Senior Chief Cook—you just promoted him, whether you know it or not—for sonar, and Master Chief Morgan Henry for radio. Harry Daniels will be the pork chop, I want Toasty O'Neal for electrical division, and Dick Van Dyne for weapons, and if there's anyone else awake at Portsmouth Naval Hospital from the *Devilfish,* you bring them here too."

"Anything else?" Patton asked, exasperated but beginning to warm to McKee's style.

"Two things. I want you to instruct Judison to go to my house and bring something up with him. The photo on my study's wall."

"Good-luck charm?"

"You might say that, sir."

It was the first time McKee had called Patton "sir" since he'd arrived at the staff plane.

"Okay. What's number two?"

"What the hell is a Mark 17 Doberman ATT?"

"Come with me, my son," Patton said, wrapping his arm around McKee's shoulders and walking him toward the NSSN assembly building, "and I'll tell you all about it."

"One last thing I forgot to ask, Admiral."

"Jesus! What now?"

"I'll need a straw broom. To hang from the mast-head when we come back."

Patton stared at him and broke into the widest grin McKee had ever seen on that cold face. "You got it, Kelly. You got it."

32

It was a few minutes after midnight on the morning of July 25. Under the floodlights of the NewCon Facility Building, the NSSN lay on the blocks of the lateral translation platform. The NSSN had originally been designed to be a close follow-on to the SSNX, and at first there had even been discussion about eliminating the distinction between the two ships, but Admiral Patton had decided that NSSN would improve on SSNX. The hull itself was identical to McKee's old *Devilfish* except for the sail, which instead of the SSNX's Russian-style teardrop shape had the more conventional vertical arrangement of the 688-class. The torpedo room had been made bigger and safer, since the SSNX's room fire during Operation *White Hope* had almost doomed the ship. The changes in the control room were among the most noticeable, including the elimination of the periscopes and the periscope stand, the "conn," in favor of a total commitment to photonics, the electronic sensors mounted on non-hull-penetrating masts in the sail able to display 360 degrees of view at once, with the output displayed on huge flat-panel displays angled in the overhead of the control room.

In order to allow the displays to be more easily

seen, the deck of the middle level where the control room was located was lowered by eighteen inches, with the upper level deck higher by the same amount. That made the headroom in the control room seem strange to submariners from previous generations of ships. The ship-control station forward, which had been designed for a single diving officer/helmsman up front, had been opened up to allow a two-seater console, for a pilot and copilot, with a relief pilot roving the room. The command console, a small station on the SSNX's conn corner, had been located in the center of the room and expanded. Gone were the eggshell canopies of the SSNX Cyclops battlecontrol display system, replaced by cubicles with doors, each three feet square and ten feet tall for virtual-reality display of the battlespace.

· The Cyclops system was improved, although the programming had not caught up with the hardware. The engineering spaces were simplified, designing in greater power density with fewer, more automated components. The sensors for acoustic daylight imaging were improved, able to identify friend or foe without the need for over-the-horizon confirmation. The system allowed the use of Mark 94 UUVs, remote unmanned underwater vehicles for reconnoitering a bay or anchorage or cubic space of ocean without the need to drive the ship into the area.

In all, Admiral Patton had maintained to Captain Kelly McKee, an SSNX captain should be able to step aboard and take immediate command with a few hours to brush up by reading through the computer files.

McKee stood on a platform level even with the middle deck of the submarine at the point of the nose cone, where the DynaCorp sign-making facility had draped a huge conformal banner reading SSN-780, USS HAMMERHEAD. Two more banners were erected on the port and starboard flanks, covering huge block letters that spelled SSN-780 VIRGINIA. There was a speaker's lectern set up there, with microphones. Below him on the floor of the mammoth building, the crew had been assembled, the members of the previous *Virginia* precommissioning personnel unit pulled from their homes by state troopers and military police. Next to them were the half-dozen survivors of the *Devilfish* well enough to come up to Groton on Patton's staff plane, including Judison and Dietz—both looking as if they were walking through a dream.

In a ceremony marked by briefness, McKee read his orders and pronounced the ship rechristened the *Hammerhead.* He didn't think that his first emotion on hearing that name echo throughout the NewCon building would be one of disappointment, but as he looked down from the platform all he saw were ninety pairs of uncomprehending eyes, some of the officers and enlisted men wondering why the ship was being renamed. He tried to shake it off, forcing himself to smile at the crowd as he hoisted up the Dom Pérignon '01 and smashed it as hard as he could against the steel plate epoxied beneath the banner at the exact center of the elliptical nose cone, cemented in place to keep the hard glass of the bottle from damaging the fiberglass of the bow. The bottle exploded into a shower of foam and bubbles, wetting him and the podium.

The crew dispersed to the building's offices, leaving McKee standing stupidly on the platform by himself. Even Patton had already left, leaving minimal orders behind. McKee had his weapon loadout information and the data disks about the NSSN, including where the ship was deficient, mostly in the command and control system. And the crew. And the war plan. And the rules of engagement. And of course, any scrap of goddamn intelligence of where the enemy was.

Or, for God's sake, *who* the enemy was.

Patton's forces suspected that the bad guys were the Ukrainians, perhaps one of the Severodvinsk units attached to the Black Sea Fleet. They had the means and the opportunity, Patton's intel briefing noted.

McKee looked around one last time, then pulled the banner off the nose cone. The parachute-size material fell to the deck far below. He put a tube of solvent to the squares of epoxy holding the steel plate, let the epoxy melt, and pulled off the plate, tossing it to the floor of the temporary platform along with the hard copy of his orders, and walked down the steps to the NewCon building floor.

He glanced at his watch. It was one in the morning. Next the lateral translation platform would be moved to the other end of the building and the submarine would be lowered into the water of the western half of the NewCon building. He could stand here and watch it in exhaustion or he could do the sensible thing and go into the low-bay complex to one of the VIP bunk rooms and sleep until six in the morning. By then the hull, which would have been moved a mere inch per minute, would be halfway into the water. He could even sleep until seven or eight, when the ship would be closer to its surfaced draft mark. The crew would embark at 0900. He should do the sensible thing and get some sleep.

But Kelly McKee, standing a few feet away from the submarine he'd just been given command of, remained standing and watching her as she inched away from the christening platform. At first he was just going to watch for a few minutes, but then decided to stay by the ship until it was time to embark. There would be time to sleep when this operation was over.

It was then that he realized that the feelings he felt now were akin to those of a man in love, and his fixed stare at the ship was much like that of a lover at his beloved.

33

Captain Kelly McKee sat in the captain's stateroom of the USS *Hammerhead,* SSN-780, eighty feet beneath the blue-green water of Long Island Sound, and read the op order on his WritePad computer.

```
251400ZJUL2018
IMMEDIATE
FM          COMUSUBCOM, NORFOLK VA
TO          USS HAMMERHEAD SSN-780
SUBJ        OPORDER 2018-0725-TS-002
COPY        CNO, WASHINGTON DC
TOP SECRET
//BT//
```

1. (S) USS HAMMERHEAD AUTHORIZED IMMEDIATE UNDERWAY 1400Z, 0900 EDT.
2. (S) USS HAMMERHEAD TO SUBMERGE ASAP IN LONG ISLAND SOUND PER LITTORAL WARFARE ATTACK PLAN 2017-1202 WITH NO LESS THAN FOUR (4) FATHOMS UNDER KEEL.
3. (TS) MISSION INITIAL PRIORITY IS TO MAKE MAXIMUM SAFE SPEED VIA SUBMARINE SAFETY LANES FROM POINT MONTAUK TO VACAPES OP AREA. SECOND PRIORITY IS SANITIZATION OF NEAR WATERS OF NORFOLK HARBOR FROM ANY HOSTILE SUB-

MERGED CONTACT, SEARCH AREA TO INCLUDE ELIZABETH RIVER, THIMBLE SHOAL CHANNEL, NORFOLK TRAFFIC SEPARATION SCHEME, TO LIMITS OF VACAPES OPAREA AS DELINEATED IN COMUSUBCOM OPPLAN 2200 REV 4 DATED 11/22/17.

4. (TS) RULES OF ENGAGEMENT: UPON DETECTION OF ANY HOSTILE SUBMERGED CONTACT, USS HAMMERHEAD AUTHORIZED ANY REASONABLE EMPLOYMENT OF SHIP'S WEAPONS AT DISCRETION OF COMMANDING OFFICER TO DESTROY HOSTILE CONTACT.

5. (TS) UPON SANITIZATION OF VACAPES OPAREA, USS HAMMERHEAD SHALL DEPART VACAPES OPAREA FOR SOUTH ATLANTIC AND PURSUE UKRAINIAN BLACK SEA FLEET BATTLE FORCE EN ROUTE WATERS OFF URUGUAY. BLACK SEA FLEET SHALL BE ENGAGED IF REQUIRED TO PROVOKE HOSTILE SUBMARINE CONTACTS.

6. (TS) UPON ENCOUNTER HOSTILE TRAFFIC AND PRIOR TO ENGAGEMENT, USS HAMMERHEAD SHALL POP SLOT BUOY SIGNAL NUMBER ONE (1) PER COMUSUBCON OPPLAN 2200 SAME REVISION. UPON COMPLETION OF ENGAGEMENT USS HAMMERHEAD SHALL CONTACT COMUSUBCOM BY MOST EXPEDITIOUS MEANS WITH SITREP TO FOLLOW. IN THE EVENT NO HOSTILE TARGETS DETECTED, USS HAMMERHEAD SHALL REPORT BY SLOT BUOY SITREP AT TWELVE (12) HOUR INTERVALS.

7. (U) REMAIN UNDETECTED.

8. (U) GOOD LUCK AND GOOD HUNTING, KELLY.

9. (U) ADMIRAL JOHN PATTON SENDS.
//BT//

McKee read the message four times. Though he probably couldn't explain it to Judison or Dietz, it was clear to him that his mission was to pause—not stop—in the VaCapes Op Area and check to make sure the hostile sub was truly gone, then head south to the equator and catch up to and sink the Black Sea Fleet. The hostile sub was obviously long gone—it had no reason to remain in the VaCapes, not now that the SSNX was scrap metal. With no acoustic daylight sensors to find it, the hostile sub was invisible, mission accomplished, and the Black Sea Fleet would be unmolested all the way to Uruguay. And to find the Ukrainian sub, he needed to find the Ukrainian fleet.

The trouble with this mission—more troublesome than finding the Ukrainian sub—was that the crew was mostly a precommissioning unit, a group of men with very little at-sea experience. The construction stage had been expected to take three to six years, and the group was seasoned with a very small cadre of experienced submariners expected to teach the "nubs," the "air-breathers" who didn't know potable water from potty water. The real leadership of this crew were the men he'd brought in from the *Devilfish*. Between him and those seven officers and chiefs, they would have to take the ship into battle and damn the torpedoes.

McKee picked up the phone to the control room forward of his stateroom and buzzed the officer of the deck. Van Dyne's voice came over the circuit.

"Get the XO and navigator to my stateroom in ten minutes, and have the galley send up two pots of coffee and three cups."

"Aye-aye, sir," Van Dyne acknowledged.

McKee wondered at the rush of pleasure he got from hearing that, from feeling the deck's slight vibration under his feet, from seeing the navigation chart with the flashing dot indicating their position, from the smell of the ship, the deep bass growl of the ventilation ducts, and the weirdness of how amazingly great the coffee tasted at sea—if hot dogs were better in a ballpark, there was nothing like coffee served four hundred feet beneath the Atlantic. All this was healing him, changing him back into the man he'd been before the trouble had begun.

"Captain?" Judison's voice said.

"Come on in, XO," McKee called, the feeling coming to him that calling Judison by Karen Patri's name and Dietz by Judison's name was extremely strange. There would be a lot of strange feelings on this run, McKee thought.

"Man . . . battlestations!" the Circuit One PA system announced throughout the ship.

Captain Kelly McKee stood aft of his command console in the control room. The commander's chair had been unbolted from the deck plates and stowed away in the fire-control stowage locker. McKee had tried it a few times but found that he was too tense to sit in it, and in point of fact did not want his officers of the deck sitting down during their watches. Sitting down during a 3-a.m. OOD midwatch during an uneventful submerged transit was an invitation to sleep on watch.

Hammerhead was eighty miles east-northeast of Norfolk, driving due south until they could accomplish the first part of the mission, the sanitization of the VaCapes Op Area. McKee pulled out a Cohiba torpedo and tapped it against his cheek. The large cigar, fragrant in its cellophane wrapper, was begging to be smoked, but he put it back in his coverall pocket and waited for the crew to arrive in the control room. When they were manned up, with Dietz as the battlestations OOD, McKee addressed the room:

"Attention in the fire-control team," he said. The watchstanders grew quiet. "Our first mission is to ensure the hostile sub that sank *Princess Dragon* is no longer in the VaCapes Op Area or in the vicinity of Hampton Roads. In my opinion this is going to be a formality. The hostile sub left long ago. But we will make sure, and every watchstander is to make the assumption that the hostile sub *is* in the area until we prove otherwise. Our orders are specific that we use whatever weapons will kill this guy the instant we detect him. And that's what we'll do.

"Step one, we'll warm up two Mark 58 Alert/ Acute torpedoes in tubes one and two with the tubes flooded, equalized with the muzzle doors open. Step two, we'll load and prepare a Mark 17 Doberman ATT antitorpedo torpedo even though we don't have the software to run it. If we need to use it, we'll have to guide it in manually, and let me tell you, gentlemen, that's a goddamn long shot. If we need to use a Doberman, every watchstander is ordered to pray as hard as he can until we have contact, and I'm dead serious."

McKee paused, deciding to light the cigar after all. He unwrapped the darkly fragrant torpedo of tobacco, the feel of it magical in his hand.

"Step three, we'll load and program a Mark 94 UUV an unmanned underwater surveillance vehicle. The Mark 94 will be my hydrophone on a leash. I'll drive it all the way through Norfolk Harbor in ultraquiet mode. If there's anything there more noisy than a sailboat, we'll have a lock on it. Step four, in ten minutes a P-5 Pegasus patrol plane will be overflying Hampton Roads from Norfolk Naval Air Station, and he'll drop two Mark 12 Yo-Yo pods, one on the west side of the Bay Bridge-Tunnel, one on the east side. We'll monitor the Mark 12 acoustic daylight output by streaming the passive high-data-rate UHF wire while we're deep. Between the Mark 12s and the Mark 94, Port Norfolk will be nailed down.

"Step five, anything we detect we have to classify. It won't do anyone any good if we launch a plasma torpedo at a container ship. I will definitely get docked command pay that week."

The watchstanders chuckled politely. McKee had clipped off the end of the cigar and raised his USS *Devilfish* lighter, firing up the tip.

"Let's say we classify a target as a hostile submerged target. Step six. We shoot his ass with the Alert/Acute Mark 58 torpedoes, with very carefully inserted settings so we don't blow up a bridge or send a torpedo into a beach house. And finally, gentlemen, step seven—if the hostile sub shoots at

us, we'll quick-reaction-launch the Mark 17 Doberman antitorpedo torpedo, with Mr. Dietz driving it.
If it's passive we'll run like hell to maximize our
distance from it, and if it's active we'll shut down
to give it zero Doppler return. If luck is with us,
Mr. Dietz bags himself a torpedo and a place in
your hearts. If it's a bad day, Dietz misses but
doesn't live long enough to experience your anger."

McKee tossed off the last while puffing the Cohiba to full flame, the billowing cloud of smoke rising to the overhead.

"Any questions on today's operation? Good.
Very well. Watchstanders, carry on. Mr. Van
Dyne? Are you ready to line up my tubes?"

For the next five hours, McKee scoured Port Norfolk. The unmanned underwater vehicle did laps
around Hampton Roads inside the Chesapeake Bay
Bridge-Tunnel, then came outside and swam
through the VaCapes Op Area, finding nothing of
note except the *Hammerhead* herself. The Mark
12 Yo-Yo pods had been dropped from the P-5,
revealing the same intelligence. Unhappy with the
result, McKee called for more Mark 12s for the
eastern area of the VaCapes Op Area, but a square
of ocean the size of the state of Maine was empty
of a hostile submerged contact.

Although McKee had expected to find nothing,
he wasn't prepared for his disappointment at the
news. He began to realize that there was a certain
bloodlust rising in him, far out of proportion to his
own personal losses. He'd practically slept through
the entire crisis. Troopers like Dietz and Judison

and Petri had done the suffering, and they should have had the desire for revenge. But McKee noticed that every time his mind brought up Petri's name, the desire for vengeance grew stronger. The hostile sub's attack had almost killed her, and now he would do anything, including violate his orders, to put the bastard down. It had become personal inside the space of a few hours. So be it. The enemy sub's commander had better be damn good, McKee thought, or he would be damn dead.

McKee had originally planned to rendezvous with the Black Sea Fleet where he had met the mockup force during the exercise, far south in the Atlantic. He sprinted toward the equator, dutifully sending his situation reports at twelve-hour intervals, but now they all just said "Situation nominal." So far no radioman had indicated they were getting any ELF signals calling them to periscope depth. And McKee had avoided periscope depth. It was good for the occasional correction to the ship's inertial navigation unit, grabbing a fix off the global positioning system satellite, but the NSSN had the UGM universal gravity module for deep ocean navigation, sensing the bottom's varying gravitational field, and an advanced passive bottom contour navigation system. The two of them made the need for excursions to periscope depth almost a thing of the past.

McKee's navigational plot had taken them along the great circle route, duplicating the path of the *Devilfish* to the South Atlantic. The great circle route crossed the equator at longitude twenty-five degrees west. With McKee's sprint at flank speed, he approached the equator in the wee hours of July 30.

McKee had reset the ship's clocks to Zulu time. Three days after they'd sanitized Norfolk Harbor, the "jet lag" was still making him tired. He climbed into his bunk in his boxers and T-shirt, after a long day of training the men and officers. Fire drills, flooding drills, tactical drills, reactor plant casualty drills. They'd been doing them whenever they did not interfere with the ship's southeastward progress. And McKee was exhausted. The job of training these men was much bigger than he'd imagined. The veterans were too few. It was unrealistic of him to take all these kids to sea and expect them to know their ship on the first time out. So drilling eighteen hours a day was McKee's way to get the crew where they needed to be.

McKee had planned on six more days of drills before they reached the South Atlantic ·hold position. He was hardly prepared for the phone call that buzzed him awake at 12:20 a.m.

"Captain," he said.

"Officer of the Deck, sir," Dietz said, getting right to the point. "Sonar reports multiple warships bearing one six five. Chief is indicating that they are Ukrainian. Ten warships, sound like deep-draft vessels, with fifteen merchants—cargo ships or troop transports or merchant vessels. Contacts are distant, sir, far over the horizon. Our target motion analysis range is being done now, but the computer is putting out a very-long-range number. Over a hundred miles."

McKee sat up, rubbing his head. "How far are we from the equator?"

"One hundred and ten miles, sir."

"Is it possible these guys are crossing the equator? Or at a hold point at the equator?"

"Chief Cook thinks they're at a hold position at or close to the equator, sir."

"Good. Station your section tracking party and slow to fifteen knots. Track the contacts and see if they have a holding pattern or a random zigzag while they're holding. And, OOD?"

"Yes, Captain."

"If this is the Black Sea Fleet, it's possible they are waiting for a submarine asset to catch up to them. Maybe even our friend from Port Norfolk. If that's the case, he's on the same great circle route we are. So keep up a max scan looking for him."

"Aye-aye, Captain. I'll talk with Cook."

"One more thing. Rig ship for ultraquiet. Shut down the port side of the engine room."

"Ultraquiet with port down, aye, sir."

"Wait a minute, OOD. Line up and prepare the Mark I Predator UAV. At sunrise we'll man battlestations and have Cyclops fly it over the surface force to confirm our targets, and to identify. We can't use satellite intelligence to backup the UAV—the software is down hard."

"Line up and prep the Mark I Predator unmanned aerial vehicle, aye, Captain. I'd recommend we keep the power off the unit until zero five hundred local, sir. Otherwise it'll overheat."

"Very well. Put in a wake-up for me at five-thirty."

"Good night, sir."

McKee hung up, debating with himself whether to grab a few hours of precious sleep or pace the control room. If he slept, with Dietz in control, he'd wake refreshed at five-thirty or earlier if something major happened. If he paced the control room he'd give the impression of being nervous and afraid, never a good image to project. That decision made, McKee rolled over and sank into a dreamless sleep.

Early the next morning the word was passed on the phone circuits in the rigged-for-ultraquiet submarine that the captain had called battlestations. The fact that the midwatch had detected the presence of a convoy a hundred miles down their great circle route had been circulated by the messenger of the watch, and even the men sleeping after the evening watch were shaken awake with the news. So when the phone circuits lit up with the word to man battlestations, the men were already up and dressed. The watchstanders filed into the control room within seconds of the order rather than the expected two to three minutes. All of them except Dietz and Judison seemed nervous, perhaps even afraid. The navigator and XO both wore frowns, war faces. McKee suspected that for them this morning's watch would be about revenge and the ghosts left behind on the bottom of the VaCapes Op Area.

Captain Kelly McKee had slept well since last night's call. He'd climbed into starched and creased black Nomex coveralls, the word MCKEE embroidered over his left pocket, his solid gold dolphins pinned above and his capital ship command emblem pinned below. On his collars were pinned the silver eagles of his new rank, Navy captain. On his left shoulder was an American flag patch. His right shoulder was missing the customary ship's unit patch, the ship's rechristening too sudden to support making a new patch.

He glanced around the control room. The room was filled with men, and even with the air-conditioning in high gear, the normally cold room was slightly stuffy. McKee had an odd feeling, finally realizing that with the periscope stand, the "conn," removed, there was now no railed-in elevated poop deck where he could pace and look down on his watchstanders. The center of the room, where the conn should have been, was now taken up with his command console with two chart tables between it and the ship-control area with open space aft where officers could stand and observe the overhead projections of the photonics sensor views on the large tilted flat-panel widescreens that ringed the room's overhead. The displays could also show the two-dimensional output of the Cyclops system, the navigation charts, or the video monitor outputs of one of the ship's cameras. McKee bit his lip. He would still function, but it wasn't instinctive. Making matters worse was that instead of having his own virtual-reality console, he would have to don what looked like a fighter pilot's helmet without the visor. The inside contained two rubber eyepieces that put the output of the Cyclops system into both eyes, making him see into the virtual battlespace in three dimensions. He'd be isolated from his control room even though he'd be standing at his command console. There was a function that would allow him to have one eye see his control-room watchstanders from a small camera mounted on the side of his helmet. Aside from the difficulty of interacting with his crew, he'd look ridiculous. And what about the intangible interaction, the expression on the captain's face? He'd spent years training his facial expressions so the crew could see his confidence or anger or concentration. That alone could make the difference in battle.

But then, he reminded himself, he hadn't liked the *Devilfish* control room at first either. But after a year aboard, he'd known he couldn't go back. He put the battlestations helmet on the console, plugged in its interface cord, and looked up at the watchstanders.

"Attention in the fire-control team." He had decided to do his war brief as a speech to the watchstanders as soon as battlestations were manned. There was always a speech by the captain to tell the watchstanders his intentions and decisions, but this speech would turn into a full-scale briefing, and with the watchstanders on their feet and tense, he was guaranteed to have their full attention.

"As you are all aware, we have multiple sonar surface-ship contacts over the horizon. By all indications onboard, these ships are warships, and they are Ukrainian. Senior Chief Cook believes we have found the Black Sea Fleet. The ships of this surface task force are distant, over the horizon, now at thirty-eight miles. The contacts are doing a diamond-shaped zig pattern, a shape they've followed all night. We believe they will continue to follow that pattern.

"We do not have satellite intelligence to confirm this, unfortunately, because our software isn't able to receive the data, so we're limited to onboard and offboard sensors."

He had a vertical launch system tube loaded with a Mark 94 Predator UAV unmanned aerial vehicle as well as a Mark 5 Sharkeye acoustic daylight over-the-horizon sensor. Between the two of them, he had the eyeballs to determine himself the contents of the entire battlespace. Or, as Petri might have said in a lighter moment, *We don't need no stinking satellites.*

"We'll launch the Mark 94 Predator UAV as soon as it's ready to go, and monitor the surface force. If the Predator escapes detection, we'll keep it up for the next phase of the battle. As soon as the Predator's up, we'll launch the Mark 5 Sharkeye over the horizon acoustic daylight pod. That way we'll have subsurface intelligence at the same time we have an aerial view. We'll put the Mark 5 on the other side of the task force by about fifteen miles, since we believe it will start to proceed south once it completes the rendezvous with the submarine. I have a concern that our launch vehicles will give us away and that either by radar or by seeing the smoke trail the surface force will know we're here. This is why I've chosen to launch now, when we're still almost eighty thousand yards away, which will minimize visual detection of the launch.

We'll evade to the east and approach the task force from the northeast. In addition, the launch vehicles will circle around to approach from the south, opposite the missile flame trails. The Mark 5 pod will be instructed to fly fifty miles east, then a hundred miles south, then fifty miles west, turn to the north and slow down, then put the pod down fifteen miles south of the convoy position. We'll program the Predator aerial vehicle the same way, except we'll have it fly in after circling around counterclockwise.

"Now, in addition to the acoustic daylight pod and the Predator aerial vehicle I intend to launch one Mark 23 Bloodhound UUV. Because the Mark 23 is an Alert/Acute torpedo body with the warhead taken out and the sound surveillance module jammed in, unavoidably it's going to sound like a torpedo. For that reason I considered not using it at all. If the surface force or their submarine pal realize there's a torpedo coming in, they'll immediately be alerted we're here and they'll reconfigure to a maximum ASW dispersion—you might even say that the surface force will go absolutely batshit looking for us." There was a nervous titter in the room. "None of us here want that, and as you all know, one of our orders is 'Remain undetected.' At the same time, people, I don't want to be blind, so I've decided to send out a Bloodhound in a decreasing spiral at ultraslow speed. The circular motion of the Bloodhound around the task force will avoid any high inbound Doppler return from a high-frequency active sonar. The Bloodhound should hear any tonals the submarine is putting out if the submarine is below the thermal layer, and I

intend to keep the Bloodhound circling for the du-
ration of the attack.

"Control of the Predator aerial vehicle will be
by software programming. I don't want to talk to
the UAV at all and put out radio frequency transmissions, not even highly secure EHF. We want to
be listening only, with passive sensors. That goes
for the Bloodhound in passive-listening sonar, the
Predator with visual and infrared and radar receiv-
ers only, and the Sharkeye—which is receive-only
anyway. If we do have to steer the Predator, we'll
absolutely minimize our EHF transmission. In addition, there will be no communication to the satellite
overhead at any time during this attack. We will
be as stealthy as is possible.

"Now listen up. This may be the only chance I
get to tell you people this. Once we launch the
Predator, the Bloodhound, and the Sharkeye, we'll
be in a tactical situation, and the only thing I want
to think about is where to put the next weapon,
not clueing watchstanders in to the reasons I'm
doing things. Do I have everyone's attention?"

Other than the sound of the ventilation ducts and
the whine of the Cyclops system, he could have
heard a pin drop. The whites of every eye were
turned toward him, the only calm faces in the house
belonging to Judison and Dietz.

"Good. Now it is my intention to confirm the
identity of the surface force as Ukrainian. Once
that is done, we will be attacking the task force,
per my orders at the start of this emergency mission
as part of the payback we're dealing out after the

Princess Dragon went down. However, there are a lot of ships, and we don't have a lot of weapons."

McKee flashed his fingers across a display on his console, and a long list of weapons flashed up on the display in the starboard corner of the room.

"It looks like a lot, but with our loadout of four antitorpedo Dobermans, two vertical-launch aerial surveillance Predators, two Bloodhound underwater surveillance vehicles, and two vertical-launch Mark 5 Sharkeyes, we only have twenty Mark 58 Alert/Acute torpedoes and eight Mod Delta Vortex missiles. That's twenty-eight weapons going against twenty-five surface contacts and a submarine, and we have to have at least four torpedoes and four Vortex missiles *dedicated* to the sub. Anything less could mean we can't box him in, and if I have a choice, I want *all* my weapons aimed at the enemy submarine. Everyone here needs to understand this—we don't *care* about the surface ships. We want the surface task force to turn back to the Ukraine so we have more weapons for the sub. We are attacking the surface force to draw the sub's fire, to make him show himself. If he shows up in our sensors, we will break off the attack against the surface ships and try to kill the sub.

"Now, we may not see the sub for a while, so if our offboard sensors have reported all the intelligence we need and we still haven't seen the sub, we'll do a time-on-target attack on the combatants. So far we think the surface ships have ten combatants—destroyers, cruisers, an aircraft carrier, a chopper carrier—and fifteen assorted cargo ships, troopships, amphibious assault ships, and maybe a command-and-control flagship. We'll target the high-value warships first, but we're going to try to identify the command-and-control platform and spare him. Now, you're probably asking yourself why the old man would want to spare the C-and-C flagship. The reason is, if we let the admiral in command of this fleet watch his ships sinking, he may give up and turn around and bring this war fleet back to the barn. We'll target the ten warships with Mark 58 Alert/Acute torpedoes with the attack planned so that every one of the ten will take a torpedo hit at the same moment in time—we don't want any of them alerted or doing evasive maneuvers, and we don't want any to survive and turn on us and do an antisubmarine search. We want to kill them in the same instant, not wound them or kill some and leave some unharmed. Everybody got that? So that's ten Alert/Acutes gone. Our loadout will go down to ten Mark 58s and eight Vortex Mod Deltas, leaving six more Mark 58s we can shoot and four Deltas before we hit our reserve battery for the sub.

"So we'll sit back and watch the combatants sink. The next phase of the battle should begin then if I'm guessing right, and that is the appearance of the escort submarine to break up our assault on the surface fleet. If there is a Severodvinsk escort sub here, he should come roaring out at us the instant he hears the first torpedo shot." At least, McKee thought, he hoped so.

"If we don't detect the sub at that point, we need to make a decision. If the troopships and cargo ships do not withdraw to the north, we'll start to target them one at a time until the admiral in command gives up and goes home. The one-at-a-time strategy will also give the submarine time to get pissed off and come at us. We'll shoot a troopship or cargo ship every twenty minutes until they withdraw or until they're all sunk, using up to six Mark 58s. If the sub still doesn't show, we'll fall back, shadow what's left of the surface force, and let a day or two pass. If it's a few days later and there's no sign of the sub and the flagship is still driving south with the remaining troopships, we'll put them all on the bottom, save two weapons for the sub, and head home after calling for backup. I sincerely doubt that will happen.

"Everyone clear on this plan?" McKee looked out over the watchstanders. Judison nodded. So did Dietz. His XO and navigator had this down. Dick Van Dyne looked cool, but the other junior officers looked white and embalmed. It would get worse for them, McKee thought.

"Very well. Carry on. XO? A word please?"

McKee turned away from the watchstanders, Judison walking up close. "Yes, Captain?"

"Those Mark 17 Dobermans. Do they work?"

Judison shrugged. "Onboard documentation says they will."

"But we don't have the software to control them."

"Right."

"Can we patch them into the VR consoles and steer them manually?"

"Yessir. Odds are slim we'd ever hit anything."

McKee gave Judison an appraising look. "You practiced it, didn't you?"

The executive officer, formerly McKee's navigator, stared at the deck plates. "Yessir, I did."

"And?"

Judison looked up, his face red, and spoke for once in a quiet voice. "I never connected. Own ship took the torpedo every time, straight up the poopchute."

McKee put on his war face. "I played football in high school. Quarterback. We came from behind to win state champs my senior year. On a crazy flea-flicker play that never once worked in practice. You get my drift?"

Judison's face's red color eased, and he grinned. "Yessir. Loud and clear, sir."

"Good. Attention in the fire-control team. Prepare to launch our three offboard sensors."

While the crew busied themselves with the sensor launch, McKee watched Judison, wondering if the XO had any idea that McKee had never played football in his life.

34

The surface of the Atlantic Ocean a little over fourteen hundred nautical miles east of the mouth of the Amazon River was unremarkable. The deep blue waves were gentle, rolling eastward in the slight ten-knot breeze. From one horizon to the next the sea was completely empty.

The placid seascape was punctured by a white foam burst as a white object came flying out of the sea. In the blink of an eye a column of smoke towered overhead in what before was a featureless sky. The roaring fury at the top of the smoke finger was at first deafening, then receded, then disappeared into the distance. The remaining smoke was blown by the slight breeze. The smoke trail ended two thousand feet above the waves, and whatever had caused the smoke trail was gone.

Twenty seconds later, a second white object appeared and roared aloft on a thread of smoke, with an identical booming roar that quickly faded and disappeared. Within a minute the smoke trails faded, resembling the contrails of a far-distant airliner.

Just below the surface of the waves, the sea was warm, stirred by wind and heated by the energy of the sun. The warmth extended to about two hundred feet below the surface—but at that point the water hovered a fraction above freezing for salty seawater, a mere twenty-eight degrees Fahrenheit. The sounds from the cold, deep water rarely were able to penetrate the line of demarcation into the warm layer, instead bouncing back down to the cold water. Similarly, sounds from above the layer rarely were able to penetrate deep, reflecting off the surface of the layer, like light on mirror. Three hundred feet below the layer depth, a twenty-one-foot projectile moved through the water like a swift shark. The skin of the machine was rubbery, like that of a dolphin. It moved by virtue of a pump jet propulsor, from water being sucked into two indented ducts on the skin and taken deep within the inside of the body and being moved aft by the vanes of an ultraquiet water pump impeller. The water was ducted out of a central nozzle at the far aft end, the underwater version of a jet.

The gas turbine, driven by the combustion of high-temperature gases resulting from a spark in contact with the peroxide self-oxidized fuel, made a rhythmic noise at a primary frequency of its rotation. In addition, there were harmonic frequencies put out at multiples of the rotational speed of the turbine as well as the natural frequency vibration of the whole machine from the disturbance of the vibrations of the turbine. But along the skin were twin hydrophones—noisemakers—that put out noise in exact opposition to the turbine noise, phase-shifted one-half wavelength so that the transmitted noise exactly canceled the turbine noise. This combination was called "active quieting."

The unit's inventors had long watched sharks and dolphins, seeing that their skin moved while they passed through the ocean, flexing and dimpling, making waves on the surface of the skin like those on the surface of the sea. The give in the sharkskin reduced the drag force on the undersea creature, allowing it to swim faster. The manmade object had been given the same low-drag skin.

The machine had a name—Mark 23, the unimaginative weapon code, and Bloodhound, the more definitive nickname that had stuck since the time of the first unit's testing. It had what could be considered a mother, for streaming from a tailfin was an ultrathin fiber-optic cable, connected miles behind it to the tube of metal that had launched it. The Bloodhound was in the water for one purpose—to sneak up on the battle fleet and listen with the array of hydrophones covering the nose of the machine in a small basketball-size hemisphere. The noise heard would be sent back to the onboard mid-body processor that did the calculations to put out the active-quieting noises.

The Bloodhound was swimming southeast, making a decreasing-radius spiral inbound to the surface battle fleet, steaming slowly in its diamond formation above the equator. In the space of an hour, the Bloodhound would be five nautical miles away from the surface ships, far to the south of them. From the ring laser compact inertial navigation module it knew its own location, and from its fiber-optic link to the mother ship, it knew the location of the surface ships, which was confirmed by very dim noises coming from the general direction it expected. But the loud surface ships were up on the waves while the Bloodhound was circling three hundred feet below the thermal layer. At the five-mile point, the Bloodhound would cautiously fly above the level of the layer, its right side toward the surface ships so that its motion would not cause a sonar pulse to be reflected back as it would be if the Bloodhound approached straight on.

A few feet above the waves and fifty miles west of the surface ships, the airframe of a jet-engine-powered missile flew over the water at two hundred miles per hour. The airframe was covered with radar-absorptive material, and the missile had a smaller radar reflection than a seagull or a wave tip. The machine flew on small carbon-fiber winglets, and the vectored thrust of its small jet, which took in air from an underbelly scoop, passed it through the gas turbine, and ejected it from the aft nozzle. The machine was carrying in its nose a package the size of a steamer trunk, destined for a spot on the ocean fifteen miles south of the surface ships, the Sharkeye acoustic daylight imaging pod. Sometime in the next twenty minutes it would reach the point where it would shut down the engine and angle upward, its velocity dying as it pointed to the heavens, and at zero speed the airframe would eject the Sharkeye package, which would drift down to the water's surface under a haze-gray silk parachute.

Far to the east of the convoy a similar missile body flew, but this one slower, at about ninety miles per hour, and this unit did not cruise clipping the waves but high above the water at an altitude

of twenty thousand feet. Its infrared scanners and
visual and light-enhanced gyrostabilized cameras
looked westward over at the battle fleet. When the
Sharkeye hit the water, the Mark 94 Predator unmanned aerial vehicle would be almost four miles
above the surface task force.

Transmitting its information down to the men
inside the submarine far beneath the waves was a
small antenna inside the mid-body. The antenna
was gyrostabilized so that its beam of extremely
high frequency transmission did not waver, but was
aimed precisely at the receiving antenna. The EHF
radio waves were nearly impossible to intercept,
but gave out only a meaningless garbled noise if
they were.

Thirty miles beyond, on the surface of the waves,
was a small object the size and shape of a football
bobbing slowly on the ocean's surface. Inside the
object was an antenna locked onto the signal coming down from the Predator. The football buoy was
connected to a cable that extended far into the
warm ocean layer in an arc, penetrated the layer,
and went deeper, ending finally at the top of the
sail of the nuclear submarine. Soon, when the Mark
5 Sharkeye package parachuted into the waves, a
small buoy much like the towed football on the
submarine would surface from a cable going down
to the Sharkeye's basketball-size acoustic daylight
imaging sensors, which would not concern themselves with the surface ships above the layer, but
would sink deep below the layer to search for the
image of a submarine approaching the convoy. The
information from the Sharkeye would be transmit-

ted upward along the thin cable to the floating football and uplink to a second antenna on the Predator UAV, which would transfer the information to downlink to the submarine's football along with the data gained by the Predator itself.

The central node of the three sensors was the Cyclops battlecontrol system, which would collect all of the intelligence and integrate it into a single four-dimensional picture of the battlespace, the fourth dimension being time. The display of this information would come into the control room in the virtual-reality display cubicles or into the command console's interface module, down the interface cable, and into the captain's command helmet.

At eleven o'clock in the morning, the Sharkeye airframe pulled hard upward while cutting off the fuel valve and shutting down the engine. The missile climbed five hundred feet, stopped in midair, and began to fall slowly downward when the skin of it blew apart. A barrel-shaped electronics package emerged, a streamer popping out to stabilize it. Then a mattress-shaped silk parachute popped out to slow the unit on its two-minute trip to the water's surface. After a small white splash, the unit disconnected from the silk and sank into the ocean. At the thermal layer the barrel shape popped open and scattered the small spheres connected by fiberoptic wires horizontally and vertically. While the spheres sank lower and spread apart, the football buoy rose above the layer, its cable connected to the central sphere, and broached the surface, bobbing gently in the small waves. Its antenna came alive and transmitted the "all nominal" signal to the Predator's antenna.

Captain Kelly McKee's helmet transmitted the data into the twin lenses connected to his eyes by soft black rubber eyepieces. His eyes blinked as the virtual-reality world opened in front of him and around him, transporting him to a three-dimensional space as real as the one the Predator was watching.

He existed in a crystal-clear ocean of infinite depth. When he looked down, his feet rested on the toy hull of a submarine pointed southwest, the hull about three feet long. High overhead, he could see the wavy surface. It looked like he could swim for it, but in between was another surface—the thermal layer—also wavy. It was as if he were submerged in a bottle of salad dressing that had separated.

Over his head, to the southwest—the direction the toy sub hull was going—the twenty-five ships of the surface fleet were steaming. They were about forty feet above him and in front of him. He could see each one, spread out, all of them about three or four feet long, clustered into a formation and steaming southeast, at a ninety-degree angle to him, baring their left flanks to him.

With the Cyclops Mark 83 Mod Echo Battlecontrol Artificial Intelligence Network Nodal System, a newer version than the Mod Bravo system on the SSNX, McKee would be able to leave his virtual station standing on top of the sub hull and fly up above the surface to see the virtual targets. He had been skeptical that the ability to maneuver would even be useful, and he'd heard that the maneuver function could give severe vertigo, but he mentally shrugged. Self-consciously, he lifted the hand up, aware that he probably looked like a child pretending that his hand was a jet fighter, but he immediately forgot what he must have looked like to the control room watchstanders, for as his hand lifted up toward the overhead his virtual body flew away from the submarine hull and up toward the surface. He could feel his head penetrating the warm layer, then he flew farther up out the water and into the sky. Below the thermal layer he could see the hull of the *Hammerhead,* a gray color, looking like a dolphin with the waves leaving moving highlights on its top flank. McKee raised his head as the surface grew distant, and then over to the southwest, below him by what looked like a hundred feet, perhaps a virtual half mile toward the horizon. He moved faster and faster, accelerating until the ships were directly beneath him. He began to plummet until the twenty-five ships of the fleet were five feet below him.

The first ship McKee looked at was the Kuznetsov-class aircraft carrier. It looked as real and sharply defined as if it were a physical model. The computer stored actual high-optical-magnification visual images of it from each angle of the flying Predator vehicle, then assembled them together to form the three-dimensional display. The ship was a canted flight deck carrier with a ski-jump bow runway. The shape of the ship was wide and flat, the navigation island home to several phrased-array radar panels, a huge central stack, and a tall cylindrical antenna, with the bridge control deck visible below. A dozen aircraft were cabled to the flight deck, including Flankers, Frogfoot and Fulcrum fighters, and two of the recently procured FireStar Japanese export-variety jets.

"Identify," McKee muttered to his boom microphone, addressing the Cyclops system. A tag appeared in front of him, listing the ship's vital statistics:

NAME: *ADMIRAL FLOTA SOJUZZA KUZNETSOV*
HULL NUMBER: 113
DISPLACEMENT, TONS: 67,500 FULL LOAD
DIMENSIONS, FEET: 999 X 229.7
MAIN MACHINERY: 8 BOILERS, 4 TURBINES,
   200,000 HORSEPOWER / 147 MEGAWATTS
MAX SPEED: 30 KNOTS
COMPLEMENT: 1,700 (200 OFFICERS)

"Registration," McKee said. The tag added the words:

NAVY OF THE UKRAINE. BLACK SEA FLEET.

"Attention in the fire-control team," McKee said into his boom microphone inside his helmet. "This task force is definitely the Black Sea Fleet battle flotilla. I'm searching to see if there is a flagship or command-and-control vessel, but other than troop carriers and cargo ships, there are only the aircraft carrier, two cruisers, two ASW destroyers, two anti-air destroyers, and three fast frigates. We will therefore target all ten warships with a time-on-target Mark 58 Alert/Acute torpedo attack. Any questions?''

Judison spoke up. "But, Captain, what about having the fleet admiral turn the ships back to the Black Sea? If we take out his aircraft carrier flagship, he won't be around to give the order. Your previous policy, sir?''

"The executive officer has raised a good point," McKee said to the room. "My logic is that I can't leave the aircraft carrier to proceed on with the task force. It is too lethal, and the aircraft embarked aboard could include ASW jets, which could come get us. As far as making the remaining troopships and cargo vessels turn back, we'll have to count on whoever is the surviving senior officer present afloat to make that call. If he makes the wrong call, we'll motivate him by conking a ship every twenty minutes. A final word. Despite the business of shooting these weapons and watching them detonate, all hands are to remain on max alert for the arrival of the Ukrainian submarine. Any other confusion? Very well, carry on."

McKee flew circling the surface force for the next few minutes while the attack was prepared.

"Captain," Kiethan Judison said in McKee's ear as he zoomed in between the two cruisers, then flew back high above the force, high enough to see the dolphinlike shape of the *Hammerhead* below. "Ship is ready for the salvo. Alert/Acute weapons are warm in tubes one, two, and four with the tube muzzle doors open. Tube three remains loaded with the Mark 17 Doberman. Do you want to download that for an Alert/Acute?''

"No," McKee said. "Even if it means we keep the Mark 58s orbiting a little longer before they run to the Black Sea flotilla, I want that tube for the Doberman. You remember our little chat, XO?"

"State champs on the flea-flicker, sir."

McKee smiled, his white teeth shining inside the helmet where no one could see him.

"Cyclops, Captain," McKee said.

"Yes, Captain," the deep-voiced computer said in his headset.

"Designate the ten combatants of the Black Sea Fleet as follows: aircraft carrier, target one. Cruiser at this position"—McKee flew to the southernmost of the two cruisers—"as target two, the other cruiser target three." He identified the four destroyers and three fast frigates, then confirmed Cyclops had the data.

"Target designation entered, Captain," the system said.

"Very well. Cyclops, insert calculations for a time-on-target torpedo attack using tubes one, two, and four with Mark 58 Alert/Acute torpedoes with wire guidance cut off, full programmed attack."

"Please specify detonation interval, sir."

The computer wanted to know whether the ten torpedoes were required to hit within a half second of each other, or sixty seconds, or three minutes.

"Plus/minus ten seconds," McKee said. Not enough time for the ships to take evasive action, and loose enough that the computer wouldn't waste torpedo fuel orchestrating an attack more precise than it needed to be.

The Cyclops system spent the next second thinking, knowing the rate at which it could launch each
torpedo, shut its muzzle door, drain the tube, open
the breech door, ram in a new weapon, plug it in,
start the gyro, shut the breech door, flood the tube,
equalize it to sea pressure, open the muzzle door,
pressurize its water-round-torpedo tank, confirm
that the weapon was warm, complete the onboard
processor's self-checks, perform the warhead self-
checks, insert the trajectory to the target to the
onboard processor and launch the weapon, then
start the entire cycle over again. The cycle time
even with the fast warmup of the Mark 58 torpedo
put the detonation time far after the launch of the
first torpedo, especially given that they were still
thirty-five miles away and that torpedo approach
velocity would be set at a stealthy thirty knots.

"Captain, from first launch to the time-on-target
interval, we are showing one hour and seventeen
minutes."

"Attention in the fire-control team. Firing-point
procedures, targets one through ten for time-on-
target assault, Cyclops data to be inserted."

"Ship ready, sir," Dietz said.

"Weapon ready," Van Dyne reported.

"Solution ready," Judison said.

"Cyclops ready," the computer said.

"Shoot on generated bearings," McKee ordered.

"Set," Judison said.

"Standby," the Cyclops computer said.

"Shoot," McKee ordered, his final chance to
abort the attack or pursue it.

"Fire," Van Dyne called, the report that the Cyclops system had control.

"Cyclops has the torpedo room," Judison said.

"Tube three launch in three, two, one, mark," Cyclops said, the word "mark" punctuated with the barking roar of a torpedo launch from the lower level.

For the next fifteen minutes, Cyclops fired torpedoes. The first-fired unit flew out of the dolphin shape below the layer, an orange trail marking its passage. McKee watched it from high above as it drove two miles from the *Hammerhead* and began a slow circle a thousand yards in diameter. The other torpedoes began to emerge from the ship below him, their hold circles spaced out so that they were a half mile apart, until there were ten torpedoes in the water. The last-fired weapon in the salvo didn't circle but proceeded on toward the surface force; then the other nine torpedoes broke off from their orbits to sail on toward the fleet.

"Forty minutes until plasma detonation, Captain," the computer said.

"Very well," McKee said. Shutting his eyes, he pulled off his helmet and put it on the console. Reality returned to him in a rush, the sky and the sea beneath him vanishing, the control room back. And vertigo came to him, not from the motion of flying in the three-dimensional virtual battlespace but from the sudden stopping of the motion. The room spun around him, and his stomach lurched. He clamped his eyes shut and held on to the console handhold. The nausea didn't seem to wear off. He considered putting the helmet back on, but didn't want to stand there with the stupid visorless box on his head for the better part of an hour.

"There's a bottle of water in your console, Skipper," Judison said, not looking at him. "And a couple of vertigo pills."

McKee took the water but ignored the pills. At last he forced himself to open his eyes.

"How was it, sir?"

"A trip to the amusement park," McKee said.

He glanced up at the tilted widescreens in the overhead. The forward port display showed the surface force as so many diamond symbols with the approaching torpedoes ellipses. The central forward display showed the camera view from the Predator circling overhead discreetly to the south.

"Cyclops, how long to impact?" he asked the overhead.

"Eight minutes, Captain."

"All right, everyone, tighten it up in here. Torpedo detonation is imminent, and we have to expect that in the next few minutes our weapons may be counterdetected. We also may need to be ready for a visit from our submarine friend. Carry on."

Where the hell was the Ukrainian submarine? McKee wondered in frustration.

35

"Check," Novskoyy said, moving the black rook to the far side of the board, in line with Grachev's king.

Grachev stared at the board. "Into my trap," Grachev said, blocking the rook with his knight.

"What did you say?"

"Nothing," Grachev said.

Novskoyy studied the board, then moved his queen diagonally to threaten the knight.

Grachev moved his own queen and stood.

"Where are you going? You've got a game to lose."

"Do I? That would be difficult, seeing as you're under checkmate." Grachev left his outer stateroom and walked up to the control compartment, a slight smile growing on his face.

Behind him in his stateroom, Al Novskoyy mentally played the chess game through five moves and lost, then tried another five moves. His third attempt ended in only four moves. He knocked over his king and pushed back from the table in disgust.

In the control compartment, Grachev's boots tapped quietly as he climbed the ladder. He stroked his fingers on the cool, smooth, oily metal of the hatch bulkhead, then emerged into the center of the room. Around him purred the bass note from the air-handling ducts, the whine from the inertial navigation cabinet and the thrum of the processor modules of the Second Captain.

He stood behind his command console, his hands in his pockets, nodding at the deck officer. He tapped through his console's software display. The navigation display came up, and it showed them 122 kilometers north of the equator, due north of longitude twenty-five. Grachev had turned the ship from its great circle route from the U.S. East Coast farther east to approach the rendezvous point from due north. This approach was apparently a submarine safety lane, so that the convoy—were they to detect a submerged contact from due north—would know that a sub coming from that direction would be a friendly vessel.

A carafe of coffee arrived, and with it Grachev's *Vepr* cup with its trademark boar's head, designed personally by Svyatoslov. A boar, Grachev thought. Only his Svyatoslov would name a combat submarine after a boar. He smiled to himself, realizing that every kilometer he made good away from the port of Norfolk gave him that much more confidence that they would return from this mission.

It had been a good day, he thought, sipping the scalding hot coffee, looking around the compartment in satisfaction.

He heard Svyatoslov enter, looking around.

"Mr. First," Grachev said. "What's going on?"

"Nothing much. Just seeing to the chart. I'd rather look from up here than on my remote in the stateroom."

"It is better," Grachev said. "Like the old days."

Out of nowhere came the ringing of the general alarm by the Second Captain.

"What is it?" Grachev asked the Second Captain while scanning display zero. "And silence the alarm."

The clanging of the emergency annunciator stopped.

"Captain, the system has picked up a possible torpedo in the water at bearing one zero one, bearing rate right, range distant," the sterile voice of the Second Captain said.

There was very little else on the status panel of display zero. While Grachev leaned over to think, he could hear the footsteps of the men hurrying into the control compartment.

"Deck Officer, man tactical stations," Grachev said, tapping his console display to show the surrounding spatial representation taken from the sonar sensors. Aux one showed ship and weapon status, aux two the raw sonar display, and aux three the processed sonar information. The other auxiliary displays he left to the Second Captain to use to show him information as it saw fit.

"Check," he said, hearing his own voice.

"Read you, Captain," Svyatoslov said.

"Attention control compartment," Grachev said. "Second Captain has detected a long-range torpedo sound from the east. We don't know if it is headed for our convoy. I'm waiting now to refine the data coming into the Second Captain on this leg. Once the computer has a steady bearing rate, I intend to drive the ship across the line-of-sight to the torpedo

to get a preliminary parallax range on the unit.
Once we get a read on range, I will move the ship
above the layer depth and analyze the sonar signals
we hear in the warm water. If this torpedo is shallow, our signal-to-noise ratio will improve. If not,
the torpedo will get quieter. We will also be listening to see if we can detect the firing platform,
which I suspect we will when we penetrate the
layer." His stomach sank. Either way this was very
bad news. "Second Captain, prepare tubes one
through four with Bora II torpedoes, then flood,
equalize, and open outer doors on the upper bank.
Apply weapon power one through four for a quick-
reaction firing."

The torpedo might be targeting them—that was
the first task on the frantic emergency checklist,
to see which direction this torpedo was going and
determine if they needed to evade it. If it wasn't
headed for the *Vepr,* where was it going? He'd
have to warn the surface force to split up, to scramble into an antisubmarine formation and disperse
to avoid the incoming torpedoes.

The next thought came in a rush. If there was a
torpedo in the water, then someone had launched
it, and it was extremely unlikely that it was an air-
craft-launched weapon, not this close to the battle
fleet with all their radars and air-search abilities.
No, this had been launched from *a submarine.* And
a hostile sub meant it had to be an American, because who else would be gunning for the formation? The sub they'd shot at was the most capable
sub in the fleet. He had to assume that the sub that
was out there was much less capable than the

SSNX ship they had put on the bottom. But less capable or not, it had managed to sneak in here and launch a weapon, and the sub would need to be destroyed, and quickly. Grachev wondered if he looked as shaken as he felt.

"Sir, ship is answering dead slow ahead," Tenukha called from the ship-control enclosure, jarring him back into the present.

Grachev looked at his display zero. The torpedo was off to the east at bearing 101, drawing farther south. The line-of-sight to the torpedo connected *Vepr* to the weapon, and both he and the torpedo were making velocity southward along the line-of-sight, a dangerous situation, possibly leading to a collision course with the torpedo, but he wanted to give the Second Captain another second to record the bearing rate with this situation. Then he would drive them off their track to the northeast and see what the torpedo did.

"Second Captain, leg status," Grachev demanded.

"Leg quality five four percent," the system's dead voice said.

Good enough, Grachev thought. Anything over 30 percent was gravy. Grachev looked over at Tenukha in the ship-control console and called, "Ahead fifty percent, left full rudder, steer course zero three zero!" This course would put *Vepr* across the line-of-sight, giving them an almost instant passive range to the distant torpedo.

"Coming around left, Captain, zero five zero, zero four zero."

"Ahead thirty percent, make your speed twenty-five clicks."

"Steady zero four zero, throttling down, speed twenty-six clicks coming to two five."

"Second Captain, report range to torpedo," Grachev said. His order was superfluous—the computer would tell whether he'd ordered it or not—but making a biting order made him feel better. For the next sixty seconds he waited while the Second Captain's computations came into focus. The error confidence interval shrank from 200 down to 80 percent, further down to 50, finally after a second minute to 30 percent, where it was good enough to report. Grachev's display zero showed the torpedo range at twenty kilometers, with a weapon speed of twenty-two kilometers per hour. The Second Captain system announced aloud the torpedo's speed and range. Slow for a torpedo, Grachev thought. The weapon's course was reported as 165, which was very odd.

"Crew, prepare to penetrate the layer," Grachev said. "Ship Control Officer, change ship's depth to thirty meters."

"Rising to thirty meters, Captain," Tenukha said.

"Very good." Grachev waited, the aux four display showing the ship's depth. The chin sonar rose through the layer depth at sixty-two meters. The aux three display of signal-to-noise ratio immediately sank to zero—the torpedo had vanished the second they had gone above-layer.

"Deep!" Grachev shouted. "Take it back down to three hundred meters! Steep angle!"

Tenukha reversed his stick, pushing it to the forward bulkhead, the deck plunging downward as the ship dived back into the colder deeper water. The signal-to-noise ratio came back up, the torpedo back where the Second Captain expected it.

"Second Captain, any indication at all of the damn launching platform?"

"None, Captain."

"Follow the course vector of the torpedo backward into the sea. What's the reciprocal course of one six five? Three four five! Follow that back and see what you have!"

"Still nothing, Captain."

"Other torpedoes?"

"No, sir."

"Where is this torpedo going?" he asked himself with a lower voice. "It's headed southeast. The convoy is twenty-three kilometers southwest of it. So, if it's attacking the convoy, why is it going southeast?"

Svyatoslov stared down at display zero, standing next to Grachev.

"Sir, it's not headed for us, and it's not headed for the convoy."

"Wait a minute. I smell a rat. Second Captain, compute the possibilities of this torpedo intercepting the task force at a future point."

Grachev waited. "Well?" he bellowed.

"Zero point zero, Captain."

"Can't get much lower than that," Novskoyy added.

"Compute intercept point with task force at farthest east point of diamond pattern, and report torpedo speed and course."

"Sir," the electronics replied, "Course one seven eight, speed ninety-seven point five clicks."

"So why would this torpedo be putt-putting along southeast when it should be going all-out headed due south?"

"It's not going southeast. It's going east," Svyatoslov said. "Now east-northeast."

"What?"

"It's circling."

"Dammit," Grachev spat. A circling torpedo meant he couldn't expect to see the launch platform approaching from the line drawn through the torpedo's course. The launching sub could be anywhere.

"Second Captain, any classification on this torpedo? Could it be helicopter-launched?"

"No classification, sir."

"Depth of the unit?"

"Below layer, Captain."

"Sir, we'd better open range to that torpedo," Svyatoslov said. "If it's circling, it could come back around and hear us."

"Are we closing the circle?"

"No. But you're still heading zero three zero, away from the convoy."

"Ship control, right full rudder steady course two one zero, ahead forty percent."

"Forty percent, ship is coming around to the right, sir, passing zero four zero to the left."

"Belay reports."

"So now what do we do, Captain?" Svyatoslov had pulled his boom mike up and held it with his hand, speaking quietly in Grachev's ear so the whole crew wouldn't hear.

"We'll pace back and forth until we hear something more."

"Sir, shouldn't you warn the convoy? And you're out of the safety lane."

"If I come to mast broach depth and transmit, we'll go above layer and lose the torpedo. I can't risk that."

"But the convoy is still orbiting. In ten minutes they'll turn to course zero four zero. They'll be driving right into the search cone of that torpedo. Look, right now they are twenty-three kilometers from the torpedo circle's closest point of approach. Once they make the turn to the northeast, they'll close the torpedo orbit to thirteen kilometers. That's almost half the distance. The torpedo will see a huge signal-to-noise-level increase. I mean huge, sir."

"You're right. Attention, crew. We're going to go upstairs and warn the task force. We'll go up quick, get out our warning, and pull the plug and go deep. Everyone got that? Tenukha, prepare the radio circuits. Mr. First, write out and insert the emergency message into the UHF, HF, EHF, and VHF frequencies and code it per the operation plan. Tell them we have a torpedo threat from the northeast, immediate fleet formation break, escape vector to the southeast or off the track of the threat axis. Got it?"

Svyatoslov was scribbling furiously on a computer clipboard, nodding. "Here, sir."

Grachev read it quickly. "Good." He shouted to the room: "Ready?" He saw Novskoyy standing next to him, still icy-calm. "Al, grab a handhold, this will be hairy." Novskoyy held on to a horizontal bar mounted on Grachev's command console. Grachev took a last look at display zero, then shouted into the boom microphone, "Second Captain, emergency mast broach with the multifrequency antenna ready *now*!"

The deck almost immediately began to rise. One second Grachev was standing on a level surface, the next on a tilted incline steeper than a staircase. The deck rumbled with power as the propulsor shot ahead to 100 percent reactor power. The ship's turbines wound up, at full throttle, and the noise in the engineering spaces almost immediately tripled as the turbines roared, then howled.

Grachev, Svyatoslov, and Novskoyy hung by the handholds of the command console as the vessel rose 250 meters, making the ascent in less than a minute. The ship's acceleration, so radical a few seconds before, was reversed as the Second Captain inserted progressively larger shunting resistors into the propulsion turbine electrical output, then reversed the polarity of the DC current feeds to the massive propulsion motor, then took the shunting resistors back out of the circuit, the maneuver causing the propulsor to go from full revolutions ahead to full revolutions astern in the space of four seconds. The hull shook violently from the backing turns. The shaking calmed after several seconds as the Second Captain throttled back, and the deck suddenly came back down level. Grachev was able to feel the slight rolling of the hull in the waves above as the Second Captain kept the vessel at

walking speed at mast broach depth, to avoid
sheering off an antenna.

The moment the ship reached the shallows, the
telephone pole of the multifrequency antenna pushed
up out of the fin and upward out of the water. The
surface of the mast felt moist sea air and began to
transmit immediately.

"How long are you staying up, Captain?" Svyatoslov asked.

"Let's see. It would be nice to get a reply from the
task force. I'd also like to see what we hear up here
above the layer. Transmission status, Second?"

"Message transmitting on all frequencies, Captain."

"Sonar contact above the layer?"

"Nothing above the threshold signal-to-noise
ratio, Captain."

"Attention, crew. We'll remain here until we get
a reply from the task force or for ten minutes of
transmitting." If the surface group didn't get the
hint in six hundred seconds of panic transmissions,
it would have to take the consequences. "After
that, we're going deep to drive a circle around the
orbit of this circling torpedo at a safe radius to see
if we can find the launching platform."

Chances were, he thought, things would develop
while they were up here, deaf, and that when they
did eventually get back below the layer, things
would be . . . different.

In the control room of the submarine thirty-two
nautical miles northeast of the *Vepr,* the executive
officer, Kiethan Judison, checked his watch at the
forward chart table and looked up at the captain.

"About time to strap our cleats on, Skipper."

Captain Kelly McKee nodded and pulled on his control glove, then picked up his helmet. He shut his eyes so that he could get contact with the rubber eyepieces. He opened his eyes once inside.

In his helmet view he saw the room almost as he would with it off, except for the odd effect when he turned his head. His eyes saw reality around him with a visual separation between his "eyes" of twelve inches instead of the usual two. He saw Judison vanish into one of the VR cubicles. Now alone in the open part of the room, he switched his vision to be part of the Cyclops system's output.

Once again he found himself back on the toy submarine under the clear water of the battlespace, below the layer depth. To the south he could see the orange marks of the trails of the torpedoes, nine of them circling in their orbits as the tenth drew alongside. As the tenth torpedo "flew" southwest, the other torpedoes broke out of their orbits and set off toward the surface fleet.

McKee raised his hand and immediately rose out of the water. The surface fleet appeared at the limits of his vision, far to the south, in the middle of its leg on the diamond-shaped path. He blinked, and the previous path of the surface group became inscribed in red on the surface of the virtual sea below him. From this view, a mile was represented as about ten feet. It was as if he hung from the scoreboard of a basketball arena, the floor below him cluttered with models.

The torpedoes were approaching in a fan about five miles wide, all of them now headed roughly southwest toward the surface convoy. The attack was progressing routinely. He had a thought that it was going well, but then became annoyed. This was the warm-up show. The headliner act, the submarine, was still nowhere to be seen. McKee had ordered that the Mark 23 Bloodhound underwater surveillance vehicle climb cautiously above the layer for thirty seconds every ten-minute interval. Even that was something of a waste of time. The surface ships stirred up the warm Atlantic with their loud cavitating screws, making an entire sector of the battlespace useless.

As the Mark 23 Bloodhound peeked above the layer this time, though, it heard the tonals of heavy rotating machinery, and the flow of something through waves. The processor onboard became flooded with information, displayed a few seconds later in McKee's battlespace representation. In it was a pulsing red ray emanating from the position of the Mark 23, only the bearing of the noise apparent. Whatever it was, it could be anywhere along that line from the Bloodhound, which was southwest of *Hammerhead* but north of the tracks of the southwest-headed torpedoes.

"Attention in the fire-control team, we have a detect above the layer heard from the Bloodhound. I have an apparent bearing going northwest from the Bloodhound's position. Immediate action will be to do target-motion analysis with the Bloodhound—and keep it above layer for the moment—and get our own ship above layer now. Carry on. Pilot, left full rudder, ahead standard, steady course west. Make your depth one two zero feet, sharp angle!"

The response came back from the pilot at the two-man ship-control console, and the deck tilted upward to a twenty-degree angle as the ship ascended to the shallow layer, then pitched back level.

"Sir, depth one two zero feet, steady course west, answering ahead standard."

"Pilot, all stop, mark speed four knots."

"All stop, Pilot aye."

Hammerhead had screamed for the layer, and now had turned west from the previous course of southeast.

"Sonar, Captain, we're above layer. Are you getting an acoustic daylight image of the Bloodhound and a contact farther northwest of it?"

"Captain, Sonar, yes, we have a detect on a submerged contact, bearing two six eight, distant contact. Should be coming into your battlespace display now," Senior Chief Cook said in McKee's headset.

Below him, from the toy *Hammerhead*'s position, a thin ray of red light burst out from the sub going almost due west. The intersection of the red ray from the Bloodhound southwest of them and the ray from own ship pulsed into a purple diamond, the triangulated position of the submerged contact.

"Sonar, Captain, designate the submerged contact target twenty-six. Classify target twenty-six."

"Captain, Sonar aye. Twenty-six is making way on one forty-two impeller propulsor jet doing three zero RPM. Unit is not a U.S. or allied submarine class, possible Russian Republic generation four hull. Contact is shallow, above layer. Possible transients indicate unit is at periscope depth—"

"Captain," Judison said, "we've got a rooster

tail, very slight, at the location of the bearing intersection. Looks like a periscope or mast. This guy's at PD!"

"Firing point procedures, tubes one, two, and four, Mark 58 Alert/Acute, target twenty-six, high-speed run to enable, passive snake, wire-guidance-enabled. Report!"

McKee moved his point of view to the camera onboard the Predator, training it to the location of the bearing intersection. There, clear as day between the blue waves with their slight whitecaps in the sea breeze, was a pole protruding from the water, a slight white wake behind it.

McKee commanded with his cursor hand that the weapon status and tube status come up on a display board hanging in space in front of him. The tubes were loaded with spun-up Mark 58s. They were ready to shoot, and they had a firing solution to a submarine that was a Severodvinsk class. So why was he hesitating? This was his mission, what he had come here to do.

"Ship ready," Dietz said.

"Tubes one, two, and four, weapons ready," Van Dyne reported.

"Solution ready," from Judison.

"Cyclops ready," the Cyclops system said.

"Shoot on generated bearing," McKee said.

"Set."

"Cyclops has the room in standby."

"Shoot!" McKee ordered.

"Fire!" Van Dyne said.

The deck jumped as the heavy torpedo was launched.

"One fired electrically," the Cyclops system said.

"Conn, Sonar, unit one, normal launch."

The deck bounced again, the second torpedo crash hitting McKee's ears.

"Conn, Sonar, two, normal launch."

The litany continued until three units were on the way to the Severodvinsk sub.

"We may go home early," McKee muttered.

"Sir, any transmission replies from the surface force?" Svyatoslov said in Grachev's headset.

"Nothing," Grachev said from the command console.

"It's been eight minutes, sir. We should really pull the plug and see what's happening with those torpedoes deep."

"Very good. Ship Control, lower all masts, three hundred meters, ten-degree down angle! Right one degree rudder, steady course zero six zero, ahead four zero percent. At three hundred meters throttle back to three zero RPM."

Grachev waited impatiently until the vessel penetrated the layer depth and leveled out deep. He looked at aux two for information, and his eyes bulged out as he saw what was coming. The original torpedo they'd found was no longer orbiting and no longer where they'd seen it, but was now a few kilometers farther southwest. In addition, it had been joined by what looked like a dozen more, all of them on the way to the surface force. But what hit him between the eyes was the torpedo coming straight at them from the east, far north of the group of torpedoes heading for the surface force.

"Torpedo in the water!" he screamed, his voice choked.

"Four torpedoes in the water, Captain," the Second Captain announced in its level voice, on top of Grachev's. "Bearing zero eight eight, zero eight seven—"

"Second, Bora II immediate launch pending tubes one and three, bearing east, immediate enable, medium speed. Autocycle to tubes two and four! Ship Control, ahead a hundred and eighty percent power, depth six hundred meters, left two degrees rudder, steady three zero zero degrees!"

Vepr came around to head northwest, diving deeper, almost to her maximum operating depth. While she was passing north, tube one fired a large-bore Bora II torpedo. When the ship was almost steady on course 330, tube three fired, forcing that weapon to have to circle back around to the east, giving it much farther to go than the tube one unit.

Once *Vepr* was steady on course 330, the Second Captain automatically cut the weapon wires, shut the outer doors, and drained the tubes, then opened the doors on the middle tube bank, doors three and four, and shot those torpedoes. The deck began to shake as the ship sped up beyond its normal full speed. The reactor was now pushing beyond the rated power level by 80 percent, as the steam plant was rated to take up to 180 percent reactor power. The additional power would gain them only a few clicks over the ship's rated speed, eighty-five clicks. If the additional 80 percent gave them fifteen more kilometers per hour, he would be more than grateful, but drag increased as velocity

squared, so to double speed they'd have to more
than quadruple power—and more, because reactor
power became diminished by all the electrical loads
the ship required, such as fast-speed recirculation
pumps, each the size of a truck, and increased air-
conditioning and steam-driven feed pumps. So
power to the turbines would give them perhaps 10
or 15 percent more speed.

In two more seconds, tubes three and four were
ready to fire, and the Second Captain launched
them. Four torpedoes down the bearing line to the
launching submarine.

In Grachev's chest his heart hammered so hard
he thought it would affect his speech. He glanced
over at Svyatoslov, his look as hard as he could
make it, but the first officer had forsaken the command console for one of the virtual-reality consoles. The first officer had left his VR cube door
open, enough that he could lift his goggles and see
Grachev. Obviously he was keeping an eye out,
because when Grachev looked over, Svyatoslov
looked over at him. Grachev glared at him, and
Svyatoslov nodded back in understanding.

Grachev put his hands in his pockets. If those torpedoes closed in on him, he could always punch out
the control room. Of course, by then the surface force
would be shredded metal. He glanced at Novskoyy,
who had moved to the chart table and was leaning
over it to try to see what the torpedoes were doing.

Who were these men who had so boldly sneaked
in here and launched a dozen weapons at the surface force—which so far had done nothing but sail
here from the Ukraine—and now four at him?

36

"Possible target zig, Captain," the Cyclops voice said in McKee's ears. Below him, target twenty-six was maneuvering, his sound changing. "Target is showing a lower frequency from his original sound signature. Target twenty-six has turned away. Target twenty-six has increased speed. Estimate velocity now at thirty-two knots, increasing to thirty-five. Still increasing."

"Attention in the fire-control team. Target twenty-six is running. I'm planning on preparing the Vortex Mod Deltas to shoot at him—"

"Torpedo in the water, Captain," Cyclops announced in its annoyingly level voice. "Two torpedoes. Both from the bearing to the target. Both are at very high attack speed—"

"Cyclops silence," McKee ordered. The system spoke too slowly—and he had not programmed it to spit out information during an emergency, mistakenly thinking that would upset the fire-control team, but now he could see the system's slow reports were frustrating all of them, making a bad situation worse. McKee watched the display: target twenty-six was turning to the north below him in the water, and the acoustic daylight of the spherical arrays showed the torpedoes. He wished he'd put

the Mark 5 Sharkeye on this side of the surface
force. It was so far south that its triangulation range
to the hostile sub, target twenty-six, was crude and
losing accuracy. But then, there had been no time,
and there was certainly no time now, because he
had a torpedo—no, two—in the water now, both
aimed for him. The enemy sub captain must have
aimed them down the bearing line to the torpedoes
that were coming in on him.

McKee took a breath, ready to shout an order
to turn east and run, but realized if he did that
he'd lose the tactical picture. Putting his machinery—screw and turbines and motors—between the
acoustic daylight spherical array and hull arrays and
target twenty-six would lose the target. It was true
that McKee could then put more distance between
the ship and the incoming torpedoes, but he *had*
to see what the enemy sub was doing. If the Severodvinsk sub managed somehow to evade
McKee's torpedoes, he could vanish, costing
McKee precious minutes and maybe more searching for him. He'd come this far looking for the
destroyer of the *Princess Dragon* and the *Devilfish,*
and he'd be damned if he'd turn tail and run.

Which reminded him. The *Hammerhead* was
moving, still at ahead one third, five knots. He
needed to freeze the ship in the sea so that they
minimized radiated noise and didn't show any "up-
Doppler," the Doppler effect upshifting a reflected
sonar pulse's frequency from an object moving
toward the listener. If he was at the same speed as
the sea around him, the sonar pulse from the torpedoes bouncing off his hull and going back to the

torpedoes would return at exactly the same frequency as the transmitted sound and the return from the surface waves. If the torpedo was transmitting active pinging sonar, it might even discard return sonar sounds that were within a few Hertz of the transmitted tone, allowing them to escape even though they would be dead in the water.

"Pilot, all stop!" McKee ordered. He was glad for a moment that he couldn't see the faces of the control room officers. To a man, they would be horrified. The standard operating procedure called for McKee to turn, put the torpedo on his rear quarter, and go to emergency flank, 200 percent reactor power. Instead he was going to stand in his boots and let the torpedoes come. It was suicidal.

"Pilot, hover at this depth, and make sure you're silent, and place the reactor on natural circulation."

If stopping was a sin, shutting down the reactor with no pumps was a mortal sin. It would take vital minutes to come back to full power, time that could mean the difference between life and death on the sea bottom. But it still made sense, because shutting down the plant would make the ship that much quieter.

"Hovering, sir, rector going to nat-circ."

"Um, Captain?" Judison said. "We should be running—"

"No, *Hammerhead* will stand and fight. Van Dyne, prepare to shoot tube three's Doberman Mark 17. XO, grab a VR cube and ride that Doberman to these torpedoes."

"State champs on the flea-flicker, I know. I want

Dietz on the circuit in VR three when I'm in two, sir. He can help back me up."

"Fine. Pilot?" McKee's calling for reports was a throwback to the ways of the past. In reality, a skilled operator should be able to get the information quicker from the Cyclops system, and McKee was going through the system's three-dimensional displays, but he still preferred to hear news from the crew, and to give orders to them instead of the computer. Otherwise, this would turn into a one-man show.

"Reactor is in nat-circ. Hovering on the trim system."

"Very well. Van Dyne?"

"Tube loading one, two, and four with Mark 17s. Tube three outer door open, Mark 17 Doberman ready."

"XO, launch tube three when you're ready. And get those damned torpedoes. When tubes one, two, and four are ready, you and Dietz take command of them, and get two units out there. Leave two units in the tubes for reserve."

"Aye, sir."

"Van Dyne, prepare vertical-launch tubes nine through twelve for immediate Vortex Mod Delta launch."

"Captain, we're too shallow. We need to be at least at eight hundred feet—"

"Pilot, flood depth control and take us to nine hundred feet."

"Flooding to nine hundred, sir."

"Muzzle doors opening VLTs nine through twelve."

"Attention in the fire-control team," McKee said to his impersonal boom mike. "We're going to counterfire with Mark 17 Doberman antitorpedo torpedoes to the incoming weapons, and we're going to put out a second salvo of Mod Deltas down this asshole's throat. Carry on."

The room was quiet for long and agonizing moments. It began to sneak into McKee's consciousness that they might not make it out of this battle in one piece, and his order to bring the sub deep didn't help their chances. Beneath them was water three miles deep, and if he and Judison and Dietz didn't get them out of this, that rocky sea bottom would be their final resting place.

"Captain, depth nine hundred feet," the pilot reported.

"Very well."

"Sir," Van Dyne said, "Vortex tubes nine through twelve are pressurized, request to open muzzle doors—"

"Open muzzle doors and launch when ready."

"Aye-aye, sir, nine through twelve assigned to target two six. Doors opening."

Come on, McKee thought impatiently. The deck jumped under his feet as Judison launched his Mark 17. McKee waited another minute, and the second Mark 17 Doberman was launched. A third barking noise sounded, much quieter, and coming from farther forward.

"Unit nine launch," Van Dyne reported.

"Very well."

The battlespace below McKee in the three-dimensional view was filling with the Mod Delta

Vortex missiles and the first two Doberman antitorpedo units. With nothing further to do but wait, he
turned to see what was going on with the torpedoes
targeting the surface force. To his surprise, the surface ships had broken formation and scattered,
most of them breaking to the south or southwest.
Apparently the Severodvinsk had been able to
warn them during its periscope-depth excursion. He
blinked and brought up tags on the ten torpedoes.
They would have extended runs now. They had
originally been scheduled to begin hitting, but the
surface force had failed to make two turns following the diamond pattern to fall into the torpedoes'
traps. Fortunately, the torpedo seeker cones would
still be seeing the target ships.

"Unit ten launch."

The enemy torpedoes were getting closer and
closer. The closest one was now about seventeen
nautical miles away, going forty-five knots. Time-
to-impact was twenty-two minutes. But the main
thing now was that McKee had to stop the firing
ship, target twenty-six, from shooting any more
weapons.

"Unit eleven launch, sir."

"Very well."

But should he fire the entire load at the Severodvinsk? And the torpedo room, too? But if he shot
more Mark 58s, he wouldn't be able to wire-guide
the Mark 17 Dobermans into the path of the incoming torpedoes. No, he decided. Anything else
he launched at target twenty-six would have to
come from the vertical-launch tubes. Vortex missiles. He had four left and four on the way. Sud-

denly the first-launched Vortex solid rocket engine ignited. The flame trail was represented as a bright white blowtorch flame in the deep layer of the virtual sea below McKee.

"Unit twelve launch and unit nine, normal rocket motor ignition, Captain."

"Very well, Weps."

"Sir," the Cyclops system reported. "Terminal speed increase on Mark 58 unit three."

McKee looked south for a second, seeing that one of the Alert/Acutes was closing rapidly on one of the fast frigates, which, in spite of its name, was one of the slower vessels in the task force. But he had no time for that. What he had said to the control room watchstanders was true: he didn't care about the surface force.

"Cyclops continue silence," he said. *Shut the hell up.*

"Unit ten normal rocket motor ignition."

"Belay reports," McKee snapped. *I can see for myself.*

Two minutes later, four of the Vortex underwater three-hundred-knot plasma-tipped missiles were on the way. Time of flight—four minutes thirty-six seconds. After that, it would be too late for the Severodvinsk. As if to punctuate his thought, the first plasma detonation sounded from the south with a roaring *BOOM*. The fast frigate exploded into iron filings, marking the first deaths in what would be a very long morning.

"Come on, let's go, get tubes one through four lined up! We need more ordnance on the target,"

Grachev said. The counterattack was going very poorly. *Vepr* was losing. Only four weapons were out down the bearing line. By fleet training standards, he should have been able to pump out at least three tube banks by now, twelve large-bore weapons. There was no time to spend thinking about why they'd been slow, but it probably was a partially clogged tube drain strainer or corrosion clogging the line that drained down the tubes. The slower drain-down meant the computer had had to wait longer to stuff the tubes.

"Mr. First," Grachev said, "what have you got on the Second Captain's analysis of incoming torpedo range?"

"We've got a very crude wiggle range, sir, but it's not like acoustic daylight—"

"Wish we were shallow enough to use a Shchuka sensor, eh, Mr. First?"

"Um, sir," Svyatoslov said, "range is less than fifteen kilometers on the near unit, about eighteen on the most distant. And there are four more launched in the past minute."

"Four more?"

"Yes, sir."

A wide, ugly streak appeared on aux two and three. Grachev stared at it, then realized Novskoyy was beside him, likewise staring.

"Second Captain, report the additional detects to the west."

"Sir, new detects are incoming torpedo units five through eight, with a louder sound signature, signal-to-noise ratio increasing by forty-five decibels."

"Second, are you sure these are *torpedoes*?"

"Captain, sound analysis indicates the presence of a solid rocket motor."

"Solid . . . rocket . . . motor."

"Sir, I think we're in deep, deep trouble."

"Captain," the Second Captain computer voice said, "incoming weapons have been analyzed for approach velocity."

The system paused.

"Well, what is it?"

"Captain, incoming torpedo units five through eight approach velocity confirmed at five hundred fifty kilometers per hour."

"What?" Grachev shouted. What was going on with his computer?

The computer began repeating its sentence, taking Grachev literally. Svyatoslov broke in. "Sir, they're underwater missiles. Over five hundred clicks. Blue laser guidance. They'll overtake the conventional torpedoes in a few seconds, and they'll be here before you finish your next sentence."

The next ten seconds were busier than entire months in Grachev's life. Novskoyy began to frown. Svyatoslov practically interrupted himself to hurry forward. Grachev stared down at the main display. The first-launched torpedoes—plotted on the main display—were overtaken by the first of the oncoming underwater rockets. Grachev shouted into his boom microphone, "Second, calculate time to impact of the first rocket torpedo!"

"Captain, impact time zero nine twenty-seven hours local time, which is seventeen seconds from now."

In the next second Grachev, thirty-four years old,
father of a toddler, and in command of the number
one nuclear attack submarine of the Navy of the
Ukraine, realized that today was the day of his
death, that for him, his thirty-fifth birthday would
never arrive. And although in Martinique's and Pavelyvich's minds he was already dead, dying today
would make it even worse. And he'd never even
gotten to say good-bye to the two of them after
Kolov and his men had brought him in the dead
of night.

Grachev pushed Svyatoslov aside and ran the five
steps to the ship-control cubicle and ripped open
the panel to the manual control compartment separation panel, the "punch-out" panel, the one they
called "the panic button."

It represented the only chance they had.

He pulled the lever that opened the panic panel.
He barely heard the alarm, a klaxon sound, wailing
in the compartment as he threw the panel cover to
the deck. The panel cover spun downward to the
deck in slow motion, sinking only a few centimeters
by the time Grachev wrapped his fist around the
third lever down and pulled it from the top detent
down to the bottom. The process of punching out
the control compartment began as ten explosive
charges received the electrical signals to detonate.
Ten explosions severed the cable and fiber-optic
lifelines connecting the control compartment to the
first compartment. The explosion happened so
quickly that by the time Grachev released the third
lever and reached back up to the first lever, the

lights had gone out, plunging the room into darkness.

Grachev put his fist on the top lever. In his peripheral vision he could see flashes of light as the battle lanterns clicked to life and then clicked out again, and in the silent-movie effect of the battle lanterns strobing to life, he could see Svyatoslov frozen in motion running toward him.

Grachev threw the top lever, the one designed to isolate the compartment. The dual inner and outer hatches dropped like the blade of a guillotine, slamming shut in their framing and isolating the compartment, making it watertight. The circuit also slammed shut massive watertight doors in the heavy-walled air ducts, further sealing the compartment.

Next, Grachev reached for and threw the second lever, which ordered the sixty explosive charges built into the structural steel and titanium to sever the structural connections between the control compartment and the hull. The lever also activated the circuits of two hundred explosive bolts designed to rip open the sail and blow it away from the control compartment, to allow the compartment to ascend to the surface. The battle lanterns clicked to life again and then went out, revealing Svyatoslov closer by almost a half meter. Grachev's hand reached the bottom lever beneath the already-thrown third lever, the one that would detonate the final explosive train and rocket motors that would thrust the control compartment upward and away from the main hull.

All four levers thrown, Grachev reached for a

handhold next to the panel. The room vibrated
with a slamming explosion—but it was only the
hatches and the air-duct doors forcefully hitting
their seating surfaces. The explosions from the second lever kicked in, a sustained, booming roar
rather than a quick report.

The emergency lights clicked again and held, and
Svyatoslov was almost all the way to him, although
what he was doing Grachev could only guess. High
overhead, the detonation of the explosive bolts
could be heard as small pinging noises, small-cali-
ber bullets ricocheting down a metal hallway.

The next sound Grachev didn't expect—the
noise of a thousand buildings falling—and he felt
as if his eardrums had ruptured and blood was
spurting out of his head. What he would not realize
until ten seconds later was that the noise was only
the first of the plasma detonations from the torpedoes sent to destroy the warships of the surface
task force he'd been ordered to guard.

Grachev had released the handhold and begun
to put his hands to his ears when the next plasma
explosion rocked the ship, and by the time his
hands did reach his ears another plasma warhead
had gone off. He was beginning to sink to the deck
when the rocket motors distributed around the bottom of the control compartment lit off, starting to
blast the compartment away from the main hull.

Grachev began to smile as he felt himself dashed
to the deck, flattened there by the acceleration of
the rocket thrust. His last-resort action had worked.
He'd been successful in punching out the compartment. The smile faded as he realized he had proba-

bly been too late. He had taken too much time. In just heartbeats, the first rocket torpedo would be impacting the hull, and the plasma explosion that came next would rip open the metal of the compartment and kill every man left aboard.

37

Kiethan Judison was not standing on the deck of the submarine *Hammerhead*. He existed instead inside the body of a Mark 17 Doberman antitorpedo torpedo, with the water rushing at him, the pulsing virtual target in front of him. It all came down to judgment, he thought. So what if the Mark 17 didn't have the computer control of the Cyclops system? That module had never worked. What it did have was Kiethan Judison. He practically felt like giving a cowboy whoop, but kept his enthusiasm to himself.

"Status, XO," McKee said.

"Catching up on unit one, the closest," Judison said. "We're calculating detonation time in less than thirty seconds."

"Go early," McKee said.

"Aye, sir, initiating Doberman sequence now."

Judison entered the command to detonate the Doberman's warhead, with the incoming torpedo now a mile away. Early, but as the captain had said, he was hitting the switch prematurely.

Out in the Atlantic some sixteen miles west of the *Hammerhead,* the Doberman onboard processor activated the warhead on the orders of the fiber-optic cable from the Cyclops system. Far to the south the first plasma explosions began to detonate as the Mark 58 torpedoes caught up with the lagging surface ships. The Doberman warhead was a densely packed carbon-fiber microstructure wrapped around an inner charge of high explosives and stuffed into a chamber with segment charges along its four seams. On the signal from the onboard processor, the segment charges exploded, ripping the skin of the chamber open on the four seams, just as the inner ovoid of high explosives blew up, further exploding the chamber walls and scattering the carbon-fiber structure. The expanding gases of the fireball drove the structure out into the water, while small hidden charges went off. These were more directional shaped rocket motors than explosives, carefully crafted to propel the carbon-fiber structure farther outward from the central explosion. In the next second the intention of the designers became clear. The carbon-fiber structure spread out, its matrix expanding into the sea. What once was a densely packed ball of carbon became a widespread finely woven net, spreading outward in a disk. The tiny rocket charges opened it out fully until it became an undersea spiderweb, waiting directly in the path of the incoming torpedo.

The Bora II torpedo, having no sensing mechanism fine enough to see the netting spread out before it, drove unsuspecting into it. The netting flexed like a drum, then tensed. The momentum of the sixty-five-knot torpedo stretched the fibers of the net more and more until they began to approach what material scientists called the elastic limit. Beyond this point, the removal of the stress would not result in the return of the material to its previous state. Instead the material would be permanently stretched, like a pair of stockings tugged on by a dog. The netting stretched farther, lengthening and absorbing the torpedo's momentum until the fibers reached the rupture point. The force required to capture the heavy torpedo was much more than the designers had calculated, and finally the netting broke and the unit sailed through.

If the weapon had fouled its propulsor vanes on the netting, it would likely not have driven on toward the *Hammerhead,* but the propulsor continued spinning. Had the torpedo been knocked downward, upward, or sideways more than forty degrees, it might have tumbled the gyro and caused the torpedo to spin out of control, sparing the *Hammerhead.* But it didn't, turning a mere ten degrees, easily able to correct its course. After a short period of lessened stability, the torpedo recovered, found the target, and continued driving on.

In the control room of the *Hammerhead,* Lieutenant Commander Kiethan Judison's jaw fell open.

The rocket charges at the base of the control compartment escape pod grew weaker as the solid fuel was exhausted. The charges died just as the first underwater missiles arrived at the main hull of the *Vepr,* some two hundred meters below. The escape pod had been rising rapidly in the warm layer from the force of the rocket charges and the buoyancy of ballast spaces at the bottom periphery and foil balloons that had filled with compressed nitrogen. The pod had risen until it was only twenty meters deep when the first plasma explosion detonated below. The shock wave blasted upward and impacted the pod.

It rolled over forty degrees but continued to rise, its pressure envelope intact, but the contents hammered. The second underwater missile's plasma warhead exploded as the pod was breaching the calm surface seastate. The pod bobbed on the sea while the next two missiles exploded.

The first plasma detonation vaporized the forward 60 percent of the main hull, turning the low-magnetic carbon steel hull into carbon and iron molecules. The plasma expanded and melted the hull in a fifty-meter radius and shredded what was left aft. The remainder began to sink to the bottom. The second missile's blue laser seeker homed on the aft remaining hull, turning it into a shovelful of the sun's surface. The next minute, nothing was left. The third missile sailed in and homed on the expanding gas cloud, which to the blue laser seeker registered as a hull. One downfall of the terminal guidance system was that if the first unit was drawn off by a decoy and detonated, the follow-on units would home on the explosion. But there was almost nothing capable of drawing off the Vortex Mod Delta missile, its design refined over five years of abject failure, and it had flown true. The fourth and final missile homed on the other explosions and added to the conflagration. None of the units saw the control compartment pod high above.

One minute after the fourth missile detonated, the sea had calmed. The four torpedoes launched earlier by the *Hammerhead* were sailing in. But their passive sonar systems saw what sound engineers referred to as a "blueout," the presence of so much noise in the water that the units were blinded, the same way a skier could become snowblind by the glare from the slopes. Ten minutes after that, the first torpedo arrived, circling the blueout, and seeing it as a curtain of noise filling the sea. Its onboard processor had a preset for this condition, because a plasma blueout would render the unit ineffective. But the present was set to detonate-on-blueout, leaving no stone unturned in a combat situation. The explosion, it was assumed, would add to the damage an enemy vessel suffered if the target had evaded the immediate vicinity of the plasma detonation. Extensive testing had shown that a ship would not need to experience a direct hit. A detonation within a nautical mile was usually enough to cripple or sink most test vessels. When the first torpedo measured the blueout, it made its predestined decision and detonated, adding to the conflagration in the cubic meters of ocean where the *Vepr* had once been. The second, third, and fourth torpedoes likewise detonated, adding to the shock waves that had already hit the floating pod above. Any Los Alamos physicist presented with the data and asked to evaluate the chances of people in the control compartment escape pod would have shaken his head in pessimism and respect for the dead.

*   *   *

Inside the pod, one disaster added to the next. The plasma detonations were so violent that no one was conscious to hear the third. The fourth explosion reverberated through the sea, reaching the men's ears, but no brains received the information. By the fifth explosion, the pod had been so tossed by the impact of the shock waves that the heartbeat of the ship control officer, Navigator Captain-Lieutenant Grigory Tenukha, stopped.

While the explosions continued, the body of Captain Pavel Grachev remained wedged between Tenukha's control couch and the bulkhead where the panic panel was. The lights had been out since the first shock wave. The pod was tossed by the following shocks until finally the sea quieted. Only the rush of bubbles from the explosions rose around the pod, the sound like boiling water, but after twenty minutes in the stuffy pod, that sound died down too, until the only sound left was the breathing of the survivors. That sound continued for some time until it was joined by sound of the flow of water as the flooding in the pod began.

Lieutenant Commander Bryan Dietz tried his hand, sailing toward the incoming torpedoes in the second-fired Mark 17 Doberman.

"Don't go early," the captain's voice said in his ear. McKee's voice still sounded iron-hard and self-assured, a miracle, Dietz thought in the background of his mind. What he needed now was a second miracle—the shooting down of the incoming torpedoes. But there were still four on the way in, and only three Dobermans. The other two were tube-loaded and ready, but McKee had held off on shooting them.

Dietz could "see" ahead of him the incoming torpedoes. A tag on his virtual world counted down the distance between him and the incoming units. The closest one's range rolled down to 2,600 yards, down to 2,200, 1,950, down, down, until the tag read 400 meters, Dietz's signal to detonate the warhead.

Like the first, this unit's canister blew apart, and the high-explosive core blew the net outward, the rocket charges at its boundary further opening the rose petals of the net. As the distance between the first-fired torpedo rolled down to zero, the Bora II torpedo hit the netting.

But like the first netting, this spiderweb was no match for the momentum of the high-speed unit. The netting material stretched and then ruptured. Slowed by the net, the unit slowly regained speed, the target ahead becoming dimly visible in its sonar seeker.

"Still inbound, Captain," Judison said, with a rising note of concern.

"I'm done with Dobermans," McKee said, pulling off his helmet in disgust. "Give me Vortex vertical-launch tubes five through eight. Webs, pressurize tubes five through eight, open outer doors, and lay in phantom targets from my console."

McKee's fingers flashed over his panel, finding the God's-eye view of the sea, the location of the incoming torpedoes relative to the position of *Hammerhead* in the center. He tapped the screen, commanding the Cyclops system to transmit to Van Dyne the locations of his finger stabs. McKee was laying out a pattern of plasma detonations. The distance of the future blasts from the ship would translate into a time delay in each missile. He hesitated at the last unit, because he would need to put a plasma detonation within a nautical mile of the ship if he wanted to make sure he either decoyed the incoming torpedoes or destroyed them from the direct blast effect or the consequent shock wave. But a plasma blast inside of one nautical mile would kill the *Hammerhead,* and her depth would make things much worse. The pressure of the deep was already stressing the hull so that when the shock wave arrived, it would rip it open like an overinflated balloon hit by a razor blade. Finally he hit the display panel, ordering the final plasma detonation to occur seventeen hundred yards away, inside the lethal radius of a plasma warhead.

"Enter the solutions and shoot when ready," McKee shouted.

"But, Captain, the distance to the final unit—"

"Shoot on generated bearing!" McKee interrupted.

The forward vertical-launch tubes began barking as their motors propelled the Vortex Mod Delta missiles away from the ship. McKee counted four launches, biting his lip as the last unit was launched. At three hundred knots and a run-to-detonation of less than a nautical mile, he had only a second after solid rocket ignition before the Vortex detonated its plasma warhead. That last-fired Vortex missile was about to make a bad day worse, McKee thought.

"Unit eight solid rocket ignition," Van Dyne said as the first missile lit off, a few hundred yards to the west.

"Sir, we're in the kill zone, hovering and deep," Judison said.

McKee looked at the XO. Judison's armpits were soaked completely through, and there was a wild look in his eyes. McKee deliberately withdrew a cigar from his pocket, praying that his hands weren't shaking.

"I know."

"Unit nine, solid rocket ignition!"

"Very well."

"Sir, we've got to run."

McKee had pulled the Cohiba's wrapper off.

"Unit ten, solid rocket ignition."

"Pilot," McKee said, the cigar between his teeth, "emergency blow forward."

"Blow forward aye! Blowing forward!"

The noise in the room became deafening as the emergency blow system blew the water out of the forward ballast tanks. The deck began to rise as the hull started upward toward the surface from a standing start near test depth.

McKee lit his cigar while watching the depth display, one hand grabbing a handhold on his console. The deck climbed upward to ten degrees, fifteen, then twenty. The room began to fill with condensation boiling up from the super-cold piping of the emergency ballast tank blow system, competing with the ball of smoke around McKee's head.

Inside that head, Kyle Liam Ellison McKee was staring at the shadows of his father, grandfather, and great-grandfather, wondering why they didn't grab for handholds in the tilted-up control room, then nodding to himself that they were ghosts, apparitions that came to a man in the final moments of madness before death. He looked away from the shadows and continued puffing on the Cohiba.

"Unit eleven, solid rocket ignition, sir."

"Depth six hundred feet, Captain."

"Pilot, emergency blow aft," McKee said calmly.

"Blowing aft, sir!"

The noise in the room became even more frenzied from the air blasting into the aft portion of the emergency blow piping. The air added to the noise of the solid rocket motors of the Vortex missiles as they blasted away from the ship.

"Unit twelve, solid rocket ignition!"

"Depth four hundred, up angle thirty degrees, sir!"

"Secure the forward blow and vent forward," McKee said between puffs. "Ahead emergency flank."

"Securing emergency blow forward, sir, venting forward, ahead emergency flank!"

The deck began to tremble violently as the engineering section aft answered the emergency flank bell.

"Secure the aft blow, vent aft."

"Securing aft, sir. Blow aft secured, venting aft."

McKee took a deep puff and blew the smoke out his nose. "Pilot, maintain depth one five zero feet, course east."

"One-fifty feet, zero nine zero, aye, sir."

The plasma detonations happened next, the initial shock wave hitting them from the closest Vortex missile. With the sea as an anvil and the explosion as a hammer, the ship took the shock wave, but it didn't take it well.

38

Captain Second Rank Pavel Grachev's cheek rested on the vinyl tile of the deck near the ship-control station. The cover of the panic panel lay on his head, and his right arm, with the wrist broken, was stretched out in front of him. He would have remained there for some time if not for the water that rose on the tile, submerging his fingers, rising to the level of his nostrils. His next breath pulled in water, and he reflexively started coughing. Raising his head, he felt the room spinning around him despite the fact that he was in complete darkness. He felt his broken wrist screaming in pain. He felt his fingers in the water, his knees in the water, water leaking into his boots.

He pushed himself to his feet with his good hand and reached for the bulkhead where the panic panel had been. Farther to starboard was a panel to energize the battle lanterns—and they should have come on automatically, but the shocks of the explosions had obviously opened the circuit breaker. He found the panel cover and threw the breaker off, then back on. The lanterns became so many strobe lights as they clicked back to life, exposing one of the ugliest scenes in Grachev's memory.

The interior of the compartment had not fared well under the multiple impacts of the plasma explosions. Panel displays had shattered, bulkheads had fallen, valves were hanging from sheared pipes. The flooding water rose slowly, but he could not find the source. And it didn't matter—they had to get out.

The next several minutes passed in blur as Grachev found the collapsible ladder to the emergency hatch—normally leading up into the free-flood space of the fin interior, the accessway for maintaining the masts in the fin—and unfolded it. He climbed up a rung to grab the wheel with his good arm and tried to open it. He had an instant of panic, wondering if the stress of the impacts had jammed the hatch shut, but it had been intentionally built with additional clearances to enable the compartment to take severe overpressure. The wheel turned, the hatch dogs rolled back, and he opened the hatch upward into the airlock space, a bare cylinder of steel leading to the upper hatch. The upper hatch was the next challenge, but its wheel spun easily. Grachev pushed the hatch up to its latch, and bright sunshine streamed downward into the compartment. Fresh-smelling sea air seemed as exotic as the surface of another world, and to an extent, it truly was. For a second he allowed himself to luxuriate in the smell and feel of the outside, then steeled himself to descend back into Hell.

The dimness of the compartment and its stuffy stench were much worse after his glimpse of the surface. Grachev walked over to Svyatoslov, who was wheezing and moaning on the deck facing the overhead, his eyes shut in pain.

"Are you hurt?"

"Leg. Broken," the first officer winced.

"Come on." Grachev pulled the big man out of the water, now five centimeters deep, and rushed him to the ladder and pushed him up to the top hatch.

"Can you pull yourself out?"

":Yes, Captain!"

Grachev found Novskoyy facedown in the water. Grachev kicked him to turn him over. The unconscious consultant sputtered and coughed in his slumber. Grachev would save him for last. He pulled the officers out of the fire-control cubicles, hauling them to the ladder, Svyatoslov hauling them up. Tenukha was dead in his couch, his body becoming stiff, his skin cold and gray. Reverently, Grachev pulled him out of his harness and pushed him upward, refusing to leave him in the compartment. Finally he turned to Novskoyy and dragged him to the ladder and up to the upper hatch.

Alone in the wreckage of what had been his control room, he looked around for a moment. The water came up to just below his knees. He found a package the size of a large emergency duffel bag, just small enough to fit through the emergency hatch, and muscled it to the opening. Water continued to pour in, although he couldn't tell from where. After the bag was up on the deck above, there was nothing more to do inside the compartment. He looked around one last time.

"Good-bye, *Vepr,*" he said.

He climbed up to the upper hatch, emerged back into the sunshine, and took a deep breath. The outer surface was not smooth, but was covered with angles and pieces of the structural steel, the former lattice that had held up the fin. He stood next to Svyatoslov, who was opening the emergency duffel, which had several life rafts, emergency food supplies, flares, and several emergency radios. The first officer had opened up one of the radios and activated the emergency beacon.

"Sir, if any of the surface ships survived, they might be able to pick us up."

They could only hope, Grachev thought.

"What's your hurry, Mr. First? Think of this as a vacation."

Novskoyy picked that moment to return to consciousness.

"Who are you?" he said to Grachev. "And where in God's name am I?"

Grachev glanced at Svyatoslov and smiled.

"What have we got?" McKee asked Judison.

"Reactor scrammed on shock. Port seawater system flooding stopped by the chicken switch. Trouble with the starboard reactor recirc pump breakers. Torpedo room monitors show a weapon fuel leak. Cyclops has sealed the torpedo room and purged it out with nitrogen gas, with liquid nitrogen spray going intermittently—"

The deck jumped as a torpedo tube was fired.

"—and is jettisoning weapons as fast as the cycle time will allow."

"Which leaves us with no torpedoes and we're out of Vortex missiles," McKee said.

"Exactly." The deck jumped again, another torpedo jettisoned below.

"How many weapons to go?"

"Three more. Then we'll need to emergency-ventilate the torpedo room. We need power first."

"Start the reactor on the port loop and the steam plant starboard side. We'll limp out of here. Any other flooding?"

"Port seawater was bad enough, Skipper. There's four feet of water in the aft compartment. Drain pump is about to take all the battery, and the emergency propulsion current to keep us level is taking as many amp-hours as we would have used starting up."

"Then get back aft and help bring the reactor up. No excuses, I want power. If you have to cut the drain pump, do it, but get the reactor online. Take Dietz. Go!"

The two experienced officers dashed aft. McKee's cigar had gone cold. He contemplated the wet chewed end and finally tossed it in the trash, deciding he'd smoked his last cigar. That had been the entire reason he'd lit it, because he'd assumed he'd be dead in minutes.

But the Vortex missiles he'd launched at the incoming torpedoes had worked. The torpedoes were gone. Most of the damage to the *Hammerhead* had been caused by his own missile exploding. Major flooding—that had been stopped—and a problem with a reactor loop, while serious, were minor compared to what could have happened. And with the torpedo room weapon fuel leak, a lesser ship would be on fire and sinking, but the Cyclops system, the sealed torpedo room, and the ship's ability to rapidly jettison weapons in a self-oxidizing fuel leak emergency would save their lives.

"Captain, XO." A voice from the overhead speaker sounded on Circuit Seven.

McKee found the mike. "Captain."

"Sir, we're going to need some time. Recommend coming to periscope depth and snorkeling on the diesel."

"Very well. Give me full report after the diesel's on the bus."

"XO aye."

"Pilot," McKee called, "make your depth seven five feet and prepare to snorkel."

After the sub had risen, he spoke into the microphone:

"Commence . . . snorkeling!"

The order was punctuated by the roar of the diesel engine starting up. It pulled in air from the snorkel mast ten feet above the top of the sail and blew its exhaust out the plenum aft of the sail. The diesel engine, once warm, would supply the DC buses, allowing the XO aft the time he needed to restart the damaged reactor plant.

"Pilot, right full rudder, steady course west."

"Aye, Captain, my rudder's right full."

He might as well drive to the position of the Severodvinsk and see if it had been hit. He glanced at the display of data coming in from the Predator, which should be running out of fuel any minute. The data was now coming in on the photonic periscope mast, since the football buoy had been damaged in the battle. One display showed the fleet far to the south, the ships reforming, the combatants largely gone. One troopship had been hit by a weapon mistake, leaving behind a destroyer with the other cargo vessels and troopships. Whoever commanded that destroyer was now in command of the fleet. The ships were turning back to the northwest, which was odd, considering that they should have been heading northeast to return home.

McKee stared up at the angled display screens, wishing for the feel of a periscope optics module. The display of the photonics mast showed the water coming toward them, the snorkel mast aft, and something strange in the distance.

"Cyclops, what do you show at bearing west?"

"Magnifying, Captain."

The image in the display grew. The jumping image looked like a boat, with the hull low in the water.

"Take the Predator over the contact."

"Captain, Predator fuel level is at low-low."

"Take it as far as the onboard fuel cell will allow. Let the unit glide to the contact."

"Aye-aye, Captain," the electronic voice said. "Predator engine shutdown. Captain, if it continues to transmit, we will not have the ability to perform the Predator self-destruct."

"Forget the self-destruct. Fly the Predator to this contact and keep the camera feed coming as long as it answers."

"Aye-aye, Captain."

McKee watched the image grow as the Predator glided in toward the contact. The view showed something round.

"Conn, Maneuvering, electric plant is in a full-power diesel lineup. Request to restart the reactor."

McKee found the microphone. "Restart the reactor."

"Restart the reactor, Conn, Maneuvering aye."

The image grew until McKee could see he was looking at a floating object with people standing on it.

It was some sort of escape pod. There were survivors from the Severodvinsk sinking! And here he was without weapons. He thought quickly—there were small arms in a cabinet in his stateroom. But then, how logical would that be, to shoot survivors with machine pistols as they stood on their escape pod?

But then, how logical would it be to let them live, after what had happened to *Princess Dragon* and *Devilfish*? And to Karen Petri?

"Conn, Maneuvering, reactor is critical."

"Maneuvering, Captain, aye."

McKee stared at the display from the photonics mast as the image grew closer.

"Captain, Predator shutdown," Cyclops reported, the display screen winking out.

"Do we have contact with the Mark 23 Bloodhound or the Mark 5 Sharkeye?"

"No, sir. Contact lost during the battle, sir."

"Sir," the pilot said. "Maintain course?"

"Keep going," McKee said absently, staring at

the photonics mast display. The men were growing clearly visible on the deck of their huge escape pod.

"Range to the pod, Cyclops?"

"Estimated range, four thousand yards."

Keep going, McKee thought.

"Radio, Captain," McKee said on the Circuit Seven mike. The speaker in the overhead rasped to life.

"Radio aye."

"Radio chief to control."

Morgan Henry took all of four seconds to arrive. "Sir, did you want to send a sitrep?"

"Sitrep?" McKee asked dumbly.

"Yessir, about the sinkings of the task force ships and the submarine?"

Sitrep, McKee thought. He'd probably go to prison for shooting the surface ships in violation of his orders.

"No. I called you in here for one reason. Get a connection with the East Coast cel phone grid. Call into Portsmouth Naval Hospital. Find out the status of Karen Petri."

"Yessir."

"And hurry."

Twenty minutes later, the reactor was online and the diesel was still running, now at no-load and cooling, and *Hammerhead* was hovering at periscope depth ten yards from the escape pod of the Severodvinsk.

"Radio, Captain, you got your phone call in to Portsmouth?"

"Yes, Captain. We're on hold."

"Let me know. Pilot, prepare to vertical-surface."

Judison showed up then, staring at the displays.

"XO," McKee said quietly, "here's the key to the small-arms locker. Go down to my stateroom and bring up five MAC-12s."

Judison stared malevolently at the display for a moment, taking the key. "With pleasure, sir."

"What the hell is that?" Svyatoslov asked, pointing at the odd-shaped pole protruding from the sea with a spherical shape on top.

"Obviously we didn't hit the submarine," Grachev said, spitting overboard. "There he is."

"What if he tries to take us captive?" the first officer said.

"Give me that nine-millimeter," Grachev said, taking the pistol and loading a clip.

He aimed it at the sphere of the photonics mast and fired, emptying the clip into it.

"Did I hit it?"

"Yes, Captain," Svyatoslov said, cradling his bad leg as he sat on the deck. "I think you got it."

"Ready to vertical-surface, Captain," the pilot said.

"Hold that thought," McKee said, at the same time the display winked out on the forward panel. "Hey, Cyclops, what happened to the photonics display?"

"Photonics mast is damaged, Captain," the computer's voice said. "Open-circuited."

"Dammit," McKee said. "You'd think they'd battle-harden these things. This is going in my report." He smiled, wondering if his report would be made from a prison cell.

Judison came in with the machine pistols. McKee took his, the gun heavy in his hands.

"Captain," a voice said from behind him. It was Morgan Henry, the radio chief. "They want to talk to you, sir."

McKee picked up a radio handset, linked into the multifrequency antenna to the cel phone transmitter.

"XO, get ready at the hatch. On my word we'll vertical-surface. Open up the bridge clamshells and open fire on these assholes."

"Yessir."

"Hello," McKee barked into the handset of the radio. "This is Captain Kelly McKee. I want to be connected to Karen Petri's room!"

"You are connected," a voice came back. It wasn't Petri, or a doctor or nurse. It was the iron voice of Admiral John Patton.

"Sir. How is she?"

"She's fine, now—"

"Let me talk to her!"

Silence for a moment, then Petri's voice. Karen Petri's sweet voice. "Hello?" she asked uncertainly.

"It's me," he said. "Are you okay?"

"I'm fine. They may release me today."

"I'm so glad," he said, relieved.

"McKee!" the phone voice said. Patton again.

"What?" McKee said belligerently.

"Why are you calling Petri's room? Why haven't you called on Nestor?"

"I've been kind of busy," McKee said.

"Be careful, you're on an open circuit. But tell me now. Did you finish?"

McKee sighed, then clicked to transmit. "We finished. We're definitely finished."

"And your friends?"

"I can honestly say, they're finished too."

"Well, come home as soon as you can."

"We'll see you soon," McKee said. He clicked off.

"Well, Captain?" Judison asked. "Vertical-surface?"

McKee looked at his executive officer, who was ready to climb out the top hatch and shoot an automatic pistol at the survivors of the Severodvinsk.

What the hell, he thought.

"No," McKee finally said. "Let the Severodvinsk sailors take their chances with their remaining surface ships. I don't have time for them anymore. Secure snorkeling, take her deep, and lay in a track for Norfolk. We're going home."

Ten minutes later, McKee was leaning over the chart table when Judison joined him.

"Sir?"

"Yes, XO?"

"About those Dobermans we had trouble with . . ."

"Don't worry about it, XO. We got away clean even without them."

"That's not it, Captain. I was talking about your football game? State champs on the flea-flicker that never worked in practice?"

"Yeah, what about it?"

"Sir, you never played football in your life." Judison was starting to smile.

"Well, you've got me, XO," McKee said, smiling himself. "How did you know?"

"I'm the executive officer, sir. I have access to all the ship's personnel files, even yours. It's my job, sir."

"So, why didn't you say you knew?"

"I assume you deceived me for a reason, Skipper."

"Of course. I wanted you going in confident."

"So now you have your answer."

McKee laughed. "You know, Kiethan, someday you just might make a decent commanding officer."

Judison smiled. "Same to you, Skipper, same to you."

McKee shook his head and went back to studying the chart, lifting his head for a moment to take in the room, beginning to realize he was enjoying himself, and that the hole in his life carved by Diana's death was starting to heal. The first thing he was going to do when he got back was drink an Anchor Steam.

"Thanks, Bruce," he whispered to no one.

Epilogue

President Jaisal Warner bent to lay a wreath gently at the base of a marble monument with a cruise ship carved into the top. The names of those lost on the *Princess Dragon* were carved on the face, the sunshine making shadows of the orderly tombstones of Arlington National Cemetery. Next to her Admiral Michael Pacino watched from his wheelchair, his gold stripes climbing to his elbows, his medals on his chest extending from his shoulder to his waist. While he watched, a tear leaked from one eye, quickly blotted away by his handkerchief. Surrounding them were thousands of officers and enlisted men, as well as the cameras and microphones of the press. The ceremony broke up after an hour. Pacino insisted on lingering until only a few photographers remained.

Finally he turned to Colleen.

"Take me back to the hospital," he said.

The admiral was pulled into the Sea King helicopter for the trip to Bethesda Naval Hospital.

Kelly McKee stood on the flying bridge on top of the sail when *Hammerhead* made the turn into the Elizabeth River Channel and sailed past the carrier piers, then the cruiser berths and the destroyer piers, and finally to the submarine pier. He'd declined the offer of tugs, and as he conned the ship into his berth, he could see the officers of ComU-SubCom staff as they stood there in their starched full-dress whites, swords, full medals, and white gloves. There were twelve of them, standing at parade rest.

Patton was there, in front of the triangular staff formation, standing directly opposite to where the gangway crane idled, ready to put the brow across when the lines came over.

"Here she comes," Patton's deputy commander, Byron DeMeers, said. "Miss America."

The USS *Hammerhead,* lead ship in the NSSN class, had just made the turn to the slip, the crew hustling on deck, getting ready to throw over the lines.

"Detail," Admiral Patton said, "atten-*hut*!"

The officers of the staff formation came to rigid attention. Twelve pairs of shoes clicked together at the heels in one synchronized thump.

Patton waited with the formation until the brow was over the hull of the *Hammerhead,* which was tied to the pier by four heavy lines, the others coming over. The gangway in place, the crane withdrew, and a lone figure wearing khakis walked slowly across the gangway. Captain Kelly McKee, his uniform blowing in the wind, his eyes squinting against the glare.

"Detail, hand sa-*lute*!" Patton ordered as McKee walked up.

The officers raised their gloved hands to the

brims of their hats in unison. McKee stepped twelve inches in front of Patton and raised a salute.

"Captain McKee, USS *Hammerhead,* reporting as ordered, *sir.*"

"Ready, two!" Patton ordered, and the formation dropped their salutes.

The admiral began to smile. He pulled off his right glove and grabbed McKee's hand, pumping it enthusiastically.

"Congratulations, Kelly," he said. "Well done out there. You and your ship avenged the deaths of our fleet. We're here to thank you. There will be an awards ceremony for you and the crew at thirteen hundred hours. Here. The President is coming."

"The President?"

"And Karen Petri."

McKee smiled. "Okay, Admiral. I'll be here."

Michael Pacino watched the ceremony on SNN from his Bethesda hospital bed, with Colleen there, young Tony slouching in a chair. Admiral Sean Murphy leaned on his cane by the window, his eyes glued to the television, where President Warner, fresh from the Arlington ceremony, stood on the pier next to the USS *Hammerhead,* placing a ribbon with the Navy Cross around Kelly McKee's neck.

"Nice job, Kelly," Pacino said, his voice weak. "I knew you could do it."

"Well, that job's done," Murphy said. "And so's mine, Admiral. I'm tired. I quit."

"So, Sean," Pacino said, "who should replace you as CNO?"

"You see that guy there in white? Two-star admiral?"

"Patton?"

"You got it."

"He's a bit young. Think he can handle it?"

"Yes, Patch. I think he can."

Pacino laughed. "Okay. What about the commander of the Unified Submarine Command? Who's going to run the shop once Patton's gone?"

Murphy pointed again. "See that other guy in white? Four-striper? Next to Patton? Wearing the Navy Cross?"

"Captain Kelly McKee? Yeah, I see him."

"You're looking at the new ComUSubCom."

"Sean, you'd better buy those guys new shoulderboards. They're out of uniform."

"Done, sir."

"And I suppose you'll have some advice to Admiral McKee on who will be taking over his *Hammerhead*?"

"I would. But I'm not sure if he'll take my advice."

"Why's that?"

"See for yourself. I don't know if he'd put her on the conn."

On the screen, Kelly McKee was holding the hand of a female officer sitting in a wheelchair, her shoulderboards showing three stripes. Karen Petri.

Pacino laughed. "I suppose it would depend on

who ends up wearing the pants in the relationship. Me, I run my marriage with an iron hand."

"Shut up, mister," Colleen said, smiling.

The jet that landed in Milan's airport pulled up to the general aviation hangar, where a man in an Italian suit stood in the fading light of dusk.

The door opened, and a squinting and confused Alexi Novskoyy climbed out.

Rafael walked up to him and shook his hand. "You did very well. Congratulations."

"Why do you say that?" he asked as the two men walked to the limousine. "The surface force headed home with its tail between its legs. The operation did not work."

"It worked well enough for us to get paid. Dolovietz had a contract, and he had to pay. So his Uruguay operation failed. That wasn't part of our contract."

"He kept up his end of the deal?" Novskoyy asked as he ducked into the limo.

"He had to, or else the press would have gotten some embarrassing videodisks. I understand he's running for election next year. And I also hear that he'll have a tough run of it. A certain Pavel Grachev is running against him."

"I hadn't heard."

"I certainly hope you were nice to him, Al. We'll be making a sales call at his campaign headquarters in the next month or two. We may even be heavy contributors to his campaign. Someday he may need us. But in the meantime, you are a very rich man. Check that out."

Rafael put a computer in front of Novskoyy's face. The statement of his bank account.

"Are you serious?"

"It's all yours, my friend. You could buy Moscow with that. I just hope you're not so rich that you would quit on us. We need your talent."

"What now?"

"Now? How about helping Suhkhula with the Saudi shipping operation? You'll be joining her with the operation in progress, but you two seem to work together well."

"I'll fly down tonight."

"Not before we celebrate. I've got the best restaurant in town waiting for us."

"Drive on," Novskoyy said.

Pavel Grachev cautiously opened the door of his house, cradling his broken wrist, wearing a cast and a sling. It was evening, and he was finally back from the endless debriefings at fleet headquarters.

"Honey?" he called. "Martinique?"

She hit him at a full run, hugging him so hard he thought he'd smash into the door. Her arms wrapped around him, her kisses covering his face, her tears flowing like faucets, her nose running too. "Pavel! Pavel! You're alive! They told us this afternoon! I can't believe it! Pavel!"

A small voice below him joined the cacophony, "Daddy! Daddy, Daddy!"

Grachev smiled, pushing his wife and son far enough away from him that he could look at them.

"Well, then," he said, grinning. "Did you miss me?"

He was immediately smothered with the body of his wife, his son's arms hugging his leg so tightly his foot fell asleep.

"You look great. Is your head okay?" McKee asked Karen Petri at their table overlooking the waves lapping gently on the sand of Sandbridge Beach.

"Almost perfect. They say I'll have headaches for some time."

"I'll have a stern talk with Mr. Dietz about clobbering you with the battle lantern."

Karen smiled, carefully, her head still throbbing. "No, you won't, Kelly. He saved my life. We're throwing a party for him."

"We? As in you and me?"

"Do you have a problem with that?"

"No, not at all." McKee smiled, raising his wineglass. "To us."

"To us," she smiled. "And to Bryan Dietz."

McKee drank, staring into her dark eyes, realizing for the first time in a year that he was truly happy.

"And to Bryan Dietz," he said.

"Admiral Patton," Byron DeMeers said, back in Patton's Norfolk headquarters, packing the office for the move to the Pentagon in Washington, where Patton would be taking over as the Chief of Naval Operations.

"Yes, Byron?"

"We have a strange report just in. Two oil carriers coming out of Saudi Arabia exploded at sea and sank."

"When did that happen?"

"This afternoon. And another supertanker out of Saudi was reported missing this morning."

"Let me see that," Patton said.

"Admiral?" his secretary called. "A Captain McDonne on the phone from Naval Intelligence?"

"Patch him into the video in here," Patton said.

McDonne's fleshy face came up on the wall-mounted flat panel. "Admiral."

"Carl. What's keeping you in the office this late?"

"Trouble, sir. Another Saudi supertanker was just reported missing, and we have a satellite detect of an explosion and sinking at sea. Along the sailing plan of another Saudi tanker. I think we have a situation here."

Patton nodded and began to issue a flurry of orders, realizing that he was doing what he'd been born to do. And loving it.

A hundred and seventy miles northeast of Sandbridge Beach, Virginia, four ships dropped anchor in the shallows of the Atlantic Ocean off the coast of the Delaware-Maryland-Virginia peninsula. The ships were heavy salvage vessels, there for an operation that would commence at sunrise.

That operation was the raising of the hull of the submarine *Devilfish*.

PENGUIN PUTNAM INC.
Online

Your Internet gateway to a virtual environment with hundreds of entertaining and enlightening books from Penguin Putnam Inc.

While you're there, get the latest buzz on the best authors and books around—

Tom Clancy, Patricia Cornwell, W.E.B. Griffin, Nora Roberts, William Gibson, Robin Cook, Brian Jacques, Catherine Coulter, Stephen King, Jacquelyn Mitchard, and many more!

**Penguin Putnam Online is located at
http://www.penguinputnam.com**

PENGUIN PUTNAM NEWS

Every month you'll get an inside look at our upcoming books and new features on our site. This is an ongoing effort to provide you with the most up-to-date information about our books and authors.

**Subscribe to Penguin Putnam News at
http://www.penguinputnam.com/ClubPPI**